THE GHOSTWRITER

MJ Stone

CONTENTS

PEN-ULTIMATUM

How do I start this story?

With a blank page: Innocent and untarnished. Snow before it hits the earth.

Its potential is limitless, but as soon as I mark it, I ruin it. Every word sullies its glorious and hypothetical possibility. I trade hope for disappointment, intangible perfection for tangible shit.

Every sentence is a decision. Every decision is wrong.

The phone rings and this internal monologue dissolves as quickly as any half-assed epiphany.

"Thank god," I say to no one in particular.

I pat around my desk, hoping to feel that familiar and comforting metal rectangle that ties me to the outside world.

I jump up and pace around my place, arbitrarily changing direction at each ring and cursing my scattered existence. Where is it coming from? I finally locate the source of the invasive droning under some loose papers on the kitchen table. Karin. Who else would it be?

Karin is my editor—or would be if I actually wrote anything for her to edit.

"Hello"

"Gabi?"

"Hi, Karin."

"I'm in Cape Town now. Just arrived... I'm going to drop my bags at the hotel and then we can meet for coffee in town in, say, an hour?"

"An hour? Um... well, I kinda ne..."

"Gabi," she scolds. "Really? I know your schedule, or lack thereof. I've spent fifteen hours on a plane to Africa so that I can see you. Well, also because of that apparently amazing restaurant, but mostly to see you," she laughs. "Meet me at um, Guy-tee-gee... at twelve. TripAdvisor says it's good and it looks nice. Good view. I'll treat you to lunch."

She thoroughly mangles the pronunciation of Gaaitjie, a rather fancy local restaurant. Understandable though, Americans usually have trouble with Afrikaans pronunciation. I do.

"Hey, you're the one who insisted you come visit," I exclaim. "But fine, okay, I'll be there."

"Thanks Gabi, byeee."

...click...

Shit.

I reach around my bedside table, for my cigarettes and a lighter, and knock down two empty wine bottles that held, just last night, a fine red Syrah. These bottles tend to litter the house, waiting for their opportunity to be topped with a candle. Not only would that be a great defense against the rolling power blackouts, but it would lend the décor a bohemian whimsy, rather than have it resemble the home of a cliched alcoholic writer. Unfortunately, I never get around to buying the candles. Instead, a few have been used as makeshift ashtrays.

I head outside to light my own candle: Marlboro.

Inhale.

I'm going to have to tell her I've still got nothing. Again. She's going to be disappointed with me. Again. Why can't I fucking write? I'm so fucking useless.

Exhale.

Here's how it will go. The first fifteen minutes will consist of chit-chat: menu-perusing. "How beautiful is Cape Town?" and the "oh the flight was okay". As if she hasn't come all this way to confront me and "fix this problem". Then she'll offer an almost-innocent, "So how's it coming?" I'll make excuses. I'm good at that. Karin will recommend all sorts of proactive solutions. She's good at that. She'll brainstorm the problem.

"So, what exactly is the reason you can't write?" she'll ask.

I'll offer a half-excuse, half-reason. As if I know exactly why I can't write. As if that's how it works. Then she'll recommend writing techniques.

"Have you read any Truby, it's for screenwriting but the structure might give..."

"Maybe use some writing prompts? Just to see if they spark something. They're all over the internet..."

"I know some writer's groups, they…"

None of it helps. It never has and won't now. The thought of sitting down and creating a novel out of an algorithm sickens me. Where's the romance in that? The creativity? The freedom? Can't I just tell a story? Well, I guess I can't. Every day, I prove that my 'method' doesn't really work. That's not really true. It worked once. Just once and that's just as many times as is required to be considered an author, apparently.

I walk along the road towards Gaaitjie, the restaurant that TripAdvisor says is nice, with a good view. I breathe the air deeply. Seaweed and seagulls. The sound of my sandals crunching against the dirt sidewalk. A cool breeze, coming in from the ocean, creeps between my tank top and skin. It offers a little relief from the summer heat. The sights and sounds reach into my brain and pull out memories from when I was last here. Back then I didn't have a book to write and a deadline to fight. Sure, I had all sorts of other problems, but they seem insignificant now.

I was thirteen when my parents brought me here, on a tour of South Africa: the country of my birth. My mom was insistent that I experience my heritage. So little Gabi got snatched from her hometown of Pensacola, Florida and dumped in Cape Town, South Africa. There wasn't that much for me to do here, not a lot I was allowed to do at least. I spent the first day sulking, but boredom changed me in a way I never expected. I started writing, mostly for lack of other entertaining pastimes. I started with a short story about a girl with numerous existential crises. When I read it now, I cringe at the autobiographical self-indulgence. Still, this city got me writing in the first place. I hoped that coming back here would spark that again. Alas, it has accomplished nothing outside of an overindulgence of wine and seafood.

We could have met at my house, but Karin knows I don't like to meet her where I live. She knows I like being able to say that I've done things I haven't, without the threat of evidence to the contrary. Over our years together, she's become so accustomed to dealing with me that my deceptions are now mutually understood for their truth. It's frustrating at times. I used to enjoy at least a certain level of opacity.

As I arrive at the restaurant, Karin is already seated, half hidden by a waist-high white wall.

"Gabi!" she stands to hug me. She smiles wide and warm. Her curly hair is tied back, and her face is covered by large designer sunglasses. I'm unused to seeing her in such casual attire: a loose white cotton top and faded jeans. She almost looks relaxed— professionally relaxed. As if someone is watching her and she has to show them how relaxed she is, like she's relaxing for a vacation magazine.

"Hi, Karin," she wraps her arms around me, pinning mine to my sides. I'm regretting that I walked here. My skin shimmers with sweat.

She motions for me to sit. Even here, entirely out of her element, she seizes control. She treats this tiny little table like her desk: smart phone, laptop and a few papers neatly ordered before her. I don't think she understands the level to which she forces me to resist her. It's instinctual for chaos to rebel against such strictly enforced order. But I guess she has traveled all this way to visit me and I've nothing to show her, besides this restaurant with a nice view. So, I contain myself and sit, limiting my resistance to a sardonic smile.

"So, how are you?" she asks.

"Good. Well, I mean," I correct my grammar, as if that would make up for something. "I am well. And you?"

"How are you sleeping?" she asks, glossing over my irrelevant small talk. This conversation isn't about her. "You're not still on those horrid pills, are you?"

"No," I lie. "No, I'm trying to wean myself off them. Just like you said."

Karin smiles, nods.

"Good," she says. "I don't think they were doing you any favors. You really needed to get off them."

I also need to sleep.

"And Cape Town! It's beautiful here. Very authentic. I can see why you love it."

I smile at her description of Cape Town as "authentic." It says more about her than the place. "It's perfect here," I reply.

"Oh, I'm sure," she says. "Perfect for inspiration?"

She raises her eyebrows as if to underline the word "inspiration." The unasked question lingers. That was quicker than I expected.

"No, I haven't yet... been inspired. I haven't started anything new. I don't even know what I'm going to write about. I need more time," I sigh. I had half considered lying, but instead the truth rolls out of me like vomit.

"I guessed as much..." Karin replies, pursing her lips to the side. Solomon brings me a cappuccino with foam shaped like a heart. He's the waiter here. I know him because of how often I come to this particular restaurant. He smiles at me but doesn't say anything. Karin thanks him on my behalf.

"You ordered me coffee?" I ask.

"It's how you like it, no?" Karin says. "One sugar cappuccino."

She wanted to avoid me ordering a drink, an actual drink.

"Yeah... I mean..." I try to stop myself from complaining. "Yeah, thanks."

"Did you want something else? I just thought, it's not even one yet."

"No, it's fine," I say. "Don't worry about it."

I have no right to be annoyed with her at something so small, considering. Still, I am annoyed.

"So, when you say you haven't been inspired, you mean . . . nothing? No premise? Ideas? Even something . . . rough?"

"That's what I mean," I reply.

"You've been here two months, Gabi," she says. She's not angry, she's disappointed.

How has it been two months? How have I written nothing?

"Two months isn't long enough to write a novel," I reply.

"It's been nine years since you wrote *Enduring Freedom*," she says quietly, preemptively rebutting the excuse I was about to give. "And you know I didn't expect you to have a finished novel. We just need . . . something. I'm not sure that time is the problem."

"No, it's not. I'm the problem. Me." I say, shrugging. "I try. I try every single day, but I get nothing. I could knock out something mediocre in a few months, I'm sure, but you don't want that. I don't want that. We've already decided we don't want that."

Karin frowns. "I know, I know. I don't want to nag. I'm here to help."

She interrupts my protests as soon as I begin.

"And I know you don't like help, or techniques, or trying to fix problems," she continues straight through my first syllable, rolling her eyes. "But unfortunately, we've moved past the point of a polite request."

"What do you mean?" I reply, crossing my arms and leaning back.

"Gabi..." Karin says. "You know I understand where you're coming from, but Milton-Hughes has effectively paid you to write a novel, and you haven't written one. I've pushed back deadlines for you. I've made excuses for you. Every directors' session I get asked when your book is coming. It became a joke."

Karin deepens her voice and puts on a strange generic male accent: "At least we've always got the new Gabrielle Rivers coming out next year..."

She mimes the laughter of rich white men in a boardroom and slaps her thigh before continuing with an abrupt transition back to earnestness.

"But they're not laughing anymore, Gabi. Anticipation is fading. Your name isn't top of mind like it used to be. Even the controversy has subsided. The directors are getting impatient. If I can't show them something by the end of April... they're going to demand your advance back, with interest."

The words hit me further back into my chair. A loud ringing creeps into my ears. That's two months away.

"I can't write a novel by then!" I almost shout. I spill some of my cappuccino into the little saucer beneath it.

"You don't need to finish it," she says, putting her hands up. "I just need something to show them, a first draft, a sample chapter, hell, even a good premise might do."

I can't do this. I am nothing. I am not an author. I just happen to have written one book. That doesn't mean I'm an author. Perhaps I was just the equivalent of a million monkeys typing away at a keyboard. At some point a human was bound to accidentally write a bestseller. Define: Fluke.

Solomon reappears. He opens his mouth, assumedly to ask us for food orders.

"Could you give us a moment?" Karin asks and he departs again.

I wouldn't mind some food right now.

"Well, how about this Gabi?" Karin leans forward. "Let's talk about what you've always managed to avoid…. somehow."

I watch her. She asks as if she's uttering something taboo.

"How did you write *Enduring Freedom*, at sixteen years old? What inspired it?"

Silence.

"It's the same question you've been asked by countless journos. You always avoid going into details. There's something more to it than that. I just know there is."

Our eyes meet, and then I look at the ground. The silence swells.

"What are you so hesitant to talk about? I mean, did you steal the idea from…" Karin looks quite nervous as she continues.

"No!" I interject. "No, it's just… I can't really explain it. I didn't steal it; it came from my own head…"

Despite an apparently strong grasp of the English language, I find myself struggling to form coherent sentences. Karin looks at me attentively. She's waiting for some nugget of understanding she can glean from my mumbling. I can't admit to her where my inspiration came from. God, it's so cheesy. She'd be insufferable about it.

"You were there, Karin." I reply. "You know how I wrote it."

"I just edited it," she says. "As important as that is, you're the one who wrote it. What inspired you?"

"I guess I was just inspired. Can you explain inspiration?" I say, shrugging. "What can I say? The reason why I've always avoided that question is that I don't know how to answer it. I don't know what possessed me to write it. I just did."

"So, I guess the question is," Karin continues. "How do we inspire you again?"

Her approach and manner remain as proactive and pragmatic as ever. There is no pause for rumination; there is no judgment. She is an algorithm incarnate. At least algorithms always come out with a solution. My rumination tends to get stuck in an infinite loop. Negative feedback cycle. Computer crash.

Me? I guess I have my own algorithm. It's far less healthy, but at least it's reliable. I slide a cigarette into my mouth and light it. Karin avoids speaking her mind as I do.

"Well, I was sixteen at the time." I say, breathing out smoke and melodrama. "I fell in love with every boy, every song made me cry. I'm old and jaded now, Karin. Do you think I can still find that sort of inspiration?"

"Gabi…" Karin consoles with equal traces of humor and annoyance. "You're still in your twenties. Don't play the age card. And by the way you are far more sensitive and perceptive than you realize. I've seen it. You experience the lives of everyone around you. You just need to break through your walls. Your defense mechanisms…"

She points at my cigarette as if it's a sword I use to keep people away. Anyone who thinks that cigarettes are anti-social hasn't ever been a smoker. I made more friends through smoking than anything else. Besides maybe drinking.

"How about this?" Karin announces as if it suddenly came to her, as if it isn't the entire reason for this meeting. "There's this guy. A psychiatrist. He specializes in nurturing genius. He's the ace up my sleeve. Apparently, he's worked with people in your position before…"

"Genius? You want a shrink to nurture my genius?" I reply, my contempt fairly overt.

"Once again, I know you don't like this stuff, but you know what Gabi? You need it. He comes highly recommended… just give it a try. If you really can't work with him then we can try something else."

I frown slightly.

She continues, "Just meet with him a few times and see what you think okay? Don't think of it as therapy, because it isn't. Think of him as a consultant, a creative consultant. We would just like you to talk to him. Maybe he can offer some insight as to why you find yourself unable to write. You don't have to say anything you don't want to."

"Really?" I say, tapping my cigarette. "I don't want to talk to a fucking psychiatrist."

"Just meet him and see how it goes." Karin says. "Please."

"I don't really have a choice, do I?" I reply.

"No, not really." Karin says with a wide smile. I can see the weight lift off her shoulders as I submit. "When is good for you?"

"You know my schedule, or lack of one. Remember?"

"Of course. Next week is good. I'll tell you the details closer to the time."

I smile nervously. "How impatient are they really getting?"

"Impatient," she says, but smiles. "Don't worry, Gabi. They throw their tantrums, but I know that they're also scared of losing your second novel. They don't want to make you pay out your contract and then have you release a hit with someone else. They also don't want the publicity of fighting you legally. We just need to make some sort of progress. Show them something." Karin looks warmly at me.

How does she always get me to do what she wants?

"Well, fine, I'll give this guy a chance," I reply. "Although I doubt it will help."

"He's famous in his own right, you know?" Karin says. "Dr Sivers. He's very well regarded. He has written case studies on some of the most talented people of the last few decades. He's published successfully both academically and in popular media. It seems he has unlocked much of the mystery surrounding genius; he says he can help people accomplish it. It's all been very well received."

After the second time I hear Karin reference the word "genius," any trace amounts of anticipation I had for seeing this psychiatrist dwindle. It sounds like that's his buzzword. His brand. I bet that he has the word genius written at least twice on both sides of all his books. I bet every blurb written about him references that word. I bet every time someone says that word, they think of him. Genius.

"If he's so famous," I ask, the thought suddenly crossing my mind. "How are you getting him to come see me in South Africa on such short notice? I mean, surely he's a bit too busy to fly halfway around the world just to see me?"

Karin looks slightly bemused. "You usually don't concern yourself with these things. He's more than happy to fly to South Africa to see you. For him, it seems, the chance to get to talk in-depth with the Gabrielle Rivers is one he would not miss for the world. He's approached us a few times about talking to you. But I knew how you would react, so I've tried to fend him off."

I imagine his wall filled with photographs of him posing with these so-called geniuses of our time. He's smiling, with sparkling white teeth, as he shakes the hand of some child prodigy piano virtuoso from India. Above there is a blank spot on the wall, labeled 'Gabrielle Rivers'.

"I think he'll be more than disappointed." I scoff. As I say it, I realize its implication. What will he say about me? The world, including him, thinks that I am some sort of genius. I just so happened to write one good novel. I feel like I have conned everyone. Even Karin. They all have so much faith in me. They have so much confidence in my ability to pen greatness that they are willing to put money behind me, lots of money. Karin has staked her career on it. My family, my fans… they all make my excuses for me. Will this doctor see through it? Will he figure out my secret, or lack thereof? Or is such a fluke impossible? Is my writing *Enduring Freedom* proof that I actually do have what it takes? Is this just the usual writer's block?

Karin is watching me throughout this internal monologue.

"Don't worry Gabi," she says. "He won't be disappointed. In my, and the world's, opinion you are a genius. You may disagree with us as usual, but I think we're right on this one. Trust us for a change."

Solomon approaches the table again.

"Do you want some food?" Karin asks, picking up her menu.

Maybe I just need a good night's sleep.

ADAPTED FOR TV

I stare into the darkness. My room is in greyscale, unfamiliar and vaguely threatening. I look at my phone. 03:34. I have been lying here for hours. My body is tired. My mind is awake. My mind drifts to my pills, sitting in the medicine cabinet. Inside is sleep: Deep dreamless sleep.

I'm just so fucking tired.

I throw off my blanket, as if it had some part to play in this cruelty. I know exactly where they are in the cabinet. I could get them so easily.

They can get me through this, but it comes at a cost. Everything comes at a cost, right? I'll wake up groggy and distant. I never really felt rested on them, despite sleep. I don't dream.

I'm not sure whether that's the best or worst part. My dreams were once vivid and disturbing. I used to wake up in the middle of the night, terrified of something I couldn't quite pin down. They were filled with pain. They were half the reason I couldn't sleep, but they were still dreams. They were still my dreams.

I spring out of bed and retrieve them from the bathroom. Hypnocil is written in pen on the box. The rest is in Chinese.

I'm so fucking tired.

Sometimes I feel like I begin dreaming before I fully fall asleep. As soon as I realize, though, it recoils. My body tries to protect me from it, as if it were Death come to take me. It frustrates me immensely. Trying to fall asleep is a paradox in itself. I've never understood how the rest of the world makes it look so easy. How do you will your own consciousness into giving itself up? How do you turn off your mind? Mine fights so hard to stay around.

I put the box next to my bed, as if I'm not going to take them. I'm not quite ready to succumb, yet. But I already know that I'm going to crumble later. That's why I fetched them. That's why I put them next to my bed. Even if I didn't, I have an emergency stash in my purse. I pretend like I've forgotten them there, but I'm well aware.

I take a sip of wine, a blend of Merlot and Cabernet Sauvignon, as a flat screen TV reflects me back at myself. A black mirror. I turn it on and flick through channels. City sponsored advertising warns me to reduce my water usage. Cape Town is facing a drought, the worst drought in a lifetime, they say. Day Zero is approaching, the day that the city turns off the taps.

"If it's yellow, let it mellow."
"Shower for 2 minutes or less!"
"Limit your water use to 50 liters a day!"

What happens when a city runs out of water? How will people be when their nature is undiluted? I shudder to think. Resource scarcity. Isn't that the route of all conflict? Maybe that's my issue. Maybe someone else is hogging all the good inspiration. Maybe that's why my taps run dry.

I flick on further, leaving the thoughts of anarchy behind

Low and behold a show catches my eyes. Another black mirror. A show about me.

Books across Borders: The Story of Gabrielle Rivers.

It's very telling that the documentary is about me, rather than *Enduring Freedom*. Should I watch it? It'll be entertaining to see what they think of me. I can't help myself. I know I'm not going to like it.

My sixth-grade English teacher appears on screen.

"She was a quiet and contemplative girl." Mrs. Swift remarks sagely. "Even at that age, you could tell there was something special about her. She had a way of understanding things the other kids couldn't..."

I was twelve for Christ's sake. I don't remember Mrs. Swift taking any particular notice of me. I was mediocre. No one treated me like I was destined for greatness.

An old video comes on screen, one of me performing a play with the other children. I'm a normal little girl with a special talent. Of course, like Sir Mix-a-Lot... they like big buts. One was coming up.

"High school saw a different time for Gabrielle, a time she had to balance the usual pressures of adolescence with becoming one of the most famous authors of the modern age," the narrator announces, as the screen shows a now-infamous video of me drinking at a high school party. The outdated home video quality gives it an air of gotcha Gonzo journalism, as if they had caught a politician with a hooker. It cuts straight from my drinking to an ad.

I give one full sweep of the channels during the ad break, but there's nothing on: only scripted reality television on what was once a music channel, movies made without intention, and a sitcom that tries too hard to be *Friends*. I swear there was more to watch on TV when there were fewer options. I click back to myself. Maybe it is a bit vain, but this black mirror is equal parts flattering and insulting. Like overhearing a conversation about myself.

What comes after the ad break is particularly strange. A face I have not seen in years, one of my old 'friends', appears on the screen. She looks different. Her hair is tied back, and she seems to have gained a bit of weight: Kari Bryson. Scary Kari, we used to call her.

"Yeah, I was friends with Gabi, but I mean, well, yeah, she didn't really open up to me. I mean, yeah, I didn't even know she was writing a book. She never told anyone. Like she had this inner world that I could never touch and um, like she would just disappear into her thoughts. And she was always into geeky stuff, like boy geeky stuff. She was one of those 'I like hanging out with boys' kinda girls. But um, like we would steal booze and stuff together. She could be fun."

I can't help but crack a smile. Clearly the only thing about Kari that has changed is her appearance. She still talks like she's in high school.

The narrator continues, "At sixteen years old Gabrielle began writing a novel. She didn't tell any of her friends about it, nor her teachers. She had never written anything before. Still, she wrote every day and every night with religious devotion."

Kari appears on the screen again.

"And then she like properly disappears." Kari makes the 'poof' hand motion. "She stopped going out with us... she started missing school. Whenever we called, she'd tell us she was swamped with homework, but she'd often show up at school without her work done. And when she did, I mean, she looked like a mess, you know. Like a drug addict. She seemed like a different person. We all just assumed she was on something... you know... like hooked on something."

Kari pulls out all the sincerity she can muster. It's not that much. The deep-voiced narration returns.

"Despite falling grades and the loss of some of her closest friends, Gabrielle continued writing. Within the span of one year, she had written her first novel, one destined to become one of the best-selling novels of the decade. She had written *Enduring Freedom*."

The screen cuts to a shot of Middle Eastern conflict. All you can see is gunfire and explosions lighting up an arid city. The war could be anywhere. But it's in Afghanistan. It's always in Afghanistan.

"Gabrielle sent her draft to multiple publishing agencies."

Karin surprises me on the screen. She's wearing her characteristic navy business suit, sitting with perfect posture at her New York desk.

"After the first chapter of *Enduring Freedom*, I was blown away. It hooked me immediately. I read the rest in three days. It floored me.... I knew at once there was a great novel in there. When I followed it up and discovered this girl who wrote it... well... needless to say I was absolutely gobsmacked. A sixteen-year-old girl, who had never written before, who lived in suburban America... How she managed to write something so nuanced, and authentic, about the experience of a young Afghan... I'll never truly know. Two days later I was meeting with her and her parents to sign the most talented author I have ever met."

I get a shiver up my spine listening to Karin speak so highly of me, despite her use of the word authentic. For a moment I feel better about my own abilities as an author. For a short moment.

"With Milton-Hughes as its publisher, *Enduring Freedom* went onto the bookshelves on June 6th, 2004."

Karin returned to the screen.

"To say it was a hit would be an understatement. We sold nearly a million copies in the first year."

A montage of press pieces flash onto my television. Little snippets of news broadcasts, talk shows and newspaper headlines all overlapping each other. They make it sound like every town in the world was talking about me. In reality it was pretty much young adults and middle-aged housewives in North America and Western Europe, but hey... that's the world, right?

All the press pieces aren't about the book though, they're about me. That's why the show is about me. Two stories were thrust into the spotlight:

Enduring Freedom, the story of Feda Ahmed, a Hazara boy's life in Kabul.

Child Prodigy, the story of Gabrielle Rivers, a young white American girl with a secret gift for writing.

The first was a better story, but the second was more suited to press coverage. It was more relatable to Americans, particularly white American teenage girls who wanted to believe they had a secret gift. I was their passive first-person protagonist in a dystopian future. I even got the leading man, for a while at least.

The footage skips to a new interviewee. The caption for this man reads "Dr Hashim Mahomed Manaf. – Professor of English Literature at Harvard University."

"There are numerous reasons for the success of *Enduring Freedom*," he says. "It was accessible and relatable. It translated a Middle Eastern experience for Western ears. Her naivety and inexperience as a writer helped her bypass what could have easily suffered from pretension. It felt earnest instead. Feda Ahmed, the protagonist, remains one of the more astute and engaging child characters ever written. Who would have ever guessed that a poor Afghan orphan would become a celebrated and tragic hero of American literature?"

An illustrated image of a Middle Eastern boy appears on screen. It doesn't quite look right. It just doesn't look like Feda, although I couldn't draw him better. Despite the still image, the video gently zooms in to create some illusion of movement, reminding the audience that they are in fact watching television. Dr. Manaf. continues.

"The biggest factor towards its success, however, was its context. Not just the story of Feda Ahmed, and his life in Kabul, but also the story of Gabrielle Rivers: the mysterious teenage girl who spontaneously wrote a bestseller. You would never imagine, reading *Enduring Freedom*, that it was written by someone so young, by someone who hadn't even been to Afghanistan. Most sixteen-year-old girls in America couldn't point it out on a map, yet Gabrielle Rivers wrote as if she grew up there."

There we go. Hit the nail on the head. How could she write it? Not even I know.

The screen shows warfare and news headlines, and the guest continues, "*Enduring Freedom* the novel became inextricably tied to its namesake: Operation Enduring Freedom, as well as the war in Iraq and subsequent military involvement in Pakistan. Soon after the 2008 election, the book - and Gabrielle Rivers herself - became embroiled in controversy."

The footage cuts to one of my first interviews. Oh, how I cringe inside every time I watch these: particularly this one. I wasn't prepared for the interview. I wasn't prepared for the world. I was only eighteen at the time.

I lounged on the couch, trying to look as cool as possible. I remember fighting with the show's make-up and hair artists. They wanted me to look pretty, but I wanted to look rebellious and edgy. I was so nervous, but looking at me now, you don't see it. When I get nervous, I tend to just spew out a stream of consciousness. I said much too much, far too quickly. I babbled like a maniac, trying desperately to match my mouth to my brain.

Of course, other people don't see the inner turmoil. To the world, and to my interviewer, I was just an opinionated, naïve and scathing teenager with an agenda to push. They don't even show the question I was responding to.

"I think we overreacted to 9/11," I say, leaning forward on the couch to engage the interviewer. "After all the death we sowed in our proxy wars against the Soviet Union. After the civil wars we stirred up in South America and Iran. But then we face a few thousand civilians' deaths on our home soil, and we use it as an excuse to attack people that had nothing to do with it. We've spent more years at war than any other country, and we are shocked, we react with absolute force when we lose two buildings and a handful of people in the continental USA. That's what gets remembered as the greatest tragedy of the last decade. You know what they would call that in Afghanistan. Tuesday."

I can feel my face flush with blood even now. I can't even remember what point I was actually trying to make.

According to the narrator, I "polarized" the nation. Everyone was expecting this "wise-beyond-her-years" and zen young author packed in an All-American girl package. Instead, they got me, with a sharper tongue than my wit. Intellectuals balked that my responses were not as nuanced or well-presented as the thematics of my fiction. The youth reveled in my "rage against the machine" and "speaking truth to power" aesthetic.

I received death threats from patriots. I received death threats from religious fundamentalists. I received dick pics from perverts. That was my last interview. Too late, I realized that the microphone is dangerous.
It was much easier to talk freely, and without consideration, before facing the outrage brigade, the witch-hunt.

The show continues, glossing over my fall into depression.

"Although Gabrielle Rivers dropped from the limelight, refusing press interviews and talk shows, she remained in the public eye thanks to a series of high-profile relationships with other celebrities. This included a very public break-up with television heartthrob Kyle Winterly. More on her messy love life, after the break."

Kyle and I appear on screen, followed by a picture of him posing without his top on.

I click off the television and top up my wine, growling as I do. I take a few deep sips. I don't fucking want to see video clips of my ex and I, fuck you very much.

I top up my wine again and stew in its juices. I feel the frustration of my celebrity hell, complete with guilt over the irony of my success bringing me misery. I guess that can't even be considered ironic anymore. Miserable and discontent celebrity is a cliché in itself. Maladapted child star, check. I'm not even an original tragedy.

I reach across to the pills. Two capsules. I place them on my tongue and swallow.

I drink my wine like juice, and my eyes open hours later.

DIFFERENTIAL

My mouth is dry. My lips crunch as I kiss them together. I'm suddenly hot.

The empty wine bottles and the box of sleeping pills on my bedside table tell me the story of last night. I breathe deeply. My mouth is toxic, like some sort of primordial soup was simmered there overnight. My mind is muddled. I have clearly been run over by a garbage truck.

And now it's already eleven in the morning. I have less than an hour until I have to meet with Dr Sivers. I'm going to cancel. I can't meet him like this.

My phone rings again: Karin reading my thoughts and preemptively correcting my course. I make my voice sound as weak and pathetic as I possibly can. I answer feebly.

"You're not sick," Karin says. "You're hungover. Don't bail on this meeting, Gabi. The doctor is already there."

"Karin."

"Gabi."

"Okay," I submit.

I find a bottle leftover from last night and swig it with some paracetamol and codeine. It's a warm and disgusting cocktail, but I'm going to need just a little bit of alcohol in me to get through this. Just enough to take the edge off the hangover.

The drive is stressful and sickening in the backseat of a taxi. I secretly wish for a car accident to rob me of my responsibilities. That would be a valid excuse for missing the meeting, right? We pull up to the Grand Daddy, a hotel in the middle of the city, forty-five minutes late. My painkillers appear to be steadily losing ground in the battle against my hangover. I start to half jog up the final stairs to the roof before noticing how terrible an idea that is. Every step makes me feel worse.

As I gain my breath, I find the doctor waiting. The man I assume to be the doctor at least.

"Ms. Rivers!" he says, extending his hand. "Pleasure to meet you."

He maintains strong eye contact as our hands meet. He's tall. He's wearing a crisp and clean gray suit. He looks put-together, as if he's put himself together out of all the symbols of European style. I caught only a glimpse of myself in a reflective window as I came in. I look more like I stumbled out of a Ke$ha music video, except I didn't bother to brush my teeth with a bottle of Jack.

"Likewise," I say, forcing a smile.

We sit at a table on the roof terrace. It would be a nice day if not for my hangover. I can see the waitress approaching out of the corner of my eye.

"I must say..." Dr Sivers starts. "I have been really looking forward to meeting you."

My eyes turn to meet his again, and I tilt my head to the side.

"Oh yeah? Why?"

He stops rather abruptly, seemingly taken aback by my response. I guess he assumed that his reason was obvious.

"You wrote one of the most influential novels of the decade. As someone who specializes in genius, it is..."

A waitress interrupts the good doctor with her presence and my eyes dart upwards. She's a pretty black lady with tight cornrows against her scalp. She looks very nice. Far more impressive than me.

"Hello hello, I'm Themba and I'll be serving you today. May I get you anything to drink?"
Her voice is honey-sweet, and she speaks with a private school accent. She looks barely twenty.

Dr Sivers beckons for me to go first. I order a double scotch on the rocks. It's an order that sparks a glimpse of interest in his eyes. Perhaps he has heard about my apparent drinking problem. Perhaps he's read the bullshit tabloids and thinks that I'm a drug-addled nympho party girl. I'm just grabbing that dog by the hair, biting back. He orders a rock shandy.

"Please continue..." I say as our waitress leaves. "You are very pleased to meet me and all that."

He smiles: "Let me just say you are of great professional interest to me. But we're not really here to talk about me, are we?"

"I was assured we would talk about whatever I wanted," I reply.

"What would you like to talk about, Ms. Rivers?"

"I'd like to talk about you, Dr Sivers."

"And what would you like to know about me?"

Our replies ping pong back and forth but stop here for a moment. In the breath between, I gaze over his shoulder towards a cloud. I feel the kickback of last night's wine in my throat. I haven't had to speak to a stranger in a long time. I already don't like it.

"Why the interest in genius?" I ask, and then pause. "You've made it your brand the world's foremost genius on genius. What's the story? Are you looking for something in particular? Are you just hovering over the shoulders of giants... trying to copy their answers?"

I often default to scathing without trying. Maybe it's the hangover. 'Babalas', they call it in South Africa. His eyes tighten in thought.

"Well..." he says. "Do you not think that they are interesting? Geniuses. The great individuals of the world?"

"I didn't say I don't find them interesting. I asked why you find them interesting. Why have you devoted your life to studying them?" I reply.

The doctor takes a moment before speaking.

"I want to know what makes certain people stand so far apart from the rest of the population," he says, pauses and then continues almost as if he is speaking to himself rather than to me. It's only now that I notice the slight German... or Swiss accent.

"Is it luck? Are they special? Are they emergent out of any mass of individuals, the inevitable outliers? Humanity has achieved so much. We tend to be cynical about it these days, but humanity has achieved so much. Yet, for the most part, it is not the accomplishments of people in general, but rather of these specific persons. Geniuses."

"Most humans do not effect much change in the world. They care about living, being entertained, finding love, finding happiness, reproducing and then dying, yes? When push comes to shove, most do not even know how they would want to change the world, let alone have the drive to change it. There is nothing wrong with that. It is necessary. In fact, it is probably the most sensible way to live."

He shrugs, as if it's not the life he has chosen, or ever would in a million years.

"It makes for a pleasant life, yes, but not an interesting one. These people, they make for uninteresting case studies. No, I prefer to learn about those with ambition, talent, and yes, even ruthlessness. Those who can harness energy, earn ungodly amounts of money, perform physical feats previously thought impossible, sway entire nations with rhetoric, wield what is magic to others, or even those who can simply communicate deeply with an entire book-reading public, as you have, Gabrielle. I want to learn about the bleeding edge of humanity: The people who drive the plot of humanity's story, the people who can change the world."

That seemed more honest than I expected, or at least less humanitarian. I imagined he would offer a far more... politically correct answer? Perhaps a more sympathetic one. This doctor is a bit more jagged around the edges than his smile would suggest.

"And what have you found? I'm afraid I haven't read your books. In all this time you've spent with geniuses, what have you learned?"

I try to indicate with a scoff that I don't consider myself a genius. Part of me even considers using air quotes, but I chicken out.

He lets out a generic chuckle, the kind that punctuates conversation rather than illustrates humor. It's his way of downplaying the aggressiveness of my questions. He's trying to defuse me.

"I did not expect you to have read my book, no, I am not quite so gifted an author as you. And as to what I have found...well, it is uh, complicated..." he says. "Too complicated to simply tell you in a sentence. That's why I wrote all those books, after all."

Our drinks dive straight into the conversation, landing delicately on the table in front of us.

"Well, what's the benefit of us meeting then? I might as well just read your books. If they're the best of you?" I ask, picking up my glass and sipping it deeply. That burns. I can feel that straight away. "I'm assuming that Karin has mentioned why I'm here."

"Because you are afraid that you have already written the best of yourself. Because you cannot write anymore," he states.

He could have phrased it as a question, but he didn't. I narrow my eyes at him.

"Karin did not use those words, no," he says. "But I assume that you're suffering from, what's the phrase, writer's block? Why else would you meet me?"

"Perhaps I'm just doing my publisher a favor?" I say.

"Perhaps they are also doing you a favor?" he replies. "Perhaps you are being offered help, not being attacked."

I swirl my whisky around my glass. I feel the pang of guilt for treating him so rudely.

"Let's just say you're right," I admit, more sincerely than habit. "Perhaps I'm having trouble with writer's block. In all your research on geniuses, is there anything you've learned that might help me write another novel?"

"I certainly hope so," he says, the warmth returning to his smile. "I would love to read another. But before I can give you advice on that, I need to know how you wrote your first one."

"Ohhh well that too is complicated," I say, reverting almost instantly into sarcasm.

"I have no doubt," he continues... "You see, I have read your book. I have seen your interviews. I have read about you, everything that I could find about you. I have researched you thoroughly, Gabrielle Rivers... and I have never found a satisfactory answer to that question."

It bothers me that I feel a little flattered.

"My apologies for not satisfying you," I say in response. "It's not a complaint I get often." The doctor ignores it and continues.

"You avoid going into details whenever you talk about your inspiration for *Enduring Freedom*. Why? Why are you so vague about it? It is the first question that every interviewer asks, and you always change the subject."

"I must say, doctor," I reply, fanning my face like a southern belle. "I expected you to be more insidious in your approach."

I bring my glass up to my mouth for a moment, for a moment with my thoughts and my whisky.

"Aren't you supposed to build a rapport, a therapeutic relationship? Slowly try to gain my trust, easing me into the more confrontational questions? I mean, where's the foreplay?"

"I could tiptoe around you for a while if you like," he replies. "I... yes... perhaps I think too much of you to be anything less than straightforward... but I am here by your permission. We can dance whatever dance you like."

"What makes you think there's anything special about how I wrote *Enduring Freedom*?" I return. "How do people usually write novels? They either vomit their thoughts onto pages and then draw patterns in it, or they build stories like houses, from foundations to furniture."

I strongly regret my choice of metaphors.

"Which did you do?" he asks.

"The former..." I can feel I am no longer smiling. "Do you mind if I smoke?"

I reach into my handbag for a newly-bought pack of Marlboro. Another one of my conversational vices, I'll admit. Every puff, as with every sip of my drink, is another few seconds to think. Every cigarette is another chance to escape a conversation for a few moments of nicotine-filled fresh air.

"Go ahead..." the doctor says. I guess he didn't know I smoked. At least I have a few secrets. "So, what can you tell me about writing it?"

The ritual holds comfort: this oral fixation. Pulling the small plastic tab to remove the transparent covering. Noting the warning in clear black and white. "SMOKING CAN KILL YOU". It disappears when I open the top and reveal the neatly ordered row of tightly packed cigarettes. I flick the bottom twice. One slightly pops up. I pinch it and slide it out. I can feel the doctor's eyes on me as I place it in between my lips and look up at him. To my surprise there is a lit zippo hovering six inches from my face. He knew that I smoked... and he wants me to know that. I lean forward and let the flame reach the tip. I breathe in deeply.

"You know, I can't remember the first time I had sex."

Our waitress approaches and I signal for another drink. I scan the doctor's face for any change at the s-word. Barely the slightest. Damn.

"I know when, where, who and how. I can recreate it mentally, but I can't actually remember the act itself. I'm not sure if what I see in my head is actually what it was like. My mind was so different back then that I feel it's incompatible with me now. Like we're different people, connected by a thread of time and memory... a separation just as profound as the distance between your brain and mine."

"And the thread of language?" the doctor offered.

I curl up a fake smile in agreement. "We can talk to each other, you and me. But I present my thoughts and you deconstruct and reconstruct them in your own image. I can't directly relay my thoughts to you. No matter how well I communicate, I can never do that purely. And I can't relay my memories to myself. I remember the memory, not the actual event."

I puff on my cigarette as my second drink closes in to replace the corpses of two blocks of ice.

"It's like that nostalgic lens we have with old movies or music. When you remember a film that you loved when you were a child, you remember your interpretation of the movie. If you watch it again, the exact same movie, it is completely different...."

I take the first sip of my next drink. It's stronger than the memory of my previous.

"Is that a roundabout way of answering my question? Or a distracting tangent?" the doctor says.

"It's an allegory, doctor," I reply. "A hidden message in a story."

"Is that what it is?" he replies. "And the hidden message is that you cannot remember how you wrote *Enduring Freedom*?"

"Why would I put it so bluntly?" I ask. "When I could dress it up as some sort of greater message about memory and experience?"

"And layer in a gratuitous sex reference," he replies. "It is almost as if you are trying to get some sort of rise out of me?"

I smile wickedly. "Well, did you rise?" I lean forward. "I'm afraid I can't quite see from here."

He doesn't break eye contact, not taken aback, nor amused. I can feel him considering how to deal with me. That's what I like to see. I prefer people being off-balance.

"What do you remember about it?" he asks, ignoring the bait.

"It wasn't quite where he expected," I say softly. "And it was quicker than I expected..."

"What do you remember about writing *Enduring Freedom*?" he insists, while his face betrays him with the slightest smile. I consider that a success, a breakthrough.

I lean back and fold my arms.

"You can avoid the subject as long as you want, but it will only delay our progress," he says. "Feel free to tell me about the first time you had sex, if that's what you want."

I look down at the table and sigh.

"I remember certain things about writing it. I remember that I wrote most of it at night and in the early morning. I remember that it felt like Feda was real, and that I experienced everything he did. I remember crying. I remember my parents and friends worrying about me. I remember that I didn't enjoy it."

My breath finishes as I stare at the table. "I don't see how that really helps me now?"

"And you haven't written anything since?" Dr Sivers asks.

"I mean I can still write," I reply. "I haven't got amnesia, or anything. I just haven't created anything that could follow *Enduring Freedom*. I mean, I don't know if you know this, but apparently it was pretty good."

The doctor smiles back; I think he's placating me.

"I have written short stories, and I'm sure I could write a decent enough novel that would be published and sold, simply because I wrote it. It wouldn't hold a candle to its predecessor, though. And that's all anyone would ever say about it."

"So you can still write, but the inspiration for the story is what eludes you?"

"Not just the story, but what I want it to do. I don't just want to write something entertaining. I want to change the reader, change their minds. I honestly believe that great stories change things, one way or another. Perhaps not all at once, but little by little. All those people that you say don't change the world. Well I think they are the world, and they do change. They change slowly. I want my next work to inspire that change, and for that to happen, it needs to be inspired itself."

I open my mouth to move on, but stop. This creates a silence. The expectation of my next sentence.

"I've got the microphone, I just don't know what to say," I continue.

"May I offer something?" the doctor asks tentatively.

I nod. Sipping once again and touching my feet against one another underneath the table.

"Perhaps you're having difficulty finding inspiration again, because part of you doesn't want to."

"What do you mean?" I purse my lips.

"Well, aside from the usual imposter syndrome." He motions with his hand like it's a given. "If writing your first novel was so psychologically traumatic, perhaps you're scared of letting yourself go back to that place. Perhaps that's why you self-medicate..."

He motions casually to my drink, but I know that's just the half of it. I know that I need to stop taking those damned pills.

"You are so worried about the anxiety and trauma that come with being inspired, with changing the world as you say, that you will not let yourself go there."

I don't say a thing.

"But I only met you today, what do I know?" he laughs. "My hunch is that you are sabotaging yourself."

I look down at my glass. Perhaps I'm too used to running and hiding... maybe that's the problem. Maybe I've internalized avoidance to such a degree that I avoid inspiration.

"Do you think I should stop drinking?" I reply, more seriously than usual.

"Normally I would not offer advice so early on, but rather investigate and understand. However, I know in your case I am here to help and that there is a time factor at play. I would be surprised if drinking is the cause of your problem, it is more likely the symptom. Perhaps you are too anxious to open yourself up to what you experienced before. *Enduring Freedom*, although there was warmth to it, was a tragedy. You do not want to go through that again. And as much success as it brought you, it also brought you pain and isolation."

I sit quietly and stare at my drink. I'm self-sabotaging? That does sound like something I'd do, doesn't it? It's funny how everyone says they appreciate honesty, until people are honest with them. We only want it when it suits us. But he's right. I have been hiding from this. That's why I can't write. It's my own fault. I'm fucked up.

"It hurts," I say. "To create someone. To give them life and snuff them out. To hold them in captivity. I tortured Feda, I killed him."

The doctor swallows as if he's swallowing my pain. What a ridiculously overt display of empathy. How absurd of me to mourn the death of my own fictional character. Surely he's feigning this for my benefit. He's just placating me. He's trying to win me over. He's layering in the right compliments, and even the right criticisms. Goddamn him. This is what he does. This is what they all do. They lure you in with fake empathy. They make you feel comfortable enough so they can find out how you work, find out your secrets. Fuck them.

"You also granted him immortality," he offers, raising one hand in the air as if it's an even trade-off. As if Feda had a choice in becoming the martyr I made him. "You told his story and through it the stories of many others. It will hurt again, but that's a part of the job."

I swirl my whisky, staring deeply into the golden abyss.

"Perhaps you're right, doctor," I say.

"You can call me Jakob if you like."

He smiles. I guess his manner of dealing with me has been a bit of a gamble. He thinks it's worked. I don't trust him.

I down the rest of my whisky as if it's the period at the end of our conversation. I stand up.

"Is that it?" he asks, his face turning to one of concern.

"That's it for today," I say.

"Would you like to meet again?" he says. "We still have a lot to talk about."

"Do we?" I ask. "I think my people will talk to your people. It was nice to meet you, doctor."

He frowns. I hold my hand out for him to shake. He rises and takes it.

"I've got just one more question for you," he says, gently shaking my hand.

He's not bad looking, looking at him closely now, although he must be in his forties or fifties. His hair is silver, and his skin is well taken care of. He's not my type though. Of all my issues, none are daddy related. Why is he still holding my hand?

27

"What about your dreams?" he asks.

"What?" I pull my hand away from his, abruptly. What? I repeat internally.

"What do you dream about?" he looks at me earnestly. I don't quite know what he's playing at. That came out of nowhere and sounded somehow desperate?. I turn to leave, ignoring the question at first. After a few steps, I stop and look back at him. I'm not quite sure why, why the question seems so odd, nor why I'm actually going to answer it.

"I don't dream," I say.

"You should," he replies. "It may help."

I look at him for a moment,

"My car's here, I um, I need to go," I mutter as I turn around.

"See you later." He says.

As I leave the hotel, it sticks with me. That was a weird thing to say at the end. I don't know if I liked that meeting.

I type a message to Karin on my phone as I sit in the back of a car.

I met with the doctor. I don't think I'll be meeting with him again. Don't worry, I'll figure out how to write the novel myself.

Send it. One tick. Two tick. Blue tick.

I know I'll get a phone call about that later. Karin hates texting.

Back at my house, I'm lying on my bed staring at the ceiling and running through the conversation in my head. The more I think about it, the more bizarre it seems.

My phone buzzes on my bedside table. I already know who it is when I glance over. As I reach out my hand, I knock over my box of Hypnocil. I sit up on the bed and bring the phone to my head while picking up the sleeping pills.

"What's wrong?" my phone says. "What happened with the doctor? Why don't you want to see him?"

I stand up, staring at the Chinese characters on the box, the ones that help me sleep, but rob me of my dreams.

"It was just weird," I say. "He is a really strange guy. Not the friendliest."

"Pot calling the kettle black," Karin replies. "Did you do that thing you do where you try to provoke people until you drive them away, so you don't have to deal with them?"

I walk into the bathroom and glance into the mirror. This one's not black. It's white with a halo of fluorescent light.

"That doesn't sound like me at all," I say.

"You're going to have to see him again," she says. "I'm sorry, but you're going to have to. I can't let you avoid this one."

"Okay," I say.

I upturn the Chinese box into the toilet. Blister packs slide out. I say a silent goodbye to the rest of the sleeping pills, the rest that I will so badly miss.

"Okay?" Karin asks.

"I guess it's not my decision to make," I say, flushing the toilet. "You're the one in charge, right?"

"Well... good... but..." she replies. "Wait, did I just hear a flush? Are you on the toilet while talking to me?"

I laugh. My pills aren't going down properly. The blister packs spiral around the bowl like boats in a whirlpool, floating above the pull of the ocean's depths.

"Not anymore," I say.

"Well, that's a relief," she replies sarcastically.

"It certainly was," I laugh back at her.

WHERE DREAMS ARE MADE OF

The city was green and gray. Rain splashed against the dry earth beneath her feet. The redwood buildings rose up around her like giant knotted elevators. A pack of rabbits and plastic bags hopped around the foot of one building stump and disappeared down a tight shady avenue. The grass grew through the cracks in the rocky pavement, hiding worms and cigarette stumps. The leafy overgrowth above her slapped at the droplets of water that fell from the sky. She started walking down the road, the siren of a bird's call echoing from a side street. She followed it, avoiding a taxi silently galloping past. It froze and stared at her for a moment before disappearing back into the forest. Timid little thing.

Her sneakers slid ever so slightly on the earth, the white dotted line in the middle of the trail dividing the critters into those coming and going. Birds sat in open windows splashing light out of apartment blocks and humming the busy themes of sitcoms. They stared down at Gabi with open mouths and sightless eyes. She continued loping slowly, looking at everything she could at once. It was all so much. She watched the frogs hopping around in the stream running down the staircase of a nearby building, a family of cats curling around its roots. The animals and garbage were hurrying into the buildings and trees as heavy raindrops pushed past large leaves and rushed to meet the ground. A neon pink flash lit up the sky, followed by electrical thunder a second afterwards.

For some reason Gabi felt at peace here. She knew the city and the forest, albeit usually individually. She knew the birdsongs and the TV shows. It all felt like a part of her. She recognized the face that leered out from behind a brown door in the apartment block opposite her. She smiled and he returned it. That was a face she hadn't seen in years. That was a face she missed.

"Hello, Gabi," he said, creeping out from his shelter.

"Feda," Gabi nodded. "It's so good to see you. What are you doing so far from home?" The world was quiet except for the softly blended forest and city sounds, and the pitter patter of rain.

"Far?" he replied sadly. " This is my home."

Gabi looked around again. "Where are we?"

"You haven't been here in so long. So much has happened. We have… so much to catch up on." He smiles like a child younger than he was, broadly and innocently.

Gabi smiled back. It felt so right. It felt so comforting to see him. Why hadn't she come here in so long? What was she so scared of?

"But you need to be careful. Everyone knows you're here. Everyone saw you. You've come crashing back in here like a stumbling child. He's coming to hurt you. He's already seen you, and I can't protect you when he comes."

His words are firm, concerned without panic.

"Who?" she asked, but another voice cut her off. This one was familiar, but less so.

"Gabrielle," came a cool and calm croon from behind her. She spun to greet the greeting. The doctor was walking towards her, wearing a crisp pin-striped suit shaped perfectly to his form. His leather shoes made no noise as they tread upon the tarmac earth. His hair showed no sign of dampness despite the rain.

"Doctor Sivers?" she said with surprise. "What are you doing here?"

Gabi motions around her with her hands, showing off the city cum forest as if it were her home: "What do you think?"

The doctor's face broke into a partial smirk. "It is certainly unrestrained. Very imaginative," he said. "Why don't you show me around?"

"I don't really know the way around…" she frowned, turning to Feda. "But I'm sure if we ask…"

Feda had disappeared silently at the doctor's approach. Why'd he go?

"Who are you talking to?" asked the doctor.

"Um…" Gabi said uneasily. "He was just here…"

She looked around as worry crept up her spine. Each look made her more frantic. There were no more animals scampering around. The doors and windows to all the buildings were closed. She heard the deep rumble of thunder again… natural thunder. The sounds of the woods and the city had faded. Her eyes met the doctor's.

"What is it?" he said, looking a bit worried himself. The expression seemed uncharacteristic on his face.

"I don't know..." she whispered. "But something's wrong here."

Now she could feel the rain against her skin, her hair matted against her forehead. A shiver ran up her spine and she clung to herself as the cold entered her.

"Let's get you inside," the doctor said, moving quickly toward her. He spun around. As he did, he pulled off a winter coat she didn't notice he was wearing and wrapped it around her. He began shepherding her towards a nearby building. She felt the roots under her feet squish as she stepped on them. A wind had started blowing strongly, collecting water droplets and pelting them against her face. She reached down to the door handle and turned it. The door wouldn't move.

"It's locked," Gabi said, turning to the doctor. Their eyes met for a brief instant and communicated their panic. The rain subsided with only a moment's goodbye, leaving wind as the last remaining sound for a few seconds. Then it too left them. If only it left them alone, that might have been okay, but instead there was something else. Something else remained. Something from long ago.

Before anything had happened, everything had changed. The sense of foreboding bore down upon them. They couldn't hear the silence sneaking up on them. The darkness swelled. It grew and swallowed everything. Only their breathing and heartbeats broke the stillness.

The doctor rushed forward and tried to push the door open. Terror grew in Gabi's chest.

She heard it then, the sound of metal scraping on the ground. The scraping of a blade. She knew that sound. Metal against metal. It reached into her memories, the worst of them, and cut open old scars.

"What the fuck is that?!" she said in a breathless panic. The noise was growing louder and approaching them along the road. The darkness was all around now... with only a solitary street light shining near them.

The scraping grew louder still, approaching. She could not tell how far.

"OPEN THE DOOR!" Gabi screamed.

The doctor reared back and aimed a powerful kick at the door. It shuddered, but did not break. The sound was almost on them. Gabi turned around and saw a shape, something, emerge out of the darkness.

The door splintered by way of the doctor's shoe and he dragged her through the doorway without a look backward. They raced through the corridor, turning to the left and up a flight of stairs. It was dark there. But it was not the same dark that was behind them.

"Where are we going!?!" Gabi asked, her panic audible.

"Somewhere safe..." he replied. "Somewhere that's not here."

Her hand was tight around his as he pulled her quickly behind him. Now there were only hurried footsteps and heavy breathing. Panic gives way to fear, which is replaced by a tiring dull ache.

Why am I doing this?

I let go of the hand and my eyes burn. I dart upwards.

I am greeted by the TV in my bedroom, flickering images of a breakfast show. I think I slept. After hours of nothing, after giving up and watching the first glimpse of sunrise from the wrong way round. After feeling it come and realizing so hard that it recoils and leaves me again. I look over at my clock on the bedside table. There is no clock on the bedside table. I rummage through the duvet covers wrapped around me in bed and find my phone.

09:33... 09:34

The last time I looked it was about seven o'clock. I must have had at least a few hours of sleep. I must have slept. I must have finally managed to sleep. It's no wonder I need those sleeping pills; my dream woke me up so quickly. I'd forgotten just how terrifying they were.

I slept, but for a moment. Still, I dreamed. I dreamed.

EPIPHANY

"Okay, I'll tell you how I wrote *Enduring Freedom*," I say, leaning back in my chair. This time, my one hand holds a lit cigarette and the other, a coffee.

The doctor shows his surprise. I like that look on him, as measured and restrained as it is. I used to surprise people all the time, even shock them. This has become more difficult. These days my reputation precedes me. Or my celebrity does.

"I'm glad to hear that," he says, smiling that warm, twinkling, book-cover smile of his. "And?"

I try to connect all these strings in my head. It's not a story, I haven't told it to anyone, which means I haven't put it all together in a meaningful way. It's just thoughts and memories loosely associated with one another. I haven't been forced to organize it. Perhaps it will dissolve if exposed to light.

"I started writing when I was a teenager. I was good, I guess, not great. I wrote what teenagers write. Angst. Sure, I could write it better than most, but it was nothing anyone who wasn't another teenage girl would appreciate. Of course, I got published in a school magazine and suddenly I'm known by my peers as the artsy one, slightly disturbed, but oh so talented."

The doctor maintains eye contact and gives me the slightest hint of a nod. All these practiced signs of visual feedback, honed to illustrate that he's listening attentively. Therapist training. I try to ignore it.

"I wrote all through middle school, although mostly for catharsis. I wrote for myself and I wrote because it made me feel like I was that person they all thought I was: the tortured, talented, unappreciated artist. If I wasn't that, then I wasn't really much at all. That was all I had. Well that's not true. There was nothing wrong with my life, but I convinced myself there was. I knew that I was miserable and I reveled in that misery as much as I could. Life seemed pointless and stupid. I was restless and discontent, and under the impression that the world had somehow wronged me. At the same time, I felt guilty. Guilty for all my privilege. Guilty for all the things I was learning about in the world... However, if I had this gift, this gift of art, well, it made me special. Especially if I suffered for it. It meant there was something different about me. Instead of my self-imposed suffering being pointless and damaging, it would rather be evidence of my depth. My suffering would instead be a sacrifice, a sacrifice on the altar or artistic expression."

I smirk at the end to try to blend irony into my confession. Despite what people think, I've never had a problem being honest. I just sneak it in with my sarcasm, hyperbole and skepticism.

"The trouble I faced, and I didn't even know this at the time, but the trouble was that I really didn't have much worth writing. All my opinions, my positions, were built in opposition to the world, but there was nothing in them that hadn't been said before. There was nothing I could say better than those before me."

I take a sip of my coffee. Perhaps to take some time to recompose myself. Perhaps to create some suspense. The storyteller in me regrets that I have said too much too quickly.

"But one night, it could have been any night, I dreamed about Feda Ahmed..."

I take this opportunity to take a long drag from my cigarette. The gray snake on the end tells its own story: how long I was speaking without pause.

The good doctor's face breaks into a genuine smile. I think that's what it is, at least.

"How did you know?" I continue. "How did you know that my dreams inspired me?"

"Just an educated guess," he shrugs. "Perhaps this old doctor has something to offer you after all."

I narrow my eyes at him, conspicuously suspicious. I continue explaining.

"Feda was that 'something' that I needed. I don't know how I came up with him, but he represented all the real tragedy and drama of the world. I just started writing about him. It wasn't even a story at first, I just wrote snippets of his life. Different moments. It just seemed to flow out of me, as though they were my own experiences. It all came so effortlessly. It was painful, and I felt it all to my core, but I didn't need to agonize over their creation. They spurted out like blood from my arteries. They wanted to get out of me. Over time, I took those snippets and I crafted them into a story. That story eventually turned into Enduring Freedom," I say.

"Why are you telling me this now?" he asks. "When you have clearly avoided talking about it before?"

"I dreamed last night, for the first time in years," I reply.

The doctor's eyes fixate on mine for a second. I feel a shiver climb up my spine. The intensity of the gaze is discomforting, especially in contrast to his usual manner, one that seems cultivated to put at ease. He opens his mouth.

The doctor asks: "You dreamed? What about?"

As clear as it seemed in my head, it all slips away like water through my hands. I realize quickly that I don't remember it as well as I thought I did - or at all, in fact. Where was it? I was in a city? Or a forest... I must try to remember.

"I was in a forest, um, or a city."

I remember being terrified... of .... something.

"Something was scary."

Fuck. I sound like an idiot.

"It's not so easy, is it? To remember your dreams," he says. "Try to remember what it looked and sounded like. Keep your eyes closed and imagine that you are there again."

"It was in a city, not Cape Town or any city in particular, but it was also in a jungle." I close my eyes and try to visualize it again. It sounds ridiculous and pointless.

"I could hear the sounds of nature, and the sounds of the city. They seemed to meld into one."

"What happens next?" he asks.

"I met someone there," I say.

"Who?" he asks.

I squint my eyes shut and think. It seems just out of my reach, but with his voice, I remember him.

"You... you were with me," I laugh. "Is that weird?"

"I end up in most of my clients' dreams at some point, to be honest. It is entirely normal, considering the work I do. Tell me more about the dream. Is there anyone else with us? Or anyone before or after?"

"Just you... actually wait, no." Parts start coming to me more clearly. "Some-one... or something else came. Something bad. I don't know what though. "

"Oh? Is this the scary thing?" he says, his voice level. "Something bad? How do you know it is bad?"

"I could feel it," I answer, as I feel just a little bit of the same fear now. "I could feel that it was evil, feel it with absolute certainty. It was vaguely fa-miliar. Like it was from some horror movie I watched as a kid."

"Describe it to me."

"I just felt this overwhelming terror and anxiety, as if I knew something bad was going to happen. I don't remember what it was, but I know it."

"Is there anyone else around you? Someone that you recognize?" he con-tinues.

"Recognize?"

"We seldom encounter strangers in our dreams. Was there anyone from your past there?"

"Ummmm whatever was coming that was dangerous, I recognized it. But I don't know how."

I take a sip of water as he looks at me. Is he waiting for more? I know there was more, but I just can't remember it.

"Thank you for sharing that with me. It's very interesting," he says. "I think that practicing your dream recall might be quite useful for you."

"Practicing?" I ask. "Remembering my dreams?"

"Perhaps," he says. "If it worked before, maybe it will work again. But it is difficult. It requires discipline to remember your dreams."

"Aren't dreams undisciplined by nature? I mean, isn't it just your imagin-ation running wild?" I ask.

"Everyone dreams, Gabi. You must have been dreaming all this time, despite saying that you have not. You have simply been unable to recall them. Un-less, well, unless there is something else you are not telling me?"

I can feel him trying to look through my eyes into my head. Like he's rum-maging around in my brain.

"Ummmmmm, well, I have been on sleeping pills..." I say sheepishly. "I think they might have stopped me from dreaming."

His eyes grow wide.

"You have been on sleeping pills?" he says, his brow furrowed in thought. "Sleeping pills usually inhibit REM sleep, which in turn limits dreaming, but they do not completely prevent it. What kind were you on?"

"I think they're called Hypnocil, I think they might also be antidepressants," I reveal. It feels like I'm being interrogated out of nowhere.

"Hypnocil?" he says without asking. "That is not exactly a sleeping pill, more like anesthesia. How long have you been on them?"

I feel a pang of guilt. My doctor prescribed it to me when I was suffering from particularly bad night terrors and months of depression, not long after releasing my book. I couldn't sleep, and when I did, I would wake up distraught. The medication is the only thing that got me through it. They were supposed to be short-term, but I never stopped. I managed to find a supplier who didn't care whether I had a prescription or not. Some things are too easy when you have money to spare. Once I became accustomed to them, it became impossible for me to sleep without them.
"I wasn't..." I say, realizing the expression on my face was changing into that caricature of feigned innocence. "They helped me sleep. I just stopped taking them yesterday. I don't know, it's been a few years."

The doctor shakes his head in incredulity. "You have been struggling to find inspiration, inspiration of the unconscious and almost divine sort..."

I already know where he's going with this.

"...and the entire time you have been taking drugs that literally inhibit your ability to dream."

"Yes..." I say, eyes downcast like I just got detention.

He breathes in. "This explains so much."

My submissive acceptance is overtaken by a heat creeping up the back of my neck. Who is he to criticize? Without the pills I couldn't sleep, and I can't dream without sleeping anyway. It was great to not dream. I fucking loved it. It's been so long, dreaming just stopped being something I think about.

"You've stopped taking them now, though, yes?" he says. "All you need to do is get used to living and sleeping without them."

My mind flashes to comical images of me as the divorcee of a bottle of white circular pills, lying in bed alone weeping over their unused pillow.

"It would also do you a lot of good to get some exercise, eat well, cut down on the drinking and smoking," the doctor goes on. "An active healthy life-style has been found to help you sleep better."

Oh god really? He's going to start giving me health advice now?

"Is that really your prescription," I ask. "An active healthy lifestyle? An apple a day will help me write another novel?"

He shrugs: "Feel free to go back on Hypnocil and see if that works out... or you can try something new and see if the result is different. Which seems like the better choice?"

Our eyes lock in my resistance.

"I'm not saying that all your problems will be fixed with some exercise and a healthy diet," he says. "But it will help."

"Ugh, fine," I reply. "I'll go drink a fucking kale smoothie. It'll make for a riveting read."

RUNNING CIRCLES

"How's it going with Doctor Sivers?" my phone says, with its usual voice. It's optimistic and pragmatic. "Sorry I didn't call earlier, I've been a bit swamped here."

The background hums with the ambient noise of "being swamped." Papers shuffle. Keyboards click.

"Don't worry about it," I reply "It's okay. It's going okay."

"Okay?" she replies. "From you, that's a ringing endorsement. He's supposed to be incredible, you know. You must hear all the work he's done."

"Yeah?" My voice operates like an input tone on a phone.

"He's worked with all sorts of top businesspeople, politicians, artists, scientists...
He's helped so many and he must have learned so much from them...
I can only imagine he is what he studies - a genius."

I fill in the blanks with gossip disguised as praise and subconsciously nod along with her.

"So tell me what happened?" she asks, as if she wants to know whether I made out with Chad under the bleachers.

"We just talked about inspiration, you know?" I say. We talked about what it was like for me writing *Enduring Freedom*. He thinks that I may have a tendency to self-sabotage, with drinking for example."

I can hear Karin's unsaid I-told-you-so all the way from the other side of the phone.

"Yes," I say. "I know you've told me a thousand times, but it's different when it comes from a doctor."

"Mmmmhuh," she says. "So are you going to play ball now? Are you going to stop rolling your eyes at me and resisting every piece of advice I offer?"

"I think I'll continue the meetings for now and see how it goes. I'm not a convert yet," I say. "Apparently I'm supposed to change some lifestyle habits: Cut down on the drinking, exercise more, eat healthy. Just generally be an adult, I guess. Ugh."

Karin laughs. "How has the doctor managed to do in a few meetings what I've failed at for years?"

"Get me off the sauce?" I reply. "And onto a treadmill? I mean let's not get ahead of ourselves here."

"I'm sure there's a good gym nearby," Karin says. "Why don't you go give it a whirl?"

"I'm hanging up now, Karin."

"Do you even have gym clothes?"

"Goodbye Karin."

"Goodbye Gabi," she replies. "Let me know how everything goes, okay?"

"Of course."

"Oh, and Gabi."

"Yes."

"You know how a treadmill works right?"

I laugh and hang up on her.

Karin is from the generation that still uses their phone as a phone. Any reasonable person would have just sent me a message - well, a string of messages. I prefer text. You get to omit whatever you want. You get to choose your words carefully and deliver them without interruption. Phone conversations are just lesser versions of actual conversations. Text is its own medium.

"Good afternoon, Mrs. Rivers," greets the lady at the front counter, handing me a small towel. "Would you like me to find you a personal trainer, or are you fine by yourself?"

I would rather die than have Karin know I was pre-emptively taking her advice. Here I am at a nearby gym.

"No personal trainer, thanks," I say. "Just browsing."

It would be far too embarrassing to have a professional watch me puff, pant and sweat. After my session with the doctor, I did some of my own research online. Apparently, regular exercise is one of the best treatments for insomnia, and generally good for a healthy dreamlife. The doctor was right, who knew? Seeing as I can't go back on my sleeping pills, and that I can't dream unless I sleep, and that I can't write unless I dream, this is all I can do. Look at me, being all proactive and shit. I'm not self-sabotaging!

I haven't exercised since high school, when I ran track. Well, when I walked track. I tended to just wander off somewhere to hide and smoke. Never quite took to the exercise thing. All that sweating and pain. I respect that other people do it, but it's never been my idea of fun. I respect them in the same way I respect
those people who jump off mountaintops in wingsuits. It's impressive and all that, but it's not something I want to do myself.

I stride my way into the gym, clad in my new color-coordinated Nike sweatpants and tank top. Matching gray. People are dotted around various machines, machines that look a bit too much like medieval torture devices for my liking. I wonder how long the line is for the iron maiden?

Who are these people exercising in the early afternoon of a weekday anyway? Don't these people have jobs?

I don't know how to use most of these machines, and there's no chance I'm going to ask one of these sado-masochists for advice. Instead I make my way to the treadmills. They're pretty self-explanatory, right? Despite my reaction to Karin's joke, I can't remember the last time I actually used one. A few pokes at a delayed and non-responsive touch-screen and the ground starts moving beneath me. Numbers start changing on the screen. It must be broken, or going through some time dilation effect, because after an hour of running the timer only reads ten minutes. Sweat dribbles down my brow into my eyes and my legs ache. My chest feels tight and breathing doesn't come easy. Is this normal? Is this how it's supposed to feel? Did it used to feel like this? My breathing is sharp and shallow. This is terrible. Who would do this?

I glance around to make sure no one is watching this embarrassing display of physical ineptitude. While scanning, I notice one person staring at me: a man. A man wearing a red cap. He is walking on another treadmill. He quickly looks away, and starts increasing the pace on his treadmill. He looks oddly familiar. My heart skips a beat, one of the five thousand it's racing through every second. He was watching me. Why's he wearing a cap inside anyway, that obnoxious red baseball cap? I feel my foot hit the side of the treadmill, and I stumble and grab the handles. I reach forward and instinctively slam the giant nuclear red button and the treadmill lurches to a standstill.

Panting like crazy I look back to the man, who is now looking purposefully at anywhere that's not me. In contrast, everyone else is now leering at me, the crazy woman fighting with exercise equipment. I hope they don't recognize me. I stand for a while trying to catch my breath. Was that guy watching me? Am I just being paranoid? My side hurts. This was a bad idea. I grab my towel and start walking towards the exit.

"Is everything okay, Mrs. Rivers?" the lady at the counter asks. I nod, fake a smile, and hurry back home. I really hope a video of me storming out of a gym doesn't end up on YouTube. Exercising is terrible. Gyms are horrible. At home I sit on the floor of my shower, tepid water splattering over my face and body. Ashamed and embarrassed. Angry. My legs hurt. It takes me a few minutes to realize that I'm wasting water in the middle of a drought. I dart up and turn off the shower, now feeling more guilty and dirty than I did before.

"Every liter counts!"

I wrap my towel around myself and lie on my hotel bed. My mind runs through all the terrible things about myself, which takes me a good while, but eventually I do find myself somehow refreshed by the whole experience. The ache in my body somehow feels good, like it's the evidence of effort. Despite it all, I did it. I did something.

Feeling smug and satisfied that I have done something productive, I reward myself with the antithesis of productivity. I start a quick and aimless browse of the internet. Scrolling pointlessly, I come across a news headline.... you've got to be fucking kidding me.

KYLE WINTERLY AND SAGE LESLIE TO MARRY

Kyle Winterly is set to marry co-star and on-screen love interest Sage Leslie. In another case of fact following fiction, the two actors grew close on the set of everyone's favorite political fantasy....

I stop reading. Of course that happened. That fucker always wanted another actor, someone as wrapped up in their own self-importance. That vile Hollywood self-importance.

I wonder if she'll get lambasted when they break up and get divorced. Everyone loves a happy ending, but it ends the story. No one wants to read a story about a happy Hollywood couple. Have you ever watched a sequel where the romantic hook-up is still a thing? No, then it has to be a new story. A story of heartache and betrayal, or redemption and sacrifice. Good luck to them, really, good luck.

I stare at his picture in the article.

The asshole with his chiseled abs and forlorn expression. He stares at me with deep brown eyes, peeking out between the strands of clumped brown bangs. All dark and mysterious. Grizzled stubble. Eyes that approximate the surface of a lake, hinting to something dark and deep beneath.

How can someone look that pensive, that sad, while working out enough to keep a 6-pack? That's not what depression looks like. He manages to look the part without anything behind it. I thought there was. His face looks like a curtain that conceals this deep well of thought and feeling, but it's just a face. It's a veneer. It's the illusion of depth. He's no glasss

He carried that façade into the bedroom. He felt like more than he was. His body convinced me that it was carrying some secret pain. It intoxicated me. But it wasn't actually there.

I remember when I saw his sex scenes with her. I had to watch him have steamy sex with her on screen while he denied anything going on.

"I'm a professional actor," he once said, when asked. "It's not me. My character is the one that makes love."

Bullshit.

You can't play someone and not feel it. You have to believe the words coming out of your mouth, at some level, even if they were written by someone else, right? Even if it's a hollow identity, it's an identity nonetheless. In his case, it's about as deep as his own persona.

Anyway.

If this had happened a month ago, it would've destroyed me. Now, I find myself oddly okay with it. Shocked, sure. Jealous, sure. More than a bit sexually frustrated, of course. But emotionally? No, I'm fine. I'm okay with it. I've got more important stuff on my mind.

I've got my plan. I've got my dream. I can't think about this shit.

This time I have done my homework. Despite my run-in with voyeurism at the gym, and learning that my ex is marrying his once-fictional girlfriend, this is actually going pretty well. Better than it usually does. Perhaps I have been overly critical of Karin's results-focused attitude. Perhaps I have just been overly critical, period. Perhaps I should try to stop thinking of Kyle and Sage Leslie having sex. Fuck.

THE FIRE WITHIN

A man shuffled through the white forest. He left deep footprints in the snow behind him. He left his honor behind him even longer ago. It remained at his post, alongside dead men. Alongside flame and blood. Alongside screams and terror.

Here, instead of screams and terror, he found cold and dread. Here, he was accompanied by the slow ache of inevitable death. His long steel blade offered no protection against this fate. Despite this, he dragged it behind him. His real protection came from a black fur-lined cloak that clung around him.

His features were dark and weary, his face sunken from lack of sleep, food and all other manner of human need. His eyes carried the depth of his regret.

The forest offered little, but sleep. It offered sleep in abundance. It called for him. Just crawl under a tree and sleep. You're so tired. It's so cold. It'll be warm there. Just lie down. He looked to the tree, an ancient tree. That tree had surely seen more men than him die at its roots.

As he turned to nestle below it, an arrow stole his spot. It lodged itself with a thud, flying mere inches past his face. The slow call of death was hard to resist. The immediate threat of being killed, however, summoned an instinctive reaction. He spun around, bringing his sword to arms as if it could save him from arrows. If anything, it simply marked him as a man-at-arms, someone to be killed guilt-free.

"You lost?" called the woman, fierce red hair distinct against her cabin. She held her bow drawn, an arrow notched and ready to ruin that black cloak of his.

He narrowed his eyes at her, and dropped his sword and body into the snow. Into darkness. Into that deep sleep. He collapsed.

Through fevered dreams of war, fire and death.

The man, Kyle, woke to war, fire and life. Steel pressed against his throat, sharpened steel. Fire floated around the woman's head above him. Another fire crackled to his right. The embers inside had survived the night.

"No lost, are you?" Her accent was as thick as the wild. "Running."

She pointed to the black cloak bundled in the corner of the cabin. He was naked underneath a heavy fur blanket. Naked save for the steel necklace pressed against him, a straight blade against his throat.

"I am lost." Kyle said, his eyes gazing into the distance.

She ran the blade down from his neck, dragging across his chest lightly.

"If you are lost and I find you," she smiled mischievously, "does that mean you are mine? You say, finders keepers?"

He turned back to look at her, his piercing blue into her wild green. She ran the knife further down, gathering the fur blanket as she did. As it crossed his stomach, he uttered a feeble attempt.

"stop"

She pulled down the blanket further, past his navel. His hand jolted up to grab her wrist.

"I can't," he said. "There is someone else."

"Is or was?" The fire-haired Sage asked, desire incarnate, burning flesh.

His cowardice showed again, his inability to resist temptation. Whether running to, or running from, the temptation of burning flesh.

He brought his mouth to hers. She dropped the knife as he held the back of her head. The blanket slid off as she crawled on top of him. The fire cackled in victory. All too easy.

Gabi gazed through glass at this, from the cold. The window of the cabin was frosted on the outside, and fogging up from within. The warmth inside, the warmth he felt that she didn't. She was on the outside, without fur or fire to keep her warm. She didn't wish him ill. She didn't want him dead. Okay, maybe just a little death.

She just needed the warmth herself.

She stumbled away from the hut, uneven footing in the heavy snow. Why was she here? She didn't want to die in this snowy forest. She needed help. She needed someone to help her. She needed someone.

She sank into the white and collapsed forwards, bitten by the touch of the snow.

"Who? Who?" an owl asked.

It was a snowy white, with its head turned towards her. Gabi took a moment to notice the red baseball cap it wore.

"You?" she asked in return. "Why were you watching me?"

It blinked its massive eyes at her, opening its beak to speak. But it stopped. Silence had fallen over the forest, unnatural silence. A silence too quiet for even an owl.

It didn't last. Somehow Gabi knew what came next. She knew it in her bones. Bones remembered things, long after the fractures healed. The piercing and violent screeching of metal against metal split the air open

"Ahh," Gabi uttered involuntarily. The noise escaped her out of fear.

If it were even possible, the red capped snowy owl's eyes widened further. It launched itself from the branch without a sound and glided away into the forest.

"Don't leave me!" Gabi called to the woodland creature.

She clambered to her feet, although they kept sinking into soft snowy earth. She started to scramble away, but couldn't even tell where the sound was coming from. It seemed to echo all around her.

As she stumbled through the dark, she felt something wrap around her leg. In only seconds she felt the sensations in order: Metal against her flesh. Searing, blinding hot pain.

She screamed. I scream. I dart up, drenched in sweat, and screaming as if my leg has been ripped off. I reach down to the pain. I can't see anything in the dark.

The room in grayscale slowly takes shape. My bedroom. I'm awake. Oh my god, it was a dream. Oh my fucking god.

I can still feel it as though it is wrapped around my leg. Whatever it was. I try to remember what happened, but it melts like snow against piping hot metal.

NEWSTORIES

London was home to many a mouse, but none quite like Dorothy. Dorothy knew these streets like the back of her paw. Every dumpster in every alley, behind every restaurant. Every apartment cat that was too lazy to fight for its food. She knew which squirrels she could trust and which were just a little bit mad. The city was her playground. What she didn't know, however, is how she would manage to get her dinner ready in time. It was already six o'clock and her parents would be over in thirty minutes. Her fondue was bubbling furiously, too furiously. It reminded her strongly of her mother. She quickly lowered the heat, simultaneously noticing the mushroom slices starting to burn.

"Oh dear, oh my, oh dear." She frantically scurried to and fro, using her tail to move the mushrooms. She heard a loud knocking at her door.

"Oh no, they're not supposed to arrive yet," she flustered, bounding across her apartment to the door and peering through the peephole. The face of a stupidly grinning fox greeted her.

She sighed in relief and unlatched her door.

"Dorothy..." crooned the fox. "Something smells scrumptious."

Dorothy laughed. "Don't you go getting any ideas, fox! It's not for you, it's for my parents."

They embraced just inside her apartment, her tail shutting the door behind him. Immediately after, the fox slunk around the kitchen, sniffing every bubbling pot and sizzling pan.

"Not enough thyme?" he joked.

She ignored him and returned to her meal preparation. After all, she had big news for her parents, and she needed them well-buttered. The meal had to be perfect.

There was another knock at the door.

"Oh goodness," she gasped again. "That must be them, and they're early. You can't be here when they arrive!"

She started shoving the fox into her kitchen cupboard. He resisted only enough to frustrate her. But his playful smirk disappeared.

"The knife!?!" he said, pointing behind her.

"Stop playing, you silly fox," she scolded.

"I ain't playin'," he said.

Dorothy turned back to her kitchen, where her chef's knife sat on the wooden counter. But it didn't just sit there. It cut. It dragged itself along her counter towards them, as if by an invisible hand. It carved a deep gouge into the wood as it progressed.

"What?" she muttered.

BANG BANG BANG. The knocking on the door grew more insistent. The knife left the wood and dragged over the stovetop, scraping metal upon metal. Dorothy plugged her fingers in her ears. The knife knocked the pots and pans, and fire erupted from her stove. A large plume of smoke attacked the ceiling; fire spread across the room.

The door ripped open

I lean back from the computer and recompose myself. This story took a very dark and unexpected turn. But I wrote it. It flowed out of me easily, like it used to. I'm not sure why I started writing a horror story about an anthropomorphic dormouse. It's not the most bankable of genres, but at least it's something. I mean, it kinda worked for *Watership Down*.

Well, it felt good writing it. I enjoy looking at the text on the screen, so I just stare at it for a while. I save it. Save as: The Fox and the Knife.

I stand in front of my clothes rack, pulling out items almost at random. I somehow expect the perfect outfit to jump out at me, but it does not. I select a white and purple sundress, holding it against myself and looking at the mirror. The woman in the mirror is smiling. She doesn't look fragile or sharp, right? She doesn't look like a girl. She looks like a confident and self-assured woman. I haven't seen her in a while. I dress and put on my makeup: all the rituals I haven't had the opportunity to take for granted in recent months.

I order a car that I somehow manage to be late for. Cruising through the city in the back of an air-conditioned sedan, I rest my head against the tinted window and idly watch cosmopolitan streets flash by. Hawkers at traffic lights - or robots as they're called here - glide between cars, holding up "handmade" and "traditional" curios that all look suspiciously like they were made by the same small Chinese hands. Beggars shuffle around, looking as conspicuously destitute and pathetic as they possibly can. At another set of lights a bunch of young white girls, dressed in bright red smiles, hand pamphlets from a local pizza chain to drivers. They are welcomed far more readily than the hawkers and beggars.

I don't truly feel present in Cape Town. I float above the city as all tourists do. Some locals too. I wish I could feel it, I wish I could get to grips with the streets and the people, but I don't. I don't quite feel that sense of place. I swing from tower to tower far above it. Admiring the view. Maybe that's just what the rich do, and nothing makes you feel rich quite like Africa. Even Cape Town.

The car pulls up to a house on the outskirts of the city center, a suburb called Tamboerskloof. Dr Sivers has rented it for his time here. It means we have somewhere more private to conduct our sessions. It's large and beautiful, nestled in the foothills of Table Mountain, with a view over the whole city and harbor. Like all the surrounding houses, it is large and secluded from view by tall trees. Like all other houses in South Africa, it is armed with electric fencing and Alcatraz walls. I wonder if they're built to keep the poor out or the rich in.

I thank my driver and ring the intercom for the house. The steady voice of the doctor answers.

"Hello."

"It's Gabi."

bzzzzzt

The door jolts as it unlocks and I open it. On the other side, I'm greeted by wooden stairs heading up to the doctor's feet. He's wearing comfortable beige slacks, a loose-fitting white cotton shirt, and sandals. He looks like he's taking his time here as an impromptu vacation. It's Cape Town, after all: everyone's either on vacation, or unemployed.

"Good afternoon, Gabi.," he says, extending his arms as I climb the staircase.

I smile up at him.

"Doctor," I nod.

He ushers me to his deck-cum-balcony, which overlooks the whole city. There's a small table flanked by chairs and a mobile bar. I glance at it.

"I thought I wasn't supposed to drink?" I ask.

"It came with the house," he smiles. "Would you like something to drink?"

I would, but...

"Water is good."

He starts pouring us spring water from a bottle, topped with ice and lemon, carefully placed with metal tongs. Everything he does seems so deliberate. I could see him individually measuring out the water for his ice blocks and weighing his lemon slices.

"So," he asks. "How has it been going?"

"I went to the gym this morning," I reply, barely managing to contain my glee. "I dreamed last night, and today, wait for it, I wrote."

I imitate an excitable drum solo in celebration.

"Congratulations," he states, nodding enthusiastically. "I'm impressed."

"I mean, don't get too excited, doctor," I continue. "It was a story about a mouse trying to cook dinner, not exactly *Ulysses*."

"No one wants to read another *Ulysses*," the doctor says under his breath, in an endearingly human moment.

I smile back, not quite knowing how to react. I haven't had to engage in conversation while sober in awhile. Where's the provocative reply, Gabi? Where's the double entendre?

"How did the writing go?" the doctor goes on. "Did it feel the same as it did before?"

"It did... although it ended up going in a weird direction," I say. "It somehow turned dark and terrifying, like the other night. Why do my dreams always turn into nightmares?"

"Do they?" he asks in response.

"Yes," I reply. "Almost always. It's one of the reasons why I took those damned sleeping pills in the first place. I think it's the reason I can't sleep. They're not just unpleasant, they're absolutely fucking terrifying."

The doctor frowns.

"There are other ways of treating that, healthier ways, rather than those pills," he says. "I can help you, if you like?"

"If I like?" I laugh sarcastically. "I mean yes, I'd like to be able to sleep without waking up drenched in sweat and fear. Yes, I'd like to be able to sleep."

"Well, what did you dream about?" he asks.

I rack my brain. All I can remember is fear. I think I dreamed about Kyle. There was snow.

"Honestly, I can't remember much," I reply. "My ex was there... but the main thing I remember is waking up with this fear in the pit of my stomach."

"The first thing you need to do is to learn how to remember your dreams," he continues.

I reply, "That kinda feels like the opposite of what I want to do."

"And you're going to need to face whatever is terrifying you. How are you going to face it if you don't know what it is?"

He points at my head. It feels weirdly invasive, even though his finger is far away from me.

"I mean, they're just dreams, right?" I counter. "That doesn't mean there's some deep dark secret, right? Do you think they mean something?"

"Of course your dreams carry meaning," the doctor says. "Your mind creates your dreams. It is impossible for anything that your mind creates to be random and meaningless. The same way that everything you write has an element of your personality in it. Their meanings are not always simple or literal. And they are often even more difficult to articulate."

"Do you remember your dreams?" I ask.

His neutral expression is betrayed by the slightest of smiles. "I make it a point to."

He speaks slowly and deliberately, with the sorts of pauses one usually hears in political speeches.

"I think dreaming is a generally underappreciated experience," he says. "Everyone dreams, no matter their race, gender, age, religion or nationality. We spend about a quarter of our lives sleeping, and most of that is spent dreaming. I think it's a wasted opportunity to not remember them."

I don't disagree with anything specific he has said. Nonetheless, I find myself wanting to disagree with him in general. Maybe that's just one of my bad habits that I need to break.

"Maybe you are right," I say, noncommittally agreeing in that way you do when you can't think of a good reason not to. "I guess I've just learned to avoid dreaming. Do you really think that dreams are the key?"

"I don't think they are necessarily important for everyone," he muses. "But I think they are important for you. You need to reclaim a part of your mind that is no longer your own, to regain your sleep and your creativity. You need to dream to be able to write, and you need to conquer your nightmares in order to dream."

"Okay okay, sure," I begrudge. "So how do I learn to remember them?"

"I can teach you," says the doctor, in a way that suggests this is what he had in mind all along. "But, as with most things, it takes practice. Write down everything you remember from your dream, as soon as you wake up. Even if you have to make up the parts in between."

He pauses.

"Think about it this way. Every dream is a story that you need to write."

DREAMCHILD

His wife had always wanted children. As far back as Adam could remember, his wife had wanted children. It's not that she would talk about it all the time, or put pressure on him, but he could see it every time she saw a child, or a baby. Whenever they thought about the future, children were a part of it. She wanted to be a mother. When they finally decided, he could see the joy and expectation creep into her. He could feel the difference when they made love straight after the conversation. There was a renewed passion in her movements. It wasn't even lust. It was a look in her eyes that he hadn't seen in years. They had sex every day that week. They fucked like teenagers. It felt incredible. He finished inside her and she clawed at his back.

When they talked to the doctor, almost half a year later, that time was gone. A heavy dread hung over them. As the doctor's mouth moved and articulated, Adam felt his entire body go numb. He heard a loud buzzing in his ears. He could barely tell that his wife was clenching his hand in hers. Neither of them cried. They wished they could, but this was beyond crying. The doctor relayed his condolences. He mentioned the other options they could try. They thanked him hollowly and left, not speaking as they climbed into their SUV.

As the car hit theirs, Adam saw a final glance of his wife's living face. A moment in time frozen in his memory, hanging in his mind like a portrait. He didn't remember anything else. Just her face and the kaleidoscopic colors of the world spinning around the car, the deafening but indistinguishable noises of metal, metal and tarmac. After that it was beeping and hospital smell, nakedness under a loose-fitting gown. A vague ache. Once again, the doctor's mouth moved and articulated. Adam's body was already numb. He couldn't feel his wife's hand clenching around his. He couldn't cry. The doctor offered his condolences. Adam just lay there, staring at the ceiling. The promise of his family was gone.

Now he sat, four years later, in that same doctor's office. That office had cost him so much.

"Adam," said the doctor, his bedside manner over a desk. "I'm so glad you came."

Adam barely looked up. Being here, being in this office, took him back there.

"Your story... what happened to you and your wife and your..." the doctor continued. "Has always stuck with me. It was just so unfortunate."

"I know." Adam replied. "I was there."

The doctor faltered for a second.

"Well, yes... of course." He half smiled as if it was a half joke. What else could he do? "But there's something happening right now that I think might interest you."

Adam looked up. What could possibly interest him?

"I'll cut right to it. There's a new experimental procedure. You could have a child, and well, it would be your wife's."

Adam's heart skipped a beat.

"What are you talking about?"

"We have your wife's DNA. We can use that to give you a daughter." The doctor smiled over the desk.

"But, who would be the mother?" Adam asked.

"Your wife. She will be carried artificially, but she will be your wife's and your daughter."

Adam sat back, thinking. He had given up on the idea of having a child. He had given up on the idea of having anything really. He was used to having nothing. There was a comfortable numbness to it.

He thought about it. He thought about it for a week. He thought about the decision he made right when he heard the news. He could never. He couldn't raise a child. He could barely take care of himself. He spent the last week eating instant noodles out of a cup and watching late night television. How could he raise a child like this? Not to mention, wouldn't that be unethical? It surely was. Anyway it didn't matter. He couldn't do it.

But for some reason he avoided answering. Until he was in the doctor's office again. Staring at the desk.

"Okay," he said, smiling for the first time in four years.

Sixteen years later he was still smiling. Lily changed his life. He felt complete. Sure it was difficult being a single father, working and raising her, but it helped him find himself again in a way he never thought he would.

Lily was so much like her mother.

"All the tests are looking good," the doctor said with his warm deskside manner. "She's as healthy as she could be."

They checked in every year, just to make sure that everything was okay. She was one of the first of her kind after all. They just wanted to make sure she was healthy and normal.

"Good to know." Adam said. The doctor could hear there was a question in his voice.

"What's up?" he asked.

"She's so similar to her mother."

The doctor smiled. "I'm sure you've heard that thing about apples not falling far from trees, Adam."

Adam's smile wasn't quite as genuine as his doctor's.

"Sure, she's her mother's daughter alright. But I mean, uhhhmmm, she looks almost identical. She even sounds the same."

The doctor's smile faltered.

"It's entirely understandable, and it's quite normal. Seeing a loved one you've lost, seeing their face in someone else. In your case, it's even more expected."

Adam glanced his eyes downwards.

"I guess that makes sense."

"Don't worry about it."

That night, Lily returned from school, moody and offish. He had no clue why, but she was fifteen, it wasn't at all unusual. She muttered a "hey" and slunk to her room. He knew she'd return for dinner, when it was announced. That was another similarity she had with her mom – never missing a meal. Adam was sitting on the couch and paging through old photo albums for a photo of his wife when she was young. He finally found a picture of her at around the same age as Lily, her sweet-sixteen party. He stared down at it. If not for the fact it was a photograph rather than a digital picture, he would have sworn it was of his daughter. He slipped the photo out of its slide and looked at it closely. He felt this burning sensation at the back of his throat and his heart beat madly. He wasn't just imagining this. That was his daughter.

"What you looking at?" came her voice over his shoulder, her hands lightly on him.

His heart jumped and he spun around in fright. He was so entranced that he didn't notice her behind him.

"God, you gave me a fright," he panted. She laughed.

"Great help you'd be if a robber broke in, wouldn't even notice a thing." She leaned on his shoulder, looked at the picture and said quite suddenly "Is that me? When was that?"

"A few decades ago..." he said.

She wrinkled her forehead.

"It's your mother," he continued solemnly. "When she was your age."

"No way!" She reached down and grabbed the photo. "That's so weird."

"You look just like her..." he said, trailing off. Looking at Lily looking at the picture was even more bizarre. She stared at it in bewilderment.

"I can see that," she said, her tone dumbfounded. "I mean, I knew that I look like her, but um, I mean wow."

"At least you know you're going to age well." Adam said, trying to lighten the tone. She didn't laugh.

"It must be really hard for you?" she said, quite softly.

"What do you mean?"

"I mean, every time you see me, you must think of her."

A lump hit his throat. The welling. He could feel all the pain and sadness in his stomach, in his heart. It was different to when it was fresh though, it felt different. There was something else in there too.

"Dad..." she said, taking his head in her hands and holding him against her. He broke as she did, with tears and sobs. He hadn't for a while, not like this. He wrapped his arms around her too. Although he felt the catharsis of the tears, he couldn't help but feel the guilt of being comforted by his daughter. She shouldn't be the strong one, he should.

"I'm sorry, Lily," he murmured, pulling his head away from her and looking up. "You shouldn't be the one consoling me."

His wife looked down at him. God they looked so similar.

He ended up spending the evening with Lily, a better night than they had spent in a long time. He hadn't enjoyed quality time with her in months, for no particular reason. Teenagers are difficult, he reminded himself. But that night was different. They stayed up together, just hanging out. They watched old movies. Eventually Lily fell asleep, curled up in a blanket next to him as Michael J. Fox rocked a *Back to the Future* guitar solo on the television set. Adam muted it. If this were a few years ago, he probably would have carried her up to her room, but she was getting a bit big for that right? He kissed her forehead, made sure she was tucked in, and went to bed himself.

His dreams that night were disturbing. The worst dreams aren't nightmares. Nightmares always end with the relief of waking up. The relief of realizing that the horror of what you experienced, and its consequences, aren't real. The worst dreams are the ones that convince you that they're real. They convince you that your wife never died and you believe them. It feels so real, so normal, until you wake up and have to realize once again that she is dead, even though you saw her only moments ago. You realize that, and you live through an echo of the worst moment of your life.

A few days later he found himself in the doctor's office again. This wasn't a regular scheduled visit, but the doctor made time for him nonetheless.

"Hi Adam, so what can I do for you today?"

"You can tell me the truth." Adam replied. His tone was severe, but measured.

"What do you mean?" the doctor frowned back.

"Lily..." Adam continued, his voice wavering a bit now. "She's not just like my wife, is she? She is my wife."

A noticeable panic flashed across the doctor's face, just for a moment. Like a single frame in a movie, replaced.

"We've talked about this..." he said.

"Don't give me that bullshit about it being normal. I know my own goddamn wife, and that's her. Lily's a younger version of her."

Even though he had come to this realization himself, there was something different about saying it out loud, to a doctor. It sounded crazy. There was no reply, so Adam continued.

"You cloned her, didn't you?"

The doctor opened his mouth, but didn't end up saying whatever he intended to.

"Oh my fucking god..." Adam stammered a bit, his anger now replaced with incredulity. "You actually fucking cloned her." He leaned back in his chair.

The color had drained from the doctor's face. It was clear as day. This was the moment of his greatest loss. This was his upside down moment in a flipping SUV. This was his mightily fear come to light.

"I can't say anything more," he said distinctly and clearly, as if speaking into a microphone.

"Fuck you." Adam said. "You coward."

The doctor was silent.

"You just wanted to clone a human, but you aren't allowed to. So you just fucking did it anyway. And you hid it by pretending it was my daughter, oh fuck..." Adam felt the lump in his throat, the bile building up. There was rage inside him, spilling out.

"You're really going to stay quiet? You're dead. Do you know how many laws you've broken? What am I saying, of course you do, you probably know better than I do. How could you... how could you think you'd get away with this? I can bury you. All it takes is a simple DNA test."

The doctor just stared down at his desk; finally he spoke.

"Hypothetically, do you know what would happen to a human clone, if it were made public?"

It was Adam's turn to stay quiet.

"I don't know what the authorities would do. But besides that, a teenage girl, finding out she's the first human clone. That might make her life quite difficult. The scientists, the media, oh imagine high school?"

Adam felt the fury once again, but there was fear too.

"What would it be like for her? Finding out that her life was not her own, but that of her own dead mother? Imagine her finding out that she was your wife? That you loved her. That you loved her romantically. That you are attracted to her. I mean talk about daddy issues."

"You piece of shit."

"Hypothetically, of course, if something like this were true… well it would destroy so many more lives than just the doctors involved. The doctors who, I might add, have an army of high-powered lawyers on retainer. Lawyers that might demand the clone be put through truly rigorous testing to determine the truth of such an allegation."

Adam knew a rehearsed speech when he heard one. He had never realized that a person, especially a person he knew, could be so indefensibly evil.

"You son of a bitch." Adam spat.

"On the other hand, it's simply not true. So everything will just go along fine the way it is now. Nothing will change. No lives will be ruined. You get both your daughter, and your wife, back. Happily ever after. Right?"

Adam stood up. The doctor did so at the same time. He wasn't quite quick enough, though. Adam swung and connected with the doctor's face, sending him back over his chair. Pain seared through Adam's hand, ignored.

"Don't ever go anywhere near her again!" Adam said through gritted teeth. "I'll keep your secrets, but know that if anything happens to her, I'll bring you all down."

He reached into his pocket and showed his phone recording. It hadn't been on the whole time, but the doctor needn't know that.

Adam turned and walked out, past the receptionist who hurried into the room behind him.

Without looking back, he returned home to his wife and daughter.

ELUCIDATE

The doctor's eyes come to a stop at the final word of my story and he looks up at me. He looks moved, unexpectedly. Did I just... strike a nerve?

"You've come a long way in quite a short span of time," he says.

At first, dream recall seemed almost impossible. Most nights I barely slept, not until the early hours of morning. I would fall asleep for the briefest time, maybe an hour, perhaps even two or three. I would dream and suddenly wake in terror. Screaming. I'd take to my notebook and squeeze out every unmemorable detail. They always seemed to be disparate recollections. I'd be in one place doing something, and then in another place, as a different person, doing a completely unrelated thing. The only part I could remember vividly was the fear at the end.

Unsurprisingly, these dream reports made for terrible stories. This is the reason that you should never bore other people with stories from your dreams. They're ridiculous. Our dreamselves benefit from the most intense suspension of belief possible. No one awake can match it. Within that moment, it makes perfect sense that your high school teacher is trying to teach you ice skating to dismantle the Russian mob. In the light of day, however...

Even if they weren't so ludicrous, dreams are framed as "This wasn't real and has no bearing on anyone or anything." Technically I guess that is true of any story, really, but you'd never want to admit it. You want to ground your story so it feels real. There's no grounding to dreams. That's what unbridled creativity looks like, I guess.

But the key, it seemed, was to apply storytelling over the experience. So, night after night, I tried. Dr Sivers helped me, guided me, during our sessions. He recommended that I draw my own lines between the dots, even if I couldn't specifically remember them. Dream-by-dream, my dream reports started resembling coherent narratives. After a week and a half of trying, this is the first one I could craft into a story. That's how I managed to remember it.

"Thanks," I reply.

"Have you thought about working on this?" he says, looking over the paper at me.

"As my next novel? No, it's not the one. I like the premise, but it's not the message I want to send out to the world. I don't know if I like where it's going," I reply.

"Where is it going?" he replies, in his typically Socratic way.

"I feel like it might get dark, you know, and not my normal kind of dark. Heavily technophobic. Maybe some incestuous and age-inappropriate sexual overtones. Far too Humbert Humbert meets Shelley for my liking." I stand and walk out onto his deck.

"Is that where it was going?" he muses. The thought seems to trouble him.

I smile. I'm pumped. I'm ready.

"So..." I ask. "What's next?"

"What do you mean?" he replies.

'Well, what's the next thing for me to do?"

"It seems as though remembering your dreams is enough to inspire you to write."

"I'm certainly feeling inspired to write again. I'm happier with what I've written in the last few days than in years previously," I say.

"Well good," he replies. "I am glad I could help."

"But I haven't written the next *Enduring Freedom*," I say. "Nor am I sleeping peacefully. Most of my dreams still terrify me."

"There is another step," the doctor says, being even more aloof than usual. "But it's difficult, dangerous and incredibly hard work."

"Dangerous," I laugh. "Come on doctor, don't hold out on me now."

"Learning to remember your dreams is only the first step down the rabbit hole. There is a whole other world down there, if you feel like you are ready to... tumble down."

"I'm ready, Morpheus," I say. "Let's say I choose the red pill. What's down the hole?"

"Morpheus?" he asks, his attention sparked. "The Greek god of dreams?"

"Morpheus, the black guy from the Matrix," I answer, feeling very non-intellectual.

"Oh," he replies. "I don't watch much TV."

"Evidently," I say.

He puts down my dream report, which he has been casually glancing over, stands and leans against the railing that overlooks the city. He is silhouetted by light.

"That's quite dramatic…" I laugh.

"You have learnt how to recall your dreams, pretty well I might add. You will have to continue practicing this, but that is only the base skill of dreaming. It is like learning the alphabet, not learning how to read."

He turns to face me.

"Tell me, have you ever heard of lucid dreaming?" he asks.

"I shake my head," I reply.

"Memory is an important element of consciousness, which is why you begin by remembering your dreams. The next step is to become conscious while you are dreaming, and most importantly, aware that you are dreaming. Once you are conscious and aware, you will be able to understand your dreams far better, and even control them to a degree."

Remembering my dreams was hard enough, how on earth do I do this?

"There are techniques that can help," the doctor continues, apparently reading my mind. "The two most common are the identification of dream signs, and reality checks."

"Should I be writing this down? Is this going to be on the exam?" I jab.

"It is entirely up to you if you want to pursue this. I can help you, but I'm not going to push you. You are already writing. You are already remembering your dreams. If that is enough for you, we can stop right here. But that won't stop your nightmares." The doctor looked at me matter-of-factly.

"Relax, Yoda, I'm interested," I reply. "Teach me the ways of the force."

He laughs. "Yoda," he says. "I understand that reference, young dreamwalker."

I involuntarily let out a chuckle, despite how terrible the joke is. Perhaps it is simply because jokes seem so out of place coming from the doctor. Especially ones based on pop culture.

"It is important for you to realize that if you are going to have any chance of success with this, you have to want it. It is not easy, and I cannot do it for you. It is all in your head, not mine."

He looks directly at me, making it clear that we're engaging in some sort of verbal contract.

"Do you want to learn how to become a lucid dreamer?"

My eyes meet his.

"I do," I say, not really knowing if I do. Maybe I'm just used to ignoring the terms and conditions.

I suspect he can sense this, but he seems to accept it.

"Let us start with dream signs," he says.

"Okay," I say. "So, what's a dream sign?"

"When you are dreaming," he answers, "certain things tend not to behave quite the same way they do in the waking world. I am sure you have noticed this. You can be in one place and then suddenly in another. Strange contradictory events can occur at once. Sometimes things happen without consequence, like you get stabbed repeatedly without dying or bleeding."

I chuckle a bit. "Cheerful. Happens all the time."

"The trouble with that example is that it is quite extreme and dramatic. There are simpler things to notice. Clocks, for example, clocks tend to have trouble keeping a consistent time, especially digital clocks. Mirrors usually do not work properly either. Light can behave in peculiar ways. You may find that you can cross through solid objects, even yourself."

I think back to my dreams as he mentions this.

"The key is to notice these dream signs and use them to help you realize that you're dreaming. Then you need to hold onto that thought and not lose track of it. One of the hardest parts is not waking up while you do."

"I see," I say slowly.

This whole process sounds quite bizarre and yet, oddly ordered. It's as if this was a subject at school that I just happened not to take. Lucid Dreaming 101: Introduction to dream signs.

"The other technique is related. It is called a reality check. In essence, you create your own permanent and personal dream sign to determine whether you are dreaming or not. For instance, one of the most common reality checks is to press your finger through the palm of your other hand. In waking reality this does not work, but in a dream it usually does."

He pushes his finger against the palm of his hand to show me, and shock-horror, it doesn't go through.

"Well, I guess you are not dreaming right now," I joke. "That's good. I would hate to know that I was just a figment of your imagination."

"It is best to use a combination of these two approaches to identify that you are dreaming. To do that; you need to develop a habit of doing reality checks throughout the day. That way, the habit sticks with you through your dreams."

"Really?" I say trying to poke my finger through my hand. "I have to poke my hand throughout the day? That's all I have to do?"

The doctor claps his hands together.

"That is the crux of it. The rest is down to practice and willpower."

"Can you? Dream lucidly?" I ask.

"Oh yes, I have been doing it for a long time." The doctor replies happily, almost proudly.

"So do you have any recommendations for my reality check?" I ask.

"Some people try to fly. Others try to do mathematics or carry a notebook that they can read from. If you read the same thing twice in a dream, it often appears differently the second time," he goes on. "All you need is something that will have a different outcome in a dream to what it would have in reality, and that the dream outcome is unusual. You can also change this check as you get more experienced."

"What's yours?"

"I have a few," he explains. "It can be useful to run through a few of them. I started with the finger through palm technique."

"I guess I'll start with that one then," I say, without much confidence.

"Remember that it is not just the action. You must sincerely attempt to push your finger through your hand, expecting it to happen. Then consider the possibility that you are dreaming while you do it. You must not be lazy about it. Every twenty minutes or so during the day, you need to do the check," he says.

"Okay, okay," I say, idly poking my hand. "And what should I do if I realize I'm dreaming?"

"Well, that is the fun part," he replies. "The reason you need to become aware in your dreams is because that is necessary for you to control them."

"I don't quite understand. How can I control my dream?"

He goes on. "We dream in much the same way as we think. Everything that happens in your dream happens in your own mind. Therefore, to a degree, everything that happens in your dream is under your own control, insofar as you exert control over your own thoughts and feelings."

Surely that's not how it works? We can't control our dreams. They're the product of our unconscious mind, I guess, unless we're conscious. It can't be that easy though, can it?

"So how does that work?"

I notice a box of cigarettes lying on the table next to me. I reach down to it.

"Do you mind?"

"Go ahead," he says. "They're yours. You left them here."

I go through my ritual. There's still comfort in it. Despite itself. I can't stop myself from this oral fixation.

"So," I say, now loosely holding my cigarette in my fingers.

"Your mind creates your dream around you. Once you're aware, you can craft your expectations and force the dream to take whatever shape you want. The entire world is yours. Once you recognize that, your will can affect it."

"So, you can make anything you want happen?" I ask.

"Not exactly," he continues. "The world behaves how you believe it to behave or expect it to behave. It requires you to be able to properly control what you think, what you expect and what you believe. For example, in the waking world, gravity works in a relatively predictable way. Things fall to earth if they are in the air. Trajectories are based on the laws of physics. For this reason, we, as humans, cannot simply take off and fly."

The doctor pauses for a second, as if suddenly focusing on something else. Then he returns to his speech.

"By default, a dream will follow roughly the same rules. In your dream, you expect gravity and physical forces to behave the same way as they do in the waking world, so they do. However, if you were dreaming that you were in space, gravity would behave differently. It would behave however you think gravity behaves in space. If you can convince yourself that you are in space in your dream, you can float."

"So if I think..." - I use bunny ear quotes with my fingers - 'I can fly' and continue, "then I can fly in my dream?"

"You cannot just think it. You have to expect it; you have to know it to be true. You have to be utterly convinced. Dreams take doubt and amplify it. If you worry, even for a moment, that you might fall, you will fall."

"This all sounds quite ummmm, how do I say, unbelievable?" I say skeptically. "If people can control their dreams so easily, why don't we?"

"Some people do," the doctor says. "There's a whole subculture of lucid dreamers. These are people who practice it every night. They lead double lives. Every night they experience incredible and surreal adventures."

"As to why more people do not practice lucid dreaming?" he continues. "Well, it requires a lot of concerted effort. It is not easy. Most people are content to not be dreamers. Most people are content to remain asleep. To have their dreams write themselves."

"All the information is out there," he says. "There have been scientific studies conducted. Lucid dreaming is not some grand supernatural conspiracy."

"So you do this every night then?" I ask.

"I do," he says. "As I have said before, I believe in taking every opportunity that life offers me. I could not imagine allowing all the time I spend sleeping to be time wasted."

I raise my eyebrow. "Oh, so you're being productive when you're dreaming?"

"More productive than if I was unconscious," he replies.

"Fair enough"" I concur. "But doesn't it rob you of a good night's sleep? If it requires so much effort?"

"You still get a full night of sleep, in fact, often better than if you were not dreaming lucidly," he replies. "Uncontrolled dreams can sometimes go badly; in fact, they have a tendency to. In your case, controlling your dream is perhaps the best way to avoid this. Perhaps if you can overcome your fear within your dreams, they will not wake you every night. Sleep will become something your body looks forward to, instead of something you resist."

I don't say anything for a short while. I just sit and think. This would have been useful last night. But it sounds like it shouldn't work, I can't quite figure out why. Surely, if everything that the doctor has claimed is true, it would be a huge part of everyday life? He must be overselling it. But, maybe, this is my ticket to a good night's sleep. Perhaps this is my ticket to writing a novel.

"So what do I do?" I ask.

"It is simple, but not easy." The doctor starts to explain in a tone that reminds me of a television narrator. "You already understand what you have to do. You're a writer after all. Write your dreams, as you have been. However, instead of writing them after the fact, try to write them as you experience them."

ESCALATE

"How're you doing there Gabi?" Karin calls back from up the path. She's power-walking up the mountain like a freight train.

"Yeah, um good," I pant, more than a few feet behind her.

I thought I was getting fit. I've been exercising, drinking less, smoking less. But here I am being utterly humiliated by a woman twice my age. I don't even think she's sweating; does she even breathe? I'm leaning on my legs as I pull myself up Table Mountain, a so-called new seventh wonder of the natural world. What a marketing campaign.

Karin was so impressed by my newfound healthiness that instead of meeting for a drink, caffeinated or alcoholic, she invited me to join her "for a walk on the mountain". Little did I know that this walk was going to entail power striding up a 45 degree incline behind someone who probably schedules "5 minute insanity workouts" between her meetings.

There's a phenomenon that I notice any time I go for a hike or walk up the mountain. I've usually lived in cities, surrounded by people day in and day out. Any time you walk anywhere, you pass hundreds of people, barely looking them in the eye or saying a word to them. As soon as you're away from people, there's this compulsion to greet everyone you see. Every other person we encounter gives us this polite head nod and perhaps even a greeting, just because we're walking up the mountain together.

I feel like as soon as we're in nature, we become people first and foremost. In the city, it's what makes you different from everyone else that makes you important. In nature, you celebrate the sameness. You are both humans... in a wild place.

Karin stops at a peak with a view, sucking on some alien-like tube that leads mysteriously into her backpack. It's like the perverse healthy equivalent to those hats at football games that feed you beer. She checks her smartwatch at the same time, assumedly reading the exact date and time of her death, every run helping to stave it off another few hours. I finally catch up to her, trying to disguise my panting by looking out over the view.

"B-eautiful..." I say, grimacing as I lean over. A stitch in my side is killing me.

"Let's just stay here for a bit and take in this view," she says, handing me a water bottle out of her bag. She must have brought it especially for me. I'm bending over leaning on my knees.

"It's better to stand upright." Her voice interrupts my discomfort. "It makes it easier to breathe if you stand up straight."

"I'm okay," I gasp, slowly regaining use of my bodily functions. Enough to find a space on a giant boulder to sit and look out over the vista.

"It really is a beautiful city," she says, looking out over Cape Town. I'm surprised she's still here. She had meant to only be here for a week, but had instead extended her impromptu vacation. She was still working of course, via video calls and email. Maybe she's been keeping an eye on me. It's been nice to have her around.

"I'm going to miss being able to do this when I'm back in New York," she says, sitting next to me on the rock. "I'm actually thinking of buying a house here."

It's a hollow threat. I can't really imagine Karin living anywhere besides her Manhattan apartment. She's be bored to tears here within two months.

"How are things with the doctor?" she asks, for her first time at this particular meeting.

"They're going well," I say, looking at her, smiling and saying nothing more. Talking is hard.

"As forthcoming as ever, Gabi," she laughs. "Give me something a bit more than that."

I don't really want to tell her about everything, which is strange. If there were ever anyone I could talk to, it would be her.

"Have you made any progress?" she continues.

"I'm writing again. I wrote a chapter the other day," I follow up quickly. "I don't think I've figured out exactly what the next book is going to be, but the writer's block has gone."

"That's incredible Gabi!" she says animatedly. "I'm so proud of you."

Despite myself, I still feel flattered by her gushing. "I don't want to get ahead of myself, but I feel like I'm on track. The doctor has helped me a lot."

She looks at me proudly, like I'm a cake she just baked. "If you don't mind me asking, how is he helping you? Is it therapy? Some sort of creative training?"

"Something like that," I laugh. "Sorry Karin, I can't really talk about it, or even explain it."

I cannot bring myself to tell Karin that I was, and am currently being, inspired by my dreams. She would be insufferable about it. Especially after all those years on the pills she said I shouldn't have been taking.

"Oh, okay. I don't mean to pry," she replies, almost defensively. "But the board keeps pushing me for progress reports. They want something."

"I know, Karin," I say. "But, you know, I don't like letting other people read my work until it's finished. It's similar to my work with the doctor. It's a black box process."

"Gabi…" Karin says. "They're pushing for me to bring in a ghostwriter."

"What?" I exclaim. "A ghostwriter for a writer? What's the point of that?"

"Ghostwriters write, Gabi," she says. "They produce books. Books sell, because they have your name on them. Franchise grows. Milton-Hughes makes money by selling more books. You need to write something."

"I know," I say. "I'll bring you something. I promise. A premise, as a short story. Would that work?"

"Yes, anything. As long as it's the one you want to pursue," she says. "The sooner the better. They can get excited about a premise."

Karin turns around to look at the view. My hands are shaking. Oh yes! I completely forgot.

I push my finger into my palm, trying my hardest to expect it to go straight through. As I bring my head up I notice someone staring at me. His face contorts in surprise as he sees me and he quickly turns away. He's standing at a ledge a bit behind us on the path, wearing a red baseball cap and a light beard. He looks familiar, but I can't place him. Why was he staring at me?

"Have you heard about Kyle getting married?" Karin asks.

"What?" I reply, taken aback. "Oh yes, yeah, I heard."

"Are you okay?" she says.

"Weirdly enough, yes," I reply. "I think I've been too distracted by my work with the doctor to sit and dwell on it like I usually would."

"Good," she replies. "Don't worry. You're going to find someone that's far better for you than him."

"Who says I'm looking for someone?" I ask, annoyed by the assumption that I'm lesser for being a single woman.

"Oh, have you already found someone?" she asks, clearly on a one-way street.

"No," I reply. "Can't I just be happy being single? You're single and successful. Why can't I be?"

"Of course you can," she replies, looking a bit wounded. "I wasn't trying to imply that you couldn't. I just know that you were torn up when things didn't work out. Don't you want to meet someone?"

"Do you?" I ask in return.

We both stay silent. Why am I lashing out at her? I know she just wants the best for me. Do I want to meet someone? Yes, I guess. I would be happy to meet someone and fall in love and be swept off my feet and go to brunch. Sure. That doesn't mean I'm unhappy without it.

"We should probably head back." Karin says suddenly, breaking my drifting thoughts. "I have a meeting that I have to get back for."

Is she angry with me? She doesn't forget about meetings. No, she's doing this so I don't have to walk up the rest of the mountain. She's still so Karin.

"Thanks," I say, as I turn to walk down the mountain path.

"For what?" She starts following me down.

I laugh. "For everything. For everything that you've done and continue to do for me on a daily basis."

She laughs in return. "I think you underestimate how much you've done for me."

"You mean, getting you promoted and making you bucketloads of money?" I harp on.

The guy who was staring at me earlier is still standing here, now playing with his phone. I look at him as we walk past, but he doesn't look at me. He hasn't looked at me once since I noticed him. At least I haven't seen him look at me.

"Should I know that guy?" I stop and ask quietly as we exit earshot. Karin looks around at him. He starts walking up the mountain again without looking at us. It's just that moment that I realize where I recognize him from. He was the one I saw at the gym. The one who was watching me on the treadmill. I remember that stupid red baseball cap. Karin looks at him.

"No, why?" she asks.

"I'm sure it's nothing, but I think he was watching me at the hotel gym, he was staring at me earlier and he is very conspicuously not looking at us now."

"Hmmmm." Karin hums. "Let's continue down."

The man continues up the mountain without turning back. He doesn't seem to follow us and we get back to the lot where Karin parked.

"Keep your eyes out for him." Karin says as we get into the car. "If you see him again, let me know. I'll organize some security for you. I'll take care of it."

"Don't be ridiculous," I reply. "I'm sure it's a coincidence."

As we drive away, I stare out the back of the car, looking for a glimpse of that red cap.

VALLEY OF DEATH

Three anonymous horsemen stood atop the mountain beside the Bamiyan valley, cloth protecting their faces from the wind and sand. Two had rifles slung over their shoulders. The other uttered a phrase and their horses began to descend to the lusher green below them. Their hooves found sure footing on the rocky ground, but kept their speed measured. The landscape blossomed around them, identifying itself as cultivated and watered. Wheat and alfalfa, rice paddies and potatoes. Streams crisscrossed the land.

Ahead of the men, a woman was working alone in front of a small building. She was wearing a bright tunic, but no niqab or hijab. She looked up from her task as the men approached. They could see that her expression didn't change. That didn't please them. They unhorsed and walked up to her, unmasking themselves as they did.

"You're not covered," the man said in Pashto. She didn't reply. He repeated himself in Dari.

She looked around obviously and replied, "I didn't know I was in company. Allah forgive me."

"Where is your husband?" the man continued. One of his companions strolled casually over to the house.

Her eyes followed the man prowling around. "He is tending to the goats. He will be back any moment."

A small pair of eyes peeked out the windows of her home for only a moment, then disappeared.

"You are Hazara, yes?" The man looked around the farm, presumably for her husband. "And Shia?"

"I am Muslim," she replied. Her eyes were downcast, but she stood still.

His eyes narrowed. "No…" The other man was now at her front door.

"My husband will be back very soon," she said, raising her voice loud enough for him to hear. He stopped in front of her door and looked back at her.

The other put his hand on her shoulder. "No... no he won't."

"You might not want to watch this." A familiar voice interrupted Gabi from behind. She turned away from the scene. Feda was standing next to her.

"Feda!?!" She exclaimed.

Feda? Feda's dead. Feda's not real. I am dreaming. Before I have a chance to recognize it, I hear a woman's scream piercing the air. She's being dragged back to her house by the men, a small boy running out to help her. The men kick him away while wrestling her to the ground.

"What's going to happen?" I ask Feda, but as quickly as he appeared, he's gone. I am alone with the screams of a woman I thought I didn't know.

Or is Feda here? Is he that young boy running towards his mother, kicked away by a Taliban boot?

As I consider this, I realize that I am standing openly in a desert watching this take place. At the same time as I realize one of the men could notice me, one of the men notices me.

"Oh shit!" I say, taking a step backward.

He raises his rifle, aiming it towards me. I see the muzzle flash, swiftly followed by a loud bang, and the rock next to me explodes. I turn and start scrambling away, tripping over the rocky ground. Another bang and a ricochet to her right. She notices a large rock and darts behind it for cover. Crouching there, she looks down at her hands, bloodied and blistered from scrambling over sharp rocks. Then I realize something I realized moments before. I nearly slipped out of it. I poke my finger through my hand and re-member that I'm dreaming. This is it. It's happening. I need to take control. This is my dream. This is my opportunity.

I stand up from behind the rock and see the men riding towards me. Okay, so this is my dream, what do I want to do? I want them to stop.

They don't stop.

They pull up in front of me and jump off their horses. I stand idle and confused. Passive. The one shouts to me in a language I cannot understand, one that I understood earlier. What's going on? He walks up to me, pulling his rifle up. He aims its butt at my face and ...

BAM. I crumple to the ground, holding my face, my nose broken. It hurts. How does it hurt in a dream? I want to wake up.

The man stands over me and aims the barrel of his rifle at my face. He's going to kill me. I'm actually going to die. I can't die. I'm dreaming.

He pulls the trigger. Click. The gun misfires. Thank God. I start scrambling away again. I feel hands gripping against my clothes. This isn't right. This is my dream. I saw Feda. I can get away from this. I fumble around the ground and grab a hand-sized rock. I spin around and throw it as hard as I can at my attacker. It strikes true. It hits him square in the face and flings him backwards. I turn and crawl away, managing to get onto my feet and into a run. It works. I sprint as fast as I can over the rocky ground. I can feel them behind me. There's nothing ahead of me except for more rocky ground. I carry on running. I don't stop. I just run. As far as the eye can see it's just dirt and rocks. Just dirt and rocks and dirt and rocks. What a desolate place. There's nothing here. Not even them. They're gone. They're not behind me anymore. I look, and they aren't there. There's nothing. Just me, entirely alone.

That's good. I'm safe. I'm alone. I take a moment to catch my breath. There's nothing here, just me. Just my mind. I'm safe. Alone is good. Alone is safe.

It takes a moment for me to regain myself. I just don't quite know how long a moment is here. It feels like it could have been a few seconds, it could have been an hour. All I've been doing is standing in this empty wasteland.

But now what? I can't just keep standing here.

I guess I can focus on taking command of my dream.

There's nothing around, but rocks and sand and smaller rocks. What should I do? At the moment, I'm barely managing to keep this place uneventful. I try not to think about all the bad things that could happen. I try to stay focused on this reality as it is. But this will get boring quickly. What's the point of controlling your dreams only to have them be safe and boring?

I look up. The sky is cloudless and blue. I'm going to fly. I'd love to fly. There's no reason I can't fly; I control this world. That seems like a good way to start.

I stare up at the sky and try to fly. Oddly enough, nothing happens. I guess I expected that. Idiot. That's the problem. Of course, it won't work if I expect it not to.

I concentrate. I am weightless. There is no gravity here. This is space. I can just fall up from the ground. There's no reason why I shouldn't just float upwards into the sky.

Nothing happens. I'm still just standing in a desert, feet firmly on the ground.

"Hmmm," I say aloud, for no particular reason. "Maybe I should…"

A cloud of dust in the distance interrupts me. It grows quickly from its appearance on the horizon. I squint to see a black sedan come into view, hurtling over the rocks and sand towards me. What's that? Surely, I should know. Somewhere inside me, I must know what's inside that car. Unless, unless that only happens once I see what's inside the car. Maybe my brain just improvises it on the spot. Maybe it's all jazz.

While this all goes on in my head, the dust cloud expands as it approaches, and then shrinks as it starts to slow. Is it slowing down so I don't get covered in dust? That's very considerate of my brain. Who is it? I think I can already guess.

"Hello Gabi," the doctor says, rolling down the window. The car slows to a stop next to me.

I nod to him, unsurprised. "Doctor."

Why do I keep summoning the doctor in my dreams?

He opens the door from the inside and invites me in. I can feel the comfort spilling out. So, I leave Afghanistan and enter Mercedes-Benz. It's far more pleasant. I slide onto leather seats and climate-controlled air wraps around my body. I didn't notice how hot and sweaty I was until now. The doctor is in a perfectly-fitted navy suit with glasses of whisky in his hands. I'm wearing jeans, a halter top and layers upon layers of dust and dirt. The car pulls away.

"Drink?" he offers.

"Why are you always here?" I ask.

"Should you not be asking yourself that question? You are the one dreaming."

"I am asking myself that question," I reply.

He pulls his mouth down as if to say: "Good point."

"This lucid dreaming thing isn't all you made it out to be," I reply moodily.

"If it came easy, everyone would do it," he says, as I notice a change in audio. The rumbling of the car over the rocks has disappeared, and I get this odd sensation in my stomach. We must have reached tarmac. No, it's too quiet even for that. No, I recognize the feeling in my stomach. It's so eerily familiar.

"Look out the window," he says, so I do.

The ground falls away from us as we rocket upwards into the sky, taking off like a jumbo jet.

"Why?" I stammer. "Why can the car fly if I can't? Are you making it fly?"

"I am here because you want me to be here," the doctor explains. "And you know that I can dream lucidly, but this is your dream."

I frown. "So, I'm dreaming that you're here controlling my dream?"

"It is all quite confusing, is it not?" he laughs.

It's surreal. Or just blatantly unreal.

"So," he says, sipping on his whisky. "The world is your oyster. What do you want to do?"

I think for a moment; that's a good question. What do I want? What do I want?

It's a far harder question than it sounds. It's the hardest question ever, isn't it? There's me: someone who spends five hours deciding which restaurant to get food from and then five hours selecting a dish, now trying to decide what I want to do, out of anything in the world. That's a nightmare. That's the agony of choice right there. That's the tyranny of indecision.

And so, I end up doing what I always end up doing. I choose the route of least resistance: The obvious choice.

"I want to fly," I reply. "But not in the backseat of a sedan. I might as well be in a plane. Although at least it's first class. No, I want to fly like a bird."

The doctor rolls his eyes jokingly. "Everyone wants to be Superman."

The car spins without warning and gravity goes haywire. The door opens and I am flung out. I feel myself flying into nothing but air. The sky and earth spin around me. I am screaming. Screaming and falling.

"There you go," the doctor says calmly. He's sitting in an armchair falling alongside me. His whisky glass is still in his hand; not a drop has been spilled. Mine has been lost in the chaos.

"Now you are flying."

My heart pounds and I try to stabilize myself in the air like a skydiver. I try to calm myself down.

"Sure, you are flying directly towards the ground, but that seems no different to me." The doctor sounds like he's enjoying himself. The smug bastard.

"This really isn't helping!" I shout, over the air rushing past me.

"How about this," he goes on. "This armchair can fly. Come sit on it."

He lifts himself off his chair and hovers forward almost as if he's walking, except without moving his legs. I fall towards the chair and grab it by the armrests, pulling myself into it. As I do, the chair starts steadily slowing in its descent. The doctor does the same while standing in front of me. Eventually it comes to a stop, still miles above the ground. I look over the side of the armchair, this familiar classic ruby armchair. Below me span the peaks of mountains, from horizon to horizon. It's breathtaking. It's magnificent. It's also just a little bit terrifying.

"Comfortable?" he asks.

I smile giddily, floating in an armchair high above the earth. I look him in the eyes and nod. The chair lurches forward silently but accelerates quickly. I fumble instinctively for my seatbelt, the safety harness built into whatever ride I'm on. It's not there. The doctor moves to the side, and I speed past him. I fly in a straight line ahead, still feeling the acceleration in my stomach. I squint my eyes as the wind hits them.

"Tell me what you want it to do." I hear the doctor's voice.

"You mean like…" I begin. "If I say down, then…."

The chair instantly responds, darting downwards. I nearly leave the seat, but I manage to grip the sides and stay in. I gasp and laugh. After a moment - "Left!" I bank to the left.

I start playing around to get the hang of it. "Do a loopdeloop!" The chair follows suit.

Screams of joy, a young girl on a roller coaster, I soar through the air.

I could get used to this. I start commanding it to do tricks and it obeys my instructions exactly as I imagine them. I start flying down towards the ground. I want to fly through the mountains to give myself a sense of reference, a sense of speed.

As I descend, I realize I'm not instructing the doctor anymore, I'm instructing the chair. The change happened so subtly I didn't even realize it. He's given me a flying chair. But it's just a chair. I'm flying around on a chair. Instead of shouting my directions to the chair, I simply think them explicitly.

The chair obeys. I rocket into a canyon like a fighter pilot, darting past sheer rock faces, through the gaps between pillars and the side. It's the most incredible feeling I've ever experienced. Piloting at breakneck speeds with perfect maneuverability.

It's exhilarating. The world is a blur of color and danger. I'm doing it. I'm lucid dreaming. I'm fucking flying.

I pull out of the canyon and onto a flat plain again. That's a pity. I was enjoying the canyon. Still the plain is breathtaking in its own way. Ahead of me, I notice some sort of settlement, a city in the desert, an oasis of concrete, abandoned and overgrown. Green and gray. Steel and leaf. I've been here before. It looks so familiar. Look at my works, ye mighty, and despair.

Without my insistence, my chair starts to slow down. Speed up, I think. Turn around. It doesn't listen to me, if it ever truly did, but rather prepares to touch down on the streets of the city. This must be the doctor? Wait, I remind myself, it's not the doctor. It's all me. This is all in my mind. I remember that I'm alone.

The armchair lands comfortably on the tarmac. The city is still. I don't know why I thought it might be teeming with life. There is nothing here. Not even a vulture picking off its carcass. It's not Kabul. Maybe it once was? It doesn't look like Kabul. I've never actually been to Kabul.

I stand out of the chair and walk along the road, through the nothing towards more nothingness.

"Hello?" I call to the city. Is this a city? Can it be a city without inhabitants? But there is someone here. I can feel a presence. "Feda?"

It's not Feda. It's something else. Whatever it is, it starts with a noise. It sounds like scraping. Metal on metal. It reaches up inside me from the bottom and grabs my heart. It pulls my hair on edge. It echoes across an empty and otherwise silent city. It's all the way inside me. It unsettles the depths of me, my heart, stomach and bowels.

I whirl around. Where is it coming from?

The sun gently disappears behind the clouds, clouds that weren't there moments before. The buildings loom over in gray, as a new filter is applied to this picture of the world.

I remind myself that this is a dream. Nothing can hurt me here. But even so, I know that's not true. Whatever this is, it can hurt me. I know, because whatever this is, it has hurt me before.

The scraping grows closer as the darkness draws in. In the distance down the street, a long street uninterrupted by buildings, I can see a darkness. A specific darkness within the general. A vague figure of black.

It moves towards me, and I freeze.

"Run," calls a familiar voice. "Run."

Feda? Doctor? Is it just me, somewhere inside my own head?

I turn to run. I sprint down the street, a street far too large for a little girl to run down. My heart pounds and sweat flings from my brow. I don't look back. I don't look for fear of what I might see.

I tear around a corner into a narrower alley. On the far end I see it. This being of black, bearing down upon me. I scream. I scream my little fucking lungs out as my room flickers into view. Back in my bedroom, still screaming. Still sweating. Where is it? The darkness around me terrifies me. I fumble the bedside lamp trying to turn it on. But this is a normal darkness. This is a darkness I'm used to.

It takes me a few minutes, with damp sheets wrapped around me, to come to terms with reality. I'm okay. It was a dream. It's over. I'm okay.

ANTAGONIST

"Well, I have good news and bad news," I say.

We're at a restaurant in the Cape Winelands. I've never been here before. The view is spectacular. Mountains of green tower over us on the one side, while the vineyards slope down the hill below us on the other. It's a world-class vista. Most of this wine gets exported overseas.

"The good news is that I became fully lucid," I smile. "It was incredible."

"It is, isn't it?" he smiles in return, his tone as measured and contained as ever. "Congratulations."

He doesn't sound unimpressed, but rather unsurprised. He acts like he's teaching me to drive the family car. I feel like I'm training to become a motherfucking fighter pilot.

We are flanked by lush vineyards, sipping oversized glasses of Pinotage under the shade of an umbrella. It's a far more pleasant place than that of my dreams.

"You have picked it up quicker than most," he continues.

"I had help," I admit. "You."

"Me?"

"You did say you would probably show up in my dreams," I say.

"I did," he replies.

"I kinda unintentionally tricked myself into using you," I say. "I dreamed that you were there and could control my dream. Then I realized that meant that I was essentially controlling you and you were controlling my dream, and thus I could just control my dream myself."

"A clever approach," he muses. "Genius."

That word sticks something into me. I feel a slight revulsion at the term.

"What did you do with your newfound power?" the doctor asks.

"I flew," I reply.

"Oh?" he says. "Interesting."

"Is it?" I ask, remembering what he said during my dream. "Isn't it one of the most common things people want to do?"

"Who told you that?" he asks, cocking his eyebrow up.

"Well…" I say. "You did. You made fun of me about it in my dream."

"Did I? That doesn't sound like me at all," he laughs a bit. "Would I ever make fun of you?"

"You're a bit different in my dreams," I say, a little embarrassed. "Which makes sense."

"Why does that make sense?"

"Well, it's not really you, is it? It's how I imagine you. Well, it's what I think of you," I say.

Every way I try to phrase it feels awkward.

"So how is the dream version of me different?" he says. I'm not sure if the smirk is real or imagined. The dream version of him would have definitely smirked.

"He's more fun," I fess up, leaning back into my chair. "Less stuffy and upright."

The doctor chuckles, despite himself. I've started to notice the difference between his intentional and unintentional laughter. Most people laugh as a conversational tool. It's the "mmmhuh" for something that's comedic, even slightly. It's the physical manifestation of LOL. It's just a trained cue to assure the speaker that you hear them. Genuine uncontrolled laughter is different. You can feel the difference. Real laughter is contagious. Sometimes exponentially growing into fits of giggles. Other times it gives a genuine quiet smile to those who hear it. This is one of only a handful of times that I have made the doctor genuinely laugh. His laugh and smile are always warm, but not always genuine.

"It sounds like you prefer him to me," the doctor says, still with this honest smile.

"Don't be jealous," I say. I feel awkward after I say it.

"So," the doctor says, changing the tone. "Do you have a dream report for me?"

I hand over my dream report. The doctor starts reading it straight away and I puff on my cigarette while enjoying the view.

"It turned into a nightmare, same as usual," I say, as he nears the end. "That's the bad news. That evil thing came back. The familiar one. I lost control of the dream, even though I was still self-aware. I couldn't do anything about it. I couldn't control it."

The doctor looks thoughtful as he comes to the end of the story.

"I thought becoming lucid would stop that from happening," I complain.

"It may, but did you really think it would be that easy to defeat your ghost?"

"My ghost?"

"It is the ghost that haunts you. The knife in your back. The insecurity you carry with you. The ghost you need to defeat in order to write your story."

"Defeat?" I ask. "You mean like I have to fight it?"

"Gabi," he says. "Surely, you of all people should know an antagonist when you see one."

SCARAB

Gabi sat by the bar, wearing an uncharacteristically elegant flapper dress. She was surrounded by a twenties prohibition-era speakeasy, smoke spiraling out of her long-filtered cigarette. Her glass was empty on the table in front of her, as was the stool next to her. Both were just waiting for a suitor to fill them. Fate, as it happened, intervened on her behalf. Her whisky was refilled. A handsome gentleman tipped his hat and the bartender.

"Is this seat taken?" he asked, as politely as he could

"Why no, no it isn't," Gabi replied in an accented English that wasn't her own.

"Please forgive me for saying," he went on. "But you are far too pretty to be sitting in such a place by yourself."

"Am I?" she said, fanning her face sarcastically. "I had no idea. Should I leave? I didn't realize I was unwelcome here."

"You misunderstand me ma'am," the man apologized. "I meant no disrespect. I only meant that it's unusual for such a beautiful woman to be unaccompanied here."

"I understand perfectly," Gabi said, bringing her hand down from her fanning motion. She absent-mindedly poked her palm, as she had done a thousand times before. Her finger slides straight through. I notice, and realize, but the gentleman doesn't. He grabs my hand with attempted delicacy and holds it in his.

"Then you understand that offending you was the last thing from my intention," he continues, earnestly looking me squarely in the eye. He's gone from harmless to threatening very quickly. I pull my hand away.

"I understand perfectly…" I repeat. "What your intention is." My expression speaks volumes more.

He presses nonetheless.

"My only intent is to see that pretty face with a smile on it," he says, shooting a boyish grin at me.

That hits a nerve.

"What should I do to you?" I think aloud. The gentleman is taken aback.

"Well, I was thinking that I could perhaps do some things to you," he proposes, thinking that we're engaging in playful banter leading up to my bedroom. "There's the smile I was looking for."

The smile is genuine, but not for his benefit. "I'm sorry, but I just don't think you're in enough control of your bodily functions to be of any good to me," I whisper, as my eyes dart to his crotch. A dampness radiates outwards.

His face falls as he tries to cover up. He stammers an apology and darts away from the table. I cackle as he scampers to the bathroom. The bar turns and watches him go, followed by a few snickers. I savor the laughs like candy.

I down my whisky, stand up, and call out. "This round's on me." To cheers from everyone. The music and dancing grow far louder than a speakeasy should.

"Enjoying yourself?" says the bartender, in a voice I recognize instantly.

I turn to face the doctor, who is idly pouring me another whisky. He looks natural in an old-school three-piece suit, behind a bar.

"'I've always wanted to do that." I grin, getting quite used to him showing up in my dreams. "It's a bit of a party, isn't it?"

"Oh, this sort of party is bound to get out of hand," he says plainly, as if he's seen it all before.

I look around and notice the rising levels of debauchery. A few shouts, broken glasses, some tussles and cackles.

"Well, what's wrong with that?" I ask.

A lady starts dancing on a table, kicking her legs up for the cheering crowds.

"Well, ma'am." The doctor goes on, polishing a glass with a rag. "If they keep this up, they are sure to attract some unwanted attention."

A glass flies past his head and smashes against the bar behind him. He doesn't flinch.

A shrill whistle echoes from upstairs, and everyone goes silent for the briefest of moments.

"Coppers!" The word rings out from the entrance through the constant whistle. It whips the patrons into action. They take off into every different direction. I look to the doctor.

"Why look at me?" he replies, chuckling. "I just work here. You own the place. Designed it yourself..." He nods a little to his left behind the bar. It takes me a second before I understand.

"I'll take the secret route out!" I say, with obvious excitement, jumping over the bar. There's a trapdoor under a rug. I pull it open and climb down, leaving it for the doctor to follow me.

The ladder seems to go on forever, as I climb down into what feels like a dank sewer. I hear the sounds of water sporadically from the ceiling. Finally, following minutes of climbing, my foot touches against a hard flat surface.

It's completely dark. I need light. I reach to my thigh and grab the flashlight strapped there. I'm starting to get the hang of this, shining the beam of light around. I see movement towards me. Black wings. I scream as hundreds of bats surround me, flapping violently.

"I fucking hate bats!" I shout, flailing my arms ineffectively at the leathery creatures. The flashlight flies out of my hand in panic.

"Then get rid of them," instructs the doctor.

"Arrrrrgh!" I scream.

I feel a surge of heat as a flame erupts next to me. It's a torch mounted on the wall. I lit it. In the faint darkness, I can see that they dot the walls on either side of the corridor.. I can light them. I can light them all. I know I can.

"Ignite!" I command, throwing up my arms in the air animatedly. Each one bursts into flame, sequentially. I smile, knowing that I did that. The tunnel fills with light, scattering the bats and illuminating the face of the doctor. His face is colored with the warm light of the fire and a gasp of surprise. I continue to slap my hands against my body to be sure that none of the flying, leathery rats is stuck to me.

"They are all gone," the doctor says. There is still a noticeable look of confusion on his face.

"I fucking hate bats," I repeat. "Stupid little winged rodents! Why do you look so surprised?"

"Nothing," he replies. "I'm just surprised you could light up the tunnel."

I smirk at him, my smile now visibly lit by the flickering light I created.

"Not just a pretty face, right?" I say, still trying to brush the remnants of any contact with the bats from my body. I turn and start off down the ancient sewer tunnel.

"Where are you going?" he asks.

"To the end," I say, pointing at the small circle of light that represents where the tunnel meets something else.

"What's at the end?" he asks again. Sometimes he feels like a wise teacher, other times he sounds like a four-year-old.

"There's only one way to find out."

The circle of light grows larger and larger as we continue down the sewer tunnel. I feel fresh air blowing against my face. It's a warm wind, a dry wind. As we reach the end, an entirely different world reveals itself. The tunnel ends abruptly into nothing, except a sheer cliff face overlooking a desert. Sand stretches as far as I can see. There is only one defining feature, apart from dunes upon dunes overlapping each other in an ocean of sand. An oversized black dome sits unnaturally in the center of the view. It's the size of a small city center, but with no visible roads leading in or out. It looks like an obsidian marble lying forgotten in some giant's sandpit. I peer around, hoping not to see the giant.

"Woah" escapes me.

"Woah indeed," the doctor murmurs.

"I want to see what's inside," I turn to him, beaming.

"So do I," he replies. "But first you should take stock of what is in your way."

I look down at the desert. It must be a thousand feet below me. I guess I'll need to fly down somehow. My eyes catch movement. Black shapes are shuffling around the sand between us and the dome. It's hard to see how big they are, or what they are, but they're living.

"What are they?" I ask the doctor.

"How should I know?" he shrugs. "But you should probably take something with which to defend yourself, should it come to that." He motions to a large blanket rolled up behind us.

I unroll it to reveal an arsenal of different weaponry. From swords to assault rifles to nunchucks. I stifle a laugh at the absurdity of it. I can't judge, though. It's my absurdity. Honestly, I thought I was subtler than this. I guess this sort of creativity is unrestrained. I grab a sword. It's a cartoonishly large sword that wouldn't look out of place in one of those Japanese animations. It's far too big for me. I'm sure any actual sword expert would cover their face with their hands at the thought of someone using it. As I try to raise it, I see why. I can barely lift the thing, let alone use it effectively. That's my own fault, I realize. As soon as I thought about how heavy it should be, that's how heavy it became.

"That one is lighter," says the doctor. "I believe it is made out of a special lightweight material."

I pick it up with one hand and twirl it around. It's light. It feels natural. I feel natural. I can be a badass here. This is my house. I make the rules. I could get used to this.

"How will you get down?" asks the doctor.

"Quickly," I say through a childish grin, fueled by bravado. The doctor looks at me curiously.

I back up, shuffling down the tunnel, before I launch into a sprint towards the opening. I imagine myself swan-diving out into the air, pirouetting, before landing on the sand like a superhero, dust spraying up around me. Anything is possible here, right?

But as I approach the edge, my body falters. In a panic, I try to slow down, stumbling clumsily. I'm not going to stop in time. I'm going to topple over the side, my heart reckons. I 'm going to topple over the side and die. Instead, I feel a ruff grasp on the back of my neck. A hand pulls me back into the tunnel like a naughty puppy. The bravado that compelled me disappeared completely.

"Do not underestimate this reality," the doctor says, as he pulls me back to safety. "It will take time before you become fully comfortable controlling it."

The wind batters me as I look over the edge. It seems to be picking up. The view is more foreboding than it was a moment ago. I look to the horizon to see a wall of sand approaching.

"A sandstorm," I mutter. "I don't have much time."

"So how will you get down?" the doctor asks again.

I put my two fingers into the sides of my mouth and let out a whistle, an idea coming to me as suddenly as the sandstorm.

"What?" he asks as we wait for the effect to become apparent.

"I thought you might already know, Gandalf," I laugh, my smile returning. "I've learnt a few things from reading."

An eagle the size of a car glides straight past the tunnel, turning her head to look at me as she does. Before my body has a chance to second guess me, I leap off the cliff as the raptor returns for her second fly-by.

I fall freely through the air, making sure to keep my sights locked on the eagle. I can't lose her for even a moment. With certainty I land, sprawling across her back. I disrupt her flight path, but she quickly corrects herself. I clamor at her feathers, trying to find a handhold. She flies level to allow me the needed stability. Once settled, I lean forward and whisper, "Take me to the dome."

She nods slightly as a response and flies where instructed, diving to gain momentum. It's less comfortable than the armchair was. Less responsive too. She has a will of her own. Is that a will I gave to her? How could it not be?

The wind blasts my eyes as we swoop down above the desert. As we get closer to the ground, I can see more details on the black figures that litter the sand. They look like massive insects, carapaced like scarabs, but built like praying mantises. I'm glad I didn't jump down as I planned. I expected a dramatic landing on the floor, before fighting my way through a horde of enemies. Looking at them, I shudder to think how that would have gone. Not well, I suspect.

The black dome rises up ahead of us. I underestimated its size from the cave. I can barely understand it. It could be the size of a mountain, it's hard to tell. The surface appears untextured and pitch black, as if it's devoid of light rather than a structure painted black. The creatures seem to be more densely packed closer to the dome, larger too. Ahead, a particularly large one raises his head to look at us. He jumps into the air, large mantis-like wings revealing themselves. My eagle rears back, raising its talons to meet the enemy.

"Ohhhhh fuck" I hear myself shout, as I slide back off my mount. I try to grasp at her feathers, dropping my sword and barely managing to stop my fall. As the two clash, the force throws me clear off and I feel myself plummeting through the air towards the sand below me.

Oh god, I'm going to die. I'm going to get killed by a thousand monstrous black insects. It takes me a moment to remind myself that I'm not going to die, that this is just a dream. This is my dream! I look around, seeing my sword flailing around in its own dive. I call to it.

Nothing.

"You are mine!" I shout, feeling an invisible thread connecting it to my hand. I pull it in quickly. The sword follows. I try to spin myself around in the air so that I hit the sand feet first. I half succeed. I grab the sword as I fall face forward into the desert, losing it again in the process.

I pull myself up as quickly as possible. It takes me a few seconds to orient myself, surrounded by these creatures. They stare at me with what must be their faces. Slick, oil dripping black faces. These alien beasts must be a part of me, right? They must represent something, right? Or is this just what I think a nameless enemy looks like?

My sword lies beside me, half buried in sand. I guess this is what I wanted: The chance to fight. I can kill these things, these ticks. I reach for my blade. My feet sink into the sand as the first mantis darts forwards. I barely manage to bring my sword up in time, meeting the claw that descends onto me. The force makes me step backwards. I try to regain my footing, and bring my sword up again, slicing upwards in an arc. The mantis feints me, charging and then sidestepping. I feel its claw slide straight through my stomach, warm blood spilling out around the wound. It feels strange. It's not painful, simply... odd. I felt the other creatures close in, ripping apart Gabi's body as I sit straight up in my bed. My surroundings slowly come into focus. I'm okay. I'm safe.

Awake again, I pat down my stomach. There's no wound, but there's still pain there. I can almost feel where I was cut. I feel as though my intestines are being pulled out of my body. I must be delirious. It's still the middle of the night. I don't feel well-rested. I guess my mind protected me from feeling the rest of that. I guess that's what the doctor meant when he said that it's real.

Instead of writing this one down, I pour myself a glass of whisky and light myself a cigarette. It helps me takes the edge off, as I reimagine my body being ripped apart by alien insects.

REVELATIONS

The doctor holds his hand out for my dream report.

"I don't have it." I say, staring at his expectant hand.

"Oh," he says, visibly disappointed. "But you did write it?"

"Yes, of course," I lie. "I just didn't know that you still wanted to see my homework."

He curls up the side of his mouth.

"Reading your writing is never work. But don't forget your basics, Gabi. Write down every dream first thing in the morning. We are trying to help you write a book after all."

"Yes sir..."

"But more importantly, don't forget to keep your reality check routine now that you're lucid dreaming."

I haven't really. I've been lax since I started lucid dreaming. Somehow, he knows that. I quickly do a reality check. I'm not dreaming. I celebrate with my other habit: lighting a cigarette.

"What happened in the rest of your dream?" he asks. "Seeing as I can't read your report."

I recall the dream for him, more vaguely than I would expect. Even with more experience, I don't remember is as clearly as I thought I did. The end though, that I remember clearly.

"I thought I was all-powerful in my own dreams," I moan. "I certainly didn't try to get eaten by a swarm of giant insects. Why can't I control my dream?"

"You can control your dreams insofar as you can control your own mind," he explains. "You do not have complete control over your own mind, no one does. Unwanted thoughts creep into our heads. We cannot simply think away pain, or painful memories. Our own minds work against us, amplifying our own weaknesses, even when we are aware of it."

"Okay, okay."

"Some people have trained their entire lives - Buddhist monks, for example, practice mindfulness every day through meditation, denying their desires and living under strict discipline. Even they only ever achieve imperfect control. You have been practicing for barely a fraction of that. Do not underestimate how difficult this will be."

I guess I struck a nerve.

"Geez, okay," I reply, throwing my hands up like the world's laziest mime. "It's just, you know, being a millennial and all, I'm used to having things happen instantly."

"Even in the eighties, everything could be accomplished with a few minutes of montage and a pop rock hit," the doctor says.

He delivers the line with such dry earnestness, that it takes me a moment to realize it's a joke. Pop culture references look unfamiliar on him.

"It is important to remember that taking control of your dreamworld is not as easy as intellectually understanding that you can. It is the difference between knowing the rules of football and being able to play."

"And that would make you my coach, yes?" I reply. "Making me run laps and, um, kick the ball."

"You don't know much about football, do you?" the doctor laughs. "Soccer, at least, as you call it."

"I thought you were talking about American football, you know, real football. Perhaps you should choose better analogies," I spit back, jokingly. "Perhaps you're more like the Alfred to my Batman."

"You are far too scared of bats to be Batman," he smiles again. It's one of his feigned smiles, I can tell. But something else sticks in my throat as I'm about to reply.

"Batman was scared of bats though. That's why he became Batman," I reply, absentmindedly.

Something doesn't add up.

"Oh really?" he says. "My mistake. I have never watched Batman."

"I honestly never thought you had," I ask.

I think back to when I explained my dream to him. What I said, and what I didn't say.

"What is wrong? Where did you go, all of a sudden?" he asks.

"Nowhere," I reply. "Never mind."

He looks uncomfortable; it's unusual for me to be quiet for this long. He's trying to figure out what he said wrong. He's noticed that I've pulled back. I open my mouth to confront him, to ask him.

How do you know I'm scared of bats?

But I don't say it. I chicken out. I don't know if I want to know the answer. No one knows that. My dream last night, I never told him about the bats.

"All you need to do is practice more, and you will get the hang of it," he says. "Don't beat yourself up."

I look down at my hand and touch my palm with my finger. It doesn't go through.

"You are not dreaming now, Gabi," he says. "But it is good that you are still doing your check."

"I'm going to go now, doctor," I say, standing and collecting my things. He can tell I am rushing.

"I'll see you," I say, as he follows me out of his apartment.

"What's wrong?" he asks. "Are you okay?"

Every interaction I've had with the doctor flashes through my head in small incoherent chunks. The bile rises in my throat, the anger welling up inside me. Something's not right here. He's been lying to me.

"I'm fine," I say, forcing a smile. "I just need to be alone for a while."

The drive home is a blur. My mind floats elsewhere: He's always been able to read me... uncannily. There's something more to it than simple intuition. There's something here that just doesn't make sense.

I exit my cab by my apartment, and visually check up and down my road for suspicious characters. Even at my most distracted, I won't forget this. It's a reality check in its own right, for anyone who lives in South Africa.

My heart stops, for just a second longer than it should. On the street corner, a familiar cap catches my attention. A red baseball cap. A red cap on a man leaning against a wall, I don't catch him well enough to know for sure that it's him. But it must be him, right? The man from before. There's no doubt now. He's following me. Or am I just being crazy. Red caps aren't that rare. Maybe I'm just being paranoid.

I hurry into my building, my fingers fumbling with my keys. I feel comfort when the front gate closes behind me, even more so when I enter my apartment and shut the door. I slam the security gate and lock the deadbolt.

For a moment, I just stand with my back against the wall. I breathe deeply. I try to calm down.

As I step forward, I notice myself kicking mail on the floor. No, not mail. Just an envelope, slipped under the door. Just a standard white envelope with my name hand-written in an untidy scrawl on the front.

Gabrielle Rivers.

No address - just my name. I rip open the top of the envelope and pull out a small piece of paper inside.

Don't trust the doctor.

I flip it over. Nothing I check in the envelope. Nothing.

Don't trust the doctor.

Who sent this? Who could have...?

It comes to me like I've forgotten the stove on: The man in the red cap. He must have slid this under the door. He must have. Why? Who is he, and why is he trying to warn me about the doctor?

It dawns on me that I don't actually know who the doctor is. Doctor Sivers. I know almost nothing about him. We've had weeks of sessions diving into my most personal feelings. I feel like he's been rummaging around inside my head and yet, I know next to nothing about him.

But he's famous...

I rush over to the computer.

I can find everything there is to know about him. I can ask the omnipresent, omnipotent and omniscient to share his secrets with me. God's only as far away as my internet browser.

Google is a magnificent and scary thing. All of humanity's thoughts at our fingertips. All connected. Indexed and searchable. Many online authors have created succinct bite-sized bios of our resident doctor.

Jakob Sivers was born in St Gilgen, Austria in 1965. He excelled academically from a young age and moved to Vienna to further his studies. He completed his medical education as a psychiatrist at the University of Vienna. It was during this time that he became increasingly interested in genius, largely based on his experiences with a specific patient. The patient, anonymously titled F, was a genius polymath who had descended into psychosis and was unable to reliably distinguish reality from delusion and hallucination. Sivers' supervisor, who was treating the patient, warned Sivers not to get taken in by the patient's rich dream life and the content of his hallucinations, but rather to focus on the more empirical areas of study. Sivers argued that it was key to helping the patient, and grew more and more interested in dreaming, hallucination and genius.

While working with the University, Sivers met the woman who would become his first wife, Rachel Gerber. She was an American student at the University of Vienna, also studying medicine. They married while he was finishing his studies. She too became interested in dreaming, although from a neurological viewpoint. They started working together on what became their most famous paper: "The Other Side: The neuro-psychological importance of dreaming in cognitive function."

After his patient committed suicide, Sivers fell into deep depression. On encouragement from his wife Rachel, Sivers started looking for other geniuses. Thus, he began the work that came to define his career and the contents of his first book. One of his early subjects was British mathematician and game-theorist Richard Cave. Cave was a notably charismatic man, and highly influential. The two quickly became close friends.

Soon after this work began, Rachel, who had recently fallen pregnant, was tragically killed by a drunk driver...

I stop reading for a moment.

There's a picture of Rachel, all blonde hair and fierce eyes. A bit disheveled. Typical post-doc. She was about my age when the photo was taken. She's smiling at the camera on what looks like a college campus. It must have been just before she died, from the date under the photo.

She was pretty, despite being unkept. It wouldn't be right to say she looked happy. Driven, perhaps? Something more than happiness. Passionate?

I continue my obsessive searching deep into the night.

"Jakob Sivers" controversy

"Jakob Sivers" red hat

"Jakob Sivers" danger

I find nothing, nothing except corroborations of his background and accomplishments. No suggestions of maleficence. The only personal details are of the deaths of those he was closest to. His online persona is far more respectable than mine.

Late enough, now early morning, I take a break from the screen to lie back on my bed and rest my eyes for a moment.

Just for a moment.

SURFACING

Gabi stared up at the sky. There wasn't much else to look at. She was on a small dinghy, surrounded on all sides by an endless ocean, staring upwards. It hurt her eyes, but what else was there but blue?

"Hello!" She shouted into silence. The word was swallowed up by the sea. All she heard in response was the lapping of water against the boat. All she could see was sea and sky. Blue, eye-aching blue. She could taste the salt, the thirst that came with water that couldn't quench it. She licked her lips.

How'd she get here? It seemed strange. She shouldn't be here.

She stared at her hands, blistered and blotched from the sun. They reminded her of something, something that seemed so far ago, something she should do. So, she did it. She pushed her finger through her hand, and it goes straight through. It goes straight through and I'm here. I'm dreaming. I slip into it far more comfortably each time, like old jeans worn by time and weight fluctuations.

So why did my mind bring me here, to the middle of an ocean? I guess I wanted to be alone. There's no one else here. There's nothing here. There's nothing for thousands of miles in either direction. I'm as alone as alone can be. Alone in my head.

During my waking life, I find it hard to remember my dreams. During my dream life, I tend to have trouble remembering my waking life. I know I was in the middle of something important, but it feels so far away. What was I doing?

"Hello!!!!" I shout again into the nothingness.

I struggle to remember why I wanted to be alone. Something drove me here. Trying to remember my real life in my dreams is sometimes as difficult as the opposite. But I do remember, practice helps, it was the doctor.

I am interrupted by the violent realization of something beneath me. The dinghy lurches to the side as a large gray mass breaks the water's surface. The skin of a whale emerges, spraying water from its blowhole. It drenches me. I fall back into the boat, trying to regain balance as the gray lump slowly disappears again below the water. The explosion of activity is gone as quickly as it arrived, leaving me nothing but a disheveled lump on the bottom of the boat. The only evidence it was here is the disturbed water rippling from where once was a whale.

"Unnerving, isn't it?" the doctor says, perched on the front of my dinghy, like some teenager smoking outside a school. "It is so easy to assume you are alone, just because you can't see anyone else around."

"Fuck!" I reply, struggling to my feet through the imbalance.

"Why are you in my dream again?" I shout at him

"Technically speaking, you are also in my dream," he replies.

"So, it's actually you," I say. "I'm not just dreaming about you, it's actually you in my dream."

"In a manner of speaking, yes," he says.

"Fuck you!" I spit. "So you've been lying to me this whole time. This doesn't make any sense. How can you be in my dream?"

I don't know what to do with my fury. Half of me wants to attack him. The other half wants to storm off, but I can't. I'm in a boat in the middle of the ocean. I cross my arms and turn in the other direction. I can't think of anything else to do, but even in my rage I realize it makes me look like a sulky teenager.

"I know you want me to answer you directly," he continues. "But I cannot answer you without explaining what dreams are. Straight answers can be more misleading than convoluted ones."

I spin around.

"Just tell me the fucking truth," I say. "How about that?"

"By learning how to become lucid in your dreams, you started to understand their importance. Dreams are not simply the day's afterthoughts. They are not random brain activity at night, to be ignored and forgotten by morning. There is a reason why sleep is a fundamental human need, and why we lose our sanity without it. There is a reason why everyone dreams, why our unconscious experience is revered by cultures and religions the world over. Our dream life is just as real and important as our waking life. Our dreamworld is the other side of our physical world, seen with different eyes. And much like in the physical world, we share it with others."

He takes a pause. I'm not quite sure I understand what he means.

"The same way that we all exist in the same physical world, we all exist in the same dreamworld," he announces.

He lets that sit for a few seconds. Is he saying what I think he's saying?

"Imagine that this ocean is the dreamworld. Here you are on your little boat, having your dream. There are three billion other boats out there as well. If you know where to go, sometimes even if you don't, you can bump into someone else."

I can't help but laugh at the absurdity, but the back of my mind reminds me that he has to be right. After all, I'm talking to him in my dream at this very moment. Unless I'm just talking to myself. How can I tell?

"So, if I paddle far enough, I'll come across someone else?" I ask.

"Metaphorically yes," he continues, undeterred. "The dreamworld is very different from the physical world. It has different dimensions. Space and time are not fixed, nor constant here. You may have noticed that yourself. Sometimes time runs the same way as it does in the physical world, other times you just skip through the boring bits. Physical laws do not apply outside of your expectation and understanding of them. The dreamworld is a purely mental space. It is constructed primarily out of qualia: the subjective experience of minds."

"I still don't understand how you travel between people's dreams."

"It is difficult to explain to someone who has limited experience," he says. "But essentially, it is not unlike doing anything in a dream. You have to will it so. But... it requires far more skill and willpower to find your way into someone else's dream in comparison to mastering your own dream experience. Furthermore, most of the time you should know them, or at least understand them, in order to find them in the dreamworld. It is even easier if they summon you."

"Summon you?" I ask.

"If they dream about you, then it is easier to slip in."

"This doesn't make any sense," I complain.

"Does it not?" he says. "I assure you that there are far less intuitive truths in the universe. Have you ever studied material physics? It is complicated. Far more complicated than this."

"So let's assume that you're telling the truth," I ask. "Why haven't you told me any of this before?"

He shrugs.

"I was in the process of telling you," he says. "I first needed to teach you the alphabet, then the language, and only then could I even begin to tell you. Unfortunately, you jumped ahead in your textbook."

"Bullshit!" I mutter.

"Think back to our first meetings," he continues. "Would you have believed me?"

I remain quiet.

The doctor jumps down off the side of the boat. He lands lightly in the water but does not sink. He stands on it as if he is the savior of mankind.

"Walking on water?" I scoff. "Really?"

"You can swim if you would prefer," he says. "But I think we should go somewhere more comfortable. Your mind has dumped us in a rather inhospitable place."

I look over the edge of the boat. I can walk on the water too. If he can, then I can. Simple as that. I step out over the edge and...

Sploooosh

I fall straight under. Saltwater stings my eyes. My senses are thrown into disarray. I kick and struggle to get back to the surface. Instinctively I pat down my body, reaching for my phone in my jeans before reminding myself that it's a dream.

"God damnit!" I splutter, trying to tread water to keep my head above the surface. "I thought I got the hang of this."

"You never fully get the hang of it," the doctor says, returning to hold his hand out for me. "At least not enough to stop trying." I take his hand, and he pulls me up into the air, over the water. He picks me up as if I weigh nothing at all, as if he's swinging his daughter around on the beach.

He drops me down onto the water next to him. The proximity to him standing on the water makes it easier, somehow. My feet touch firm, albeit slightly squishy, ground.

"Also," the doctor continues, "I am trying to graduate you from your training wheels."

"What do you mean?" I ask, still soaking wet. "Training wheels?"

"I may have helped you a bit in the past," he replies, almost guiltily. "Helped you control things in your dreams."

He starts walking along the ocean, assumedly in a specific direction. I follow as I feel the redness of embarrassment climbing up my neck. My mind flashes to moments with the doctor along the way. Flying through the desert. In the speakeasy. It was always him.

"How can you help me?" I ask. "I don't understand, can you control my dreams?"

"Strictly speaking, it is not the case of me being in your dream or you being in mine. When we are together, we are both sharing the same dream space. If someone else were here, they would be sharing it too. That is what we have been doing all along. We can both control this dreamspace, in fact, it is created by both our minds together, like a mutual story, or a conversation."

"So, all this time, you were controlling our dreams?"

"We both were," he smiles. "Together. I tried to leave as much up to you as possible, but sometimes I would give you a little push in the right direction. After all, I am a lot more practiced at this than you are."

"Like a learner driver..." I say.

He nods.

I look across the endless ocean.

"I still have a lot of questions," I say.

"I'm sure you do," he replies. "But some things cannot be explained simply."

"So why don't you just show me then?" I ask.

"What would you like me to show you?" he asks.

"Well, let's go visit someone's dream," I say, getting rather excited at the thought. "Rather than walking aimlessly around an ocean while you explain it to me."

"I suspected it would come to this," he says. "Do you promise to behave? Remember that although we are in the dreamworld, this is all real."

"But I mean, we can't get hurt or anything. I mean properly hurt," I ask. "The whole dying in your dream, dying in real life, thing is a myth, right?"

"Most things here will not affect you physically, usually, over and above physiological responses. Your heart rate, sweating, these things are affected," he says. "But everything that happens here happens, it happens to your mind, your memory, your experience. You can be damaged mentally, or emotionally, by whatever happens in the dreamworld."

"I think I'll be okay then," I laugh. "I'm already emotionally damaged."

"It is not only your wellbeing that concerns me," he says, stopping me. "We are going to interrupt and take part in someone's dream, their most private sanctum. Only today you understood the invasiveness of that act."

"Oh, I remember," I reply. "You're the one who's been invading my dreams for the last month."

He reaches into his pocket, ignoring my jibe. He pulls something from it and holds it above my head, sprinkling dust over me.

"What on earth are you doing now?" I ask.

"It will make you invisible," he says. "See?"

I look at my arms. As the dust collects, they blend into the background. Eventually, I cannot see them at all. "Invisibility dust? Really? Tinkerbell?"

"Easier than a cloak," he laughs, sprinkling it on himself. He disappears as I watch.

"You're making this a lot less cool than it should be," I mutter.

I gaze around in incredulity. I am now a disembodied point of view along on the surface of the ocean.

"So where do you want to go?" he asks. "Anyone you have in mind?"

"Anyone, except someone I know," I say. "Take me somewhere strange."

BULLETPROOF BIKINI

James sits in his lounge, surrounded by his loving family. The kids play with cars on the carpet as colors spit into the dim light from a color television. His wife leans on him, but they both look straight ahead. A familiar theme song fills the air.

"Would you like some coffee?" his wife asks.

"Sure, sweetie," he replies.

She pulls herself off the couch and into the kitchen. Why does everything sound so tinny?

Knock, knock, knock.

"Could you get the door?" she says.

James sighs, getting out of his comfortable spot. He'd spent all day looking forward to just relaxing at home and now there's some unannounced visitor arriving. Who would call on them at this time of night? He opens the door to an unexpected face, one he hasn't seen for years upon years. A face he doesn't much care for, and a face he no longer needs to.

"Frank..." he stammers. "But you're dead?"

"Meeeeh." His father waves it off. He would never die unless he felt like it. "I'm not. You will be though, soon." He points his finger accusingly at his son, a wrinkly and crooked digit. "The Russians will see to that."

He pushes his way in, with no resistance from a son far stronger than him. He glances at the kids and grimaces. "Them too!" The children look up at him in fear.

"Stop scaring them," James whines. His dad barely registers it.

"And where's Helen?" he asks.

"In the kitchen," James says but regrets it. She walks out that very moment, holding two cups of coffee. One falls to the floor and shatters.

James' father closes his eyes and grimaces at the noise. He flails out with his cane, seemingly out of instinct, which hits James and throws him clear across the room. His wife screams.

"You think that's something, that's nothing," his father rants. "I'll show you something. You don't even know."

"Stay away from my children," James says from the floor, more forcefully than he had resisted before.

"I'm protecting them!" his dad shouts. "I'm protecting them again."

James tries to get up, but he can't. He's too wounded; he can't even get to his feet.

"Useless," says his father. "You can't protect them. You're soft. You've always been soft. Just a chickenshit."

"Fuck you." James spits from the floor. His father laughs.

"Big talk," he mocks. "But as usual, that's all."

I can barely bear it, the hairs on the back of my neck raise themselves. This is James' great fear come to life. It's mocking him. Taunting him.

I won't let it.

As his father leans back onto his cane, it snaps in half, letting him collapse onto the floor. Never have I been so pleased watching an old man fall. I stifle a laugh, one I'm pretty sure James notices.

I feel a hand grip on my shoulder. The doctor. I can't see him, but I know he's there. He can tell when I'm interfering in the dream.

James pulls himself onto his feet, unsure of whether to offer his aged father help, or take advantage. He approaches his father, appearing to choose the former.

"I don't need your help," his father says. He uses his knee to get onto his feet and brushes away James' hand. "They do." He motions towards the kids.

His sentence ends with a knock on the door, the loud and insistent knocking of an unwelcome authority.

"Don't answer it!" says the grizzled old man, his voice now laced with fear rather than anger. "It's them."

"Don't be ridiculous," says his son, his voice less sure than intended.

The knock turns into a bang, the bang into a bash. They hear the splintering of wood as the door starts to cave inwards. His father whips out a pistol that looks roughly his age. James stands petrified in place as uniformed men from a past era storm through the front door into his lounge. A bullet from the pistol finds the heads of the first, second and third soldiers into the house. The fourth leaps over his comrades to pin James' father with his bayonet rifle. They wrestle on the floor as more troops storm in.

"Do something," I whisper. James looks around frantically.

"The gun." I don't know if I'm speaking or not. "You keep a gun under the table."

James reaches there, under the table, for the gun he never knew he had. He manages to find it. He looks at it for a moment. It's loaded and ready to go. Just point and squeeze. His father had taught him that much at least. His first shot finds the wall, his second the shoulder of the nearest soldier. The man slumps back and falls over. Another soldier raises his rifle, the barrel aimed straight at James's face. This is his death. His father was right. He can't protect his family. He's just a chickenshit.

Instead of watching a muzzle flare end his life, he witnesses a knife embedding itself into the eye of his attacker. His wife, his beautiful wife, has emerged from the kitchen, not willing to let her home be invaded. He smiles before turning to kick the soldier off his father. He holds a hand to lift his dad off the ground for a second time, this time with success. The old man grunts as he pulls himself up.

What might have been a touching moment is interrupted by a flash of light from the window. The color of the room changes. All eyes turn to the view. In the distance, a distinctive mushroom cloud sprouts out of America's horizon. A fungus that will grow and absorb them all, growing ever bigger every second.

"I told you," says the father. "I told you what would happen." His voice is steadier than it has been.

They should get to the bomb shelter.

"We need to get to the bomb shelter," James says.

His father laughs. "A bomb shelter? You think a bomb shelter will save you from that nuke? We're already dead."

James looks to his kids and his wife.

I don't know what to do. A nuclear bomb? How can I stop that? The silence is uncomfortable for only a moment, but it's a moment that stretches for an age. James moves to sit with his family. Well, not all of them. His father stands sentinel at the window, glaring at the inevitable proof that his paranoia was right. His son looks up at him.

"Frank... dad. Come sit down," James says, motioning with his head for his father to join them. Frank looks down at the family he was never allowed to know.

"The bomb," Frank mutters. His son shrugs.

"It doesn't matter."

James motions to his daughter. "This is Katie." Katie meets eyes with her grandad for a moment. "And this is David."

Frank feels the warmth of his own tear touch the top of his cheek. His throat swells with a pain unlike any he has known. A feeling he didn't even know he longed for.

"Hi..." he stammers through it.

"Come sit with us grandpa," David says.

Frank breaks. A smile under what could be a sob or a laugh. He moves his ancient bones towards his children.

The window shatters. Glass sprays the room. They are deafened by the force of human nature. The shockwave has hit them, sound and power. Frank is thrown from his feet against the wall where his son lay not moments ago.

"Dad!" shouts James.

Frank reaches out to him, but he can see the wall of the explosion on the horizon approaching too quickly. He won't make it. No one could save them. He doesn't expect a hand grabbing the back of his neck. He doesn't expect a woman, appearing out of nothingness, to drag him across the floor. He doesn't even look at the angel. He wraps his arms around his family as the flames enter the house and envelope them. Incinerated into indistinguishable ash.

The flames twirl around, but they don't reach me. I look down at my now visible hands, entirely unburnt. The doctor's hand is on my shoulder in the eye of a maelstrom. The world is on fire, but some sort of force protects us.

"We are alone again, Gabi."

"James woke up?" I ask.

"James, no…" he says. "No, Frank woke up."

I watch as the last of Frank blows away with the family he never knew. It was Frank's dream.

"At least he found some redemption."

"He likely won't remember much of it when he wakes," the doctor says. "But he might have some vague sense of it."

The inferno around us begins to subside.

"I can't fucking believe we just witnessed someone else's dream," I say. "I mean, how did we do that? Well, how did you do that?"

"You can travel somewhere in the dreamworld, as long as you know where it is. The more you know about the dreamer, or the dream, the easier it is to find." The doctor looks pleased with himself.

"Was he a friend of yours?" I ask. I try to think about the fact that he didn't die in a nuclear explosion and that he has probably just woken up somewhere.

"I would not call him a friend, no," he says. "But I know him."

"What's his story?" I ask. "Why did he dream about a nuclear strike on his nuclear family?"

"I thought you were the storyteller. Why don't you tell me?" he replies.

"Ha." I should have been expecting this, I guess. The world around has calmed slightly, only glowing ash remains in all directions.

"Frank, a veteran of the cold-war era, could never adjust to family life after being a soldier. His violence towards his children and family drove them to abandon him. As such, he's never been a part of his grandchildren's lives. He regrets this distance, especially as his life draws to a close, but he doesn't know how, or even if, he could reconnect with his estranged son."

"An interesting premise?" asks the doctor.

I look at the wasteland around us.

"I've written enough about war," I say.

"War is so last decade," the doctor muses.

I wrinkle my forehead at him. "The zeitgeist has changed. No one needs reminding that war is bad."

"What are the new relevant issues to the world? Now that global war and the threat of a nuclear holocaust are things of the past," he asks. "Funny how no one stops to really appreciate that, isn't it?"

He's not wrong. It's easy to take for granted the things that don't happen.

"Climate change. Structural, racial, and gender inequality. The perils of capitalism. The perils of populism. Mass surveillance. Fake news. Worldwide pandemics," I reply, listing off each thing on my fingers.

"All very topical... " he says. I can never help but feel like the doctor floats above the world, like somehow he's concerned with something far grander and more important than anything petty like global politics or the fate of the planet.

"You make it sound like celebrity gossip," I say. "But these are the most important themes of our age."

"Which one do you want to write about?" he asks. "We all pick and choose our causes. Which one is yours?"

I don't know how to respond to that. I hope my procrastination, or indecision, presents itself as thoughtfulness. Instead of answering, I let my eyes wander over the world around us.

It starts to change. Is it part of the explosion? No, it's time. Time is speeding up. It becomes visible, its geographic impact. The ash clears, leaving just a crater on what were once the rural fields of a world superpower. Clouds race past. The sun rockets across the sky like a shooting star. Seasons come and go in seconds as nature begins to take over. The grass shoots up. Rain falls and fills rivers. Trees sprout and rise tall into the sky, birds even appearing in between them.

"Can we go to another dream?" I ask.

"Sure," he replies. "But not tonight."

"Why not tonight?" I ask.

"We have no time," he says looking down at his watch. I can see the hands on his clock-face, but it makes no sense to me. I don't know why.

"Good morning," he says.

"What?"

The doctor opens his mouth to say something, but no voice comes out. Instead, artificial chiming emerges. He is replaced by the polyphonic tones of my phone waking me up. I slap at the scream clumsily to turn it off.

I am lying uncomfortable on top of my comforter at an off angle on my bed, my phone lying next to me.

THE RISING TIDE

Gabi casually strolled along a rock path on the side of Table Mountain. She was taking her sweet time. Karin strode ahead of her. Her pace was that of an 18-wheeler, seemingly with an equal stopping distance.

"What are you looking for?" she called back, stopping to see what was taking so long. Gabi was idly glancing around off the side of the rock path.

"I'm not sure," Gabi said. "I feel like I've forgotten something, something important."

"Oh?" she replied. "Well, I'll come help you, then hopefully it'll go more quickly. But we can't take too long."

Gabi started looking around in the bushes, shrubs and under rocks. She wasn't looking for anything in particular; she just knew she was looking for something, something vital. Karin returned to help her.

"What are we looking for then?" Karin asked. "It'd be easier if I knew what it was."

"That would make it easier, wouldn't it?" Gabi said absent-mindedly. Something was distracting her.

"Will you know it when you see it?" Karin asked, rising to look at her.

Why does this seem so familiar?

"I hope so," Gabi said, looking down at her hand.

Karin looked worried. "I certainly hope so too. We don't have much time."

I'm dreaming. I don't even need my reality check. I slide straight into the dream, like a finger through a hand. I'm back here again. I can't even remember the last time I wasn't dreaming.

"Why don't we have much time?" I ask.

"The ocean's rising, Gabi," she says, pointing out at the ocean rising. "The high ground is the only place where we'll be safe."

I gasp animatedly and look out to the waters beyond the city of Cape Town.

She's right. The tide is rising. It's slow. It's steady, but it's noticeable to the naked eye. Even from here, I can see it creeping up the beaches.

"Oh my god," I whisper. Even though I know it's a dream, it's unnerving to see this happen so suddenly, to a place that is so familiar.

"Careful," she says, pulling me to the side. A crowd of people hustle past, pushing me out the way. I nearly slip from the mountain face.

"Everyone's evacuating the city, trying to get to the top of the mountain. They'll be safe there."

The water starts to run through the streets of the city. Dark as death, it gobbles up people and cars like they are hermit crabs on the beach. The tide rises over the masts of the few ships still tied to their jetties in the harbor. It swallows them whole and without mercy. I swear it's getting faster.

"We need to go, Gabi," Karin says, insistently. "Did you find what you were looking for?"

"Maybe," I say. The fear grips me, despite all my better judgment. "Let's go."

Karin leads the way up the mountain, through increasingly thicker and more aggressive crowds. Elbows stick out as everyone struggles to clamber up. Rather than using the path, people are now bundu-bashing up the side of the mountain, grabbing rocks and bushes as they do. One man slips as a rock gives way beneath him. He manages to cling on, but the rock falls onto a woman below him. It hits her head, and then accompanies her as she tumbles into the distance below. The crowd continues upwards despite her death. What would normally be a tragedy is now only a footnote on everyone else's climb to the top.

Another elbow rams me in the side of my face as an older lady charges up the path next to me.

"Fuck this."

This is my dream. I can't let myself be its victim.

I grab the woman by her shoulder and pull myself up into the air. I am light enough to launch myself upwards reaching to the top of a nearby tree. I know that I can do this. Faces turn to me in shock.

"How did she do that?"

I'm a fucking superhero, that's how.

But Karin is still trapped below. Some superhero I am. She's being swamped as the panic of people rise around her. Even with her strength, I can see her struggling.

Looking further down, to the city that was once Cape Town, the water floods through the streets and buildings. Wave after wave rises up the side of the mountain. Bodies, blood and debris crash against rocks, shredding those unfortunate enough to be stuck at the bottom.

The carnage is interrupted by the hum of rotor blades slicing through air. A helicopter appears as if from nowhere. It balances on the wind only a few feet away from me. I can recognize the figure in the cockpit. Who else would it be? The door opens for me to jump in.

I look down at Karin, trying to remind myself that she's not in any real danger. This is a dream. That's not even Karin down there...

Unless.

What if that actually is Karin? What if this is Karin's dream? Am I in her dream? I didn't even consider that possibility. I can't abandon her.

How could I do that to her? Even in a dream.

I jump back down into the frenzy of people, churning against the trees and rocks. Hands grab me; people force their way past. I feel like I'm being pulled down into a river, a torrent of people. I start ripping them away to get to Karin. These lobsters are all crawling over each other trying to get out of the boiling pot. They are crushing each other under their own self-interest. They're dragging me down with them, scrambling over me.

I don't need to take this. They are nothing but my thoughts. I am all-powerful here. They are merely figments of my mind, or perhaps Karin's.

I scream, spreading my arms wide, and release a force that repels everyone around me. They fly off like ragdolls. Some skip down the side of the mountain as pebbles would across a still lake. Karin stares at me as I reach my hand out to her.

"Take my hand," I command.

"Gabi..." she stammers.

I hold her against me like an action hero and leap back into the tree. I barely manage to balance as I land on the branch with Karin pressed against me. I hear screams erupting up the mountain.

"Help!"

"Please help us!"

But I can't. Can I? And why should I? If they're not even real?

As I leap into the chopper, Karin pressed against me, the ground below us floods with water. The doctor pulls the helicopter up to safety. I can't help but admit how powerful it makes me feel. This is Rambo leaving the war-zone. I half expect my theme song to start playing as we fly into the sunset.

"Good morning!" says the doctor, piloting the chopper away from the choppy water. It continues to rise up the mountain. The wind torments my hair as we reach the top. Below us, people are still climbing as the tide overtakes them. The water crushes them against the jagged sides, churning them mercilessly into bits.

What was once the edge of the table-top of the mountain is now a seafront cliff. There are mansions built along the shore. Massive, sprawling mansions, complete with helipads and boat-docks, line up on the cliff face. Each is more impressive than the last. We approach one of the biggest. The water creeps up but comes to rest just below the level of the house, converting it into a prime seafront property. The helicopter gently touches down at the helipad and the three of us exit to a greeting of staff.

"Good morning, sirs and madams," the butler says. He is shouting over the roar of the helicopter blades powering down. He offers us champagne from a stainless-steel platter. "Everything has been prepared just the way you like it."

I look around aghast as Karin and the doctor take their glasses. They make their way towards an elegantly set dining room table overlooking a glass-sided infinity pool. Karin and the doctor take their places at the table and beckon for me to join them.

"What the fuck's going on?" I ask, walking over.

"What do you mean?" Karin says innocently, as a waiter starts serving all manner of food. "Oh, this looks delicious."

"It certainly does," says the doctor, scooping food onto his plate. I make eye contact with him, my mouth open. Is that the real doctor in my dream? Or am I just dreaming about the doctor? This world is confusing.

"When in Rome…" he shrugs as he digs into his food.

"Sit down Gabi," Karin continues. "Have some food. This quail has been imported all the way from Europe." She starts breaking apart the tiny, cooked bird.

I sit down at the table, still shocked at the scene. I can see the bodies of those who didn't make it. They are floating in the water on the other side of the infinity pool, rubbing lifelessly against the glass.

I try to remind myself that they are not real.

"I was so lucky to get this place." Karin says, taking a sip of wine. "When I heard the ocean was going to cover the city, I knew I would just have to get a place up here."

"What happened?" I ask. "Why did the ocean rise? So many people died   " my voice trails off.

"I know, I know." Karin repeats, a faux-sadness in her voice. "It's really such a pity, but it couldn't be helped."

"What do you mean? What happened?"

"Well, Antarctica has always just been such a waste of space, because it's just so cold. A group of investors gathered together and saw how much potential it had. Did you know it used to be a lush jungle back in ancient times? So, they found a way to heat it up and free all that land from the ice."

"So, the water? It's the melted ice from Antarctica?" I ask.

"Oh, yes." Karin goes on. "They first tried bottling and selling it, but it wasn't cost-effective. So now it's raised the sea levels around the world. Of course, the change in sea levels means a new opportunity to buy seafront property. I was lucky enough to snag this place."

I throw the doctor a shocked glance. He's taking a big swig of wine. He raises his eyebrows at me as if to say, "Crazy huh?"

"How could you?" I stammer to Karin.

"Me?" she replies, looking affronted. "I didn't do it. I actually opposed the whole thing, even spoke out against it, signed a petition, but it happened anyway. It was already happening. I just took the chance to buy some land here. I wasn't going to let myself lose out on it."

I turn to the doctor. "Is she real?" I ask. "Are you?"

The doctor finally takes his focus off the food and puts down his drink.

"What do you think?" he asks in response. That certainly sounds like him, but wouldn't he sound like himself in my dream anyway?

"She's not like this," I reply, almost defensively. "Although I guess it's a side to her. I mean, she's a businesswoman at the end of the day."

Karin looks between the two of us, while digging into her food. "What are you two on about?"

"How do I tell?" I ask the doctor. "How do you know whether someone is their real self dreaming, or just your dream version of them? How do I know that you're the real you?"

Karin looks at us in confusion.

"That's a really good question. It can be very difficult, but there are little clues," the doctor replies. "Our brains usually have trouble creating truly authentic copies of other people. They tend to behave like caricatures of themselves, strawmen of certain aspects of their personalities. They are side-characters."

I watch Karin. She does seem different. The real Karin would never be like this, would she?

"So, I have to tell the difference between how I expect they'll act, and how they'll really act?" I say. "That sounds impossible."

The doctor continues. "It's even more difficult. Dreams connect us to one another; dreaming of someone strengthens that connection. It makes it far easier for that person to enter your dream, sometimes without them even knowing. In such a situation, another dreamer might enter as the projection of themselves. Other times, they may even enter as an incorporeal point of view, watching their own projection in a shared dream, or even, on rare occasions, as another character entirely."

"That sounds convoluted," I complain. "Impossibly complicated."

"Would you expect anything less?" the doctor says. "The dreamworld is as complicated as the physical world. Imagine how long it would take to learn the rules of the physical world from scratch?"

"Fair enough," I concede.

"Dreamers can also wake up, leaving their projections behind," he says, stretching his arms out.

"So, is this a projection of Karin or the real Karin?" I ask.

"You should be able to recognize that better than me," he says. "You know Karin."

"Excuse me?" Karin chirps up. "What are you two talking about?"

"Apologies Karin," I say, sheepishly. I find it hard to be mean to her, even if it's not her.

"I must ask, Gabi," she continues. "How are things going with the new book? Have you found inspiration yet? Has the doctor been of help?"

It instantly knocks me off balance. It's the real-world creeping into my escapism. This sounds more like the real Karin.

"Oh, um," I reply "Yeah, it's going well." I look to the doctor. He shrugs.

"Why are you looking at me? You are the one who is supposed to be writing a book," he replies. "Have you been inspired yet?"

I look out over what once was Cape Town, now a port for the super-rich. Yachts make their way through floating bodies to dock at their mega-mansions.

"The view will be a lot nicer once they get rid of the bodies," Karin goes on, as though she's self-conscious about how nice her new place is.

I feel the bile rise in my throat.

"Yes," I say. "I think I just might know what I want to write about."

THIS MONKEY'S GONE
TO HEAVEN

Jason shared a shitty apartment with Cara. In return, she shared her shitty politics with him.

"How can you participate in this, this mockery of humanity?" she said. "You're complicit."

He pulled off his headset, pulling himself out of another world, a far better one. Cara stood next to his bed, her purple hair challenging him to argument. She pointed at his tablet, which had a notification for an email with a distinctive sender and subject line.

Ark recruitment   *Re. Your application to Ark 25: Dias*

"Complicit in what?" he replied. "Ensuring the survival of humanity? What a monster I am. How dare I?"

Cara opened her mouth and raised her hands, frowning.

"Do you really think that they're saving humanity? They're leaving humanity here to die while they look for new places to plunder. They're not even human anymore. They've left their own humanity behind like they left us. That's why they need you, and you're enabling them," she exclaimed.

He'd heard it all before. Cara was a revolutionary at heart. Jason liked that about her, even agreed about many of her points. It also made her kinda sexy, in that rebellious punk girl way. Where she differed from him, however, is that her answer was to burn everything to the ground. Burn the system. Down with the rich and enhanced. He, on the other hand, felt that destroying the status quo would leave the world far worse off than it was. Inevitably all realities aren't perfect, but as romantic as anarchy is, order tends to be better for all those involved. Never underestimate how much worse things could be.

"Please could you give me some space, Cara?" he said. "I really don't need to deal with your non-existent revolution right now."

He stared at his tablet and then at Cara. Her heart started to fight him, but her mind intervened. Or maybe it was the other way around. She shrugged.

"Okay," she said. "I hope you get all the space you need up there in your never-ending sleep."

She turned and walked out, leaving Jason alone, hands shaking, to read his message: To find out.

Dear Jason

Congratulations, you have been selected for recruitment as a frontiersperson in the Ark Program. You will be one of the one hundred unmodified humans on-board the 25th Ark: Dias as it pushes the frontiers of the human race. Please complete the attached documentation to confirm your acceptance....

"Yesss!" Jason yelled, nearly dropping his tablet on the table. He pumped his fist in the air. "Fucking yesssss!"

He wished he could share his excitement with Cara, but he knew that wouldn't end well. This represented the epitome of everything she stood against. She lamented what the world had become, just as he did. He wanted to escape. She wanted to fight.

Cara and Jason were the useless, the vast majority. There were no jobs left, not for humans like them. There was little an unmodified human was good for. Working outdoors was far too dangerous with the high temperatures and ozone radiation. Robots worked there. There was little left indoors that A.I. couldn't do better and more cheaply. For unmodified humans, the main source of income came from government subsidies. UDI (Universal Daily Income) provided them enough to get by. Entertainment was plentiful. Many of them spent most of their time in VR, exploring worlds they'd never get the chance to see in real life. Some played with others; Jason played alone.

"They pay us to exist and survive and shut up." Cara said. "They give us just enough so that we are comfortable, docile, content to consume entertainment and go down with this sinking earth."

"And you flip them off and take their money with your other hand." Jason replied.

"What else can I do?" she asked.

She was right about the dying planet, though. There's an old wives' tale about frogs in boiling water. The crux of the story is that a frog thrown into boiling water will hop out, lest it boil to death. However, if thrown into tepid water, the frog will remain, even if the water is slowly heated. Despite the water reaching boiling point, the frog will never jump out and instead will remain until it inevitably boils to death. The truth of this with regards to the actual behavior of frogs was up for debate, but with humanity, at least, it seemed to hold true.

For decades, the great northern ice sheets cracked and melted away. The imperialistic deserts spread far and wide, claiming new territories in Africa. The water rose, along with the temperature, beyond the degree humanity was comfortable with. There were mass extinctions, the likes of which had never been seen before. To say that humans did nothing to prevent it would be disingenuous. They talked. They made declarations in Paris. They signed agreements. They patted themselves on their backs. All of it was far too little, much too late. The world had changed, and they were the ones who had changed it.

It was understandable. For a long time, the idea was ludicrous. It was barely conceivable. The idea that human activity was having such a fundamental impact on the world. On God's green earth. Oh, the hubris of the thought. That humanity's much-needed economic growth was a cancer to the planet? Blasphemy. To both God and to Adam. That's Adam Smith, of course.

"They still go hiking, swimming, surfing though," Cara explained. "Their parents paid for that privilege, with the blood money they got from pillaging the earth."

"We all killed the earth. They got rich doing it, but humanity as a whole did that." Jason replied.

"But they're the only ones getting away with it..." she said.

Three broad areas of technology changed everything. First, Artificial Intelligence and robotics, in various forms, started replacing human jobs from the bottom to the top. It started with transport, manufacturing, waiters... low-skilled, medium-skilled, even high-skilled jobs started disappearing. But the second two technologies remedied that.

For those who could afford it, genetic engineering allowed them to become the best humans that humans could be. At first, it simply robbed them of their weaknesses. No alcoholism. No mental illness. No genetic disorders. It was a logical step from there to improvements. Intelligence. Creativity. Physical strength. Even diligence and charisma. It took time, but soon the wealthy's children were all born with every "natural" gift possible. They managed to take all the top jobs, because average humans couldn't even compete. Meritocracy became meaningless as soon as you could buy real merit.

Bio-augmentation completed the transcendence. These same perfect humans, the smartest minds humanity had ever seen, were supplemented with advanced A.I., additional computing power and storage. Data connections were built into their brains so that their minds could access vast repositories of information instantly. They became something beyond anything the smartest unmodified was capable of. Even AI could not compete with them, as their minds were a mixture of artificial and human intelligence. Their bodies were also further enhanced. They could walk in the sun without fear of burning. Their skin was treated to deal with the new UV levels. They could sprint without tiring, rip through metal with bio-engineered muscles, leap from building to building if they wanted. They became superhumans, stronger, faster and smarter than anything ever seen before. They vacationed in the few spots of natural splendor still remaining, hopping up the sides of mountains to meet the gods.

"They are not human!" Cara looked incredulous.

"You say that like it's a bad thing." Jason replied. "They're so much better than us. They've taken evolution into their own hands."

"They don't yet understand what they've sacrificed to become what they are."

"Us," Jason replied. "They sacrificed us."

This is why the modified were the ones sent to colonize other planets and solar systems. The new worlds needed to be founded by the best of them. The useless remained on earth, on what was once Earth. The useless were not even allowed to build their arks. Work was a luxury the useless could not afford. Human error was a luxury that even the rich couldn't afford.

Twenty-four arcs had been sent out thus far, each loaded with a few thousand mods. A few thousand mods, and a handful of useless. Why a handful of useless? What was their value? Why would these superhumans include a token number of weak idiots? Emergency unmodified DNA. Eggs and semen. Jizz. That was the only value that the useless had left, simultaneously their greatest weakness and most valuable asset.

There were billions of them, almost 20 billion of them in fact. All useless. All thoroughly useless. Generations upon generations of useless and purposeless people. All could afford to eat. All stayed in warm apartments, albeit small. They masturbated and fucked a lot, with pills to help. But only the smallest fraction, one-in-a-billion, had ever done something productive. Only the flukest of flukes. One in a generation might find some success. Entertainment. Usually, it was in the entertainment industry. They were relatable after all.

It wasn't even their fault. They didn't get lazy, no more so than anyone else. There was just nothing they could do that couldn't be done more efficiently and cheaply by a robot. And if it needed a human touch? Well, they could never compete with the mods, the superhumans. So, instead they just existed: Dying on a dying earth.

Not Jason though. Jason had a plan. His jizz was getting him off this planet.

The application was open to any unmodified, but they had extensive screening procedures. No criminal record. No history of mental problems. No background of activism. No history of physical problems. No history of genetic modification. Strongly fertile. Breeding stock. They didn't care much for intelligence or attractiveness. That was all covered by the mods. Useless intelligence barely registered on their level. He would be around in case something went wrong with their genetic line. For all their playing god, the mods were terrified of some unforeseen consequence, something they overlooked. He would be there in case they needed something untouched. Something untouched from an untouchable.

Jason applied to the program years ago. He had jumped through every hoop they had given him. Fulfilled every criterion, passed every test.

"You're in, aren't you?" Cara asked, standing in the doorway again.

"Yes," he replied.

"Congratulations," she said without changing her expression.

"Thank you."

They both replied with silence. Some things hurt too much to fight about.

"I'm going out tonight," Cara said finally. "I'll see you tomorrow."

"Oh, okay," he said. "Enjoy yourself."

She stalked off into the apartment. Jason messaged a friend; he wanted to celebrate. Cara had soured his joy somehow. She left first. Purple hair and leather jacket. Jason left later. He met his friend at a bar they usually didn't frequent. Zeitgeist. It was a bar that Cara had raved about. Apparently, it was all the rage these days.

"Tā mā de!" Li said. "You're going to be a fucking spaceman!"

Jason smiled sheepishly. "I'm going to be asleep for most of it, but yeah."

"That's fucking INCREDIBLE MAN!" Li shouted the last part as if Jason was a superhero named incredible man.

"Keep it down, hey?" Jason said. "Not everyone appreciates it as much as you."

Li swept his eyes around the room, as conspicuously as he could, but abruptly stopped and sank back into his seat.

"What?"

"Speak of Cao Cao," Li replied, looking a bit embarrassed.

"What?"

"Your girlfriend is here," he said, throwing his thumb over his shoulder.

Purple hair pulled Jason's gaze to a booth on the opposite side of the bar. Cara sat in intense conversation with a group, none of whom he recognized.

"She's not my girlfriend," Jason said, sounding like he had just reverted to his teen self.

"There's that girl you live with and fuck often," Li repeated.

Jason smiled. "That's better."

"She can't be too happy about this, can she?" Li said, taking a swig of his beer. "Does she know?"

"Yeah, she knows," Jason sighed. "I've already gotten an earful from her about it."

Li chose not to reply.

"I need to go piss; I'll be right back." Jason scooted out of his seat and walked across the bar to the bathroom.

He kept the purple hair in sight but tried to remain unnoticed as he moved past the group. He picked up a few sentences from their conversation.

"He won't be a problem, I'm sure," Cara's voice was as distinctive as her hair. "I take full responsibility for him."

"You're damn right you will. I can't believe you've put this entire operation in jeopardy to get your fuck toy a spot." The other voice sounded pissed. Actually, pissed barely covered it.

Jason couldn't believe what he was hearing. This had to be about him. He turned and ducked into the booth next to theirs, dropping all his eaves as he did.

"How exactly did I compromise the operation?" Cara said quietly, but insistently. "I was already editing the selections. He was an applicant like everyone on our team. It took me a whole ten extra seconds to add him to the selection. Ten seconds to potentially give us an extra team member and make a friend's dream come true."

"And if someone finds it suspicious that two applicants live in the same apartment?" The fury in the voice was buried shallow. "That you and your boyfriend were both mysteriously selected? Maybe they decide to randomly select another hundred people from the shortlist. Maybe they look into it. Do not underestimate them, they're all goddamned geniuses. God Cara!"

"Quiet."

This voice was different. It carried authority beyond Cara or the other.

"It is done," the voice continued. The words sank into the air as if pulling in all other sounds around it. "We will carry on as planned."

Both Cara and her detractor remained quiet.

"Humanity deserves the chance in this new frontier, normal natural humans," the voice stated. "And that includes your lover, Cara."

"Thank you," Cara said.

"We should not speak any more here. I'm afraid you have gone into too much detail in public. This is not a place to discuss things. You all should know what your next steps are. We will not need to meet again until we wake up. Good luck."

Jason ducked under the table to hide while the group left. He waited for longer than necessary, just in case. Finally, another set of legs joined opposite him.

"She's gone man," Li said as Jason pulled himself up to the table. "God man, please don't tell me that's where you're pissing?"

"I think…" Jason stammered a bit. "I think that someone else may have had a hand in making my dreams come true."

THE THIRTEENTH APOSTASY

I look up from my laptop, from the first solid chapter I have written in a long time.

The world off-page seems utterly dream-like and surreal, as unreal as the world I just created. I'm once again perched on the side of a mountain, overlooking the ocean. This time it is not rising up against me, nor is a crowd rushing past. There are no superhumans climbing up the side. Instead, I am accompanied by twelve Apostles, the name of the twelve rocky outcroppings that mark this side of the mountain. The Twelve Apostles itself, is also a five-star luxury hotel nestled here, a bastion of old-school colonial elegance as foreign as the name. It's the kind of place that still has a smoking lounge and animal trophies on the wall.

I am fully aware of the irony of this location, but what better place to write about the divide between class, the disconnect of humanity and the earth, than such a place. It might as well be an ark. The rich come in, two by two, hoorah! The poor get washed away outside.

But is this story any good? I'm not even sure if I can tell right now. Can I show this to Karin? I don't think it's the kind of story anyone would expect from me. I'm not sure it's my kind of story. Outside of *Enduring Freedom*, I don't really know what my kind of story is. Karin could probably tell you which genres indexed highly with my fans. She probably uses software that segments my audience and highlights key themes that appeal to them.

"You should include a non-binary character," she would say. "And have another character maliciously misuse their pronouns. LGBQT+ rights are very popular amongst your readers."

Speak of the devil, and she appears, probably wearing Prada. My phone hums on the table in front of me. Any other time, this would spark apprehension. Usually this would signal the world reaching into my life and grabbing me, pulling me out of my safe space. "Hey Gabi, I'm still here and I'm not going away. Hey Gabi, here are those responsibilities you forgot about."

This time, however, I'm ready. I'm out in the world and in control. I'm armed with a first draft of a chapter and a second draft of a locally brewed Indian Pale Ale.

"Hi Karin," I say, bringing the phone up to my ear.

"Gabi!" Karin replies. "How are you?'

She emphasizes the **are** as if we haven't talked in ages. I forget that we haven't. The last time we spoke was in my dream. Even if it were actually her, she wouldn't remember, would she? Was it her? Did it affect her?

"I'm good, er, well," I say. "Just enjoying the view from the Twelve Apostles."

"Ohhhh," she says, with gusto. "I love that place. I went there when I was last in Cape Town. You must get a massage. They're marvelous. Ask for ummmm I think my girl's name was Patricia."

My skin crawls as she harkens back to the Karin from my dreams, the one who watched the world drown from the comfort of her back patio. I keep trying to remind myself that it wasn't her. That isn't her.

"Yeah, maybe I'll get one later..." I say.

There's a short silence. I suspect Karin may be multitasking on her end. I can hear the shuffling of paper and background noise.

"So how are things going? With the doctor?" she says. "Have you um, well, how are things going?"

I laugh. "You'll be happy to know I'm sitting in front of a sample chapter right now."

"Oh my god!" Karin exclaims. "That's fantastic! Congratulations. Gabi, I'm so proud of you."

"Thanks," I reply. "I mean... I'm not sure it's any good..."

"Can I see it?" she asks. "Or can you at least tell me what it's about?"

"Ummmm." I pause. I don't know if I want to commit to this just yet. "I mean it's just a rough draft you know. A lot could still change."

"I understand how first drafts work, Gabi," she laughs.

"Okay," I reply. "I know. It's just..."

"You know that I wouldn't force the issue, but... you know the deal," she continues. "There's a lot of pressure on this. I need to show them something. Could you send it to me? I won't send it on, but just so I can look at it."

"Sure," I submit. "I'll send it. But don't get too excited."

"Perfect!" She says. "That's perfect. So... how'd you do it? Was it because of your work with the doctor?"

"I think he helped, yes," I reply. "I think I just needed to get out of my own head. He helped with that."

"Mmmmhuh," she says. "I'm glad. So, what do you two do? Is it therapy? Do you delve into your unconscious..."

"Karin..." I say sharply. "We've talked about this..."

"Fine, fine," she replies, with a bite of annoyance. "You keep your black box. Even though I'm the one who set you up with it."

I click the send button on my email and hear the whoosh of its departure. Karin is getting what she wants. I hope it's what she wants. I don't know if it's what I want, but... I felt the same way about *Enduring Freedom*. I didn't know if it was good. My parents thought it was good, but... well they also thought my poetry was good. It wasn't.

"I've sent it," I say. "Just remember that it's still early days..."

As my email reverts to my inbox, something catches my attention: A wedding invitation. Who do I know that would be getting married?

"You've got to be fucking kidding me," I mutter, to myself and to Karin.

"What?" she asks seriously.

"I just got an invitation to the wedding, to Kyle and Sage's wedding," I laugh. It's not a good laugh. It's a laugh for lack of another reaction. Another humorless laugh being born into the world. Every time it happens, an angel must lose their wings.

"Oh," says Karin. "I didn't think he would invite you."

"Neither did I!?!" I say.

I stare at the invite in incredulity.

"Why did they invite me?" I ask, out loud. "I mean who invites their ex to their wedding?"

"Someone with a PR person," Karin says. Her tone is somber.

"Uuuuugh, really?" I say, making a fake vomit sound. "You really think that's what this is?"

Despite myself, despite desperately not wanting it to, I feel it hit me. My heart tenses up and the hairs on my arms stand up. There's buzzing in my ears. This must be that fight or flight response I've heard so much about. There's a predator in front of me. An email. It's one that I can easily just ignore and could just forget about. Yet instead, my body has decided that I'm in a life-or-death struggle. Why do I have to be so damn fragile?

"I don't know," Karin continues. "I shouldn't really assume that. Perhaps Sage is trying to send an olive branch. Perhaps Kyle really wants you to be there. Don't listen to a cynical old woman like me."

"You're not old Karin. You're also not cynical," I say. "But you're probably right. That sounds like something he'd do. His team runs his life. I can only imagine what it's like with Sage's people too. What an asshole."

"You don't have to go," says Karin. "Don't feel pressured just because he invited you. It looks like it's going to be a big wedding anyway."

"Were... were you also invited?" I ask.

"Yes," she replies. "And I will be going. It's going to be jam-packed full of talent, talent who might be convinced to write autobiographies at some point."

"Of course," I sigh. "You've got an angle."

"A girl's gotta make a living," says Karin. "And at least other celebrities usually don't complain when I hire ghostwriters for them."

"Wow," I laugh honestly this time. "Wow. Low blow Karin, low blow."

"You know I'm joking," she says. "But genuinely... are you okay? You seem like you've been doing well. I would hate for this silly wedding invite to throw you off."

"You mean you don't want it to stop me writing my book?"

"Hey, if you would prefer to write an angry memoir about your famous ex-boyfriend, I can make that fly off the shelves."

I smile. This is definitely the real Karin.

"Maybe that should be my backup plan," I joke. *Enduring Winter.* Spoiler alert: It ends badly."

"It'll be a best seller for sure," Karin replies.

We chat for a bit, with Karin trying to distract me from the looming threat of an unsolicited invitation. Soon enough, she gets called back into her busy life of meetings and corporate responsibilities. Big publishing, who would have thought? Her days seem filled with so much, I wonder how she has time to think.

I stare out over the ocean and do just that. I think. I have plenty of time to think. Unfortunately, my thoughts often lead me down dark and winding roads. They take me past rationality and reasonability. Rather they choose the worst possible path at every crossroads. They compare my worst traits against the best of others. They hold my life up against an impossibly ideal standard and lament when it comes short. Even worse, they criticize their own self-indulgence, these thoughts of mine. So maybe they aren't all they're cracked up to be. Perhaps the secret to being happy is being too happy to think. Or too busy.

"You good?"

I spin around.

"What?"

"Would you like another one?" the waiter asks, pointing at my glass. A thin band of foamy gold sits at the bottom. He reminds me a bit of Kyle. Maybe it's just because he's a good-looking white guy with a beard. Not as good-looking though. His chin is different. Hasn't quite got the bone structure. He looks at me expectantly, like I should already know what I want.

"Uhhhhhh."

He hovers, half-leaning over my table, waiting for my response. I sit, frozen in indecision. My mind is still somewhere else and now I'm panicking at the simplest possible task. Do I want another drink?

"I'll come back, okay?" he says, turning away.

"Yeah... I'll have something else," I say, interrupting him. "Double Balvenie. On the rocks."

It's one way to get rid of thoughts.

CUT

A man paced around a formal English waiting room. This man was not Kyle, although he looked remarkably similar. He had the same chin, the same bone structure. Except he was not dressed like Kyle. Instead, he held a darkly colored bowler hat to his chest, against an ill-fitting 3-piece suit. He hunched slightly, awkwardly. His eyes darted to the three walls surrounding him and the paintings that decorated them. Each portrait was framed by ornate oak and gold trim. The frames whispered of class and money. Old European money, the oldest of money.

One of the pictures was of a man, a man that was also not quite himself. This man looked like himself, but old and wrinkled. His eyes danced with malice and pain, although they were only paint and canvas. This was a man weathered by time, a man eroded into a frail and sharp edge by a harsh world and his even harsher reaction to it. How many sins and years were held in the eyes of that portrait, Kyle wondered, but because these eyes weren't his, they didn't linger long. Why should they have? What would have been the purpose of lingering too long on a picture and frame? Only a glance was needed. That was enough.

"Private Roland Harry."

That was his name, for now. Roland turned away from the picture and faced the door where the voice entered. There was a woman standing there, uniformed and tightly wound around the general's reputation. She was not Kyle's fiancé. Not now. Not anymore. Not yet. There was no warmth in her eyes. Her red hair was tied back neatly, out of the way. She looked at him as a stranger would.

"Yes?" he replied, with a blank slate of confusion.

"The General will see you now," she said. "You may go in."

It struck him as odd that she would have this position, this not-quite-wife of his. Yet here she was, standing between him and this thing he must do. He had no desire to. But he had to. She beckoned him to walk past her, and so he did.

"Yes ma'am," he said, bowing slightly and self-consciously. He was not the strong and silent warrior he once was, or at least pretended to be. Now he was a different man altogether. He was shy and timid. He was softly spoken. He was awkward. He was intentionally the antithesis of his previous self. Otherwise, he would have been trapped as that other man forever. His face would be recognizable as only that. The warrior. No, this was the right decision.

As he entered, he noticed all the trinkets of the general's office. He scanned lightly over them, focusing on each for only a second; just long enough for the gist to be communicated. Each trinket helped introduce the general, a highly respected and decorated man of the military. A tough, but fair man. A war hero. There were photographs of him shaking hands with the PM. Medals upon medals. A metal cross hanging from purple fabric, with a date in the middle. The award itself was such a simple thing. Merely a prop. Yet, it could communicate so clearly, so powerfully, so quickly, so efficiently.

"Roland, my boy," said the general in the warmest tones. "I see you're in civvies as asked. Good. How are you doing?"

He extended his hand and they met outside of their levels and titles. This was supposed to put Roland at ease, but it didn't. Such familiarity often preceded bad news. Besides, Roland knew what was coming. It was foretold.

The general motioned generally towards the chair on the other side of the desk, the smaller of the two. Roland complied with the order.

"Roland…" He said, pausing dramatically and enunciating clearly. "I have good news."

"Good news?" Roland replied, knowing the news wasn't good to him.

"You're being transferred."

"Transferred, sir?"

"Yes," he said. "Congratulations! You're going home!"

"Home, sir?"

"CUT!"

The shout ripped through the fake walls of the fake office. Reality broke. The fall of a pretense. Like a psychopath revealing his dark side for the first time. A side of the world, the invisible side, erupted with activity. All of it was directed and purposeful. Credits rolled across the set, looking as busy as possible.

"Kyle…" he said, this director of reality. "Kyle."

"Yes?" Kyle returned absently. He's not quite here either.

"Kyle!" His voice jumped into a shout. "You're being torn away from the one you love! Show a little emotion, man. You love her. And you're being transferred away from her. Feel it, man. Act!"

"Sorry," Kyle apologized, or is it Roland?

"Don't say you're sorry," the director continued. "Just be better."

The woman from earlier, his fiancé, caught his eye past eye make-up. Her face was expressionless. Maybe she wasn't not his fiancé, Sage. Maybe she was just the actress who played his fiancé, Sage.

"Are we ready to try again, Kyle?" the director sighed. "Are you ready to act?"

"Yes..." Kyle replied, without much affect.

"Fuck me," said the director. "Sage, can you do something about this sack of potatoes? Make him better! That's why you're here."

Sage sighed from behind the hands and brushed them away. She reached behind herself and let down her hair. It fell around her and bounced in the light. As it did the smile returned to her face. That warm smile. That loving smile. It was her after all. She became recognizable again, sauntering over to him, all bedroom eyes and familiarity.

"Kyyyyle," she purred. "What's going on, sweetie?"

"Sage?" he said... unsure of himself again. He remains still in his smaller chair.

"Why are you being so difficult?" she said. "This is what you wanted."

"I'm not being difficult," he replied.

"You're being difficult," she repeated. "Everyone here is relying on you to perform. It's not just you, remember. You're the face. You need to represent what the body is feeling. That's what the face is for."

She softly patted his cheek as she stared at his face. Her own face cycled through a myriad of emotions, all convincing except for being obviously fake.

"You're this beautiful face," she said. "You're the beautiful face that tells the story. All of it. All of it needs to come through this face, Kyle. You need to create the ripples of every emotion in this face, with this body. You've done it before. I've seen it. I've felt it."

Where was the wild warrior woman he met? She was so much less convoluted. She spoke so much more simply than this.

"Your wife is missing!" Sage's pantomime sprang into action. She swung her head around as if she might find Kyle's wife. "The love of your life is lost, and this man, this bureaucratic figure of authority is trying to send you away. Are you going to stand for that?"

She clenched her fist. Her face matched her words in intensity, as if she meant them. It unnerved him.

"But I'm a coward," he replied. "Isn't that what I'm supposed to be?"

"You're a hero," Sage insisted. "You're a hero trapped inside a coward. Your face needs to show us that hero. Little by little, show us the hero. The hero makes the right choice."

Kyle rolled his head to the side. For a moment he looks directly at me. My heart jumps. The world lurches with it. Everything shakes. The ground itself attacks us. An earthquake in L.A., who could have predicted this? The thin walls crack and split. Props scatter as the extra credits grab hold. Sage reaches out to her husband for support. He instinctively offers it, but he's not thinking of her. He's thinking of me. The woman he saw. The woman he saw without seeing. The lack of her. How could he see the lack of someone? He doesn't know, but somehow, he did. He saw her absence.

"Jesus cactus-fucking Christ!" shouts the director. "You've got to be fucking kidding me. Hours of watching this sack of Idaho potatoes and the earth is the first thing to move me."

He throws his headset on the ground theatrically. He does everything theatrically.

"Okay, let's fix this shit up," he continues. "Sage. You and Kyle have fifteen. Get him sorted. We're paying him enough to feed a small country. If he can't get his shit together, I'm going to outsource his job to a small Indian man."

Kyle continues to glance in my direction. Can he see me? Sage wrestles his gaze back.

"What's wrong, my sweet?" she asks, grabbing him by the chin and pulling his face to hers. The soft touch couldn't hide the insistence behind the gesture.

"No one," he said. "Nothing."

"No one?"

All heads turn to me, in the same moment that I realize that I am there. I am corporeal and standing alone on the movie set, staring at my ex-lover and his wife. Did he summon me here? No, I came here. I wanted to be here. Why?

I lament the loss of my voyeurism, my fourth wall, the safety that comes with being an audience. Kyle's eyes fix on me.

Before I can stop myself, I wave awkwardly.

"Hi."

Urrrrrrrgh. I could crawl up into a ball and wither into nothingness.

"Gabi?" Kyle asks, pushing his wife off his lap. That was a mistake.

Why did I come here? I'm dreaming. I must be dreaming, but this doesn't feel quite like a dream. This is Kyle's life, and I am inserting myself into it. I shouldn't be here. For a moment, I wanted it. That's why I appeared. That must be why I came here. But I shouldn't be here. Why do I want to be here?

I start backing away.

"I'm going to go," I say. "I didn't mean to bother you two."

"Don't!" he calls out to me.

He jogs towards me, leaving Sage idling in silent fury. I stand frozen as he approaches: apparently dear to him, in his headlights. I don't resist as he grabs me, forcefully and urgently. Oh god, I missed this. I don't resist as he kisses me. This kiss, that was so commonplace in another life, is now torrid and electric with immorality. My heart pounds. The hairs on the back of my neck rise. But my mind, my mind goes blank.

As our lips part, our eyes meet again. The intensity disappears within the moment. His eyes glaze over as if his brain melted for an instant, but quickly refocus on me. A hand pulls him back into his previous life. Out of the picture. Sage charges at me. She is once again the warrior woman she once was. Hair of fire. She pushes me backwards and I stumble.

"What the fuck do you think you're doing!?!" she shouts at me. A crowd is gathering around us.

"I'm, uh," I stammer with my hands raised. "I'm sorry."

I don't know what I'm doing. Why did I come here?

"You're sorry?" she rushes over me. "That's my soon-to-be husband you were making out with and you're fucking sorry?"

She pushes me again and I fall to the ground. I don't want to be here anymore, not without the protection of the fourth wall. I only wanted to watch, to be a voyeur. I didn't want this.

"Are you still in love with him?" she says, pulling the belt off of her uniform. She wraps it around her hand.

"No," I say, in barely a whimper. "Please no."

"Is that why you still fantasize about him? Is that why you watch him make love to me," she says, laughing with a sadistic edge. "You stupid girl. Is that why you're here?"

She holds the belt aloft, preparing to strike me.

"You know why he left you, don't you?" she says. "You know why he came to someone strong like me? He chose the opposite of you. He chose someone better than you. He chose all the things that you're not."

I brace myself for the impact, cringing on the floor in a puddle of self-pity and guilt. My eyes are tightly shut. What's worse is that she's right. I know what she's going to say before she does.

"You are nothing, nothing but a memory of something great," she continues. "Just a shadow. You're insubstantial… and you," she laughs. "You thought he was the hollow one. Even now, you want to write for a cause that's not yours. Saving the planet? Climate change? Class division?" she berates me. "Ha! Since when have you lifted a finger to help the planet? Or help anyone for that matter? What have you done besides enjoy your money? You're such a fucking poser."

I can hear the swish of the leather through the air, but I never feel the impact. Seconds pass. I'm okay. I'm okay.

I hazard a glance upwards, between the gaps in my fingers. Instead of the stormy redhead whipping me with her belt, I see the doctor standing above me with his hand held down. I look around to confirm the coast is clear. Sage is gone. The cast and crew are gone. Kyle is gone. Only the doctor and I remain on the empty set.

"You're safe," he says. "Don't worry."

"What happened?" I ask, grabbing his hand and letting him help me to my feet.

"I believe that you gate-crashed your ex-boyfriend's dream, kissed him in front of his fiancée and then proceeded to have her berate you, and possibly beat you, until I intervened." the doctor says plainly. "And that brings us to now."

I glare at him, without a word.

"Are you okay?" he asks, switching quickly to sincerity.

I wipe away the remnants of tears from my face with my sleeves. They are long and cover my hands. I used to wear them like this when I was a teenager. Artsy girls always did. To hide their wrists.

"What was all that about?" I ask.

"You tell me," he says. "It was your dream. Were you even lucid?"

What's the last thing I remember? I remember the bar, the Twelve Apostles.

"How did I get here?" I ask.

The doctor frowns.

"I am halfway between impressed and appalled. Somehow, unwittingly, and, I think intoxicated, you managed to dream travel by yourself. But Kyle's dream got the better of you. Soon after, your own dream got the better of you."

The deserted film set is eerie without the crew hustling around. No magic is being made here anymore.

"That wasn't nearly as fun as I expected," I say, sullenly. "You know, I didn't really expect the dreamworld to be like this."

"What did you expect?" the doctor asks.

"I don't know," I reply, still bleary eyed. "Less psychologically traumatic, more fantastical. Fewer consequences."

"Most dreams are like most lives." The doctor replies. "They are reflections of their dreamers, of their insecurities and their relationships, their greatest anxieties, and about what they do all day."

"Why?" I ask. "Why do we dream about that? Why don't we dream about awesome stuff, happy stuff, fun stuff, you know? Why don't I dream about frolicking gayly through a meadow?"

"Because at the end of the day, you're not really that interested in that. People are interested in people. We care about people. Especially ourselves and those with whom we have relationships. Or those we used to."

The doctor removes his spectacles and cleans the lenses. It suddenly occurs to me that he surely has no need to. He's doing it exclusively for effect.

"That's exactly why we don't dream about people we don't know," he continues. "We don't care about strangers, so why would we dream about them?"

CRITICAL RECEPTION

The morning begins with me awkwardly scribbling down my dream. I cringe as I do, wondering about the doctor's words. Why did I dream about Kyle? Why did I go there, of all places? Is it because I care about him? Of course, I care about him. He was once the most important person to me, during one of the most difficult times of my life. If I didn't care, he wouldn't bother me. I still think about him.

That's not the real question, though. The real question is, why did he kiss me? Or perhaps why did I make him kiss me, because maybe I did that.

I watch the elements of my toaster glow as it burns and crisps the edges of a slice of bread. I watch it intently while thinking, waiting for it to pop up. Somehow it still gives me a surprise when it does.

I lather it thickly and unevenly with butter. I love the crunch of it, and the smell of it. The aroma mixes with that of the freshly-brewed coffee. It smells real. This helps me appreciate reality again. It's one of the things that isn't ever quite the same in the dreamworld. The experience of food. With this exception, reality has started to feel more and more like the hangover from the dreamworld.

My phone rattles on the table, interrupting my breakfast. That must be Karin. She must have feedback on my draft.

Oh god. She must have feedback on my draft. Am I ready for this? This is my usual apprehension when my phone rings.

I grab the phone with my right hand, trying not to get my buttery fingers on the screen. Unfamiliar number, that's weird. I try to push the green button with my butter-free left hand.

"Herro," I mumble through a mouthful of toast and butter.

"Gabi?" comes a familiar voice, but one that is decidedly not Karin. For a start, it's a man. A leading man. One with a certain chin, and that incredible bone structure.

"Kyle?" I say, now trying to clean my fingers with a napkin. "Hi, um, what's up?"

Oh god. Oh god. Oh god. I can feel the anxiety sweeping up my body. The hairs on my neck stand up as if they too are trying to escape me. They'd be far better off shed.

"I'm okay," he says, sheepishly. "Sorry to disturb you, are you available to talk, right now?"

"I mean, yeah," I reply. Emotions flash like neurons in my brain, and the rest of me. Nervousness gives way to a sudden flare of anger. Why is he calling me? Does he remember the dream? Fear returns, with anxiety. "What do you want, Kyle?"

"Ummm," He continues. "Yeah, I just wanted to apologize."

"..."

"Okay," I reply. "So, apologize then."

He laughs a bit. Chuckles. I used to find it so endearing how he laughed when he was nervous. Now? Now I don't know what I think of it.

"Did you get the invitation?" he asks.

"Your wedding invitation?" I reply. "Yeah, I got it. I tagged it as promotions."

"Ha" he responds. Just a single one this time. Not exactly nervousness. He sighs.

"That's the Gabi I remember," he says. "You always were quick."

"Couldn't say the same for you," I reply.

"No," he says, taking his time. "No, you couldn't."

There's silence for the moment except for breathing.

"So, is this the apology?" I ask. "Are you calling to uninvite me from your wedding?"

"No, no," he says, switching tones. "No, that's not what I'm doing, no I..." he breathes in. "I just wanted to apologize for inviting you like that. Sending you an email like that out of nowhere. Not talking to you before. I shouldn't have let that happen."

"Why'd you invite me? Or was it Sage?" I reply.

He sighs again. He communicates with them. Three sighs mean he needs food.

"No, it was me. I just didn't properly think it through. It just seemed weird to not invite you, but equally weird to invite you, I dunno. I should have called you first or something."

"Don't worry," I say. "I'll save you the trouble. I cordially refuse your invitation. No harm, no foul."

"That's not..." He says. "I mean, you're more than welcome not to come. If you don't want to, but it would be nice to have you there. If, you know, you want to. It would be great to see you again. To be on good terms."

"You want to be friends?" I reply. "And you want this friendship to start on your wedding day? What good will come of that? For either of us?"

"I don't know," he says. "I guess getting married just makes you think about things. you know? Like the people you care about. When your name came up, I just, I didn't like the thought of never seeing you again."

"When my name came up?"

"When we were making the list, yes."

"You and Sage and your entourage?"

"Well yes, they are involved in planning the wedding. That doesn't mean that it was their decision. It was mine and Sage's. We thought it would be the right thing to do. I mean, we invited Karin too."

"I understand. You've always made the right decision, the one that your team agreed with. That's fine. But please just leave me out of it. Tell your team that when they decided that I wasn't the right fit for your future, that a good celebrity like Sage Leslie would be better, when they decided that, they gave up the right to summon me back into your life."

"They didn't...."

"Look, it's worked," I spit out. Now I'm just vomiting up words again. If only it were so easy on the page. "It worked perfectly. You're on the A-list. You're out of my league now. You're Hollywood's hottest couple. You're on the freaking cover of ... whatever fucking magazine you want to be on the cover of. Are you happy? Does that make you happy?"

Silence for a few seconds.

"Okay. okay," he says. "Maybe this was a mistake. I... I didn't want to fight with you. Maybe you're right. This isn't a good idea. Um... yeah. I guess I hope you have a good life."

"Fuck you, Kyle."

"Okay."

--Call Ended--

I scream in frustration, throw the phone down and return to my bed. I flop down onto the duvet, which puffs up in response. He's such a fucking idiot. Why do I let him rile me up like this? Still. What gives him the right to flit back into my life on a whim, on the whim of his fucking scum-sucking team, to try and cast me as an extra in his wedding. Like a cameo.

I guess the doctor was right. We do care about people. People make us fucking furious, because people are fucking assholes. We fall in love with people, then we hurt each other. Then we take our hurt out on each other. Again and again. We whip each other with our own weaknesses. Kyle whipped me with his, and I whipped back with mine. And in the end, both of us are worse off. Both of us are spun up in one another.

My phone vibrates again. Humming on the table like a knock on the door. I pull myself up from my bed and walk over to it.

--Karin Calling--

--Answer--Reject--

Her face peers over the options. I can almost see her nudging me to answer it. I reach down and push the silence button, letting it end the call naturally. I pick up my phone and return to my bed. Flopping down again, the duvet doesn't puff up around me like it did before. Even my bed has grown tired of my self-pity. Fuck you bed. After all the great nights we've spent together, how can you be so cold?

For a moment, for a split second, my personified bed distracts me. As soon as I notice though, I reprimand myself for it. I remind myself how angry I am, how hurt. I don't even know why I do.

My phone vibrates again. Short and sweet this time. The sweetness of a text message. There's no need to interact. It's from Karin, of course.

Hey Gabi. I tried to call. I've finished your draft. It's great! I really enjoyed it. I do just have some small pieces of feedback I'd like to talk to you about. When you get the chance. Give me a call. Love. K

Typical. She's doing that thing where she leads with the overall positive, before diving into the criticism. It's some management technique or something. It reminds me of the break-up speech.

"Gabi, you're so amazing... you're so beautiful... I really care about you... BUT I just don't think that this relationship is the best thing for me right now."

What's the saying? The better you sound at the beginning of the speech, the more dumped you are at the end. Or is it that everything said before a BUT is horseshit. Either way it holds true.

I distinctly remember Kyle breaking up with me. Vividly.

"I just don't think I'm the right person for you," he said. "I'm just not strong enough."

Maybe he was right. Lord knows, I have enough trouble dealing with myself. I can't imagine what it must be like for someone else to have to do it. In fact, perhaps the better question is why he ever fucking loved me in the first place? Why does he still care about me enough to invite me to his wedding, to kiss me in his dream, to phone me up afterwards?

My phone vibrates again.

I know you're ignoring my calls, so I just wanted to add one important thing about the draft. Especially because it's science fiction. Don't get hung up on the world. Remember it's about the characters. Focus on Jason, or Cara. Remember that Enduring Freedom didn't work because of Afghanistan, it worked because of Feda.

She's right. Of course, she's right. The doctor was right. It's always about people. It's about characters. We care about the characters. That's why we don't dream about strangers. That's why...

But.

But I have dreamed about a stranger before. So why did I care? Why did anyone?

THREE LITTLE WOLVES

Feda's kite darted under Hassan's, but not quickly enough to catch it. Hassan was counting on this move. It was a feint. It was not even a particularly cunning one, but it did the trick. It left Feda exposed. When Hassan's kite dropped suddenly, his tar cut straight through Feda's. This sent Feda's kite tumbling away in the air. Another loss.

"Idiot," muttered Feda to himself. Hassan was confident enough to not even celebrate winning. He was never in any doubt that this would be the outcome. He beat Feda almost every time they played.

"You're too transparent, Feda. Your movements never lie," Hassan said. "That's why you never win."

"You're just too good," Feda said.

"You might be right," Hassan smiled as he started pulling his kite in. "You might want to go collect your kite. Otherwise you won't be able to practice anymore, and then you won't have any chance of beating me."

Feda took a long loop around Hassan's kite. He had heard far too many stories of necks and tars meeting. His mother made sure to tell him a different one every time he played. The necks always came off second best. She was watching now, peering out the window of their house. She liked Hassan. He was a smart boy. He seemed like a good boy. But he was also older and rougher than Feda. He grew up in Kabul: the new Kabul, not the old Kabul. She wasn't quite sure what had become of the place. She hadn't been there in a long time. She wasn't quite sure what one had to do now simply to survive there. She hoped that whatever he did there, it didn't follow him here.

Feda needed friends. He was a sensitive child. He was kind and peaceful, unlike many boys his age. He didn't enjoy fighting, even kite fighting. He only did it so that Hassan would come over.

No, Feda was a dreamer. He saw things. He saw things that he shouldn't know, things from places far away, and people long ago. He was blessed by Allah, surely. As Elaha watched her son smiling, playing carelessly with a friend, this thought filled her with both pride and with sadness. To be one such as this is a gift and a curse. To be marked in such a way, it ensures a difficult life. Especially in The Hazarajat. Especially with the Taliban.

Weeks later, it happened.

Three men rode up to the house. Three Taliban. She saw the glint of gold under the one's loose-fitting perahan. They eschewed modern sins, but the old sins, those were fine. Or perhaps they were just paid soldiers. In the end, she wasn't sure if there was a difference.

"Salam dooet e man," she greeted.

"You're not covered," the one man said, removing the cloth protecting his mouth. They should hold no sway here, nor their rules. This isn't Kabul. Nevertheless, they are men, and she is alone.

Elaha replied as strongly as it was wise to. "I didn't know I was in company Allah forgive me."

"Where is your husband?" the man asked. The other men started looking around at the house. They were looking purposefully. What for?

"He is tending to the goats," she said. "He will be back any moment."

Feda glanced out of his window, unseen. He also wondered what they were doing here. He had a suspicion. His suspicion filled him with guilt.

"You are Hazara, yes?" the man asked "Shia?"

"I am Muslim," she replied, with pride. But the menace in his voice was evident. She was worried. They wouldn't be bold enough to come attack her out here though, would they? She cursed herself for not preparing for this.

He glared at her. "No..." he said. He does not recognize her.

"My husband will be back very soon," she said, with all the authority she could muster.

She felt a hand on her shoulder. "No... no he won't," the man says. "We know your husband isn't here. We know you are a widow."

She knew now, without doubt, what was happening. They were here for a purpose. They had information. She prayed to Allah that whatever the purpose was, Feda would be safe from it.

"We have heard that there has been kite-fighting here. We have a reliable source," the man continued. His tone was severe. "Is that true?"

Elaha almost laughed.

"Kite fighting?"

"You understand that it is banned?"

"I was not aware that it was banned here," she replied. "Since when are you concerned over what happened outside your cities?"

"You think that no one sees your blasphemy out here?" he said. "You think that we don't rule The Hazarajat?"

Elaha said nothing.

"Where is your son?"

Elaha said nothing.

"We know he's been kite fighting. Where is he?"

"Maybe you should check in the mud-oven?" Elaha replied.

"What?" the man was brought to anger.

He grabbed her and she fought back. It was an unequal struggle, as it usually is: flailing against a hardened warrior. She kicked and bit. He punched and she fell.

Feda sprang from the house like a hare. He ran straight for his mom, with tears in his eyes.

"I'm sorry, I'm sorry, I'm sorry!" he screamed, as if that was why they were here. As if kite fighting brought three men to the remote house of a widow and her son. His arrival hit Elaha far harder than the fist. Why didn't he run away? She had told him to run away if this ever happened.

"Run, Feda!" she shouted from the ground. A kick stopped her. Another sent Feda sprawling across the ground.

"Spare him!" she pleaded with the men as they dragged her into the house. "He is special, he is different."

They were indifferent to his difference.

"He sees things. He sees things in his dreams. True things."

The men stopped for a moment and exchanged glances.

"He has a gift," she sobbed. "Let him live, Allah is great, let him live."

They took heed of her. Not enough to stop. There was no chance of them stopping at that point. But what she said made them reconsider Feda. Dreams were important to them. Elaha had said what she needed to. Just enough to consider him. Enough to take him in.

But he never saw her again, at least, never with his eyes open.

THE HEART OF A LION

Over time, Feda grew accustomed to his imprisonment with the Taliban. He grew accustomed to his cold cell and his cold guards. Over even more time, his prison changed shape. The bars became invisible. Although the door was no longer locked, the dependency remained. Indoctrination was intended to follow.

The problem with this manner of prison is that the bars are invisible to both prisoner and guard. So it was that his captors never knew that Feda was actually free. He had set himself free only a few months after being captured. Every night he crawled out of his cage, into a world bigger than anything they understood. He flew between continents, stood upon snow-capped mountain peaks and walked through wet jungles. He watched the birth of the world and the cosmos. He even re-joined his mom in his child-hood home. In the morning they would find him lying quietly in the corner of his cell. His captors never realized he left. He could see out, but they could not see in.

The Feda that remained appeared to be subservient. He obeyed without objection, accepted without rejection. He too was incensed by the injustices they fought against. They showed him the blasphemy of the modern influence that had seeped into much of the city, and he was disgusted. Within no time, it seemed that they might have a solid recruit, albeit one that didn't have the stomach for violence. That was essential for their mission, but he was still young. He would learn.

And learn he did. As they asked him questions about his dreams, he replied with half-truths. He responded with questions instead of answers, like any mystic would. He wanted to learn as much as possible about every one of them. He familiarized himself with each of their names and faces. They were all different, and they were all there for different reasons.

Some were true believers, through and through. Perhaps they lamented the violence and brutality, which were not supposed to be their way. But they knew that violence was the only way to achieve their goals.

Some were psychopaths, cruel and barbaric to the point of inhumanity. They used the Taliban as an excuse to exert power over anyone they could, especially women and children. The city was their playground, and the only form of entertainment allowed was violence. They felt no remorse. They joked and bragged about their murders like teenagers. Some of them were teenagers.

Some were just angry, angry over what had happened to them. They talked about the loved ones they lost, the lives left behind. Especially those who had been in Kabul during the fighting. Which fighting? Did it matter? Maybe it was the Taliban that killed their family? Was it the Soviets? Mujahideen? Was it those warlords, the heroes of a previous generation? It could even be the Americans, who always had people around. It didn't matter who at this point, not really. The vengeance was never precisely aimed.

The Taliban filled his days, and soon his nights too. At first it unnerved him to meet them there. His dreams were his escape. That was supposed to be his place, not theirs. They had no right to reach that far into him. Slowly, but surely, he realized that they could not hurt him there. The dreamworld was his place, not theirs. They had no power, but what his fear gave them.

Once he understood that, he stopped fearing them. Instead, he took advantage of his power. He repaid their violence in kind. Dream after dream, he took out every ounce of anger, every drip of self-righteous rage. They deserved every second of it.

He always ensured that the context was appropriate. He'd catch them in the middle of their own act of violence. They'd be beating up a kid, abusing a woman. He'd interrupt and they would attack first. They would always attack first. He would be far too quick for them, too strong, too smart. He'd steal their Kalashnikoffs out of their fumbling hands and butt their heads in. Others would cheer as he embarrassed them in the streets. It was revenge dressed up like justice. He was a lone vigilante, the super-hero of Kabul, stalking down Taliban thugs. Beating them enough that they lay down their arms and promised to change their ways. He never killed anyone. He only saved people.

He felt like a hero. Until he didn't.

One day, it could have been any day, he saw them silencing a baby with a loud bang. A crying baby. They didn't even have the decency to kill his mother first. She watched her child die. It was the last thing she saw. All she had left was enough time to comprehend it. That's all they gave her, before they beat her to death. It could have been his mother. It could have been. If she was around. Instead, it was someone else's mother.

"To be a soldier, you must have the heart of a lion," said Mullah Abdul, as he taught the boys around him what it took to become the devil.

Mullah Abdul was the one left in charge of their education. He was their teacher. He was one of the merciless, but he was not a psychopath. No, he felt pain. He had empathy. Instead of making him kinder, it fed his belief. It powered his violence.

He would say, "Mercy is for God alone. All we can do is follow his laws."

That night was different for Feda. When he dreamed, he found himself faced with the same situation almost immediately. He knew he would find his way there. There was no doubt. There was no hesitation. He watched from the exact same vantage point as he had during the day. But when he saw Abdul, he did not wait for the first move. There was no pretense of justice. There was no excuse, just brutality. Feda pounced on him. He beat his face until his head cracked inwards. Blood congratulated him for the violence. Blood, and all the other things that exist inside a human head.

He heard screaming, her screaming. It was the same screaming as he had heard before. Looking over at the mother, she must share in his vindication. She must understand. She must know that he has saved her. But, instead, she looked at him in horror. Her mouth hung aghast as if she was mouthing a description of indescribable evil. She was mouthing a description of him, him and his act. It bore through him.

How could his mother look at him like that? As if he were like them? He was not like them. There is no evil in fighting evil. Eye for an eye. Tooth for a tooth. How was his act not vindicated? He looked down at the bloody face of Mullah Abdul, who was still alive save for his crushed skull. He spoke through what remained of his face.

"Don't worry, Talib, you need the heart of a lion to be a soldier."

Feda's hands closed around the neck, and he squeezed all he could. Tears escaped him as Abdul cackled up a bloody lung. The sobbing overtook Feda, uncontrollably, until he lay curled on his cell floor. He cried for hours. His body rocked with every lunge of his throat. The others ignored him. It was not unusual for that sound to echo across the building. The crying of a child. It was as familiar as the pops of small arms fire in the distance.

That was not him. Even in his dreams, he didn't want to become that. That thought terrified him more than anything else they could do to him. There were enough good people doing evil already, he didn't want to become another one.

Feda asked Abdul for extra blankets that night; Kabul's winters are cold. There was a fire, but that was for Abdul, not for him.

Abdul's reply was short. "There are not enough blankets, but there is no shortage of orphans."

He was right. Kabul was filled with dirt-poor children, scrounging the ground and refuse for food like foxes. Kabul was barely a city anymore, if it had ever been. Feda saw real cities on the television, and in his dreams. They had skyscrapers and fire hydrants. They had police and traffic and neon signage. They were not Kabul. Feda didn't like cities too well, in general. He preferred wild places. Feda had never known the old Kabul, the one he had only heard about. Now, the city was in ruins. Most of the people had fled, Feda had not seen a woman's face since he had come to the city.

Although he played a part in it, Abdul seemed to lament what had happened to the city. He was under no illusion about what the Taliban were doing or where it would lead. He wanted the Pushtun ways back again, but he didn't care for all of the Taliban law.

"They say I cannot ride and play Buzkashi?" he said once, smoking his chillum pipe. "They say it is against Islam. We rule over smoldering rubble. They say we are going back to the old ways. But this is not how it was before."

Buzkashi was one of Abdul's few joys, one that the Taliban had taken away from him. Even the Soviets hadn't done that. These sorts of sentiments made him less than popular with many of the others. These sorts of sentiments were why he was stationed as a lone Talib looking after children like Feda. These children who painfully reminded him of those he had lost.

Feda learned this of Abdul, through his dreams. As nights went on, Feda learned many things about his captor, things that seemed to hold true in real life. Feda realized that these were Abdul's real dreams, and Feda was visiting them. He had always suspected, but now he understood why he was special. He used his power. He used it to understand Abdul more deeply. As he did, it became easier to find him every night. Feda trailed him to his dreams. Eventually he used what he learned to ingratiate himself to Abdul, and in return he received more freedom. He visited more dreams of his other captors, keeping himself hidden all the while. He learned all he could. This allowed him to get by without offending the wrong people. He learned the right thing to say to the right man. He learned how to use the dreamworld to his advantage, a source of knowledge available to no one else but himself.

He started visiting other children in Kabul, starting with those in the Taliban. He visited mothers and fathers. He wandered from dream to dream, every night, trying to understand the people that surrounded him. He learned their fears, their desires. He learned whose threats were hollow and whose weren't.

He started developing a reputation. He was the boy who knew things. He kept the expectations as subdued as possible, but the rumors spread.

Soon he learned that he could control their dreams like he did his own. This power changed everything. Not even holy men claimed they could control the dreams of others. No, only the devil claimed that power.

That was the power that helped me escape. It helped me survive. For a while at least. This you know. This you have turned into a best-selling novel, a version of this at least.

Feda turns to me, pulling us both into existence. I was not aware of myself before, but now I am directly addressed. "But you know the rest of the story. It was about that time when I stumbled into the dreams of another," he says. "Not Taliban. Not anyone I knew. A stranger. A stranger from a foreign land."

I feel the world lurch.

"I found myself stumbling across the dreams of an American girl," he says.

A GOAT AND A WOLF

"But this isn't the story I told," I say. "You weren't a dreamer."

Feda and I sit on a patch of lush green grass, next to an orchard. Towering cliffs and massive Buddhist statues surround us. Their faces are uncomfortable with nostalgia. They've seen what's happened here. So have I. I've been here before. It's Feda's home, or once was. I recognize it. It's the Bamiyan valley. This is where he grew up with his mother. This is where he was taken from her. He lies down on his back and faces the sky.

"No, it isn't. You told a slightly different story. One with a different center," he replies. "But it seemed to do pretty well. Made you lots of money, no?"

"Yeah," I say, unsure of how to react. "Um thanks, I guess, for that."

"Don't mention it." He runs his arms back and forth in the grass, grinning. He points his finger straight up. "Look. Let me tell you another story."

I lie down on the grass with him and stare upwards, into the blue. He flicks his finger across the sky and a long wispy trail of clouds is left in its wake. I watch in rapt attention as he starts drawing in the sky as if it were a chalkboard. Slowly the image starts to take shape. A goat, I think. Feda starts singing next to me as he paints. It's not English, but I understand the words, nonetheless. He animates the story as we go.

"I am Buz -e Chini
I have two horns.
I am obedient to neither human nor genie.
My eyes are like radiant beads,
Jade inside a ring
My ears are like soup spoons."

It's oddly catchy, if a bit of a strange song. I look over at Feda. "What is that?"

"It's from a story my mom used to tell me," he goes on. "About a goat that lived here in the Bamiyan valley. Buz -e Chini was her name and she had three kids: Algag, Bulgag and Chulgag. Before she left them for the day, she warned them not to open the door to anyone. She told them that there are those out there with ill intent, those who might do them harm. Later that day, the hungry and treacherous wolf came to their house. He said he was sick and needed help. Although they didn't want to open the door, the wolf convinced them. He snatched the two, but the third, the youngest and smartest, hid in the mud-oven. When Buz -e Chini came home and discovered what the wolf had done, she became enraged. So, she challenged the wolf to a fight. The wolf accepted but underestimated her. She won, and the wolf was forced to return her kids. They lived happily ever after in the Bamiyan valley."

He points to a rocky outcrop not far away. A mother goat stands majestically on the rock, as her three little kids mill around the bottom. The kids play and kick one another, happily. I search desperately to connect the dots between that story and his.

"Sounds like the wolf got what was coming to him," I reply, noticing the look on his face.

"The wolf just did what wolves do," he says. "The kids did what kids do. Buz -e Chini did what a mother should do. They all were just playing their parts of the story."

We lie in silence for a while. I have so many questions to ask him. I don't even know where to begin.

"Why didn't you tell me you were a dreamer?" I ask, still trying to wrap my mind around this new truth. "Why did you choose me?"

"I didn't choose you," he says. "I don't know why I stumbled into your dreams. I wasn't looking for anyone. I just bumped into you and thought, hey, she could be a friend."

He grins at me childishly.

"Why didn't I tell you I was a dreamer? I don't know. That's a good question. I have asked myself the same question ever since. I should have. Why haven't you told Karin you're a dreamer?"

"What?" I ask. "What do you mean?"

"Have you told anyone about the dreamworld? About what you are doing with the doctor?" Feda asks. "Karin? Your parents? Anyone?"

I haven't. I kept it a secret. Why is that? I don't know. I have never even considered telling anyone. It just felt like something I shouldn't tell people. I barely even understand it yet. How can I tell other people about it?

"I don't know," I reply. "I just haven't. How... how do you know about Karin?"

"I've lived in your head for a while," he says. "So, I know you haven't told anyone. It just doesn't feel like you should tell anyone, right? It's your playground, why should you share it?"

"I... hadn't really considered telling anyone until you mentioned it now," I reply.

"At first this place felt like my own secret gift," Feda says, almost wistfully. "I guess that's why I didn't tell you. That's why I didn't tell anyone, not that I had anyone to tell. I was floating above the earth, observing everyone from the shadows. It's a powerful gift, the gift of being the observer. It's intoxicating. It's addicting."

Feda breathes in through his nose like he's inhaling the intoxicant itself.

"I thought I alone was a watcher, but I was not. While I watched from the shadow, the shadow, well it watched me back. And it saw you too."

His eyes narrow at me. The shadow?

"There are other things that live here, and something in particular, something that has tasted you before. It has tasted me too. It wants to eat us again. It wants to eat us up. It does what the wolf does."

"What?" I ask. "What do you mean?"

"I cannot speak about it," he says. "You have felt it too. You know it. I have already said too much."

I can feel it now. The tension in my chest. Fear creeps up into me. It radiates from the inside out. I remember this fear.

"We need to leave. It's not safe here. I have pulled you out of the pot and into the fire," Feda says, his manner sinking with gravity. "I thought we'd have more time. There is more for me to tell you. But it is coming for you again, and I can't protect you."

"What's coming for me?" I ask, the panic rising in my voice. "Feda, you're scaring me."

"The wolf is coming," he says. "You should be scared. You need to wake up. We need to run."

"I don't understand," I plead.

In a brazen display of pathetic fallacy, the sky darkens in apprehension. Clouds block out the sun. Wind rips through the valley, carrying with it an unnatural, but familiar chill.

"Follow me," Feda says. "Don't look back."

He jumps to his feet. I follow suit. He takes off across the grass at a sprint, his kaftan rippling in the wind behind him. I can barely keep up. How does he run so fast? In the distance ahead, I can see a familiar city. A city built of nature and concrete. It's too far. How are we going to run there?

Feda reaches back for my hand. I reach out to grab it. As soon as I feel his grip around me, I am pulled into the air. My feet scrape the ground as we rise up, flying at a breakneck pace. Sand scatters from our departure. Clouds swirl around us, as they continue to gather. Lighting strikes. Sparks dance between the clouds. We fly higher and faster. I can barely keep hold of Feda's hand. It's slipping out from the moisture in the air. The rain pelts against my face. Thunder erupts.

Below us, I can see a black shape in the valley. It tears its way towards the city. Behind is a wake of sand in the air, like a rally car.

"Don't look!" shouts Feda, too late for what I have already seen. In a flash of light and pain, I find my hand leaving Feda's. I am falling. I am plummeting through the sky towards this ancient city of green and gray.

I scream until I can't anymore, but I've still got time before I hit the ground. Why am I scared? None of this is real. I know this. I'm asleep somewhere. I know this. This is my world. This is my dream. I am not plummeting towards the earth. I am gently landing. The rooftop is soft with thick foliage. I am slowing down to land safely. This is my world. I am in control.

The world obeys hesitantly, like an untrained dog. I crash onto a rooftop through thickets of greenery. It is a landing I can walk away from, but not one I am proud of. I tumble through bushes and trees, scraping and scratching myself. I crawl out of the foliage, slick with what used to be rain. It has stopped. So has the wind. Now it is silent. Except for the growing scraping of metal on metal. It rises from the street below me. This thing is down there. It is coming for me.

I look around the city. Where the fuck can I go?

What am I talking about? This is my dream. I can go wherever the fuck I want, do whatever the fuck I want. I look across the street, to the next building, conveniently a story or two shorter than this one. Without hesitation, I sprint for it. As I reach the end, I leap with all my strength. I know I can just make it. No hesitation. No doubt. These are things I can do. This jump is no more difficult than climbing a ladder or driving a car.

As I fly across the street, far above the tarmac, time slows. I can't help but glance down. At it. At him. The silhouetted figure in the distance is still now. Without movement, he stares straight into me. I can't see how, but I know. He's pain. He's pure fucking pain. He raises his hands in the air, and my world lurches. My trajectory changes. I feel myself being pulled towards him. Trees rip off the buildings around me. Glass shatters. Buildings bend and break as the world distorts.

I scream as I accelerate through the air, I contort my body to look ahead, quickly enough to slap onto the tar of the road. Skin splits from flesh as I scrape against blackness. Pain. I come to a stop, face against the world.

I want to wake up. This doesn't feel like a dream. This doesn't even feel like a nightmare. Why can't I wake up? I try to push myself upwards, to stand up. The agony is overwhelming. My arms nearly give out. What's that feeling?

"Bleaaaaurgh…" Blood forces itself out of my mouth and nose, mixed with bile and vomit. Dotted with tears.

I try to look up. What is this? Who is this? I see his feet on the ground in front of me, not five feet away, but they are still silhouettes. They are darkness on darkness, between the night and the tar. I look further up to see the rest of him, but I am interrupted. I feel something wrap around my arms and legs, piercing my skin at every point of contact. Barbed wire pulls me up off the ground and holds me spread eagle in the air, facing the sky. It sears my skin, burning every inch of me it can. I am in agony. Nothing has ever felt like this. I have never known pain before, not pain like this. Intentional, inflicted pain. Torture.

"Stop!" I scream as best I can, my voice failing. "Please stop," I beg. I would do anything to make it stop. I would die if given the choice.

It doesn't. Not for years. Years or seconds I can't tell. I can't tell.

"Fight him," I hear a softly spoken voice whisper in my ear. "Fight him."

The wires around me disappear and I fall to the ground. Even the pain of the impact is nothing on the relief that sweeps over me.

"You are alive. You live. You can fight him. You can win," says the familiar whisper. "The pain is nothing."

I hear a massive explosion. I look up to see the dark figure disappear under a building, crashing down over where he stood. Even as I am trying to stand, I am flung backwards. Dust and debris fill the air.

"Land on your feet."

I try, barely managing. Once again pain jolts through every limb. I keep my balance with my hand and my knee, scraped through to the bone.

"This is your reality. Make it obey you."

I look to my left, following the voice with my eyes. Feda is standing against a tree growing out of the side of a building.

"Fight him, Gabi," he says. He motions his glance ahead of me. Through the fire and smoke, a figure makes itself visible. The only distinct features I can make out are his eyes, faintly white. He raises his arm towards me.

I don't know why yet, but I jump vertically into the air. As I do, the ground below me erupts into a pit of snakes. They slither around each other, rising towards me like a rope. I grab onto a bent lamppost and flick myself away like a gymnast, smashing through the window of a nearby building. My arms cover my face as I break into the empty apartment. I'm channeling everything I've seen on TV and movies. That is what I need to be. An action hero.

I know I've only got a few seconds. Should I fight or should I run? How can I fight this thing? I glance around; there are no doors out of this room. I spin around frantically. Even the window is gone. It's just an empty room, featureless. It is featureless except for a slight sheen over all its surfaces. A sudden flame is spreading across the floor. Fuck.

The flames lick up against me. The room, the air, catches alight. I try to run from them, but they're everywhere. My clothes are on fire, my nerves igniting under my skin in explosions of pain. My hair is aflame. I scream and scream as I feel my skin melting.

Pain.

Only pain.

It doesn't end.

When I think it can't go on anymore, it does.

It hurts so much that I should escape into shock, or death. But I don't.

Just pain.

I can't take it anymore, but I have no choice.

The wall explodes and water floods into the room, dousing the fire and knocking me over, before spilling out of the building.

I can barely open my eyes. All I feel is pain searing through every inch of me.

All I can see is the silhouette walking towards me.

"Please no more."

My eyes can just about focus, my mouth can barely move. I can only make out his face.

The doctor stands in front of me and raises his hand, a pistol. Why? You?

The last thing I hear is a gunshot. A bullet tears through my brain.

FULL RETREAT

I don't wake up with a start. There's no rude expulsion back into the world, with an immediate realization of "Oh god, I'm alive." This is not how my nightmares usually leave me. I'm not relieved I'm alive. I'm here for hours. I edge towards being awake. I lie in bed and hurt, floating somewhere between alive and dead, asleep and awake. Nothing works as it is supposed to. Not just sadness. Delirium.

I finally claw back a few thoughts. Am I awake? Am I alive? Was that real? Can I ever be whole again?

I pissed myself at some point, I think so at least. I can feel the dampness where I lie. Maybe I'm just doused in sweat. Perhaps its blood. I wish I could cry.

At this point, I'm well trained to keep my dream journal up to date, but I don't write this one down. I know I should, but I don't fucking care. I know that makes it more likely I won't remember it, good. I don't want to remember that experience.

What was that thing? Was that the doctor?

I don't want to think about it, but I can't help it. These intrusive thoughts crowd out everything else. The details slip away from memory, but the experience remains. Perhaps it was a mistake to not write it down. At least then perhaps I'd be better able to understand it.

Is that the moral of this whole story? Is that what the doctor keeps trying to teach me? We cannot control our own minds. We have as little control over our own thoughts and feelings as we do over the world around us. Well big fucking surprise. I've been fighting with my own head since I was old enough to write a novel and become famous beyond my ability. I am the poster child of someone at odds with their own mind. And for some reason that convinced the world that my mind is special.

It's the stereotype of genius, isn't it? Kurt Cobain. Geniuses are tortured. Geniuses are just too smart for their own good. Especially artists. Van Gogh. You can't be a great novelist and also a balanced person. That would be unfair. No, you must suffer for your art. Or maybe art can only be created through that suffering. Robin Williams. This is all just part of my penance for success. What did I expect? There wouldn't be a cost? I was convinced that I wouldn't be one of those rich and famous people who lament their own success. Marilyn Monroe. It's lonely at the top. Could I be more of a cliché?

But now I know that there's something more. If my journey into the dream-world has taught me anything, it's that there is depth to the world. It's a depth we cannot see, and one that most people are only vaguely aware of. It is a depth that is depraved and disgusting and quite frankly, no better than the waking world.

Last night... was that me? Was that thing in my dream a part of me? Was it some deeply repressed and dangerous part of my psyche that comes out from time to time? Or was it something else entirely? Another person? Another entity? Something alien? A demon? Was it the doctor? Why couldn't Feda help me? Is Feda... is Feda alive?

Don't trust the doctor

The note is still on my bedside table, as unexplained as a monster that just tried to kill me. As unexplained as the man in the red hat who has been following me. What have I stumbled into?

The questions flow into one another and meld into a vague confusion. It takes eons for it to clear, millennia of me lying in bed staring blankly at the wall. Eventually discomfort forces me to leave my bed, like an itch I can't scratch. The sun streams in through windows highlighting the warmth in the air. The curtains flapping hints of a light cool breeze.

I don't know if I can ever be whole again. It's not the pain. It's the helplessness I felt. The inability to escape. That's what is sticking with me.

I shower myself as clean as I can. Apparently as simple an act as showering can help you recover from trauma. Something about cleansing yourself of the past. Something about the water cleaning the air, thus giving you more oxygen per breath. It doesn't work. Perhaps it's because I'm sitting in the shower, wallowing in the tepid shallows. Perhaps it's because I sit there until my fingers and toes prune. I don't even care about the drought. Well, I want not to care. Instead, I feel guilty, but do it anyway.

I might wander around my house naked. Now, I can barely be alone, there's no way I could be naked. Instead, I have a towel wrapped around me like a damp hug.

Minutes drag on in agony as I sit and do nothing. Even as I sit here, I feel the memory of the pain slipping away. I don't know why I try to hold onto it. I don't want it, but I don't want to let it go either. It would feel like I was diminishing it. It deserves to be felt. My brain reminds me of it every time I forget. Am I doing that or is my brain? Is there a difference?

I need to escape this. It's not worth it. I didn't sign up for this. I don't really need to write another novel. Milton-Hughes can take my money. I'll figure out something else. Maybe I'll just write a shit book and call it a day. I'm in over my head. I'm not cut out for this. Whatever this is.

I give up.

I reach for my phone and type up a message to Karin.

I don't think this is going to work. Forget the chapter I wrote. You can go ahead and find a ghostwriter. I'm not going to be able to deliver otherwise.

Send.

Done. It's done.

Now I can retreat somewhere and get away from this.

I open my laptop, but instead of a blank Word document, I search for air tickets for today. Tickets back to America for as soon as possible. Back home. To my real home. To my parents.

I just want to go home.

THOSE WHO HOLD ME CLOSE

"Welcome home sweetie," my dad says, his arms open wide. I bury my face in his chest and wrap my arms around him. I didn't realize how much I missed them, but I feel it now. Perhaps that's just the fatigue of 22 hours of flying and no sleep. Perhaps it's because I was tortured by a dream demon not even a day ago. Perhaps it's that I've given up on my only talent, my reason for being. Maybe it's for none of these reasons, but I feel my insides churning.

My father pats me on my back as he embraces me. I've got just a little bit of saline running down my cheek as I rear back up to face my mom.

"Oh, come here you!"

She throws her arms around me as well, hugging me as tightly as she can. Her mouth is practically exploding with sobs.

"It's good to have you back, sweetheart," my dad says over both of our heads.

After a teary greeting, we head inside. Home.

I haven't been home in a long time, but it's still home. In fact, it's barely changed. The hallway is a poorly disguised shrine to my success. Alongside the photographs are the best of my fame: framed and displayed. Flattering articles, photoshoots and awards litter the walls and cabinets.

My father drags my bags and dumps them in my old bedroom while my mother puts the kettle on. "Tea?"

I collapse onto the couch like a teenager. The cushions envelope me as I sink deeply into its inescapable embrace. I remember this couch. This couch has comforted me many times before.

"Coffee please."

"Oh of course. Sorry," she replies as if she had just caused a great offense. She always offers me tea, despite me never drinking it. It's a hangover from her growing up in South Africa, one of the colonies. But I'm American. I need my cup of joe.

"How was South Africa?" she asks.

"Good," I reply. "I forgot how windy Cape Town can get."

"Ja," she says. "It's no joke."

My dad walks in. "So how was Cape Town?"

"She was just saying it was windy," Mom replies.

"Oh yeah," he replies. "I remember. It really does get so windy down there doesn't it."

Their inane banter is familiar and comforting. They fiddle around in the kitchen making coffee and tea as I look around the family room where I spent so much of my childhood. The television looks small sitting atop an ornate chest of drawers. I remember when we bought it. It was a "big-screen", a luxury item. Now it would embarrass an average college student. The coffee table is littered with magazines, newspapers and coffee table books with crisp untouched glossy pages.

"So, it sounds like South Africa is having a rough time of it at the moment. Ag, shame. I hope everything was okay down there," my mom says, her and my dad carrying our coffee and tea down to the table. "I was reading about the corruption charges against the chief of police. And the president implicated as well."

"Yeah," I reply, trying to reach my mind back to the snippets of news I absorbed. "It's been quite a big story down there."

"They really haven't done well with the country..." my mom continues, but my dad cuts in.

"Let's not talk about politics," he says. "At least not this early in the day."

My dad's seen far too many conversations devolve into arguments between my mother and me. She won't choose her words carefully. I'll jump on what she says as evidence of her underlying and outdated beliefs. "What do you mean 'they'? You mean black people?" We'll both polarize each other until I come across as a "woke" socialist anarchist and she as the love child of Ayn Rand and David Duke. Neither of these positions is quite accurate. Then we'll "agree to move on" but we'll both stew in the injustice or naiveté of the other's view.

I don't know where my father sits between us, but he has apparently grown tired of it.

"I wasn't saying anything about politics..." my mom says, her face reddening. "But sure."

"What do you want to do while you're home?" Dad asks. "Also, what would you like for dinner?"

I know this is the true question. Meals are the great moments of my father's life. The in-between time is merely time to plan and anticipate the next meal. My homecoming must have thrown his plans into disarray. Now this is a special occasion. That means that anything goes: restaurants, smoky barbecued ribs, pulled pork, ratatouille, all the dishes he's had in his mind for a "special occasion". Not that I mind, I haven't eaten home cooked food in a while, let alone my parents'. They are objectively the best cooks in the world. I miss the warmth of food cooked with love. Love and usually more butter than is strictly required.

I grin sheepishly at my dad. "What are you thinking? I know you've got something in mind."

He smiles back. "I have got a piece of beef tenderloin that I've had my eye on…"

"Sold!" I say, giving him the permission that he so sorely needed.

My mom tuts. "Your only daughter is back and all you can think about is food."

He shrugs and rushes off, presumably to defrost or marinade the meat or something.

"I really don't mind," I reply.

That is an understatement, this is exactly what I need. To be home and normal again. It takes some small talk, and "quality time", but eventually my parents stop treating me like a guest and start treating me as a part of the family. My mom returns to the book she's reading, and my dad wanders around fiddling with never ending projects. It's their usual routine. There's comfort in it, even for me. It almost makes me forget. Almost.

I take the chance to return to my old room to unpack. It looks just the same as I remember, except smaller and lighter. I run my hand over my old desk, and my now outdated computer. It seems so ludicrous: this big gray box that looks like a fridge. This is what computers used to look like. This is the keyboard on which I typed *Enduring Freedom*. My shiny and advanced Mac-Book Pro has not helped me write better than this brutalist tower with its fishbowl monitor. I turn it on and sit down.

I reach past the monitor to turn on the speakers, two stereo speakers that awkwardly sit at the back of the desk. After a few moments, and quite a few moments after that, I am greeted by the polyphonic Windows startup tune, 100% A-grade nostalgia. My dad pops his head around the corner.

"I haven't heard that in ages," he chimes in.

"Do you guys not use this computer?" I ask, as the screen tries to catch up with itself.

"Not at all," he replies. "You know us with computers. Your mother is hopeless, and I will only use it when necessary. Our laptop is enough for us."

After years, I had convinced them to at least get their own laptop. I'm a bit surprised to hear that they actually use it.

"That computer should be exactly as you left it," he continues, before he turns and heads off again. "I'm glad it still works."

I start browsing. It's like browsing around the mind of a teenage me. There are disorganized untitled Word documents of prose and poetry littering the desktop. There are folders full of alternative and prog rock MP3s. Other folders have voice recordings of me journaling and freestyling spoken word. It's simultaneously endearing and embarrassing, yet also oddly relatable. The painful malaise that I felt then is something like what I feel now.

There's also a folder named Feda, the working title for *Enduring Freedom*. It only took on its final name later, in editing. Originally it was just about a boy named Feda. That's all.

The folder is littered with unfinished thoughts and chapters, scenes that never made it in: Multiple versions of the opening paragraph, alternates of the final chapter. Some of them are okay. Some of them are terrible. I can't remember exactly why I kept what I kept and why I discarded others. Some I can't remember at all. There are long monologues by Feda that don't further the plot. In retrospect, I guess that's because not everything we say is meant to further our plot. There are side characters who never made it into the final novel, whose significance got absorbed into another more efficient character, or who simply weren't deemed important enough. I realize now these could have all been real people. I took all of these messy truths and ruthlessly discarded what was inconvenient to me. What could be more insulting? To be discarded as a character for not being interesting or compelling enough.

There are PDFs full of research on Afghanistan, the Taliban and Kabul, and notes about them. I did a lot of research: More research than I remember. I trawl through it all, looking for anything I have missed: Hints, clues, anything that spoke to the other side of Feda's life.

They are there now, the clues, although they weren't apparent at the time. They reveal themselves once exposed to light, like reading a novel for the second time, knowing how it ends. Feda always seemed to be able to guess the intentions of others, identify their desires and weaknesses. He was so worldly. He seemed like he was wise beyond his years, he seemed like he was protected by plot armor. It all made him an insightful narrator.

It made him an insightful storyteller. God, it was all him.

I read through pages and pages of his thoughts, his actions, his understanding of the world. I've spent so much time wondering why I could never write anything as good again. It's because I never wrote *Enduring Freedom* in the first place. I have never written a great story. Sure, these are my words, but it's Feda's story. He told me his story, and I wrote it down. My dictator. My literal ghostwriter. It was always him.

So… I can write. I simply can't create a story. At least now that I know that, I don't have to wrestle with it anymore. I can accept it and move on. I cannot write another novel. I never had it in me in the first place. I guess I need to find something else to do. Maybe I could write a screenplay. Or an adaptation. Perhaps I could just write myself some awkward fan fiction. Maybe I could do another job altogether.

What if I had never met Feda? What would I have done then? I never would have become a famous author.

I probably would have gone on to get some thoroughly useless liberal arts degree from a second-rate college. I can see it now, it's right in front of me.

A life I never had.

Walking around campus with a disposable coffee cup in my hand. Sitting with an unrealistically multi-ethnic group of friends laughing on college steps. My arms slung around a boy's neck, my head against his chest. A sly smile underneath my hair. Hundreds of Instagram pictures of me jumping into pools, holding sunsets and pulling faces with friends. It's a magazine-dressed me ready for my first day of work. Dressed in this winter's coat, those shoes and that bag. I'm going to be a big girl now, interning at this up-and-coming trash-news site. I learn to write click-bait and listicles. I work. I work my ass off. I stay late and come early. I meet a man. He stays even later and comes even earlier. He makes more than me, but I work. We travel. Not much, just a bit. Maybe once every two years. I see Paris and Bangkok. Enough to sate me. I have friends. I fall pregnant. I leave my job, because well, he earns more than I do. I post inspirational quotes on Facebook with pictures of people who never said them. I change my diet to something sketchy because I read on blogs about how many things can hurt my baby. I do Pilates. I do yoga. I have phases. We get married. Pet dog. Buy house. I pop out another child. I love it, but also, I hate it, but also I love it. And him. He cheats, once, but I forgive him. I cheat once, but never tell him. Our children grow up. One's gay. That's fine. They leave us. We sit on a sofa. He dies. So do I. I was somewhat happy.

Would that be so bad? Maybe that life's still an option for me? I mean, what else do I want?

"And that's a sight I haven't seen in a while." My dad's voice interrupts my errant thoughts. He's standing in the doorway, leaning against the wall.

"Gabrielle Rivers, back where it all started," he says proudly. If only he knew. I'm glad he doesn't.

I smile weakly at him.

"I remember that time so clearly," he continues. "You were up at all hours bashing that keyboard into submission."

"Yeah, I remember," I say.

"We were worried about you, you know," he says. "You always seemed like you were in so much pain. Just didn't seem healthy."

"It wasn't," I reply.

"But I remember one conversation I had with you." He walks into the room and sits on my old bed. "I asked you about it, asked if you were okay. I mean, we'd asked you before but…"

"Yeah, I would snap at you for interfering in my life, I remember," I admit.

Dad chuckles a bit. "You never talked much about your book. But one time you did. One time you opened up to me. I think you hadn't slept all night, and I found you in the morning. You had rings under your eyes. You looked a bit… tweaky, a little bit unhinged. It scared me. You were supposed to go to school that morning, but you didn't look like that was going to be a possibility. I asked if you were okay and, well, you burst into tears."

I feel a lump in my throat now.

"I don't remember that," I reply.

"I'm not surprised. You weren't exactly compos mentis. You told me about Feda Ahmed dying. He was going to die, and you were distraught. I tried to convince you to change the ending, to just let him live."

"That's not how his story ends," I replied.

"That's exactly what you said," Dad says. "I didn't understand at the time. I thought, well, that if it's your story, surely you can do whatever you want? He's your character. It's your story. It didn't make sense to me that your own story could unfold in a way that you can't quite control. He seemed to have some life of his own at that point."

I stay silent. It wasn't my story.

"You never seemed quite the same after writing that book," he says.

He puts his arm around me, and I rest my head on him.

"Why are you telling me this now?" I ask.

"Because I know you didn't just come home to stop in and say hi," he says. "It was far too sudden for that. I know you're trying to write your second novel. I know you're having trouble finding inspiration again."

"Did Karin tell you?" I ask.

"Yeah, she talked to us," he replies. "She's worried about you. She said you were seeing this man. A psychiatrist. And, I mean, we haven't heard from you in months, but we're used to that. Karin said that you had stopped talking to her. That you spent all your time with this shrink."

I am about to interrupt to chastise my dad for calling him a shrink, but I know that I had the exact same reaction at first.

"Dr Sivers," I say.

"Yeah, that's him." Dad replies. "We didn't even know you were seeing someone."

"I'm not there for therapy, it's just for my work," I say quickly. "He helps me, uh, find inspiration I guess."

My dad cocks his eyebrow up. "Has it been working?"

"It's complicated," I answer. "I don't really want to talk about it."

"I'm not trying to catch you out for anything. I'm just, we're just concerned about you, you know. You've been off-the-grid, and now well..." He says, with audible empathy. "Is everything okay? It's not that we don't appreciate you coming home to visit, but it was very sudden. Did something go bad? Was it with this doctor?"

I open my mouth to speak and stop. I'm struck by my conflicting desires to tell him my full story, and an absolute inability to do just that. I think about the torture. I think about the pain and the fear. I feel the burning on my skin. I think about how I would even begin to explain this.

"Yeah..." I mouth and pause. "I just don't think I can continue with him."

"What happened?" he asks.

"I don't..." I reply. "I just don't really want to talk about it. Is that okay?"

There's a pained expression on his face.

"Of course, sweetie," he says.

"Don't worry, everything's okay," I say. "It's not what you think, at all. I promise. I just don't want to think about it for a while."

"I understand," says my dad.

He sits with me for a few seconds in silence before leaving with, "Just remember, you can talk to us, if you want. Whenever you're ready."

"I know."

I return to my computer, closing the many Word documents that litter the desktop. I need to take a break from this. I need to clear my mind. That's why I came home after all, to escape from all this. Why am I delving straight back in?

Despite literally having just reprimanding myself for it, I look through the desk drawer. Here is my even rougher work. Writing from when I was away from my computer. Poems I wanted to include. Drawings of how I imagined the Bamiyan valley. Drawings of a city overgrown by jungle...

One page has a figure sketched in black ink. Smeared.

A familiar figure in black ink, with no discernible features.

Paging through my notes, he is all over the place. A black silhouette. Page after page. He is hastily scrawled in corners.

I know this figure. This is the creature from my nightmares, the one who hurt me: My torture. I knew he was familiar.

Written below, what I assume is his name:

The Knife.

IGQIRHA

Gabi lay awake that night, in her childhood bed. She couldn't sleep. She was close, but her body wouldn't let her cross that invisible boundary. It knew what falling asleep meant. There was something in that darkness, something inside the night. Gabi peered into the eerie greyscale of her room, checking every corner, every shadow within the shadow. The duvet ensconced her body like a protective cocoon. She could feel something coming. Something in the darkness.

"Gabi."

Her eyes darted to the source of the voice, a small figure in the corner of her room.

"Who are you?" she shouted.

"Gabi," he said quietly. "It's me, Feda. Don't worry. You're dreaming."

Feda? Oh my god. I didn't even notice I'd fallen asleep. I'm dreaming. I must be dreaming. I don't even need to do my reality check. But I do one anyway. Slides through my hand, like a hot knife through butter... a.. knife...

"Feda," I say. "What was that thing? That creature that... the knife?"

"Shhhh." Feda whispers, shushing me. "Don't mention him, he might hear us. I have so much I need to tell you, but first we need to go somewhere safe."

"What?" I pull off my duvet and turn on my bedside lamp. "What do you mean he'll hear us?"

Feda is illuminated by 60 watts of light bulb power. He groans and holds up his hand to block it. He squints at me.

"Thinking about him, talking about him and referring to him is like you switching on that light. It's like a beacon to him. He can see it. That's how the dreamworld works."

"Oh. Shit," I turn off the light.

"No, the light is fine," Feda laughs, dropping his hand. "Just don't talk about him here."

I turn on the light again. Feda groans as it assaults his eyes for the second time.

"Sorry," I say.

"Ugh. You're the only person I know who can control light in the dream-world, and somehow you make it annoying. Anyway, follow me," he says. "Let's go."

Feda turns on his heels in a flash and stalks out of the backdoor of my room. I slide out of my bed and follow him barefoot into the backyard, rushing, but trying my hardest not to wake my parents. Of course, I'm not going to wake my parents. I'm dreaming. They're not even here. Idiot Gabi! Get your head in the game.

"I don't want to do this!" I call out.

"You don't have a choice," Feda replies, forging ahead.

I wince when my feet touch the cold grass of the lawn. There is dew on the ground already. I tentatively follow Feda past a lemon tree I have known since I was a kid. Instead of defining a small suburban backyard, it watches over grassland that stretches far into the distance.

Feda strolls ahead, while my feet sting from the wetness and frost. The seconds turn into minutes. I'm still following, walking behind him in the cold. Time takes its toll and the mildly annoying becomes a grave chill.

"Where are we going?" I half-shout half-whisper to him. Time has dulled my wariness.

"We're meeting a friend of mine," he says, turning back to me as he walks.

"Can they help us against that thing?" I ask.

"He won't follow us there," Feda says.

"Is he following us now?" I ask.

"Don't worry about it," Feda says. "And I mean: Do not worry about it. He'll find us if you do."

"Well, that's a relief!" I sigh. "That really helps me not think about it."

It's not the pain I remember. I remember that it was painful, mentally I know it was, but I don't feel the pain now. The fear. The fear and the inability to make it stop, that's what still lives within me. I feel like it's only inches away, like it could return at any moment. That experience of being tortured for nothing else than someone else's amusement, it reaches deep inside me now. The doctor's face flashes through my mind. He was there. He killed me. Is the Knife the doctor?

"Stop it!" Feda says, spinning around in front of me. "Do you want to invite him here again?"

My eyes widen. I didn't even realize it. I was picturing the Knife in my head. Stop thinking about him, Gabi.

"Stop!" Feda starts walking back towards me. I've never seen him look at me in anger before.

"I can't help it," I shout. "What should I think about?"

"You need to learn to clear your mind if you're going to..." he stops abruptly.

"What?"

"Shhhh."

I feel the wind change; it picks up speed. There's a new chill in the air. Not just the morning frost, but a chill on the wind. I know this feeling. I remember this feeling. I know where it leads. He appears in my mind again. The Knife.

"Fuck!" I shout, looking at Feda.

"Run," he says, before spinning around and sprinting away. I follow. My bare feet slip and slide over the grass, over the hills. My pajama pants and t-shirt cling to me in the wet.

The wind goes silent, as it has always done before. I can feel him. Close in. The sky is lighting up.

"We're almost there!" Feda says. He points towards the horizon. The sun is just starting to peek up.

We don't stop running. I hear the faint sound of metal on metal in the distance: the snapping of chains, but as the warmth of the sun bathes the landscape in light, another tune takes over. It drowns out the sounds of pain and metal. It's a song, a beautiful song. It's a song that I recognize: One I heard being sung in my youth. It's the last thing I expected to hear right now.

It's a famous isiXhosa song, but I can't remember its name.

Igqira lendlela nguqo ngqothwane
Igqirha lendlela kuthwa nguqo ngqothwane
Seleqabele gqi thapha nguqo ngqothwane
Selequbule gqi thapha nguqo ngqothwane

It's famously called the click song, because white people have trouble with its real name. Like me.

I gaze ahead. Uneven green and yellow grass rolls over the horizon like an off-color ocean. Under a UmThombe tree, a Wild Fig, stands a large Xhosa woman. She is singing, and her voice rings out powerfully across the landscape. All thoughts of before, all concerns of what was following us, disappear. I am somewhere entirely new, but entirely old.

She wears a headscarf, a long skirt, a bright multi-colored shawl and two aprons. She looks over a world that struggles to remain. There are great herds visible in the distance, but no other humans in sight, save for her.

The song ends and she turns to me. She turns to face me directly. How did I end up right in front of her?

She asks me, without surprise. "What are you doing here?"

She speaks in Xhosa, her words punctuated by clicks and tone changes. I understand her nonetheless. The same way I understand Farsi, Dari and Pashto, I guess.

"I apologize," I say. "I don't mean any disrespect. My friend brought me here."

"You don't need to mean disrespect, to be disrespectful," she replies sharply.

"Mama Busi," Feda says, poking his head out from behind the tree. "Unjani?"

"You?" she says. "Suka wena! Why are you always bringing your trouble here?"

She casually swipes at Feda with a sjambok, a large thick stick, which emerges in a flash from under her shawl. Feda ducks out the way. I only notice the strike once the sjambok has disappeared again, back under the shawl. How quickly can she move? It was quicker than a snake.

"What trouble?" I ask, as she glares at us. "What makes you think we're bringing trouble?"

"This boy always brings trouble," she says. She looks between the two of us suspiciously, as if she's trying to figure something out. "I can tell you're the same. Exactly the same. That makes sense."

"He brought me here to protect me. He said you could help me," I reply.

She shakes her head. "Did he? He wants to bring everyone here. Even those who don't belong. I think it is a mistake: a mistake we have made before."

"We all belong here," Feda says. "We are all here already. I'm not bringing anyone here. I'm just waking them up."

"You are here, and I am here," she says. "Just because the rest can come here, doesn't mean they should."

"They just haven't discovered it yet," Feda continues.

"This is the home of my ancestors. This is the home of my people. This is my home. It does not need to be discovered. It already exists. It's the only home I have left. Why would I want others to invade here like they invaded my homeland?"

"What do you mean?" I ask.

"The Xhosa have been traveling dreams for generations, little one. Before you were even a naughty thought in your father's head," she says. "It is the gift from our ancestors."

I look at her intently, prompting her for more.

"You look at me like you are waiting for me to tell you about our history, our people," she says, bearing down over me. "As if it is your right to know. You have no right to our story. You have done nothing to earn that knowledge."

"Why do you not want to tell me?" I ask.

"Why do you want to know? Do you want to discover everything? Discovery is a violent thing. It forces others to become known. It forces places to become owned. The world is not yours to discover. You do not have the right to know everything."

I open my mouth to argue.

"Everything you touch changes," she says. "And once it is changed, there's no changing it back."

She raises her hands and the entire world lurches around us.

"Even coming here, you bring trouble with you," she says. "You were followed."

"The Knife would not dare come here," Feda says. "He would not dare approach you."

Busi looks thoughtful for a moment, even peaceful.

"You are right, Feda," Busi says, the earth calming around her for a moment. "But perhaps it is not the Knife I am worried about. There are others, far more dangerous than that Mara, that creature of pain."

Feda and Busi exchange a glance and a moment of silence.

"Maybe we should go, Feda?" I suggest. This woman scares me.

"If she wanted us gone, we wouldn't be standing here." Feda says.

Busi smiles ever so slightly.

"I find you curious. That is all. I don't know if there has ever been one like you before. I'm not sure why you exist," she says. I'm not sure if she's speaking to Feda, me or both of us. "But I don't want anything to do with your plans. And especially nothing to do with another one of your idiot protégés."

"Idiot?" I ask, raising my voice.

I realize at once that I have made a mistake. Busi turns to me, I feel my body pull uncontrollably towards her until I'm inches from her face. I flinch. She holds me there.

"Do you disagree?" she says quietly, her eyes fixed on mine. "You who ignorantly stomps through the undergrowth like a child, crushing beetles underfoot. You, one who does not understand this place at all. You wouldn't know your own reflection if you saw it in the mirror."

I stay quiet, trying to look away from her. Why does she hate me so much?

"Leave her alone," Feda says. "This place is hers as much as ours."

Busi turns my head to face hers, her thick hand clenching my jaw. I feel like I'm a horse having my teeth inspected.

"Ohhhhhh, I know exactly who she is: Your author," she says, a curious look flitting over her face. "But she's not fully awake yet."

"I'm not awake?" I ask, swatting at her hand. She lets go and I stumble backwards. "What are you talking about?"

"Your boy," Busi says. "He wants to invite everyone here. He wants to invite them all into this world and encourage them to feel at home. To take a little of it for themselves. I assume you're of the same mind?"

"What do you mean?" I ask.

"You want to tell the world about the dreamworld?" she asks. "Open it to the public? Charge a fee to enter."

"Are you scared of new people coming into the dreamworld?" I ask.

"Scared?" she says. "I am scared of them like I'm scared of catching fleas from my dog."

"They're humans, like you," I say. "Don't they deserve to share this place?"

"Like they shared my homeland with me?" she says, the ground rumbling as it had done earlier. "You think I don't remember when the white scum washed up onto our beaches."

I stumble as the ground shakes below me.

"The sea spat you out onto our land," she thunders. "How well did we do to share it with you?"

"That was a long time ago," I say, noticing the wild fig tree flailing in the wind. "People are different now."

"PEOPLE ARE NO DIFFERENT NOW," she booms. Her voice throws me back through the air and I land with a crash on the ground. It sucks me down into it, pulling my legs deep under the earth. I struggle against it, but it envelops me and hardens. It traps me there, helpless, as Busi approaches.

She stands over me, lowering her voice to a whisper now that I am sufficiently disempowered.

"We should have had the strength and foresight to throw you white devils back into the sea then," she says. "We might have been able to, if we had used all our weapons. But Nongqawuse was tricked. We were tricked."

"She doesn't know what you're talking about, Busi." Feda says. "She's young. Why don't you tell her the story of Nongqawuse?

"I don't owe her that story," Busi replies.

"You told me," Feda says. "You might as well tell her."

Busi gazes out over the grassland, a remnant of a land that once was. She takes the moment she needs, for whatever reason.

"Nongqawuse was one of us. She was an Igqirha, like me. She was one of the greatest."

In the shallow valley below, a young girl walks by herself.

"She had the gift of dreams, as all of us do: the calling to speak to our ancestors. This is where we meet them. In the dreamworld."

A deep sadness replaces Busi's anger for a moment, only for a moment.

"The ancestors told Nongqawuse that the white men were dangerous for us. They warned her that we would need to fight them. They showed her the way for us to beat them."

The young girl in the valley speaks loudly and confidently.

"We must kill the cattle," she says. "We must sacrifice our cows. It is the only way. If we do this, the dead will rise up and fight off these white devils, under a red sun."

Busi looks down.

"Many were wary of her prophecy. It was dangerous. But she told us that our cattle would infect us with the diseases of these foreigners, diseases that they brought with them. The dangers of diseases were more than those of hunger. These were the words of our ancestors, our forefathers and mothers. They were the ones who looked after us. They were those who knew better."

Across the grasslands, cows are slaughtered. I watch in horror. Busi stands mute. Necks are cut. The grass, once green and yellow, is now red. Rivers of blood run into the valleys.

"We sacrificed cattle by the hundreds of thousands." Busi continues. "It was a massacre. Cows were our livelihood, the symbol of our wealth and prosperity. We killed them and burned the bodies."

Plumes of smoke rise from foul-smelling fires across the landscape.

"There were some who didn't obey. They refused the call. They kept their cattle and split away."

Busi clenches her fist.

"Instead of helping against the whites, we crippled ourselves. Tens of thousands of us died from starvation. The British fell upon us with ease, we were only a fraction of what we were before. And we were fighting amongst ourselves. Those who slaughtered their cattle blamed those who didn't. They thought the prophecy hadn't been fulfilled because the others had held back. Those who hadn't obeyed blamed those who had, for starving and weakening our people. We descended into infighting. In the end, we could do nothing but watch as our land was stolen from us."

Redcoats march over the red grasslands, bayonets at the ready.

"Nongqawuse's dreams lied to her. It was not our ancestors." Busi says. "It was a trick. It was the devil's trick. Their trick."

"Their trick?" I ask.

"The devil tricked Nongqawuse," she continues. "The devil came to her in her dreams and showed her a false future. They promised that it was the right thing for her people. She was only fourteen at the time. Imagine how easily you could be tricked by the devil at such an age. Tricked to betray your own people."

She looks at me with one eye closed, up and down my body.

"So many of us turned from the old ways after that," she says. "One trick by the devil and everything changed. So, understand why I am wary of those who travel to my dreams with instructions. I will not be tricked into giving up my homeland again. I will not be tricked by another devil. Especially one with two faces."

She turns to Feda as if to point a finger at him.

"I'm sorry about Nongqawuse," I say, from my prison in the ground. "But we only came to escape our own devil: the one that haunts me. The Knife."

She turns back to me and squints her eyes. She thinks for a few long moments.

She turns away from us both and starts walking over the grassland. She shuffles away over grass and hill. The blood has sunk into the soil, and the uneven green and yellow grass shows once again. The vista is as it was when we arrived. Everything is at peace on the plains of Africa.

"I know the devil you speak of," she says, as she walks away. "He will not come to this place. You can stay here for now. You will be safe. But don't make it a habit. I'm not always so... accommodating. I will keep my eye on you. That other devil I know, but you, you I do not."

She hobbles away down the hill, picking up her tune again. She wanders slowly, at her own pace. Eventually she disappears into the grassland. Feda and I are left alone, under the UmThombe tree.

"That's Busi," Feda says to me, sitting down against the tree. "She's friendly."

"Very," I comment, my head still the only thing above the ground. "Could you get me out of this hole?"

LE RÉVEIL

"What was she talking about?" I ask, dusting the dirt off my shoulders and sitting next to Feda under the tree.

He helped pull me out of the ground after Busi had left. "You want to bring everyone here? How do you know her? What... what is that creature? Feda... I have so many questions."

"I'm sure you do," he replies. "And perhaps I can answer some of them for you. But I don't have all the answers."

"First," I ask. "What, or who, is the Knife?"

"To be honest I don't really know. A Mara, a dream demon?" Feda answers, as if the utterance isn't ridiculous.

"A demon?" I say. "Like a real demon from hell?"

Feda shrugs. "Would that be so ridiculous?" he asks. "I don't know if that's what it is, but it's as good a description as any. He's a being of anger and pain. He roams the dreamworld and hunts dreamers, feeding on their pain somehow. Beyond that, no one really knows."

"But he came for me so long ago." I say. "I saw pictures of him that I drew from when I was a teenager. Why does he hunt me?"

"I don't know," he says. "But it's a curse I share."

"He came for you too?" I ask.

"I guess it was poetic justice." Feda says. "I floated through the dreamworld, arrogant in my own power, watching dreams unseen. I thought it was my refuge from the world. I thought I was in a safe place. But evil exists everywhere, even the dreamworld. The whole time I watched, I was also being watched, stalked."

Feda touches his stomach, as if there was some old wound there.

"He inflicts pain," Feda continues. "As much of it as possible. He tortures into madness if he can. He came for me too."

I don't need to ask.

"He only got a taste, like he did with you. I tried to fight him off. It didn't work. I had never even encountered another lucid dreamer, yet alone this demon. I was completely outmatched. I couldn't defend myself." Feda's eyes are downcast.

"I understand," I say.

"I know you do," he replies.

"How did you get away?" I ask.

"The same way you did," he replies. "The doctor saved me."

The doctor?

"My doctor?" I ask.

"Is he yours? Or are you more his?" Feda asks.

"What do you mean?" I ask. "How do you know the doctor?"

"He found me." Feda says. "He found me, like he found you. That's what he does. He finds us."

I feel a buzzing rising in my ears. The doctor didn't just know that Feda was real, he actually knew Feda. He lied to me. He didn't just avoid the truth, he lied to me directly.

"He searches the world, and dreamworld, for dreamers and other useful people. Then he recruits them for his collection. Gently, of course."

Genius.

Our surroundings around us change as the story evolves. A silhouetted figure stands on the cliff-face, watching us.

"I noticed quickly that things were different, when the Knife came for me. The weather changed without my consent. You know the signs."

Clouds gather above us. These clouds only gather for one purpose: to bring rain, lots of rain. The figure approaches. Softly, the sound of metal against metal rings in the distance. I remember this fear. I remember this figure. I grip into the grass beneath us.

"Don't bring him here," I whisper.

"Don't worry Gabi," Feda replies. "We're safe here. This is one of the few places where we are safe enough to talk about him."

I ask, "But why did the doctor kill me?"

"The doctor killed you to wake you up. He saved you from torture. That's the easiest way to help someone escape the dreamworld, killing them awake."

"Oh..." I say, feeling a pang of guilt for my mistrust.

"The doctor arrived to help me too. He fought off the Knife and helped me escape."

Feda takes a bite of an apple that must have appeared in his hand at some point.

"You want one?" he asks, holding another one out to me.

"What?" I react. "No, um why would I want an apple in my dream? I could just eat one in real life. Just... just carry on with your story."

Feda looks surprised and a little embarrassed. He drops one but takes another bite of his before continuing.

"It was incredible, terrifying, but awe-inspiring. They fought in the most magnificent way imaginable. The landscape bent to their will as they battled with every superpower I've ever heard of. Fire, ice, chains, blades. They flew through the air like angels. It was like watching Mik'ail fight Iblis. It was like one of those American comic books we would read in secret as children."

Feda illustrates the battle in front of us, like a kid playing with toys. Characters in the distance fly at each other, hurling different powers at one another.

"I managed to escape while they fought," he goes on. "The doctor found me later. I trusted him immediately. After all, he had just saved me from a monster."

An air of overwhelming sadness falls across Feda's face.

"He showed me that I wasn't alone. He showed me that I was not the only one with this special gift, and that he could teach me, train me to become even more powerful," Feda says. "He said that few people had the gift, and how even fewer got to my level of skill without training. He had sought me out to help me and so that I could help him. He wanted me to help him make the world a better place..."

Feda grips his fist around the apple for a second, before loosening it.

"The Taliban... we could put an end to them. Slowly, but surely, we could use our power together to make the Hazarajat safe again. We could make the world a better place. He always said that. We were going to stop the global power struggles that laid the groundwork for groups like the Taliban."

"How?" I reply. These aims, described in the past-tense, land with a hollow thud.

"Ever so gradually, he introduced me to his organization," he says in a conspiratorial whisper.

He looks around.

"Le Réveil," Feda says quietly.

"What?" I ask, confused.

"That's what they call themselves."

"Le Réveil?" I ask. "Are they..."

"Don't say their name so casually," he hisses. "We shouldn't say it again."

"Why?" I ask. "I thought we could talk freely here?"

Feda explains. "Not about them. We'll call them to us. Names are powerful things, especially this one. They are far more dangerous than the Knife. Using their name may draw their attention here."

"Why are you afraid of them?" I reply, now confused. "What are they?"

"They're the closest thing to rulers that exist in the dreamworld. The doctor described them to me as a collective of dreamers, all working together for the good of the world."

"For the good of the world?"

"What else would cause an organization to spring up where there was none before?"

I let out a short and sharp laugh.

"I guess they would frame themselves as some sort of board, or council. The doctor is one of them," Feda says. "He's in recruitment. He explained to me how those in the organization learned to come together, rather than work individually towards their own personal goals. Collaboration rather than competition. To help guide the dreamworld and, well, the real world."

"The doctor hasn't told me any of this," I muse.

"I imagine he's waiting for the right moment. He's still grooming you for membership. Their aims, they claim, are noble. By working together, they strive to have an impact on the highest levels of government, to influence the attitudes of the public. Together they have the power to change the world."

I can see the lump in his throat.

"It wasn't just about war. They were concerned with the rights of women and children, racism, violence, corruption, the environment... All the things we would all want to fight for."

"Sounds too good to be true," I reply.

"Doesn't it?" Feda pushes himself up onto his feet. "That's what I thought. Even then, I had seen enough of the world to think it sounded optimistic at the least. The doctor agreed of course. Perhaps it was too noble an aim. But they weren't trying to establish some utopia on earth in a sweeping coup. They did not expect the world to become a fairy-tale overnight. Their aim was to steer the world gently but purposefully in the right direction. And isn't that the aim of every good person on the planet? Slow change. To make little changes to Earth? And hasn't that been the case thus far? Is the world not slowly, but surely getting better?"

I consider this for a moment. Is it? I guess, generally speaking, is the life of the average person on Earth getting better or worse? Better, probably. I guess. Despite what it says on the news. Average quality of life is going up for most people. Poverty is decreasing. Is that because of this group? Really? No way they can claim that.

"He convinced me. It didn't happen quickly, but he convinced me. He was a part of this movement for good. I could be a part of it too."

"So, what's the catch?" I ask.

"What makes you think there's a catch?" he replies, with a sly smile.

"There's always a catch," I say.

"Secrecy," he says. "Don't tell anyone. That was the condition. Not just about them, either. I couldn't tell anyone about anything. Not about the organization, any of the members, not even about the dreamworld. And how did the organization make decisions? How did it decide what was the right course for humanity? Who all were members? The structure? What was everyone else doing? They wouldn't tell me."

"And you wanted to go public?"

"I wanted to tell you," he says.

"Me?" I ask, with the kind of shock that accompanies being mentioned when you don't expect it.

"At first it didn't occur to me at all to tell anyone about it, even you. It didn't feel like a cover-up or a conspiracy. It felt more like something intensely private: secret by nature. Like what happens in a bedroom between husband and wife. I never told anyone about the dreamworld. It never dawned on me to tell someone, possibly because I had no one to tell. I thought it was my own secret, my own superpower. It felt natural not to tell."

"I haven't told anyone about it either," I say.

"I understand. I know why. But the truth is that this place can't be ours alone, nor only for a gifted few." Feda says, his excitement leaking out through his words. "It belongs to humanity. We need to trust humanity with it otherwise, well, we shouldn't be trusted with it. It's not our secret to keep."

"It's just like Busi said, you want to invite the whole world here," I say.

"Yes. I do," he replies. "This wasn't some instant epiphany. It started as a sense of unease at the back of my mind. It just sat there. The more I showed you, the stronger it grew. The more I talked to the doctor, the stronger it grew. The more atrocities I witnessed in my waking life, the stronger it grew. It evolved from a sense of unease into something deeper."

"How can we keep something this important a secret from the world?" I say.

"What right do we have to do such a thing?" he agrees.

"Did you talk to the doctor about this?" I ask.

"Of course," Feda goes on. "It would have defeated my point not to. We had a frank academic debate over it. He heard my points and felt that they were valid. He said that sharing this with the world would destroy it, would corrupt it, and would set humanity further back. He gave me many reasons, justifications... None of them swayed me."

"So, what did you do?" I say.

"Well, that's a longer story. We can talk about it another day," he says. "While we've still got time, there's something far more important we need to do."

"What?" I utter in response. "How can you stop there?"

"Because first, we need to train you."

"Train me?" I ask.

"You need to learn how to hide yourself," Feda says. "You need to learn how to be a dreamer."

"Feda, there's still so much I don't under.." I begin.

"I know you have a lot of other questions, but this is more important," he continues. "You're a walking target at this point. Right now, in this place, we're protected by Busi, but you need to be able to survive in this world."

"Survive?" I ask. "What do you mean?"

"At the moment you stomp around the dreamworld like a noisy toddler. Your thoughts are all over the place. You think about the things you shouldn't think about, even when you know you shouldn't think about them. It's like you're walking down the street shouting random things at the top of your lungs. It's like you're sitting in an apartment with the lights on at night. Everyone else can see in, but you can't see out. You've been safe from the Knife when the doctor's been with you, but you need to be able to stand on your own two feet."

"Okay, okay, I get the point. So how?" I ask.

"You need to learn how to control how you think," he says, as if it is the simplest thing in the world. "Your thoughts need to be like your physical movements. Everything that enters your head needs to be intentional. This means restraint. This means constantly being conscious of your own mind. This requires attention and self-control."

"That does not sound like something I would be good at," I sigh.

"You don't have a choice. You need to be safe here," he says. "Unless you want to be tortured for eternity?"

The memory of my torture flashes into my brain.

"No!" Feda says. "Do not let a memory enter your head without your permission."

I stop. I need to think about something else. What should I think about? Thousands of other thoughts rush into my head. The doctor. Karin. Kyle. Feda. The Knife. All of them involve people.

Feda bows his head into his palm.

"We have a lot of work to do."

DISTRACTION

My father flips over a butterflied chicken on the grill. Peri-peri marinade, a relic from our time in South Africa, drips into the flames, popping and bursting into smoke. My mom is in the kitchen, roasting root vegetables drizzled in olive oil and seasoned with rosemary and garlic. I stand by idly as if I am being helpful. I'm supposed to be cutting feta cheese into small squares.

"Could you pass me the tomatoes?" my mom says, switching to preparing the salad.

I can't stop thinking about Feda and my training. I need to learn to control my mind. I have to focus on staying focused, not letting my thoughts wander.

"Tomatoes?!?" my mom repeats.

"Oh sorry," I reply. "Here you go."

"Is everything okay?" she asks. "You seem distracted."

I am. I have a lot to think about. I have a lot not to think about. I'm continually trying to keep my mind empty, but I find myself thinking about the doctor and the Knife. There are so many things I don't understand. And Feda's training is not quite as polished as the doctor's. The doctor taught like a teacher. He limited his lessons to the lessons at hand. He taught as a school would, with a curriculum. Feda doesn't teach me so much as train me, coach me. It's haphazard and organic, more like how you would imagine a bear would teach its cub. It feels a little bit like being tutored by a friend at school, that smart kid who implicitly understands the material but doesn't quite know why. He teaches through doing; I learn through mistakes. I learn through immersion. There are fewer rules than there are rules of thumb. Heuristics. Patterns. Not all of them are fully thought-out or explained.

"Yeah," I say, noticing the long silence I had left in my wake. "My mind's just in my book, you know?"

It's a lie I've used often enough in my life. No one questions it. One of the benefits of being a writer.

"Oh, so you're actually writing one then?" she says, stopping for a moment and facing me. I regret my reply immediately.

"Well, barely writing," I say. "I've started something, but I'm not sure if it's right..."

"Well, I'm glad you've started something," she says.

"Gaaaaabi." My father's voice reverberates across the house. "Could you bring me the garlic bread?"

He returns to whistling as he grills, confident the garlic bread would soon deliver itself to him. I turn away from my mother to collect it and take it to hlttt.

Keeping intrusive thoughts out of my head has been difficult enough, but there are all sorts of other things Feda has mentioned:

- Lucid dreaming attracts far more attention than non-lucid dreaming. I don't quite know why.

- New dreamers are especially noticeable, with their unrestrained imagination running wild. "It's like sitting in your apartment with the lights on at night," he said. I guess that's something you learn not to do in a city with frequent gunfire.

- The easiest concept to notice in the dreamworld is that of yourself. If someone dreams about you, or references you, you can feel it. This is especially true if they know you well. Even saying their name attracts their attention

"Thanks sweetie," my dad says, smiling broadly. He's sauntering around the grill, his kingdom of flame and coals.

"No problem dad."

"I heard you say something about writing again," he asks, laying the garlic bread on the grill.

News travels fast in families.

"I've been writing yes," I admit. "I'm just exploring a few ideas."

"We thought so."

"Why?"

"You've been acting a bit like you did back then," he says. "A bit detached from reality. Awake and asleep at odd hours. Shouting and carrying on in your sleep. It reminds me of what you were like when you were writing *Enduring Freedom.*"

"Oh," I say, taken aback. Sleeping at odd hours was another one of Feda's recommendations: *If you know who is looking for you, sleep when they're awake. Be wary of time zones.*

"Don't take it badly," my dad hurriedly says. "I mean, surely that's a good thing? Isn't that what you want?"

"Well of course I want to write, but I don't want to inconvenience you guys."

"Don't worry about us," he says warmly. "Just do whatever you need to do. I know you don't want to talk to us about what's going on, but we're here to help as much as we can."

"Why won't you talk to us?"

He didn't say it, but I could feel him think it. Behind his warm smile, there's this pain in his eyes. He feels like he doesn't know me anymore.

"GAAAAABIIIII!" My mom calls from the kitchen. "You're riiiiiinging!"

I walk back over to the kitchen to find my mom holding my phone with two hands like it's some radioactive isotope. She has two fingers on each side.

"I think it's Karin," she says, handing me the dangerous technological contraption.

Shit. The panic I get when my phone rings triples when I realize it's exactly who I worried it was.

"Hiiii Karin," I say, holding the phone to my ear.

"Long time, no see," says Karin on the other side. "How are you enjoying being back at your parents' house?"

How does she always know what's going on in my life?

"It's good. Yeah, I mean, yeah, it's good. How are you?" I reply.

"So, I got your text. Oh, and I heard you've up and disappeared on Doctor Sivers?" she says, her words shorter than usual. "In true Gabi fashion. Is everything okay?"

"Yes. Everything's okay. Everything's fine. I'm okay," I say, walking my phone out into another room. I'm running through things I can say to explain this to Karin. I sit in my parents' fancy, but never-used dining room. It's another remnant of my mother's colonial past, the untouchable room that's set up just in case the Queen were to come to visit. There's a glass-fronted cabinet filled with china.

"Are you sure?" she says. "Did something happen? The doctor seemed very worried about you."

Of course, the doctor contacted Karin. I've just inexplicably slipped out of his grasp. The last he saw of me, he shot me in the head.

"No, nothing happened," I lie. "But, but I'm not sure that's the story I want to tell. The chapter I sent you. I think... I think I might need to write some-thing else."

"Okay..." Karin says, obviously not sold on my excuse. "So, nothing happened, but you decided to give up and leave the country without warning or telling anyone, including me, just after receiving a wedding invitation from your ex-boyfriend? You move back in with your parents and cut contact with the doctor you're seeing. Is that about right?"

"I always thought of him as more of a creative consultant than a doctor," I reply.

Karin sighs. I haven't heard her this frustrated with me in a while.

"All this after you've already written a chapter?" she says, with exasperation. "I thought the doctor was helping? I hope you didn't get discouraged by my feedback. I don't..."

"No, it wasn't that. I just... I just... I think there may be another novel I want to write," I say.

"So, you don't want me to call in a ghostwriter?" she asks. "But you also don't want me to put forward your previous work?"

"Yes," I say.

"So you want to go back to exactly where you were two months ago," she says, resigning herself to whatever she thinks this is. "Okay then. I'll see what I can do. But I don't think that this is going to fly."

"I know. I'm sorry. Thank you," I reply. "I mean, really, thank you for understanding. I'm sorry..."

"Okay," she says. "I just... when can you give me a new direction, or sample?"

"Ummmm," I say. "I don't know."

"Gabi..." Karin says. "What's going on?"

"Please just trust me on this," I reply.

"I'll see what I can do," she says. "Gabi. Please don't fuck me on this."

"I'll try not to."

"That really inspires confidence."

"Thanks, Karin. I mean it."

"Okay," she says and hangs up.

I stare at my phone for a few long moments. Why am I doing this? Whatever's happening with Feda, it's got to be the answer, right? There's something there, right? I can't write some other silly sci-fi book about the future, no, not when I'm stumbling across this incredible secret.

"How's Karin?" my dad asks, as I absent-mindedly walk out to him. My mom is sitting nearby drinking a gin and tonic.

"She's okay," I say. "Just you know, worried about her book."

"I'm sure she's more worried about you, Gabi," my mom says. "You sometimes forget that you don't live in your own head. You live here in the real world, with people who care about you."

My dad shoots a look at my mom like they had mutually decided not to reproach me about this.

I don't reply. Instead, we sit in silence for a few minutes as fat and peri-peri sauce drips and pops on the gas grill. There are just too many things. I don't know what to do. I don't know who to trust. Now I'm talking to someone in my head. I don't even know for sure if he is real. What the fuck am I doing? No, Gabi, stop thinking about it. Relax. Control your thoughts. Take charge of your mind. Clear away the intrusive negative thoughts. Meditate. There is no point worrying. There is nothing to worry about.

"So, what is your new book about anyway?" my mom asks, sipping on her G&T.

KEEP FIGHTING

Feda and I are at the center of a football stadium, facing one another as if we are rival teams at the big game. Instead of hordes of blue coeds in the stands, empty benches watch over us. Only the argonaut watches, sword in hand. This is UWF stadium. I remember coming here at the end of high school.

"If you are discovered by someone, someone you don't want to be discovered by," Feda explains, or muses; it feels like he's thinking of what to say as he goes along. "You could wake up... waking up is the quickest way out of the dreamworld. But it's not easy to wake yourself when immersed in a dream, even for experienced dreamers. In fact, I think it might get more difficult the more experienced you are. Normal dreamers often wake up more easily, even accidentally; they are less attached to the dreamworld. They can't help but wake up."

Feda is wearing his perahan-u-tunban, white and rippling in the breeze, like some esoteric martial artist.

"Dying works," he says. "So long as death is sure and non-debatable. Outright dying can jolt you awake. Unfortunately, it can be quite difficult. Your mind actively resists it. You'll find ways of saving yourself out of fear of dying. You can end up just crippling yourself."

"So, if you die in your dream, you don't die in real life?" I ask Feda, remembering the old wives' tale.

"No, no. I don't think so," he replies, scratching his head. "No, I'm pretty sure not. I mean, you didn't, did you?"

That's reassuring.

"Today's lesson is for when you can't wake up," Feda says.

"Sometimes I need to fight?" I ask.

"Sometimes you need to fight," he replies. His face betrays the child-like grin of a boy about to play a new video game.

He widens his stance with one hand out in front, his fingers towards me.

"Stop trying to hit me and hit me," I say, lowering my voice into a caricature. "You think that's air you're breathing?"

Feda narrows his eyes at me. "What?"

"Never mind," I reply. I forget that Feda didn't grow up watching the movies that I did.

"Just remember that fighting in the dreamworld is a battle of thought and will," he goes on. "The fact that you're a woman, or that I'm a child, doesn't mean anything here. It doesn't matter if I'm a seven-foot-tall mountain of muscle. Unless you think it does."

Finally, some sort of equality in the world. In the dreamworld at least.

"Although..." he muses, "that being said, it can be a disadvantage, if you let it..."

"What do you mean it can be a disadvantage?" I frown at him.

"Men are used to being physically stronger than women, and likewise women expect to be weaker. That expectation is powerful. The real world spills over into the dreamworld."

"So, I can't even escape the patriarchy here," I mumble, half seriously. Go figure.

"Don't think about that though, because it is only the belief in it that gives it power," Feda explains. "There's no reason why you cannot fight and defeat a man here. He is not stronger than you, unless you assume that he is."

"Then why did you tell me about it?" I reply. "If you need me to not think about it?"

"Because you need to know that you think it, to unthink it," he replies. "And the men you encounter will certainly believe it. They might be used to beating down women. Even without realizing it, they are likely to be more... well, cocksure, of their power over you. Make that your advantage rather than your weakness."

"How can I make that their weakness?" I ask.

"Men have their own specific weaknesses that women do not."

"Like what?" I ask.

"Insecurity. Fragility. Sexuality. Women can hit specific fears in men, that other men won't, or can't," Feda continues. "Some men are trained never to hit women. Others aren't used to women hitting back and hitting hard. You need to identify their weakness and frame it to your advantage."

"Like in a conversation?" I ask. "You can turn privilege into a source of shame with only a few well-chosen words, or beauty into a curse."

"Exactly," Feda smiles.

"Okay, but I assume I don't just speak at them."

"Well, if you can, do that," he laughs a bit "But, when you can't... then you need to convince your opponent that you've beaten them, or in some cases, you might need to convince them that you've killed them. This can be done through pain, fear or overpowering them. Sooo.... yeah, you just fight them."

"Like with my fists?" I hold them up.

Feda flies towards me without any warning, landing a punch that stops an inch from my face. Far too late I duck down with my hands up. His movement was a blur. It took less than a second for him to cross the fifty feet between us. How?

"What the fuck?!?" I shout.

"I'm not going to pull the next punch," he says. "Either dodge it, block it, or get hit."

I jump backwards and he flies after me. I see his fist rounding from the side. I swat it away. He spins in the air and his foot comes crashing down towards me. I manage to weave to my left, but Feda uses his foot to launch himself after me. After one or two more punches, I miss one. His fist impacts my stomach. I fall to the ground, reeling over.

I groan... "fuuuuuck."

"Get up Gabi, it's nothing." Feda says, walking around me.

I try to stand up, wobbling a bit on my feet. I try to catch my breath. "Yeah, yeah," I say. "It's nothing my ass."

"I've seen you stand up after worse wounds than that," he says. "Just remember, you've been burnt and beaten and ripped apart. Do you remember that?"

I look up at him. "I do."

I remember chains wrapping around my skin and tearing... I stop myself. No. I don't need to think about that now. I need to think about fighting.

"And you're still alive and you're still fighting," Feda goes on.

"I am."

"So, keep fighting," he announces, pouncing on me.

I grab his hand and thrust a counter-strike into his chest. His eyes lock into mine as my fist hits him. It has no impact. My hand crunches against him as if I were striking a brick wall.

"What?" I shout, holding my fist in my hand. Pain darts through it. "You've got to be fucking kidding me."

Feda laughs. "You have to know that your punches are going to hurt me. You can't let me tell you that they don't."

He counter-attacks, his arms exploring every gap in my defense they can find.

"Keep fighting!" he shouts.

So, I do. For hours. We just fight, hand to hand. Every punch makes me quicker. Every kick makes me stronger. Every time I hit Feda, I hit him a little harder.

"Good," he says when I hit him, wiping away a bloody lip. "Keep fighting."

So we do.

A TORRENT OF MEMORIES

Lucidity comes quicker every night. I barely even need my reality check anymore.

"Feda," I call.

I'm walking down the corridors of my old high school, my peers shuffling past me to get to their classrooms and lockers. I look from face to face, each familiar but barely known. So many names I can't remember. I withdrew from all of them: First to write, then to become famous. I was barely there for my final years.

They whisper and peer at me. There was a remarkable distance that developed between us when I became famous. They all reached out to me, but I kept them at arm's length.

"Feda!" I call, louder this time.

They stare at me, judgey judgey eyes. A few sniggers.

"Oh fuck off," I say, waving them into their classrooms. They scuttle away like crabs caught on the wrong side of a rock. The corridor is now empty, save for a few scraps of paper and utter silence. I cherish my power over the world around me.

"Why do you hate them so much?" Feda's voice echoes off the walls towards me. "These strangers in your dreams, you think so little of them."

"They're not even people, they're just parts of my mind. Right?" I reply.

"Should you treat parts of yourself so badly?" Feda walks down the deserted corridor towards me.

"I've always been hard on myself," I say, readying myself for a fight. Over the past few weeks I've learned to be ready for Feda to attack me without warning or reason. It's part of his training. And by Feda attacking me, I mean anything or anyone around me attacking me. Doors fly at me. Animals appear out of nowhere to maul me. When you're dreaming, reality itself can turn against you. It's terrifying. I know it's not going to happen now, though; I won't let it.

"Feda," I say.

"Yes?" he replies.

"I'm ready," I say.

"Are you?" he says. "Ready for what?"

"I'm ready to know more," I say. "There's so much you haven't told me. I still have questions."

'Of course you do," he says. "Why wouldn't you?"

"So?" I ask.

"Well, what do you want to know?" he says.

He walks into the classroom. I follow him, trying to decide how to formulate the right question. He sits on the teacher's table; he grabs an apple from it and takes a bite. We're alone here. I sit at a desk, marked with the graffiti of countless bored children.

"What happened to you?" I ask. "You said you wanted to tell me about the dreamworld. You said you wanted to tell the world. What happened?"

"You already know what happened to me. You were there."

"I don't understand."

Feda laughs grimly. "Well, I died."

"You died?" I ask.

"Yes," he says. "I was blown up."

"So, you're dead?" I ask.

"Yes. I think."

"How are you dead?"

"I blew up. Bombs were dropped on my house. My body was torn apart by an explosion. It was difficult to stay alive during that."

"How are you here if you're dead?"

"Have you never dreamed of a dead person before?" he asks. "I have dreamed of plenty. Too many."

"Then... are you a dream character? A figment of my imagination? You certainly don't seem like it," I say.

"Perhaps I am. Maybe that's one way of putting it," he muses. "That certainly would make sense. But I guess I wouldn't know, would I? Dream characters usually don't seem to know that they're not self-aware, if in fact they aren't."

"Are you?" I ask.

"Am I self-aware, sure. Am I real? I'm not sure if I'm the best person to ask," he answers. "Or am I the only person who would know that? I guess I am."

"But you know things that I don't. You can control dreams. You can't just be a character in my head," I say.

"You know many things that you just don't remember. I could just be your dream controlling itself. For the longest time you thought I was just a character in your head," he says. "You've admitted that you can't tell the difference between dream characters and real people."

"But you remember dying, right?" I ask and he nods. "Well, what do you remember after that?"

"I died. I saw a white light. I saw my loved ones. It was surreal, like a dream. But it never stopped. I just ... carried on," he says.

He's sitting cross legged on the teacher's desk.

"For the longest time I was just trapped alone in my own dream, memories of my life swirling around my mind. I'm not sure how long, but for a long time there wasn't much of anything, besides me and my mind. There was no traveling. My memory of that time is unclear. I was vaguely aware of my own existence, even more vaguely aware of yours, but I could not touch you like I had before. Over time, things became clearer, more vivid. Slowly but surely, I became more lucid. I lost track of you, but I continued to exist, somehow. Those were long and lonely times. Unfathomably lonely. It is difficult to tell time in a permanent dream. There were no days, no nights, unless I wanted them to be. Hours passed, but I was never sure whether they were hours or not."

"Eventually, I found someone else," he continues. "Not a dreamer, but a person dreaming. I entered their dream. You won't believe what that meant to me. From what felt like an eternity in a borderless cell of solitary confinement, I finally encountered another person. For a moment I touched another person again. It suggested that I wasn't dead and in hell. At least I wasn't all-dead. It proved that I was still connected to the world, to humanity. That was something I could work with."

I don't even know how to react to this.

"Slowly, but surely, I learned to travel again, as I had before. I made my way through the dreamworld: The ever-changing ethereal dreamworld, I have learned so much about it since I died. I have learned so much more than I knew before. I have met many other dreamers... and even other... other things. I have seen worlds that cannot exist. Colors no one else can imagine. I've learned things even the doctor doesn't know. There is so much more to it than they know. I have returned to the shadow, truly a watcher now. I move in complete silence, attracting no attention."

His eyes and voice drift away from me at that moment, as if he's distracted. The words ring a bit, although it's not a threat. I have never been afraid of Feda before, but now it grabs me by the spine. He isn't human, at least not like I am. He's not my dream character. He is something... otherworldly. I don't know what he is. He is a ghost.

He smiles at me again, as if he knows what I'm thinking and the warmth returns. Perhaps he does know what I'm thinking. He's still Feda though. I have felt his malice before, but he is a good person. He was a good person; at least, back when he was a person.

"I don't understand," I say. "So, what are you? Are you a ghost? Are you just a part of my imagination?"

Feda shrugs. "I don't know. My body died, but maybe my consciousness lives on in the dreamworld. Something like that," he says.

"And you're, you're immortal?" I ask.

"That, I'm not so sure about," he says. "I haven't died again yet. In the dreamworld."

I think about that for a second.

"The thing is: I have no presence in the real world," he continues. "So, I can only influence things from here."

"And that's why you need me," I say, as it finally clicks in my mind. "You want me to finish your mission. You want me to tell the world about this place, don't you? You can't do it yourself. You need me to be your messenger."

"I want you to write the book you were always supposed to write: the one that I should have had you write in the first place," he says. "You have the world's attention. You could put all this power in the hands of the people, rather than the elite few. You have the power to do that."

God, why does everyone want me to write a goddamned book?

"You want me to expose Le Réveil?" I ask.

"Don't say their name!" he hisses.

"Why not?" I say. "Because we'll attract their attention? So what if they find us?"

"Do I really need to say it?" Feda says.

"What will happen if they find us, Feda?" I ask, my frustration spilling out. "This organization that you say is so powerful, the one that you're asking me to help you bring down, what would they do if they found out you were working against them?"

"Well, last time they found out I was trying to expose them..." he says. "I was killed by an explosion."

VISITING HOURS

My mother is outside watering the garden. I watch her, remembering that same lawn stretching out into the grasslands of the Eastern Cape of South Africa. I remember a tree towering over the landscape and a scary African woman with two aprons. My mom could have been watering a garden there too. She could have stayed true to her colonial roots. She could have had a house similar to this one but nestled on the southern tip of Africa. If she hadn't met my father, that would have been her life. If it wasn't for the "naughty thought in his head" she would have probably married a South African man.

My entire life could be different, it might not even exist, if it were for a few small decisions made differently. Some weren't even decisions, some were mistakes. Who knows where the better choice would have led?

My father is sitting on the sofa doing a crossword puzzle. Does he think about this sort of thing? As we grow up, do we put childish things aside? These childish things like existential worry? No, I know we don't. When I was a teenager, I used to wonder about adults. Somehow, they seemed so put together, but also, so thoughtless. They knew the rules of their game so well, but they seemed unaware that it was a game, a farce. Oh, but us teenagers knew. We were going to resist the game, the rat-race, the cycle of unhappiness. We weren't going to work nine to five. We were young, liberal and free.

Slowly, but surely, you sink into the game. Perhaps it's when you realize that there's comfort in the game. Everyone else plays the game, and you're just so tired. Also, you need money. You need purpose.

I laugh as I realize just how bad I am doing with my training. I should be meditating. I should be clearing my mind. Instead, I'm having an internal monologue.

Perhaps I should be using this opportunity, my waking life, to think about whatever I want. I'm not allowed to let my mind wander at night anymore. Lucid dreaming has robbed me of that. Perhaps I should be thinking about Le Réveil, Feda or what I might have inadvertently gotten myself into. What is this organization? Do they even exist? If they do, are they really the sinister presence that Feda implies? Is the doctor really a part of that? Is my life in danger? I sound like a conspiracy theorist.

I lay down on my bed and stare at the roof.

What should I do?

Bzzzzt.

The door buzzer interrupts my train of thought. I hear my mom call from the garden as she turns off the hose.

"Gaaaaaabi!" she shouts. "Are you expecting anyone?

"Nooooo," I reply. God, they always shout across the house, and it annoys the hell out of me, especially when I catch myself doing it in return.

I hear my mom turning off the hose and walking around to the front of the house. Who the hell comes over unannounced these days? All it takes is a text.

Then it hits me, this small suggestion becomes a piece of kindling in my mind. A spark ignites and spreads. Who comes over unannounced these days? It can't be Karin. Is it them? Am I in danger? I'm surely being paranoid. I know it's going to just be a friend of my parents, maybe some Jehovah's Witness or something. It couldn't be them. What would they do? How would they know? Have they been listening? Who are they?

I haven't done anything wrong.

"Gaaaaabi!" my mom calls again, from the front door. "There's someone here for you."

My heart sinks. I pull myself off my bed and across my bedroom floor. It can't be. Maybe it's not them, maybe it's something else. Karin?

As I round the corner, the relief I hoped for doesn't come. The doctor is standing there, tall, dark and imposing.

"Here she is, doctor," my mom says, as if she's presenting me as a gift.

The doctor looks at me and smiles. It's that same goddamned smile of his, dripping with fake warmth. That smarmy smile that is scientifically engineered to put one at ease.

"Good afternoon, Gabi," he says. "Apologies for the house call."

"Would you like something to drink?" my mom asks, never forgetting her guest protocol. "Tea, coffee?"

"Oh yes, coffee would be perfect, Mrs. Rivers," he replies. "If Gabi doesn't mind me coming over for a quick chat?"

I swallow air. My voice comes out as a croak.

"No, of course," I say." Come in."

My mother offers to take his jacket, but the doctor refuses. She guides him into the house in his full suit and I float along behind, like a balloon trailing in the wind.

What is he doing here?

My dad stands to meet him. They shake hands in the way that old men do: firm, assertive, but just below the threshold for aggressive.

"Doctor Sivers, I presume?" my dad says.

"Correct," he replies. "Thank you for welcoming me into your home."

"A friend of Gabi's is a friend of ours," my dad says. He shoots me a glance. I think he's asking me if I want him gone. I purse my lips as if to tell him that I'm not happy he's here, but don't need him removed. Somehow, he seems to understand.

My father returns to his seat, and I lead the doctor out onto our back porch. It's not particularly private, but it's the best we have.

Why is he here? Does he know?

"How have you been, Gabi?" he asks, sitting down at our cast-iron chair and table. Deja-vu drips from the moment. It's as if I'm right back at one of our meetings, showing him my dream reports and yearning for praise on my progress.

"I'm okay," I say. "Just taking some time to write, you know, practicing some of the techniques you taught me."

We are both well aware that my parents can hear us, even if they aren't listening.

"Good, good," he says. "So why did you disappear all of a sudden? I looked everywhere I could think of, but I couldn't find you, almost as if you were... avoiding me."

My mom chooses that moment to interrupt us with coffee for the doctor and me. She puts the French press down on the table and turns to the doctor. "Milk or sugar?"

"Black, thank you," he replies.

My mom smiles at him and leaves.

"No," I continue our conversation. "It wasn't about you... I just had something of an attack, a panic attack. I haven't really been sleeping well since. I came home to be with my family and recover."

The doctor leans forward and pours himself some coffee. He pours for me too.

"I know about the panic attack, Gabi," he says. "I know it can be difficult to remember anything from such a traumatic event, but I was there. I helped you. I helped you snap out of it. Do you remember?"

"I only remember it vaguely," I say. "I do remember you helping me. Thank you. I don't know what would have happened if not for you."

"Do you remember what happened that might have triggered it? Normally I would have been there, but I was called away for an emergency. However, that emergency proved to be a… let's call it a false alarm. When I returned, I found you in a bad state."

He takes a deep sip from his coffee.

"I apologize for not being there to help earlier, but I promise that won't happen again. I didn't realize the danger I left you in."

"It's okay doctor, I understand," I say, trying to reassure him. I am surprised at how well I have managed to lie my way through this.

I move to add some sugar to my own cup but stop. My hand is shaking. The doctor is watching me. I lean back.

"There wasn't someone else with you," he asks. "When you had the attack?"

I look up at him. My heart freezes.

"Someone else?" I ask.

"Yes," he says. His voice and tone continue without the slightest change. "I hope that you would tell me if you've received conflicting advice."

I stay silent and try to look confused.

"There are other doctors out there with very… unorthodox approaches, those who are only interested in their own agenda. I would hate to hear you were acting on the advice of someone untrustworthy. It could potentially be quite… dangerous."

I narrow my eyes at him. "I don't know what you're talking about."

He meets my eyes. "I cannot overstate how dangerous they can be, despite how convincing they may seem."

"Okay," I say, putting up my hands. "I'll remember that. But I think I'm going to be okay."

He leans back into his chair, seemingly comfortable that he's delivered his message, warning or threat? I'm not quite sure.

"If you are having trouble sleeping, because of the panic attacks," he continues. "I can help you, if I am around."

"Thanks doctor," I say, putting on my best smile. "I'll remember that. I know all I need to do is say your name, and you'll be right there."

He smiles. How much does he know? No, Gabi, keep your mind blank. You could be in danger.

"Yes," he says. "I will make sure to keep an ear to the ground, so to speak. So how is the book going?"

"You know me," I shrug. "Always procrastinating. I've given something to Karin though."

"Congratulations," he says. "I would love to read what you have written so far. Are you still writing about climate change, as you called it, the greatest danger facing the world today?"

"Um," I say. "Yes, in a roundabout way. I'm still whittling it down, you know?"

"I understand," he says. "Please feel free to reach out though, I believe I may still be able to help answer a lot of your questions."

He takes a sip out of his cup of coffee, and I pause in front of mine. I hope my parents assume that I'm just a terrible conversationalist and not cotton on to how tense this is. He puts his cup down.

"Well, I guess I should let you get back to writing then," he says. "Hopefully it's not too long until I see you again."

We both stand and shake hands. I walk him to the front door, lost in my own head as he says goodbye to my parents. I catch snippets of their farewell.

"You have an amazing daughter."

"We're well aware."

At the front door he utters a final, "see you soon, Gabi," and leaves me to my own thoughts again.

I wander through to the lounge.

"He seems nice," my mom says, smiling.

I grab one of my parents' bottles of wine, a glass and smile back at her.

"Yeah, he's nice." I take a sip, and continue ad nauseum, deep into the night.

THE OTHERS

"What have you gotten me into?" I ask.

Although no one is around, I speak to a particular someone. I know he will arrive soon enough. The world spins just a bit.

"I didn't ask for this," I shout into nothingness. "I didn't ask to be a part of your war."

"Then don't be," Feda says.

He emerges partially out of the darkness. For this moment, he's something sinister, flanked by dark green hedges and blackness. Where are we?

"But don't pretend that you haven't already made choices. You could have told the doctor about me. You chose not to. You could have told your family, or Karin, about the dreamworld. You chose not to. The path of least resistance is still a path."

"This isn't some hypothetical philosophy lesson," I reply. "This is my life."

"What life?"

"What?"

"What life?" he says. "What life are you worried about ruining? The one where you float around purposelessly? The one where you're unwilling to do exactly what you want to do? The one where you live uncomfortably on the profits of the story of my death?"

"Fuck off," I reply. "That's unfair."

"No, fuck you Gabi," he says. "You clamor for something to believe in, something to fight for. And then chicken out the moment you find it. If you aren't going to fight this battle, then accept the fact that you aren't going to fight any. You're barely willing to live for something, let alone die for it. You're a coward."

I say nothing. I back up. Away from him. My back is poked by the twigs of the hedge behind me. I'm in a giant hedge maze. I'm in a labyrinth.

"If you want to be lost on your own, be lost on your own," he says. He disappears backwards into the darkness. "I will leave you to your absolute freedom."

The last glimpse of him is replaced by a shroud of blackness. I am plunged into solitude.

I call for him. I reach out for him as soon as I chase him away. Instead of comfort, I feel cold. I'm alone in this labyrinth. I'm surrounded by opaque pathways leading off to unknown futures. Even in my despair, I lament my own on-the-nose metaphor. A maze? Really? Surely, I could have done so much better than this. Surely my subconscious could do more?

But no, I couldn't. I am not my potential. I'm not what I imagine I could do. I'm what I put down to paper. This is me. I'm third-rate symbolism. I'm insecurity.

I am collapsed inward on the ground at the center of my own labyrinth, paralyzed by indecision. I don't even try any of the available routes.

Time moves haphazardly. It sees me crumpled against a hedge fingering my own hand. I am dreaming. I am dreaming. It sees me standing in the middle, befuddled by the options.

Feda is right. What the fuck do I want to do? What do I want? I can go anywhere. I can go anywhere I want, and I don't even fucking know where I want to go.

What am I going to do with this life I'm so protective of?

Am I going to sit in the middle of this maze? Am I going to criticize and mock those who take an unknown path for the failures they inevitably face?

It's so great that I'm so self-aware of my weakness though, right? That changes everything.

God!

I pull myself to my feet, conspicuously aware of how unsteady they are.

I just need to do it. I just need to choose a path. I just need to choose a path and go down it. Maybe it'll be the wrong path; maybe every path is wrong. Maybe it's all about the least wrong choice.

I take off, I stumble down the path opposite me. The darkness doesn't subside as I enter. I can barely see a foot in front of me as I meander my way forwards.

The hedge is barely visible in my peripheral vision as I continue aimlessly.

I hoped to go forward. I hoped to strive into an unknown future, brave and undeterred. Instead, I feel myself regressing. I feel myself sliding backwards as if I'm ice-skating uphill. I'm falling back into a history I don't care for, but one that defines me. It's just as real now as it was then. It's been sleeping below the surface. It's been waiting to break through the ice and grab my ankles from below. It's a horror movie villain. It always returns from the dead at least once. Perhaps for multiple sequels.

I slap to the floor. It's damp and cold against me, it seeps through my clothes. Fingers grip around my ankles. I feel the ground sucking me down into the earth. The mud envelopes my hands as I try to push myself up.

My hands. Why am I letting this happen to myself? It was getting so much better. I thought I had this covered.

"You never fully get the hang of it," the doctor said. "At least, not enough to stop trying."

I remember those words, from when I was underwater. The doctor helped me up then. He helped me make the water sure enough to stand on.

I've stopped trying. That's why I'm sinking. Things don't become easier; we just get better at them. We get better by trying. Some battles will always need to be fought. Especially this one.

By now, my legs are submerged in the mud, but I can still pull myself out. I know because I've done it before. My hands squelch unpleasantly as I push upwards. The sound of suction is all I can hear, as I try to rip myself out of the bog.

I scrape and pull, for ages it seems. Slowly, but surely, but inches, not far. I slide back and claw back the lost ground. Finally, I feel my feet come loose. I pull myself to my knees and stand. Every inch of me is covered with mud and dirt.

The labyrinth stands tall around me, still imposing, still treacherous. As big as it is, as much as it looms over me with uncertainty, I remember. I remember my training. I remember all the lessons I have learned. I remember my strength. There is always an escape. There is always another dimension that you can break through.

I look up. A drip lands on my nose. It's starting to drizzle. Water is falling from the sky. Sometimes light shows you the way, sometimes water does. Wherever it comes from, there's an exit. The way out is up. As the drops grow more numerous, I lift my legs off the earth. I rise up as rain pelts me. It cleans me of the dirt and mud of the earth.

I take off into the sky, into the rain, my clothes hugging me tightly. I cut against the sheets of water, and tear through the clouds above them. It's darker and colder here, but I can see sunshine ahead. I blossom out into blue sky and the sun bakes my goose-pimpled skin. Oh god, I need every ounce of that warmth. It's just so cold. I hover and look down at the world below, rubbing myself to keep warm.

It's a mixture of awe-inspiring and terrifying up here. I have to try to not let gravity pull me down. It's so tempting. It calls to me. It would feel so natural to plummet to earth, to smash my body against the ground. But no, I can fly.

I charge forward, shivering as I hit the cold air ahead. I want to find somewhere warm. I need warmth.

It feels so strange to be alone in my dream for a change. What do I do now? Hasn't this always been my problem? The agony of choice.

Maybe I should visit another dreamer? Now I'm finally free to do what I want. I know there are others. Maybe I should meet them?

Where should I go? Who should I visit? Who do I know well enough? Not Kyle this time. Fuck Kyle.

Who do I know at all? Karin?

Karin... yes. Karin.

"I'm going to visit Karin," I say, as if I could make it true by simply verbalizing it.

I need to cover ground; I need to cover it quickly. That means flying and flying fast. I tear towards the horizon. I think about Karin. I think about her office, her home. I think about what she might be thinking or feeling; what she might dream about. These are all the things that Feda taught me to do.

The clouds below give way to a city, they give way to the inevitability of industry. I fly lower and weave between the tall chimneys and smoke like a falcon through a forest, bearing down on my prey. She's my target. She's a queen at the top of the tallest tower in the Kingdom. She's a woman of authority, of power. A force of nature. She's confident. She's strength and surety.

No.

"She's more than that," I say, without trying. I know she's more than that. She's not just what she seems. I know her better than that. I swerve and continue in a slightly different direction.

Towards Karin: alone in the city. Never married. No children. Addicted to self-improvement. Fueled by a deep belief that whatever she is now isn't quite good enough. Checklists upon checklists of things that should make her perfect. A progress bar that's an asymptote.

I swoop down towards the heart of the city, towards the twisted foundations of ambition. Under each skyscraper is a deep imperfection, an instability from growing too tall too fast. And instability that drove them higher than they should have gone.

I rip through concrete like it's paper, deep under the city. Parking lot and sewers. Dripping water echoes down long corridors. But I am alone, save for a voice and darkness. It's my voice.

No.

I won't find her here. We are not our deepest insecurities. We do not dream about our life's central driving force. I know Karin already, I don't need to intellectualize her.

I pace down the sewers thinking about how to find her. Nothing in this place comes easy. As far as I've come, I'm only scratching the surface. It requires a self-discipline of thought, a permanent level of awareness I never thought possible.

I think of Karin. Not her name. Not a description of her. Not what I think about her. Just her. Her face. Her voice. Her sense of humor. Who she is to me. The feel of her. Our times together. I close my eyes and imagine her. For a few moments, that's all I do.

As I open them, I notice a light at the end of the sewer tunnel. Poignant. Cliches can be useful, sometimes there's no need to reinvent the wheel. I walk towards it, feeling Karin the whole way. I am hit by a wave of familiarity as I approach it, deja-vu that I have to fight. That is not the right memory for now. I hear the call of a seagull, and instantly the sea air hits my nostrils. I take a deep breath. Ahhhh, that's the stuff.

As the light becomes reality, my bare feet feel the sand that's crept into the tunnel. The sounds of a beach, a beach I know, greet my ears like old friends. The sun does the same for my skin, its heat reminding me how cold I was moments before.

In the middle of this beach sits a table. It's a nice restaurant, good view. Very authentic. Sitting across at the other end of the table is Karin, the spirit of holiday calmness. A loose-fitting white cotton shirt covers her. My heart lifts to see her here. Her phone calls give me anxiety; her presence gives me comfort.

"Gabi!" She stands to hug me. I smile and throw my arms around her, squeezing her more tightly than I have in a long time. I can feel her smile against my shoulder.

"I thought you weren't going to make it," she says. "I've been waiting for hours."

She motions for me to sit down. I remain standing.

"You've been waiting?" I reply.

"Yes," she says. She looks hurt. "I... I was worried about you. I thought I'd lost you."

She sounds more sensitive than I'm used to. Is this her? How do I know? How can I tell the difference between what I expect her to be, and what she is?

"I thought we could go for a walk instead," I say.

Karin just looks at me. She doesn't say anything for a moment and then agrees. "Sure."

She smiles and joins me for a walk along the beachfront, strolling along arm in arm.

"How are you?" she asks. "How are things with the doctor?"

"I don't see him anymore," I say. "You know that…"

"Oh," she replies. "That's a shame. You two seemed good together."

I am about to chastise her for this when I stop myself. There's no reason to let a confrontation interrupt her. Let's see how she goes.

"What makes you say that?" I ask.

"Well, you couldn't write. Then you were with him. Then you could write," she says. "That seems like a good relationship to me."

I laugh. "That's very pragmatic of you."

"That's me," she replies, looking away. "Always thinking about work, right?"

Karin stops, now staring at the ocean. "Look at that."

"What is it?" I say, trying not to interfere with the direction of her dream.

"I think that someone's drowning," she says, walking towards the water. She breaks into a run, lifting her legs high as she enters the knee-level waves.

I hover behind her and then follow. While Karin struggles against the current, I walk across the surface of the water. There's no reason for me to get wet.

Karin fights her way towards what now looks like a young well-built man barely keeping his eyes above the water. Despite swimming strongly, it seems she cannot reach him. The harder she pushes the further away he floats. The waves are far stronger than they appeared at first. Karin doesn't look like she's going anywhere in the tumult.

"Chester," she splutters as the man finally disappears below the surface, not to return.

Chester? Does she know this man? We rarely dream about strangers, I guess.

"Don't worry," I shout to Karin. This is definitely her, fuck not getting involved.

I run forward and dive down into the water. He's sinking into the depth of it, eyes closed and unmoving. Chester? Who is he?

I reach for him and grab his hand. It's easy enough to pull him up. The world does not resist me. Karin's eyes are wide as she watches me while treading water. I pick up the man, as waterlogged as he is, and carry him back to the shore. Karin follows, swimming strongly as she does. Still, she lags behind me. I put Chester down on the sand. He does not look like a living man should.

"Gabi?!?" Karin splutters as she runs out of the water and onto the beach. She rushes over to us.

"He's not breathing!" she screams, preparing to give him mouth to mouth. She pounds on his chest and tries in vain to kiss life into him.

He wakes up with water spluttering out of his mouth… but he doesn't. He lies there dead. He doesn't come back to life, no matter how much I insist on that reality, no matter how much Karin pounds at his chest like a scared girl on a door. In this, her dream resists me. It knocks me. The sense of power I have cultivated shatters in a moment. I cannot bring him back to life any more than she can.

Karin shouts at him. In anger. In frustration.

"What were you doing in there? Why didn't you survive, you asshole!" She's in tears over his body. This isn't the Karin I know. 'Why did you do this? Why did you have to be so weak?"

Who is he? Why can't I bring him back to life? Is he a dreamer?

"Who is he?" I ask.

She finally stops trying, and instead looks up at me. Her eyes are red from loss, both of him and of herself. She opens her mouth to speak and stops. She seems confused.

"But he died…" she says. "Long ago."

I can feel her pain. It pours out of her like blood from a wound. It's an old scar reopened, stitches torn. It's a familiar pain, a familiar sound. It's the familiar sound of a cold wind rising from the sea. It's the sting of sand against my ankles. It's the aura before a migraine. It's the electricity in the air preceding the storm. The dogs barking. The water receding from the coast. Oh my god. It's the signal. The scraping of metal against metal. A slow intermittent beep. The silence and the cold. It's him.

I won't let him catch me again. I need to get out of here. I turn to run before

I realize; I can't leave Karin behind. I can't let him get her either.

"Karin," I say. "We need to go. Now!"

She just looks at me. This signal means nothing to her. Her eyes are still bloodshot.

"How could I lose him?" she blabbers. "How could he let this happen? How could I?"

"Karin!" I say, shaking her by the shoulder. "We need to go. Fuck! You're supposed to be the responsible one out of the two of us."

Karin's eyes focus on mine, as if that snapped something inside of her. She gets to her feet.

"What is it, Gabi?" she says. "How can I help?"

"Help?" I grab her hand. "You can help by following me. We need to leave."

I start pulling her away. I can feel the panic enveloping me again. I can hear the silence of his approach. Karin doesn't move.

"I can't leave him here," she says.

"He's not real!" I shout. "Leave him."

"What?!?" she replies.

It's already too late. As I turn back to Karin, as I am about to start explaining, as I am about to tie myself up in knots trying to tell her a half-truth, as I do this, I see him. The Knife. Even the sun has hidden. The darkness sweeps across the beach. He stands in the distance, barely anything. He's a shadow on the horizon.

Karin notices my expression change. She must feel it too. It's palpable. What can I do? I can't run. I can't get away with Karin in tow. I can't abandon her here. Fuck.

"What is that? Gabi. Who is that?" she mutters.

What the fuck should I do? No one's coming to help me this time. No one knows where I am. I can't run to Busi or the doctor or... that's it! I've been learning how to stay hidden all this time. I guess it's time to break the rules.

"Busi!" I shout. "Igqirha! Busi, I need you! Please help."

Will Busi come? I don't know.

The shadow extends, the silhouette moves closer. He's still just a dark shape growing, growing closer.

"Who's Busi?" Karin asks as she looks at me imploringly. She stands in front of me as if to protect me. This is her role.

"Stay back," she says. "You should run. I will try to hold it off, whatever it is."

"Doctor Sivers!" I call out to the darkness. "You said I could call if I needed you. I need you!"

I imagine him. I think about him. I try to feel his presence.

Nothing. Instead, there is only the Knife standing before us.

"What are you?!?" Karin shouts, adopting some sort of fighting pose. "Stay back!"

No one's coming. No one's going to come to save us. The doctor isn't going to come and shoot me in the head so that I wake up, but I can do that for her. I can save Karin. I reach to my side, to the gun I have holstered there. I draw it, disengage the safety and cock it.

The Knife stops advancing and watches.

"Karin."

"Run!" Karin says to me. "I'll hold it off."

"Karin," I say softly. "I'm sorry."

She turns to face the gun pointed directly at her head.

WHICH DOCTOR?

Her eyes widen as she looks at me. She mouths a few words before a noise comes out. It kills me to see it. It hits my resolve off center.

"Gabi?" she asks.

Shoot her, shoot her. I know I need to. The Knife has stopped.

"Gabi, what are you doing?"

"I'm so sorry."

I am. I can't do this. I can't kill Karin, even though I know she'll be fine. She'll wake up in her bed after a bad dream. Not even the worst dream, just a bad one. But what if she remembers? What if she remembers?

"Why would you think that dreams are not real?" the doctor had once said. "They are as real as your thoughts or feelings."

I turn the gun towards the Knife and squeeze the trigger. Karin stumbles back holding her ears. She falls onto the ground screaming in pain. My ears also ring from the blasts. The gun kicks back in my hand, but the bullets find their way.

Nothing happens. The darkness is unfazed. All I sense is his disappointment that I didn't shoot my friend in the head. How do I know he feels that? I don't know. There's no expression there.

The sand beneath us ripples. Too slowly I realize. The metal chains dart out of the sand and wrap around Karin's limbs. She screams in agony.

I smell her flesh burning. Oh my god, it's happening again. It's going to happen to her too. I have to...

"Gabi!" she screams.

I squeeze the trigger and her head explodes into blood and skull fragments. Her body slumps limply, still held aloft by the chains.

I crumble equally. I collapse to the sand. Sobs escape me, they erupt out of me as I look at her body. She's safe at last.

The Knife watches me, unmoving, unmoved.

"Are you happy!?!" I shout at him. "Is this what you want?"

I can't see any reaction, except the void of darkness. I turn the gun on myself. I put it in my mouth. That's what you do, right? I scrunch my eyes tight and squeeze the trigger.

Nothing, besides the click of an empty chamber. I squeeze again. Nothing. Again and again.

I open my eyes to find the Knife still staring at me. Is he enjoying this? Of course he is. Why?

A hand touches my shoulder.

"You had the right idea."

I turn around to see the doctor standing beside me. His eyes are fixed on the Knife. The Knife looks... well, I have no idea if he even has eyes.

"Doctor?" I ask. "You came?"

"I did say I would, didn't I?" he says, standing out in front of me. "Don't act so surprised."

He's facing down the Knife like he's facing down a bear. I stay on the ground behind him.

Karin's body drops lifelessly, and the chains retract into the sand, winding their way back to their owner. The sand ripples once again as they spread out around us.

"Leave," says the doctor. He does not shout it, but his voice booms like a fog-horn. The sand scatters away from him. The Knife, however, does not.

Instead, the Knife moves one step forward, as if he's about to attack, but he stops. In barely an instant he melts into the ground and disappears. His darkness becomes the coarse beach material beneath him. I can trace the river of sand that illustrates his route away.

"Thank god," I say. I can see the relief in the doctor's stance. His shoulders drop and he turns.

But before the tension could lift, another voice interrupts.

"Do you think you can summon me just to scare him away?"

The doctor and I turn. Busi stands on the sand, as if she had always been there. The doctor steps back, spinning around.

"I'm sorry, Busi," I say, trying to stand up. "I had to."

The doctor's eyes dart between the two of us as he slowly walks backwards.

"You had to?" Busi says, her voice barely containing its anger. I can hear it below the surface. It's bubbling. "And when I come, I find you in strange company. A demon and a devil, one black, one white. Tell me, girl. Did you call us both here, in a panic?"

The doctor takes a moment to regain his composure.

"I..." I stammer. "I am so sorry, Busi."

"Busi," the doctor says, finding his voice again. "I was not aware you had made friends with our young writer here."

"Is she yours?" Busi replies. "I found her alone. It's frustrating when your children run off while your back is turned, isn't it?"

His eyes dart again between Busi and I.

"All you can do is hope they don't run into someone dangerous," he replies. "I am glad it was you that she encountered."

"Does that mean you don't think me dangerous, Jakob?" Busi cocks her head at the doctor.

The tension between these two has me in a vice grip. The doctor smiles unpleasantly. It's not one of the smiles I've seen before. I don't get the impression he relishes this confrontation the way that Busi does.

"May I ask what your interest in Gabi is?" he asks. "You've never been one to take kindly to new faces in the dreamworld."

"Kevin was an idiot," Busi laughs. "But I gave him a klap, sent him on his way. But don't you worry Jakob, our agreement is still intact. This girl just happened to stumble across my path while trying to avoid that Mara I, ahem, I mean, we just scared away."

The doctor sighs.

"And what is your interest in this girl?" Busi continues. "Does she perhaps... remind you of someone?"

The doctor narrows his eyes. He opens his mouth as if he is about to say something, but then changes his mind. He disengages from the banter.

"Gabi," he says. "You should come find me when you are ready to talk. I had hoped that I would have more time to explain things to you in a structured way, but it seems that you may be getting conflicting information. We have a lot to discuss. I have many of the answers you seek."

Busi laughs, heartily. "Yes, yes, you and your friends are always so open with information, yes?"

He looks at me for a moment and then away, glancing at the body of Karin as he does.

"You can go now," Busi says, shooing away the doctor with her hand. "I need to scold this child for calling me so recklessly."

The doctor narrows his eyes at her.

"Busi," he says. "The Frenchman has a special interest in her. Don't take our acceptance of your... independence as a license to move against us."

Busi remains quiet. Her casual bravado is replaced by quiet intensity. Rather than push the issue, neither party says any more.

"I will see you soon, Gabi," says the doctor, turning away.

He walks off without looking back. His exit is unhurried and painfully slow. Busi and I watch him all the way until he phases out into a haze of nothingness. This leaves Busi and me alone, and my prospects uncertain.

"Girl," Busi says. "That was a bold move. You're playing a dangerous game."

"I'm not playing a game!" I say, putting my hands up.

"Are you playing me against them? I might have been wrong in thinking Feda was the bold half of your strange duo," she says. "I should skin you for this."

"Please, Busi," I say. "I panicked. I called both of you. That's all."

"You're good at playing stupid," she says. "It suits you."

I stay silent, worried that anything I say may trigger her temper. I feel like I'm about to be spanked by the grandmother I never had.

"They've grown bold too. That man, Jakob Sivers, should not threaten me," she says.

"He threatened you?" I reply.

"He used his name. He called his attention upon me," she says. "Maybe he just panicked himself. Maybe. Maybe Feda was right. Maybe you are right. Maybe we should be fighting them."

Busi's rage has been tempered by thoughtfulness, for the moment.

"Just what do you know about them?" I ask. "This organization that we're not speaking about."

She seems surprised by my continued existence, as if she had forgotten I was here.

"What?" she says. "You are testing my patience girl. You are trying to play a game with the adults."

She looks at Karin's body before continuing.

"You have gone through enough today, I think. I won't punish you further, but do not call on me again," she turns to me and narrows her eyes. Her voice travels through me as she speaks, as if she is speaking to someone who is not me.

"I will not fight your war for you."

"War?" I ask

She turns to walk away, to leave me behind and return to her solitude. I reply, despite knowing better, a thought popping into my head entirely out of nowhere.

"In that story you told me, about a young girl..." I say.

She stops, without turning to face me.

"What was her name?" I ask.

"Nongqawuse. What about her?" Busi says.

"Do you know who tricked Nongqawuse?" I ask.

She remains quiet.

"How old is this organization?" I ask. "Because they seem to make a habit of targeting young, impressionable dreamers. Perhaps they're doing to me what they did to her?"

She is uncharacteristically still.

"Perhaps I can see Feda in you after all," she says. "For better and for worse."

She swipes her hand at me and my eyes open. I am instantly awake. It's not quite morning yet. It's still dark outside.

VERISIMILITUDE

Gabi floats around the mall, hoodie up and earphones in. Large sunglasses hide her face. She's hiding from the world and hiding from herself. She's free to move through the amphitheater like a regular person. In other places, this disguise wouldn't be needed, after all, author-famous isn't real-famous. But here, in her hometown... here her name is household. Every-one here has mapped out their degrees of separation to her.

"Gabrielle Rivers was at the same high school as my friend!"

Shielded from the noise outside, her ears are instead filled with the music she listened to growing up. She never evolved to listen to anything new since she left high school. What she would once proudly badge herself with now feels like an embarrassment. If she were to pull out her earphones, she would treat the world around her to the unfiltered angst of college cool. She would cringe.

The world around her moved on. Who is big now? She wonders. What do the kids listen to? What do her peers listen to? What do they care about? Is she still one of them? What has she become instead, while everyone else was growing up?

The air glints as the sun hits dust. It makes her feel as though she is under-water. Someone sings in her ears. At one stage he represented everything that Gabi loved in the world. It takes her somewhere else, a long time ago. Now it sounds far away.

Did they all lie to her, all these voices that spoke to her throughout her young life? They talked about pain, and meaning, and love and life. They all talked to her about a world that was fleeting. It was a dream. Everyone else woke up and Gabi was too preoccupied to notice that she was alone. Now she is alone.

She wafts into the movie theater. At least the movie theater never changes. The movies come; the movies go. The theater itself remains. It still charges too much for popcorn and soda. The zit-faced adolescents that run the place still don't really give a fuck. They still sneak off to the parking lot to smoke, sometimes cigarettes, sometimes reefer.

What is she doing back in time?

What is she doing walking into this theater and sitting down on this stale old chair, breathing this stale old air thick with nostalgia? This doesn't feel real. She came here to get away. To get away from her thoughts, her dreams. Her book. Her house.

But is she dreaming again?

She pulls off her glasses and is about to check her hand, but is interrupted by a voice from directly behind her.

"Please don't freak out," it says. "And don't turn around."

It's a male voice, one that is unfamiliar. Who is this? What am I doing here?

"What are you talking about?" I reply.

"I'm a friend of Feda, and I'm here to help you. You're in far more danger than you think," he says. "This is the first time I've been able to talk to you."

"What do you mean?" I reply again.

Something flies over my shoulder and lands on the seat next to me: a red cap, a familiar red baseball cap. Oh god. My heart skips a beat.

"You!" I shout, spinning around to face him in the dark.

"Turn around," he whispers insistently. "Just sit and face the screen. They'll see us."

"Fuck that," I say. "Why should I listen to you? You've been stalking me."

"I haven't been stalking you," he says. "I'm with Feda. I've been trying to protect you. Please just sit down."

I frown at him, looking around at the empty theater.

"Okay. Fine," I say sliding down into my seat. "Explain yourself. You've got until the movie starts."

"You don't realize how much danger you're in," he says. "Jakob Sivers isn't who you think he is."

"You're behind the curve, buddy," I reply. "I know who he is. You, on the other hand, I have no fucking clue who you are."

"How much do you know?" he asks.

"How much do you know?" I reply.

We stay quiet for a while as the movie trailers pull up onto the screen. Stars jump out of them, winking slyly at the camera as their names are called. Trailers specialize in making each film look as uniform as possible. Each genre has its own soundtrack and format. The deep and loud boom of epics landing. The heartfelt piano behind a drama's tear-jerking. The reveal of the returning character in the sequel. But I thought he died? Oh, is that a sparsely composed and emotional rendition of an 80's classic?

I grab the man's red cap and throw it back to him. "This is yours."

"I think we got off on the wrong foot," he says. "My name is Kevin and I'm a friend, I promise."

"You're not my friend," I reply. "I don't know you. But I think you already know my name."

"I'm here to help you. I sent you that note," he says. "I worked with Feda, working against Le Réveil. You know they killed him."

I reply, "Did they kill him?"

"Yes," he goes on. "So, you know who Le Réveil is? That's good. They orchestrated his death to get rid of him because of the threat he posed to them. Obviously, they didn't do it directly. That's not how they work, well, it's not normally how they work. I think they're going to do the same to you."

"I'm getting out of here," I say. "Please leave me alone."

I stand quickly and start walking out of the theater.

"They've got a man on you," he says, following me out of the cinema. "Trailing you. Monitoring you."

"Just like you," I say.

I burst out of the doors into the light, my eyes straining as if I am just waking up. But my nightmare follows me, Kevin walks closely behind, trying to grab my arm.

"Please just stop and listen to me for fuck's sake," he says. "You're going to get yourself killed."

A few heads turn as we hurriedly walk through the foyer.

"Fuck!" Kevin exclaims. "He's seen us. Follow me. Now!"

I notice, seemingly at the same time, a man bee-lining towards me through the crowded mall. He's a tall and well-built black guy, wearing jeans and a hoodie. He looks distinctly normal, except for the fact that he's charging towards me. His eyes are fixated on us, and he parts the crowd with distinct purpose.

Kevin grabs my hand and pulls. I falter, for a moment, but follow. He drags me towards what looks like an emergency exit, pushes it open, into a parking lot.

Oh my god, am I dreaming?

Bleep. Lights flash, a car unlocks.

Kevin and I crash against it as he frantically tries to open it. I look at the exit we escaped from to see the man emerging from it. Kevin leans back, aiming a gun at him. A gun? He has a fucking gun!

Oh god, please tell me I'm dreaming.

The man at the door retreats quickly.

"Get in the car," Kevin says.

I scramble into the back seat. I look out the back window as we screech away through the parking lot. The man sprints after us fruitlessly, for a few seconds, before darting in between some parked cars to the right. I push my finger into my hand. It bends as it presses against my palm, repeatedly as I don't believe it the first time. Fuck. We make a sharp right turn. Kevin is trying to drive as quickly as possible through the tight confines of a parking lot.

"Thank god," he says. We arrive at an exit without a line of cars. He pulls up to the machine, tries to force his ticket in. Please wait. Please wait. $4.80. I see Kevin looking around the machine frantically, cash in hand.

"It doesn't take cash, only card," I say.

"FUCK," he says. "I don't have a card."

"Take mine." I pull one out of my jeans pocket. "Who doesn't have a fucking card?"

I look out the window as I'm about to hand him my card, to see the other man erupt from the line of parked cars. He is sprinting towards us.

"Fuck! He's coming!" I say.

Kevin fumbles my card into the machine, cursing loudly.

"We don't have time!" I scream.

Kevin floors it at the exact moment that the man reaches us. He manages to jump on top of the trunk of the car, as we smash through the barrier gate in front of us. We tear out of the parking lot. The man jumps from the trunk and rolls neatly on the tarmac. We fly down the road, swerving erratically through, fortunately, minimal traffic. He rises and watches us as we race away, finally pulling out a phone and bringing it to his face. A corner swipes him from my view.

"Thank fuck," says Kevin, breathing heavily. "Do you believe me now?"

I continue staring out the back of the window. My heart is racing. Sweat is dripping down my face. What the fuck just happened?

"My life is in danger," I repeat what he said earlier. "Yes, I believe that."

"You need to get rid of your phone, now," he says. "Just throw it out the window."

The window automatically rolls down in the back.

"What?" I reply.

"They can track you by your phone," he says, his driving slowing to that of a normal driver. "Get rid of it or they'll find us."

"They'll find us?" I say. "I'm staying at my parents' house, pretty easy to find."

"No, you're not," he says. "Not anymore. I can take you somewhere safer."

What have I gotten myself into? I look at my phone in my hand. I pretend to throw it out the window but slide it up the sleeve of my hoodie.

"Why are they trying to kill me?" I ask.

"I assume they're trying to protect their secret and you're planning to write a book telling the whole world about it. Is that it?" he says.

I don't reply. How does he know about this? Did Feda tell him?

"I just don't think the doctor would have me killed," I say.

"You don't think he would have you killed?" Kevin replies, still watching the road. "You're talking about an organization that controls the world. They lie and murder as daily business. Even if the doctor himself didn't want you dead. Maybe the Frenchman did. Knowing what you know, there are two choices. Join them or disappear. Right now, you're just a walking liability to them."

I breathe deeply. How the fuck did I end up here? With this guy.

I stare out of the window at America. It's a screen of scenery, on repeat. Tree, tree, tree, powerlines, tree, off-ramp, gas-station, tree, rest-stop, trees, road-side motel. It grows darker and darker every minute that passes.

We have left the city, and driven. The frantic escape has calmed to a marathon. It's been hours of us driving, deep into the night. The adrenaline ran its course long ago. My body is tired now, and I want sleep.

"Where are we going?" I have asked multiple times.

"'Somewhere safe." He has replied again and again.

"Is this what I have to get used to?" I ask. "Is this how you live?"

"I don't think you understand what you're into," he responds. "I think you're greatly underestimating the forces at play here."

"Perhaps you're overestimating them?" I say. "Or maybe just misunderstanding them?"

Kevin doesn't say much, until he explodes into disjointed rants.

"Perhaps you're right. Maybe you understand a shady, para-governmental organization far better than me. They're probably not after us. I'm sure they've got the best interests of humanity at heart. I'm sure that everything the doctor has told you is true. I'm sure that the Frenchman has reassured you that they are the only hope the world has. I'm sure a powerful organization like that would never tap their opposition's phones, monitor their dreams or kill them with drones. That's totally unrealistic, right? I'm sure the reasons why everyone who gets in their way mysteriously disappears are completely coincidental, huh? Yeah, that sounds about right."

"The Frenchman? You keep mentioning the Frenchman," I ask. "Who's the Frenchman?"

Kevin doesn't answer. Instead, he pulls off from Interstate 65 towards a motel.

"Don't tell me," I say. "Is this where we're staying?"

Again, he doesn't answer, but his actions confirm the worst. He's clearly done this often. It doesn't take him much time to book us in, in cash, at the joyless reception.

"You two kids have fun," says the receptionist in the raspy voice that tells of a thousand cigarettes. She smiles at me. I try to smile back, but I feel sick to my stomach. I just want to be alone.

A DREAM OF FREEDOM

Sun filters through broken factory windows decorating the concrete floor as if it were furnished by a madman. Dust litters the air, sparkling. And the smell. That smell. At some point crackheads must have pissed themselves and died here. Broken glass and bodily fluids hide in every corner, where concrete meets brick, and humanity meets inhumanity.

"This is even worse than the motel." I say.

"This is the safest spot for you at the moment," he says.

"Is this what I have to get used to?" I ask. "Is this how you live? Even here?"

"I didn't take you for the princess type," he retorts. "Did you think we'd be staying in the Hilton?"

"Oh, this is still better than a Hilton," I joke. "But seriously, you need to explain to me why we're hiding like hobos in this dump."

"It's the last place they'd look for you. What would you prefer?" he says.

"How about this?" I reply, walking around the corner of the broken wall. The view on the other side is glorious. Grass and greenery have reclaimed most of the building this side. Flowers grow out of cracks. Mice scuttle from hole to hole. A broken wall reveals the landscape beyond, green mountains ranging as far as the eye can see.

"Well, it's certainly scenic," he says. "Sure, we can have this for a while."

"For a while?"

"It works the same as in the real world, right? A change in scenery is a good way of not being discovered," Kevin says, repositioning his cap. "Never anywhere familiar, never anywhere connected to you. You should hide in the last place they'd look. And his eyes are everywhere."

"Whose eyes?" I ask. "The Frenchman?"

Kevin has started pacing to and fro while he was talking. He stops and looks at me.

"God, don't say his name. Fuck! God. Fuck! This is bad."

He glances around nervously, noticing the clouds peeking over the mountaintops.

"We should go," he says. " He might have noticed."

"Who is he?"

"Stop talking about him," Kevin hisses through his teeth. "He's always listening. He's everywhere."

"Listen to yourself," I say. "You sound like a conspiracy nut."

"It's not paranoia if they're actually after you," he says, starting to walk away. "And you already got into the car with me. You're sleeping in a motel with me right now. You came when I called you into my dream. You've made your decision. Don't stop unless you actually think I'm wrong."

"I'm not sleeping with you, just in the same room as you. Goddamnit," I mutter and jog after him. "Where are you going, anyway?"

He points to a small door hidden in the side of a hill; I hadn't noticed it before.

"An even safer place," he says, pulling out a key and unlocking the padlock on the door as we arrive.

The smell inside it is that of long undisturbed darkness. A damp and stale air rushes out against us. We enter and he locks the door behind us. He grabs an unlit torch off the wall. I gaze down the corridor, hearing the click of the lighter next to me. It clicks once, then twice, then a third. It doesn't light. Kevin curses under his breath. The torch lights, finally, and no thanks to the lighter. That was me.

"Let's go," he says, and shuffles down the corridor.

"What are we doing down here?" I ask.

"It's a confined space with few controlled entrance points. It makes it harder for others to find their way into our dreamspace."

"You really don't want to be found," I say.

"I really don't," he replies.

We eventually arrive at a chamber, more sizable than the corridor. It looks like the den of an animal, one that's also a freshman at college. There are bean bag chairs in the corner, a puffy couch, rugs on the floor and a lantern hanging at an off angle from the roof. I almost expect there to be a Fight Club poster on the wall and a trashcan full of used Kleenex by the computer.

"Home sweet home," Kevin says, lying back down on the couch. "Make yourself comfortable."

I look around the room. There are no exits from this place, not even back through the way we came in. It inconspicuously disappeared as I entered. I flop down awkwardly on one of the bean bag chairs.

"I'm sorry about the cramped space," he says. "I guess this is the price of our freedom."

"I never expected freedom to be so... prison-like."

"No one expects that," he replies. "Here I still can't say his name, but I can tell you about him, and the others."

"Who?" I ask.

"The man I referred to earlier, by his nationality," he continues. "The leader of a certain organization."

"He's the leader?"

"That's what everyone assumes," Kevin says. "I've never met him, and I don't know his name, his real name. I don't think anyone does. But he's the hand behind the organization. I've only heard him referred to."

"You're so terrified of him, but you don't even know if he actually exists?"

"I guess I don't know if he exists," Kevin shrugs. "But someone has to. Someone is behind the curtain. And can you imagine the man that is powerful enough to control someone like the doctor?"

"Do you know he's a man?" I ask.

"I don't, but he's been referred to as masculine," Kevin says, reaching to his right for a beer. "I suppose it could even be a collective, all behind one identity."

"Oh..."

Kevin takes a sip of his beer and I look around the silent room. I feel like I'm in a basement.

"Would you like one?" he asks, holding a beer out for me. I shake my head.

"So, what's your plan?" I ask. "You're living in resistance to this organization, what are you planning to do?"

"Oh, well that's where you come in," he replies. "You're going to write a book telling the world all about lucid dreaming, dream-sharing and the organization. You're a celebrity author, so everyone will read it. You're going to write this book, and I'm going to keep you safe while you do. That's the plan."

He smiles at me, raises his beer, and then takes another swig.

"So...." I say. "Does keeping me safe involve living from motel to campsite and sleeping in this underground bunker while writing a book?"

"Yeah," he says, smiling at me. "Pretty much. Do you have a better idea?"

"I don't know if I can do that, at least not yet," I reply.

Kevin sits up. "Why not?"

"I still know next to nothing about them?" I say. "I need to find out more from the doctor. I need to learn about this Frenchman."

"Don't say his..." Kevin interrupts, but I continue.

"I don't understand this world yet, and I can't learn about it while trapped in this fucking bomb shelter."

Kevin stands up. "Don't you understand you can't trust them? It's not safe out there for you. They'll kill you, or worse, they'll entice you to become one of them."

"I have to take that chance," I say.

"I can't take that chance," he says.

The silence hangs in the air like a threat, a threat I haven't contemplated fully yet.

"I'm leaving," I announce. Admittedly, the dramatic impact of this declaration is lessened by the awkward movements involved in getting out of a bean bag chair.

"You can't leave," he says, not moving from his position. He takes another swig of his beer.

"Are you going to stop me?" I ask, now on my feet.

He motions around the room. "Where are you going to go?"

He's not wrong. I spin around the room, completely ensconced in rock, without any doors or windows.

"Let's talk," he says, sitting up and facing me. "We're on the same side. There's no reason for us to fight about this. I'm trying to be a nice guy about it, but you're making it really difficult."

I do not trust this man. I need to get out of here. I've made a horrible mistake. But there's a way out. There's always a way out. There must be a way out of here. I reach up to the badly hung lantern and pull it down; the force pulls down the trapdoor hidden in the roof. The ladder slides down after it.

Kevin looks up at me in surprise.

"You didn't know that was there, did you?" I smile at him, before starting up the ladder.

"Come back!" he shouts. I continue climbing.

"You're going to get yourself killed, you stupid girl," he says, now apparently climbing the ladder behind me. I feel his hand grabbing on my ankle. He starts trying to pull me down. I kick. After a few misses I connect with his hand, stamping it against the rock.

"Ahhhhh fuck you, bitch!" he shouts. I feel a sick satisfaction at the term. I continue my way upwards, now increasing my speed. I can see light trickling in above, around what must be the exit trapdoor. I push it open as I get to the top, allowing light to shower over me. I crawl out of the hole and slam it behind me. I've exited onto the same mountainside from before, lying on the green grass. I can hear Kevin coming up the tunnel where I exited. I reach over, pulling a large padlock from my pocket and locking the latch closed. I hear him pounding at the door from below.

I climb to my feet. It's time to leave.

"He's always been a bit of an idiot."

I turn to find a certain Afghan boy lying in the grass a few feet away.

"Feda!" I call. "Where have you been?"

Bang bang bang. The sounds come from the other side of the trapdoor.

"I have been around," he says. "But you told me you wanted nothing to do with me, remember. Also, I have other friends too, you know?"

"I've heard," I reply. "I've just escaped from the underground dungeon of one of your other friends."

A fist slams through the trapdoor.

"I'm not sure I would count Kevin as a friend," says Feda.

"I'm glad to hear that," I say. "But he describes it differently."

Kevin rips through the wood of the trapdoor and finally manages to climb through. I stand and face him.

"I'm not standing with you Kevin," I say, as he gets to his feet covered in dust and wooden splinters.

"Okay, Gabrielle Rivers," he says, brushing himself off. "So, you're going to stand with them instead?"

He notices Feda. "And you? You're the one who planned this all. Why don't you talk some sense into her?"

"Sense?" Feda laughs. "I think she's already shown more sense than me."

"We're all on the same side," Kevin throws his hands up, seemingly unable to understand why things aren't going his way. "We have the same enemies."

"We have very different methods," Feda says. "I've told you before that I'm not willing to do the things you are."

"That is why you will never succeed!" Kevin starts yelling. "How do you think we're going to beat these people? You think that we're going to win a war without fighting? How do you see that working?"

"What war?" I say quietly. "No one wants a war."

"You might not be fighting a war, but they are," he says. "They're lying, and murdering, and thieving. Manipulating the public."

"The only thing that separates us is our methods, otherwise we'd be the same as them." Feda asks.

"We're not the least bit like them," Kevin says. "Don't pretend like we are."

"Are you going to let me leave?" I ask.

He looks at me for a moment, but his silence tells me enough. He won't let me go willingly.

"You understand that I don't have a problem with you," he says. "But you have the ability to create something so much more important than yourself."

"And you think you have a right to it?" I say. "I guess you're not so different from them after all."

He turns to Feda.

"She's right here! She's right next to me in the real world!" he says emphatically. "All she needs to do is write her fucking book. What are you waiting for? This is all part of the plan, but you can tell she's teetering on going over to their side; we can't just let her do that."

"I can't stop her." Feda shrugs. "She has to make her own choice."

Kevin grimaces. "I know you can't stop her, but I can," he says. "And you can't do anything about it."

I turn to Feda.

"He can't help you," Kevin calls. "He has no power here."

"What?" I ask.

"For all his apparent knowledge, even though he lives in the dreamworld, Feda is dead. In case you didn't know," Kevin says. "He cannot influence my dream. He has no real power here. As soon as you realize that, he's no more powerful than a part of your own mind. That's why he needs people like us. We can actually change things; he can just talk about it."

I look at Feda. He nods his head.

"You have all the training and strength you need to beat him here. You don't need me to intervene."

"Don't try to play it cool like that," shouts Kevin. "Pretending like you won't intervene. You can't intervene. You're dead, Feda. Just because you're in denial doesn't mean that you're alive."

Oh fuck. This is really going to happen. It's crept up on me, the realization. I'm going to have to fight him. I can't call Busi again. I certainly can't call the doctor.

"So, I guess it comes down to this," says the man standing across from me, his hands at his sides like he's fucking John Wayne or something. My mouth goes dry. There's sweat dripping down my arms. My brain runs through everything that Feda has taught me. Don't focus too much on him as my enemy. Have confidence in my strikes and parries; I am stronger than he is.

"What's your plan, Kevin?" I shout. "Are you legitimately going to fight me? You're going to attack a girl who won't do what you say? Does that make you feel tough?"

"I don't care about feeling tough," he says. "But sometimes you need to fight for the right cause. I'm willing to do just that."

He starts walking towards me slowly, arms lowered. My heart is thumping in my chest like a rabbit in danger.

"Just write the fucking book, Gabrielle," he says more insistently as he approaches. "Just do the right thing, write the book, and there's no reason for us to fight."

Don't let him distract you. He's already tried asking. He's trying to dominate you into submission.

Only then do I feel it: The vines climbing up my legs, wrapping themselves around my ankles. As I pull my feet up, they tighten.

"Too easy," his smug voice sweeps past me.

The more I struggle, the more tangled I become. Stop, Gabi, think. You're bound. Cut the cord. I carry a knife for this very situation. I drop to my haunches, blade in hand, slicing at the vines around my ankles. As I do, more spring up from the ground, grabbing my arms and pulling them towards the earth. My knife drops as my hands get held against the ground. I'm now bent over awkwardly on my hands and feet, more flexibly than my body is comfortable with.

I look up, as Kevin walks directly in front of me. He reaches me and pats me on the head, which now only reaches up to his waist.

"So now," he says. "Now I should have your attention. Perhaps your respect?"

How can you get out of vines? They love the dark. They love the damp. So, make a fire! I can be the fire.

"Maybe we should just stay like this for a while?" he continues, disturbingly positioned in front of me. "Is this what your dreams with the doctor are like?"

"Fuck you," I mumble through gritted teeth.

I smell the smoke; I feel it in my nostrils. The warmth on my skin. As soon as the grayish white cloud billows past my face I know that it has worked. I erupt into flames.

"What the fuck?" Kevin stumbles backwards from me.

I pull myself up, feeling the vines crack and break as I rise. My clothes peel off me, but I do not feel the pain. I surge forwards, and flames lick the air around me. Kevin brings his hands up to his face, catching my fist just in time to protect himself. He holds it for a second, but his face gives him away. He lets go and spins backwards, screaming in pain.

The warmth around me starts to grow more intense. Too intense.

As Kevin stumbles backwards, I see him reaching to his side. It's the same movement he made in the cinema yesterday. He's going for his gun. I charge towards him, slamming into him and knocking his pistol out of his hand. I wrap myself around him. He screams as his flesh sizzles against mine. He falls backwards, my flaming self still clinging to him. As we hit the grass, I feel the world change. We plunge into water, water out of nowhere. My skin rapidly cools, and the crackle of fire is replaced by the silence of being underwater. I feel us sinking down. I can't breathe. I try to pull away, but this time it's Kevin holding me. I look up at his face, burnt and blackened, smiling at me as he holds me against him. He pulls me down with him, down into the depths. I can't breathe down here. He's pulling me deeper and deeper.

This is exactly what he wants: To pull me down into this dark place. This dark place is his. Dark and wet, with the sun barely filtering through. The basement of the world. This is who Kevin is. He looks at the world from this dark and wet place. He looks at a world that is all wrong. It needs to change. Anything would be better than this. That change is worth any cost.

He lives alone here.

As I think, my heartbeat slows. I relax. I don't need to hold my breath. I've lived in this place too. If he doesn't need to breathe here, then neither do I.

His smile turns into a sneer. He pulls his hands from around me and slides them around my neck. He presses his thumbs into my throat. He's going to strangle me. I can't believe he's going to strangle me. As his thumbs push against my windpipe, I struggle with the absurdity of it all. I just stare blankly at Kevin's face. His dumb nondescript face. He's not a murderer, is he, a real murderer? Strangling is personal. This is oddly intimate for a murder. This is more intimate than he's comfortable with.

No, what he wants isn't for me to die. He wants me to submit to him. He wants me. He wants something else from me.

The thought seems to be occurring to him as well. I feel his thumbs lightening on my throat. He leaves his hands loose around my neck and stares at me. His expression is muted and thoughtful now. He doesn't want to kill me. No, he wants to kiss me. He repositions his hands at the back of my neck and pulls me towards him... Oh fuck no. I react instinctively.

He pulls me in to kiss me, pressing his lips roughly against mine. I put my hands against his chest and push away from him, kicking furiously. He lets go of me in surprise, either at himself or at my reaction. Whatever just happened has thrown him. I frown and kick away, swimming towards what I assume to be upwards. The water, previously calm, has grown tumultuous and threatening. I break the surface in the middle of a dark ocean. The swells push me up and drop me down what must be over three stories high. The roar of the wind is deafening, as foam sprays up off the crest of the swells.

I try to keep my head above the surface, desperately treading water. Repeatedly I am thrust under as waves overtake me. As I resurface, I see a rogue wave, far larger than any before. It travels fast and alone, towering above others. I dip as it approaches and am pulled deep underwater as it crashes over me. My body spins and turns. Sweat drips from my brow.

And I open my eyes to darkness. A vaguely familiar motel room. A man standing over me.

REALITY CALL

"I'm sorry, Gabrielle," he says, standing over me.

"For trying to kill me or for kissing me?" I reply.

My eyes dart around the motel room. Kevin is hovering over my bed, wearing boxer shorts and a white t-shirt. His face is hard to make out in the darkness.

"Both," he replies. "I... I don't know why I tried to kiss you. But you know I didn't want to kill you. You wouldn't have died. I just want to make you understand."

"Understand what?" I say, covering myself up with the blanket around me. "Understand that you can overpower me? Make me understand that I have no choice in the matter?"

"You are supposed to be the one who helps us," he says. "You're supposed to the herald of the revolution."

"Herald of the fucking revolution!?" I sit up in bed. He doesn't move. "Listen to yourself."

I slide out of bed on the side away from where he's standing and pull out my phone from the pocket of my jeans that were lying on the floor.

"You've still got your phone?" he says in a panic. "Fuck. I told you to throw it away."

"You also tried to strangle me, so forgive me if I don't take your words to heart."

Five missed calls, messages from Karin? Why would she call me so many times? She must have heard I was missing. Shit, Gabi.

"You need to get rid of that phone."

"Fuck off."

I start looking at the messages.

Hi Gabi. Could you please call me back when you get this. There's something I would like to talk to you about. Please. Whenever you get the chance.

Another one.

Are you okay? Where are you? Your parents are looking for you. Please call me. I need to talk to you.

Did something happen?

Gabi, your parents are worried sick. I hope you're alright. Please call me as soon as possible.

I dial her number and put the phone up to my face.

"Don't fucking call someone." Kevin moves towards me. I put my hand up to stop him. Somehow it does. This isn't even the dreamworld, but still, he obeys some of my instructions.

The voice that answers is not Karin's. It carries all the correct timbre, but none of the spirit.

"Oh, thank god, Gabi," it says. "Thank god you're alright."

"I'm fine, Karin, don't worry." I reply. "But what about you? It sounds like something happened."

"Me? Oh, don't worry about me. I was just being silly. It's not important. I'm just so glad you're okay," she babbles a bit, unlike her. "I'll be okay, I don't know why I even mentioned it to you. Considering."

Kevin is mouthing at me to get off the phone. As he moves towards me, I push my hand facing outwards to keep him away.

"What happened, Karin?" I say.

"Nothing happened. I just haven't been sleeping well, that's all. Like I said, not important. Just wanted to know if you had any of those sleeping pills left. I'm just having a spell of bad dreams I guess... I'll be okay, don't worry about me. How are you?" she mumbles.

"Karin..."

"I've been having these nightmares, that's all. Nightmares, that's all. I just know that you've had some experience in the area," she says, adopting her more measured and usual matter-of-fact tone. "I just need a good night's sleep. I feel like I haven't slept in days."

"You wouldn't have mentioned it if it wasn't serious," I say. "I'll come around straight away."

Kevin lurches forward and grabs the phone out of my hand. He throws it against the wall at full force. He stomps on the remaining smashed corpse as it hits the floor.

"What the fuck are you doing?" I shout at him.

"They're luring you there," he says, pointing his finger at my face. "They're using her to lure you back. You can't go."

"I don't really care if they're luring me there," I reply. "I'm going back. The only thing you've done is break my phone. Thanks for that."

He steps in front of the door, arms outstretched to represent just how blocked it is. I consider him for a moment. Is he really going to stop me? I think he will. I need to get out of here, but even if I could get past him, I have no phone. I have no credit card. I guess I could go to the front desk of the motel. Maybe I could call someone from there. Unfortunately, this isn't the dreamworld; I can't just conjure things into existence.

"You can't go," he says.

"This again?" I reply. "Are you going to fight me?"

"This isn't the dreamworld," he says. "It won't be much of a fight."

"This isn't the dreamworld," I say. "You're going to have to kill me for real to make me stay."

He opens his mouth, but no words come out.

"You think you can do that?" I ask. "Are you really going to kill me, and still pretend that you're the good guy in all this?"

"I'm not going to kill you," he says, through gritted teeth. "But I will stop you from leaving."

"Maybe you're just going to kiss me again?" I say, turning my head to the side. "Hmmm?"

He opens his mouth, and then closes it again.

"What?" I ask. "I didn't hear you."

"I don't want to hurt you," he says. "But I can't let you go."

"Fine!" I say and put my hands on my waist. "So, let's talk then, seeing as I'm stuck here with you. How long have you been watching me? Stalking me?" I ask.

I walk back around to my bed and sit down, as if to symbolically gesture that I'm no longer trying to get out the door. He watches me as I do, but he doesn't move from his position.

"Since you started dreaming again," he says. "I couldn't get close to you in your dreams, with the doctor always being around, so I watched you in the real world. It was dangerous, but... but I needed to be sure about you."

"Sure of what?" I ask.

"Sure that you weren't working for them," he says. "I needed to make sure I could trust you."

"I'm not working for them," I say, trying to sound as earnest as possible. "But you have to understand why you made me nervous. You stalked me, kidnapped me, imprisoned me and then tried to kill me. I think I have the right to be a little freaked out."

He laughs guiltily, as if to say aw shucks, I didn't mean to try and murder you.

"I guess you're right. I'm sorry about that," he admits. "I just... I mean, you did kick me."

"You were trying to grab my legs as I was climbing out of your dungeon," I say, giving him a faux smile. "And why did you kiss me? That was a bold move, my friend. Normally I wait for the third fight to the death before I kiss a guy."

He laughs.

"I don't know. It just felt like the right thing to do. I guess I just feel like I know so well. I have been watching you for so long," he says. "I forget that you don't know me like I know you. Honestly, I'm a nice guy. I think we just got off on the wrong foot."

"I mean, it was pretty intense," I say, trying to maintain eye contact. Then I look away. "Anyway. Maybe you're right."

"Right about what?" he asks.

"Maybe I can create something far bigger than myself," I say. "Maybe I do have that responsibility. I don't know."

He remains in the doorway, but his posture has changed. His arms are lowered, and he's resting his weight on one leg. His jacket and clothes lay discarded next to his bed. I assume that the motel keys are in there.

"Do you realize how much you can do?" he says. "You can change the world forever, like you did with *Enduring Freedom*, only even bigger. So much bigger."

"I understand," I say. "It's just scary, you know. I've always run away from it. This, well Le Réveil just seems too big and powerful. How can I go up against them?"

I look down and away from him.

"I know," he says, sitting down next to me. "That's why I'm here, though. I'm here to protect you. I can help you."

"Can you though?" I ask. "You keep saying how powerful they are? How could we go up against them?"

"I'm very careful. This is what I do," he says. "I've been doing it a long time.

They haven't caught me yet."

"Why?" I ask. "Why are you doing this? What's in it for you?"

I look back at him. Now it's his turn to look away, almost like he's blushing.

"Well, you," he says.

"What?" I reply, dropping my doe-eyed girl facade for a second.

"Yeah," he turns back and smiles at me. He wants to kiss me again. This time, I didn't put that thought into his head.

"Why me?" I ask.

"Well," he says. "I read *Enduring Freedom*, like most people. Then I read it again. Then a few more times. I, uh, am a bit of a fan. So, naturally I tried to find out everything I could about you… and Afghanistan. And then, well, I started dreaming about Feda."

"Feda came to you too?" I ask.

"He did," he says. "In retrospect it makes sense. He was still recomposing himself after being killed. He was trying to find dreamers, something to hold onto. He found me, probably because I knew him. Because I knew him and I knew you, even though you didn't know me. At the time I just thought I was dreaming about Feda. I didn't know he was real. But he showed me the truth. He introduced me to the dreamworld."

Why didn't Feda tell me about this?

"Feda helped me," Kevin continues. "He shared his mission with me. His purpose. His plan. Together, we tried to find you. We tried to find you, because you're the only one who can take this public."

He smiles at me. There is no light shining into the motel room. Neither of us had time to turn on the lights. It feels like it's the middle of the night, but it must only be evening. We only got to sleep in the morning, after hours of driving. Sleep when your enemies are awake, Kevin had said. So now we sit here in darkness, talking about Kevin's past, while he looks at me with an intimacy we don't share.

"What happened between you and Feda?" I ask.

Kevin's face changes. There's anger underneath it. "We had a disagreement about methods."

I look at him to prompt him for more.

"Feda, being what he is, doesn't feel the urgency. I don't think he truly feels anything anymore. He's not able to do anything to help the cause. I am," he says. "That's why the torch has passed to me. And, well to you."

"The torch?"

"We're the resistance," he says, proudly.

"Is that what we are?" I ask, looking around the dark motel room. "Okay."

"Okay?" he asks. "Does that mean you're in?"

"Yes," I reply, smiling. "I'm in. Let's take these fuckers down."

He looks pleased in response for a moment, but it fades after a second. He doesn't trust me, but he wants to. I need to get out of here. I need to get to Karin. I regret throwing out my sleeping pills, but I should... oh shit. I still have my emergency stash in my purse.

"I'm glad you understand," Kevin says, half-smiling. "We should get moving though, we shouldn't stay here for too long."

He stands up abruptly and grabs a water bottle from next to his bed and takes a sip from it.

"Can I shower first?" I ask, laughing. "And get myself ready?"

He looks a little bit embarrassed at the question. "Yes of course, go ahead. I brought you some clothes and toiletries. They're in the car."

"Okay, cool," I say, standing up.

"No, don't worry," he grabs his jacket from the floor, looking sheepish. "I'll grab them."

He's trying to downplay the fact that I'm still a captive here. He won't let me have the keys to the car. I hear the door lock behind him as he leaves to go to the car. As soon as it closes, I rush over to my bed and grab my purse. I rustle around inside and pull out a double blister pack of pills: Only two pills. I look over to his water bottle, one that he placed on the table before leaving. As quickly as possible, I push a pill out of the blister pack. I open the water bottle and crack the contents of the pill inside. White powder drops into the bottle. I can hear his footsteps coming towards the door as I close the bottle and shake it. To my horror, the water turns milky white as I do. Instantly noticeable. Fuck.

I hear the door unlocking.

Bottle in hand, I rush to the bathroom and start pouring the water down the drain.

"I've got your stuff here," he says, from the door. "What are you doing?"

I start refilling the water from the tap.

"Sorry, I drank your water," I say, hoping I don't show my anxiety. "I'm just filling it up again."

"Oh," he says. "Don't worry about that. I have a few other bottles. I only drink from sealed containers. Do you want one?"

He reaches for one of his bags, which has a six-pack of small, bottled water.

"Nah, it's fine," I say, now pouring out the water I had just filled into the bottle, just to make sure it's clear. I drop the empty vessel in the bathroom trash basket.

"I didn't really know your size, so I just went with practicality. I hope you don't mind," he says as he dumps a duffel bag of clothes and toiletries on the bathroom floor in front of me. He looks at me like I should be thanking him.

"Thanks," I reply.

"No problem," he says, smiling back and watching me.

"Okay," I reach down and pull the bag in and close the bathroom door. Relief sweeps over me the moment it closes, a moment to be alone and honest. That is the sanctity of bathrooms. Even the most heinous of bathrooms can be a refuge. From a club night gone wrong. From a tense relationship. From a creepy kidnapper. Bathrooms are an escape from life. I shiver. I look through the bag of clothing that Kevin has brought me, wondering what to expect. Kevin certainly has been true to his word. A few simple one-color t-shirts, stretchy sweatpants, and plain cotton panties. No bra.

I use the shower to plot. I've wasted one of my two sleeping pills already. That was stupid. I need to calm down and come up with a better plan. I have a few options. I could wait for another drink to be open and try to slip him the pill. That might be difficult. I've seen him drinking a coke. That would work. Maybe I could empty it in his food. Would that work? Otherwise, maybe I could just run for it. If we're in public, I'm sure someone would help me. Right?

I finish my shower, dress up like plain Jane, and head out into the motel room. Everything has been packed up and Kevin stands ready to go at the door, as if he's a dad waiting for me to get in the car for the family vacation. He's swinging the car keys in his fingers. I notice his eyes dart to my chest, and then up and down my body. He seems to admire his own handiwork.

"They fit okay?" he says. It could be a question.

"Yup," I feign through a smile.

We get into the car under the sinking darkness of evening, driving out of the motel past a liquor store that's about to close. I put my hand on his forearm to attract his attention and to make physical contact.

"Can I grab something in there?" I ask. He rolls to a stop and looks at me, the liquor store and me again.

"Really?"

"If you want me to write, I need a drink," I say.

He crunches his lips up, apparently deciding whether the risk of me pulling one over him is worth the prospect of getting me a little liquored up.

"Listen," I announce. "If you want me to work with you, you have to stop treating me like a prisoner."

He stares at my eyes. I doubt he can see past them. Nevertheless, he starts pulling into the liquor store parking lot.

It's any old liquor store. The welcome relief of the air conditioner washes over me as we enter. The cashier nods at us, Kevin right behind me. I consider it. Could this cashier help me? Would he? But while I'm thinking about it, we've already walked past

"Beer?" Kevin asks, reaching into the fridge.

"Sure," I reply, reaching to grab some scotch whisky off one of the higher shelves. Balvanie 21 years old. Kevin cocks his eye at me for some reason.

"What?" I reply. "It's not like it's morning or something."

"It's expensive," he says, softly.

I feel myself flush despite myself. I don't really look at prices. I don't have my credit card. I can't pay for this. I'm guessing that Kevin wouldn't want me using my credit card anyway.

"Is it?" I ask and look at the price. $166. That's not expensive, is it? What's expensive for scotch? "It's only $160."

"Okay, okay. Fine," he says. "Just that though."

Hey man, you can't expect your kidnapping victim to be paying their own way. That's just unreasonable. Kevin shepherds me towards the cashier, clearly starting to get impatient.

"And two boxes of Marlboro Gold please," I say, as he scans the items.

Kevin glares at me again as the man pulls down the cigarettes from the wall.

"Trust me," I say. "You'll prefer me with them."

"ID?" the cashier asks as he drops the cigarettes on the table. He's a middle-aged and balding white man, wearing a sweaty blue wife-beater.

Kevin is already pulling out cash from his pocket. He stops. "Really?"

"No ID, no sale," says the man.

Kevin stands frozen, as if this is the greatest decision of his life. I sigh and pass my ID over the counter.

"No!" He hisses as I do, adding a conspicuous tension to the interaction. The cashier side-eyes him as he holds the ID and looks at it.

"Gab-ri-elle Rivers," he says phonetically. "Like the writer?"

He looks at me, disheveled hair and misfitting clothes.

I smile. "Yup, that's me."

"Wow," he says, grinning. "You're famous. What are you doing here?"

I can feel Kevin's apprehension growing next to me. He restlessly rocks from one leg to another. I know he has his gun on him. Is the cashier armed? What would happen if I asked him for help? Would Kevin shoot him?

"I'm just grabbing some liquid inspiration," I say, picking up the bottle of whisky from the table. "You know?"

He laughs and winks at me.

"I hope you and your boyfriend enjoy," he says, handing the ID back and starting to put the bottles into a brown paper bag. I notice that Kevin's hand relaxes. It had been hovering towards his side.

"Thanks," he says, barely feigning a smile, and reaches for the brown paper bag. He quickly turns to walk away.

"Wait!" the cashier calls. Kevin freezes again.

"Could I have your autograph?" He reaches over with a scrap of paper and the pen that they usually use for the till slip. "My niece would be over the moon."

I take it and press it down on the uneven counter.

"What's her name?" I ask.

"Mary," He says. "And she's an absolute sweetheart."

"I'm sure she is," I say. "I'll write her a message."

The pen pierces through the paper on several occasions as I write my short message, alongside a swooping signature.

This man has kidnapped me. He has a gun. Please call the police.

I quickly pass it over to him, smiling and making eye contact as I do. Please don't do anything stupid. Kevin is glaring at me as I walk back towards him, past him and push open the glass door to the wall of humid air outside. Kevin follows me.

"What did you write?" he asks, as he follows me with the clink of bottles.

"Nothing worth reading," I say as I climb into the car. "Same as usual."

JAILBREAK

I may have become more paranoid than Kevin, if that is at all possible. Every noise grabs me by the spine. Is that the police? What happens if they show up? How will Kevin react? Would he abandon me and run? Perhaps death by police is more his style: guns out in a blaze of glory. What would he say if we were interviewed? Would he tell them about the dreamworld? About Le Réveil? Would I? That would be an easy way of getting the story out.

Today was a long drive. I'm not sure why we're going in the direction we're going in. This Virginia motel, well, it looks just like the last motel. I guess that's the point of motels, right? Like airports and fast food. Everyone knows how they work because they're all the same. There's comfort in the familiarity. It's like that old sitcom we watch again and again, knowing exactly what to expect. Ross and Rachel will end up together, so will Pam and Jim. Things will reset, more or less. The hum back to the drum and then the hum again.

I sit on the bed as I listen to the birds starting to chirp. Morning is on its way. That means it's time for bed. Welcome to the upside-down world. Kevin's home. Night is day. Hate is love. I am his.

I pull out the scotch from the brown paper bag. The beers are already in the tiny motel fridge. This is my little area of responsibility in our supposedly Stockholm relationship. I am on drinks duty. But there is no ice. I need ice for scotch.

"We need ice," I say. I assume that you can get ice somewhere in a motel. This is only my second night ever in a motel.

"They usually have ice by the front," Kevin says, peering out past the curtain.

He looks so suspicious peeking out the window. Perhaps a sniper is going to take him out. Where's the red dot on his chest? Who am I kidding? That's not how the cops work, right?

"Should I go get some?" I ask.

Kevin pauses from his idle guard duty. He turns to me.

"You and your whisky..." he says. "I'm starting to think you have a problem."

I pour an iceless glass for myself, nonetheless. Friendliness and humor have been my best defenses against Kevin thus far.

"I have many problems," I reply. "Whisky just happens to be the tastiest."

I pour a second glass at the same time.

"Are you going to drink with me or what?" I say, swirling the glass at him. "I'm going to need more than one if we're going to continue staying in places like this."

"I thought you wanted me to go get ice?" he says.

"You seem like you might be capable of both," I shrug and take a sip of my tepid drink. I get that involuntary shiver.

"Fine," he says. "How could I refuse such an elegant lady?"

He pats down his body, checking gun, car keys, motel keys... as I flip him off.

"How could I expect a boy to have ice in his freezer?" he smirks as he slides out the motel, locking the door behind him.

I wait for a few moments, as many moments as his footsteps take to trail away. I spring to action, rummaging through my pocket for the remaining blister pill. This is my last chance. This is my one remaining pill. I push it out of its container. My hands start to shake as I do.

I'm about to crack it into the glass of whisky, but I stop myself. I hold the amber liquid to the light. It's pretty clear. Dark, but clear. What if he notices?

I put the glass down and crawl over to the fridge, grabbing one of the beers out of its pack. I remember Kevin's words: "I only drink from sealed containers."

Course you do, buddy, course you do.

Channeling my inner-seventeen-year-old, I use the room's beer bottle opener to carefully open the brown bottle of cheap lager. I hear the satisfying sound of bubbles escaping. You go, bubbles! Escape your cage.

I crack open the pill into the beer, and quickly place the cap back on the top. Now for the party trick. I reverse the bottle opener on the outsides of the cap to press it back down around the bottle top. It takes some finagling, but the end result closely resembles the original. I give the bottle a little shake, just enough to get that fizz back. I place it back in its case, close the fridge and crawl back over to the bed.

My heart is racing as I sit and wait for Kevin to return. My mind tries to rush through all the ways this could go wrong, but instead I stop. Instead, I sip my whisky and embrace mindlessness. I embrace mindlessness and I wait. I embrace mindlessness. I embrace mindlessness.

The footsteps return, followed by the door unlocking, and Kevin himself.

He's carrying a plastic bag full of ice.

"I've got your ice, but that ice machine was pretty disgusting," he says. "I'm not sure you want to use this."

He holds up the ice. I believe him. There's the slightest gray tinge.

"I'm sure I've had worse things than that in my mouth," I joke, holding out my hand. He shakes his head and hands it to me. I pop two blocks into my whisky. "And besides, whisky's a disinfectant. Would you like some?"

"I'll stick with good old-fashioned beer, thank you," he says, walking over to the mini fridge. "I don't trust that ice."

"Suit yourself," I say, my eyes following his hand closely as it reaches towards the beer-trap. He grabs the closest one to the front, just as did. I sip deeply of my whisky.

"I guess we're going to need to get you something to write on," he says, as he foots the fridge closed and grabs the bottle opener.

"What?"

"I'm going to have to get you an air-gapped computer," he says. I cough as he flips the cap off. It gives a muted crack underneath the noise. "You won't be able to write using pen and paper, will you?"

"Not if you want anyone to be able to read it," I say. "I have the handwriting of an epileptic chicken."

He grunts, conspicuously not taking a sip from his beer.

"Air-gapped computers are expensive," he says.

"Do you want me to pay for it?" I reply. Kevin stops midway through raising the bottle to his lips.

"How are you going to do that?" he says. "You can't use any of your cards. That would defeat the whole point of buying an air-gapped computer."

I raise my arms in the air, spilling a bit of whisky out of my glass.

"Hey, I'm sorry I'm not as good as being on the lam as you," I say. "But it's not like you gave me time to prepare and pack. I think I'm being pretty reasonable, all things considered."

He frowns and admits, "I guess you're right. I just forget how much I've gotten used to this. It must be hard for someone like you."

Urgh.

I theatrically take a sip of my whisky and put on an overdone British accent. "Oh, it was horrendous, darling. I had to drink my scotch with motel ice.

Motel ice, I tell you. Like some sort of common peasant."

He cracks a smile despite himself.

"Have a drink with me and lighten up," I say, smiling at him with all the manic pixie dream girl I can muster. I raise my glass to him, and he returns the salute.

"To the revolution," he says.

"To writing our own destiny," I reply.

He smiles at that and takes a sip of his beer, as I have another of my whisky, which is mostly gone already. I've done a lot of nervous drinking. I want a cigarette, but I can't leave this room. I watch closely, monitoring for any signs that he's noticed it, that he's tasted it. I don't even know if this is going to work, diluted in beer. I've never done that before. Sure, I've taken them with alcohol before, but never dissolved them. I hope it doesn't kill him. Actually, I don't know if I hope that. No, I don't think I want him to die. But I don't want to be trapped here with him either.

"Thank you," he says, taking another swig. "I know that this is all real hard for you. I know you don't want to be stuck in this shitty motel room with me. Thank you for making the right choice."

I reach down next to me and pour a little more whisky into my glass, careful not to be too heavy-handed. I guess I'm going to need my sobriety, what remains of it. Kevin slumps down onto the one bed and sighs.

"It's nice to have someone to talk to," he says. "I've been doing this by myself for a long time."

I keep my eyes fixed forward, trying not to look at him. "Doing what?" I ask

"Fighting," he replies, straight from the hip, as if he was poised for it. "Living life on the run, from place to place. Sleeping with one eye open."

"Why?" I ask.

"Why?" he replies. "What do you mean?"

I motion around.

"What's your stake in this? Why are you fighting a one-man war against an enemy that you think is all-powerful?"

He stays silent for a while. Is he trying to organize his thoughts, or is he coming up with the reason? Perhaps he doesn't have one.

"I'm not an idiot," he says. "I know what you're doing."

My heart panics.

"What am I doing?" I ask.

"Trying to get me to open up," he says, with an air of sullenness. "Pretending like you're on my side. I know it's all an act. You can stop pretending."

"Half a beer, and you get all depro," I reply. "I'm glad you turned down the whisky."

"Always with the jokes," he says. "Always saying something smart. But you don't really care, do you?"

"Care about what?" I ask.

Kevin takes a swig of his beer, finishing the bottle. He holds it in his hands and stares into it. I suspect he's simply staring into space, but I can't risk him seeing any residue in there.

"Do you mean, I don't really care about you?" I ask.

"No," he says quickly, getting up and fetching another one. "No, not me. The cause…"

He cracks it open and stands while taking his first sip.

"You want one?" he asks. "Or you good?"

"I'm good," I say. "So, you were saying? The cause?"

He sits back down on the motel bed, rolling back slightly further than expected. He's lightly holding his beer bottle by the neck, and it swings beneath his fingers loosely, like a body hanged.

"What's there to say about the cause?" he says. "You know what they are. Feda's told you. They're the puppet masters ruling the world. They're the shadows behind the curtain. They're the reason the world is so fucked up. Why the world's gone to shit."

"Has the world gone to shit though?" I ask.

"Have you looked around? Or turned on the news?" he exclaims, emphatically.

"Yes, I have done both those things," I reply. "And what do you see when you look around? What do you see that disturbs you so much?"

"I knew you were on their side," he says. "How can you defend what they are?"

"I'm not on their side. I just want to understand why you have devoted your life to fighting them," I say. "I mean, you're living from motel room to motel room, kidnapping authors, waving that gun around… what's your skin in this game? What's the story?"

He sighs as if this is the kind of shit he deals with all day.

"So, you think that this is how we're meant to live?" he proclaims, perched upon his bed as if it were a box for soap. "As sheep consuming mass media while the elite do whatever they want with us? That's what they want, fat entertained pigs that are happy to earn them more money and power, while they sit and reap the interest. Are you happy for humanity to be reduced to this, to this miseducated mob that cares more about reality TV and YouTubers than freedom, while the system profits off us?"

I stay silent.

"They're asleep," he says. "They're asleep and someone needs to wake them up."

I remain silent.

"I think that we could do that," he says. "We could wake them up. We could show them a new world. A new world of absolute freedom. A new world where the rules do not apply. A new world where they don't need the elite to tell them what to do, what to want. A new world. The world of their dreams."

I have to stifle a laugh, but I don't think he notices. I take a sip from my empty whisky glass without thinking. Whisky-flavored water slips down my throat.

"Doncha want that?" Kevin says, calling my attention back to him.

"Do you really think that's what's going to happen?" I ask. "If I write this book, that's what you think is going to happen?"

He leans back, as if knocked back by my pessimism. "Maybe not. But I gotta try, right?"

As he sits back against the wall on his motel bed, he yawns while continuing with his next sentence. "I mean, what else can I do?"

"Literally anything else," I reply.

He tsks at me through his teeth, as if he's disappointed.

"Always such a smart-ass," he says. "But what would you be without Feda's balls?"

"What?" I reply.

"You heard me," he says. "If Feda hadn't, then what, what would you be?"

"If Feda hadn't what?" I ask, noticing the effects in him, even if he hasn't yet.

"Without Feda..." he continues. "What would you be?"

"I'd still be me," I say. "What would you be?"

Kevin laughs, with edge.

"Always so smart."

"Always so dumb," I reply.

He frowns at me.

"Why do you hate me so much?" he says. His eyes are failing horribly in their attempt to fix on me. I can see his eyelids drooping slightly.

I lean forward and put my glass down.

"Why?" I ask. "Really, why?"

His expression is even more dumb than usual. He yawns again.

"You really don't understand, do you?" I ask.

"What?" he says, his eyes now closing. "You're pretty. I just want you to know that I think you're pretty."

"Of course, you do," I say standing up and gathering my things. "That's probably the most truthful thing you've said all night."

"Yeah…" he mumbles, his beer spilling on his leg as he passes out.

I reach into his pocket for the keys: car and motel. I turn off the light as I leave and lock the door from the outside.

THE INESCAPABLE CELL

I gradually make my way through Midtown Manhattan. It took hundreds of miles to get here, but the last few are the slowest. I have never driven in New York City before. I don't really drive in general, not since I was a teenager. Now I'm facing the tumult of drivers and taxis and pedestrians that litter this beehive. But me, I'm here to see the Queen. She lives near the top of one of the tallest trees.

It's extraordinarily difficult to find it without maps on my phone. It's even more difficult to find a parking space.

The elevator symbolically recreates the journey from the bottom to the top, every trip. Who thought there was so much money left in books? These outdated things. These pre-screenplays. Who thought that in this day and age, these archaic tombs would still provide the starting point for most good stories? Maybe the creative spark still requires paper to ignite. Not film, but pages. The movies and games and merchandise, tie-ins, celebrity, social media and frills all bring in the money, but the idea... The idea is born from pen and paper. Or keyboard, but that's not important to this metaphor.

There's a reason for this.

Movies require producers, budgets, an audience. Games and apps require developers and teams of marketers. Even the most low-budget indie film or online video series requires a team, a framework, a formula, capital.

Books have no limitations, except the mind and language of one person.

Books are dictatorships. The author dictates the truth, the story, the reality, to the readers. They craft this story themselves. They don't need to concern themselves with what the audience wants. They decide what the audience needs.

In fact, you should never give the audience what they think they want. They won't enjoy that. Nothing is more disappointing than getting exactly what you asked for, what you expect. Nothing is less attractive than pandering. You give them something they don't know that they need. Be whiskey, not water.. Give it some ice so it goes down more easily, but be the fucking acquired taste.

Maybe the editor is the ice, the blocks in your glass. They temper you just the slightest amount. The dictator's advisor, so to speak.

And Karin was one of the best advisors around.

But I was no dictator. I was a figurehead, a puppet. I was being ghost written. By Feda. By the doctor. By a Frenchman and an organization that I'm not even sure exists. Very nearly by Kevin. Perhaps that's true of all the best dictators. Perhaps there are always puppet masters behind the scenes.

This is what happens when I'm left alone with my thoughts for too long, like sitting in a car for a full day.

The elevator opens and spits me straight into Karin's apartment. She's sitting on her couch: Books and papers sprawled over her glass coffee table. It's heading into evening, but her apartment is a mess. Uncharacteristically so.

"Gabi!" she cries, and stands up to hug me. "I'm so glad you came. Did you run out of battery? You cut out halfway through our call and I couldn't get hold of you. Where have you been? I'm so glad you're okay!"

"Yeah, I ran out of battery," I reply, meeting her with a full-body hug. She holds me tightly, tighter than usual. It's an unfamiliar hug, one that is not only giving support but also asking for it.

"What happened to you?" she says, rubbing away the earliest trickle of a tear from her eye. "Your parents called me. You have to stop just dropping off the face of the earth."

"Don't worry about it," I say. I don't feel like explaining the details of my kidnapping to her right now. I'm not sure I ever will.

"Do you want a drink? I'll get you a drink," she asks as she moves to the kitchen while continuing the conversation with me on the couch. "Come on, what happened?"

"Nothing of importance," I say, looking around the lounge for changes. A few new pictures. Plenty of new books. The notes littering the coffee table have her handwriting scribbled all over them. Neat and controlled. Powerful, but restrained swoops in cursive. Never red pen. She read somewhere that a red pen sends a negative message. Instead, she uses a blue pen. This leaves your drafts battered but not bloodied.
"And yes, I'd love a drink."

Although not a narrative, her notes tell a story. The manuscripts are many, the notes even more so. She usually works on one piece at a time, rather than flitting between many. There are doodles on her notes. Karin doesn't doodle, at least not on her work. I pull the paper towards me. It's a person, I think, scribbled. A figure more than a person. Scribbled in dark blue. I feel it in the pit of my stomach. I recognize that figure, as unrecognizable as it is. That figure has ripped apart my skin and burnt my flesh. That figure is the Knife.

Oh god. He found her. He found her and no one was there to help her. No one was there to wake her up.

She walks back into the lounge, carrying two glasses, a bottle of red wine, and a fake smile. Her hands are shaking. She's spilling out. I reach out to help her.

"Oh, thank you," she says, sounding so much older than she is. I take over the job, pouring wine for the both of us. She didn't even give the bottle its own introduction, explaining its cultivar and region. Everything about her is off.

I can recognize the exhaustion in her. She hasn't slept properly in days. I know that look. I feel something near it myself. It's been over a day since I last slept. But she wears something deeper. The deep tiredness of someone who wrestles with each night.

"What's wrong, Karin?"

"Nothing," she says, trying to collect and organize the papers on her table.

"Karin..."

"You're the one who's been missing for days," she says. "I'm fine. What have you been doing?"

She wipes her blackened eyes.

"God, Karin," I say. "It's okay. I understand. I've been there. It doesn't mean you're weak. Just tell me what's wrong. I know you haven't been sleeping. That's not like you."

"Did you manage to find those pills?" she asks, looking up at me almost imploringly.

"I got rid of them all," I reply. "I'm sorry. But trust me, you don't want to get into the habit of using them."

"I sound so stupid..." she says, not meeting my eyes.

"What do you dream about?" I ask.

She looks at me like a wounded deer.

"Whaa... what?" she asks.

"What are you dreaming about when you sleep?" I repeat.

"I don't sleep," she says. "Well, I haven't been sleeping."

"Not a wink?" I ask. "What's the last thing you remember dreaming about?"

"I don't even know, well, I don't remember," she continues. "But I can barely even function. I can't find any joy in anything. I don't feel anything really.

I can't focus. I can't work properly. I'm exhausted and I can't fall asleep. I'm going to the doctor tomorrow..."

A doctor won't help. Well, besides maybe one.

"Every time I close my eyes, I get this, this dread in the pit of my stomach," she says, her voice faltering. "Like the worst thing possible is happening. I thought you were dead, Gabi. I thought *I* was dead."

I've never seen her like this, nothing even close. This is my fault. I have brought this down upon her. She has cared and supported me for years. She has been my champion, my protector. She has guided me through life. Safeguarded me from the perils of the entertainment business. All kinds of perils. All I can do now is sit next to her uselessly, with my hand on her back.

"I'm so weak," she says.

"It isn't weakness," I say quietly. "You're not weak."

"I saw him die again. He was alive again. And then he died again. Over and over again." She breaks into tears. Sobs spill out of her. Chokes interrupt them.

"Who?"

"My brother," she says. "Chester. He couldn't breathe."

"I didn't know you have a brother," I reply

"I don't," she says.

"Oh," I say. "I'm sorry."

How did I not know that? How has she never told me about her brother?

"Why'd this suddenly happen now? I don't understand," she says. "I guess I thought I had dealt with things, but I've really just been bottling them up inside. I never understood. I thought I was stronger than this. I... is that what his life was like? All the time? Did he always feel like this?"

She rambles on. I can't quite make it out. I don't know how to support her. I can't tell her the truth. How would I even start? You're depressed because some sort of dream demon, sometimes called a Mara, has targeted you? Even Karin, with her nondescript spirituality, would laugh at me. Maybe that'll cheer her up at least.

"Is there anything I can do to help?" I ask.

She looks at me like she never has before, lost in her own head. She's thinking about something from long ago. Someone else. I don't know how I know, but I know. I can feel it in her head. She's remembering her brother.

"No..." she says. "That's the thing. You can't just fix it. It hurts. And you can't just fix it. Maybe that's why he gave up..."

No, I can fix it. If it's the Knife doing this to her, then I can help her. Is it using her to get to me? Or is she its new target? Either way, I made this happen. I guess I'll have to face it. I'll have to fight it. Lord help me, I'm going to have to find some way to fight that thing.

I think I may need some help. Feda? No, Feda can't do anything. Feda's dead. Busi made it clear that she won't help me.

There's only one person who I can go to.

There's only the doctor.

A DREAM OF HEAVEN

"I'm sorry I ran from you before," I say, lighting a cigarette as I exit Karin's building.

"I can understand why," the man replies. He's leaning against the wall outside the door. I can still see the scrapes on him from when he jumped off our car. "I try not to take it personally."

"You're not here to kill me, are you?" I ask.

"No, I'm not," he says. "I was never hunting you. I was trying to protect you from Mr. Young."

"Mr. Young? Kevin?" I ask.

"Yes," he replies.

"Are you part of Le Réveil?"

He smiles.

"You throw that name around so casually," he says. "Like you don't understand what it means."

"Are you?"

"Surely I don't need to answer that," he says. "You already know, and I don't make a habit of saying unnecessary things."

"Is that why you're the muscle?" I reply. "Man of few words. Don't ask questions. Strong and silent."

He gives me a smirk.

"No, that's not why I'm the muscle," he says. "The doctor would like to see you. Will you come with me?"

"You are lucky that I want to see the doctor too," I respond. "So yes, I will come with you. As long as you promise you will bring me back here afterwards."

"I will," he says, motioning for me to follow him.

His car is parked a few blocks down. I guess even secret organizations struggle to find parking in New York. The man walks briskly. He divides the crowds of people coming and going on the sidewalk. I stick close behind, shielded from them in his wake. We finally reach his car and drive off. It's only a few seconds before we're stuck at a traffic light.

"So, were you protecting me?" I ask, as the minutes wear on. "Or watching over me?"

He keeps his eyes on the road and his mouth closed, as we sit in traffic. It moves and then it doesn't.

"Can you at least tell me how far it is?" I ask, staring out of the window at near gridlock. If no one in New York drives, then why is there so much traffic?

He says nothing.

"What about your name? So I don't have to refer to you as 'big intimidating man number one'."

"Gugu," he replies. "Call me Gugu."

We eventually pull into the parking garage of a skyscraper I don't recognize by name.

"Let me guess…" I say as we pull in. "He's on the top floor?"

Gugu smiles. "Bingo."

We head towards a service elevator, one for which Gugu has a key. He opens it and pushes number 104.

I remain quiet as the elevator rumbles upwards. I find my bravado fading away as the elevator climbs. Have I made a terrible mistake?

"You're not going to kill me, are you?" I ask.

"If I was going to kill you, why would I bring you to the top of a skyscraper to do it?" he replies, apparently unsurprised by the question. Perhaps people ask him that question all the time. That's a worrying thing to be used to.

"It just feels like a poetic place for that to happen, for me to die," I say, shrugging. "I'm an author, you know."

Gugu replies, without expression.

"People don't die where it's most poetic," he says. "They die where they die."

"Besides," he continues. "If I were to take you somewhere to kill you, it would be a far more practical location than the top floor of a skyscraper."

"Well, that's reassuring then," I joke. "And what's up with *Mr. I don't like to say unnecessary things*? As soon as the subject is murder, you turn into a regular chatterbox."

Gugu purposefully shuts his mouth and replies with silence. The only noise now is the rumble of the non-soundproofed elevator, as it hurtles up to-wards whatever lies in wait at the top of the tower. It moves noticeably quickly, noticeably because it is not enclosed and sealed like most elevators. I feel as though I'm about to be flung out of the top of the building and thrown through the atmosphere into space.

Perhaps I'm reaching too high too quickly.

"I didn't mean to offend you," I say quietly.

"Because I'm a murderer?" he says, with an air that suggests he is offended. "Not the kind of person you want to offend."

"Are you?" I ask. "A murderer?"

He looks straight ahead. The elevator slows and comes to a stop, with a jolt. The doors open, revealing what is clearly a mechanical floor. Exposed pipes run along bare concrete walls, identifiable by distinct colors. Gugu walks out, turns and waits for me to follow him. I glance at the control panel of the elevator.

"What are we doing here?" I ask, staying within the threshold.

"You're meeting with the doctor," he says. "I thought that's what you wanted."

"Here?" I ask. This doesn't feel right.

I touch my hand. My finger pushes against my palm. I'm awake.

It feels unreal. Increasingly this is how the world feels. Like the dream world used to feel. I can't control what happens around me. I can't control the world. It feels so threatening. I am at its mercy. After almost two days without sleep, my consciousness feels just a bit further away. All of this combined with the high stakes and bizarre occurrences of the last few days, I'm unsure if I feel more alive than ever before or whether I feel like none of this is real.

"You're not dreaming," Gugu says. "This wouldn't take so long if you were."

He beckons me to follow him and walks on ahead, leading me through increasingly labyrinthine corridors. Deeper and deeper we go. He's walking me to my doom. I can feel it. I look around. Could I find my way out of here if I needed to? Would that service elevator even work for me?

I notice a slender wooden pole lying on a construction bin, about an arm in length. I grab it as I walk past and hold it behind my back. I'm going to need it. A whack to the face. A stake through the heart. I don't even know if he has a gun. I can still get out. There must be a fire escape. It's a skyscraper in New York, for crying out loud.

We finally get to a door: A plain door. A maintenance door. Locked. There is a number pad next to it. Gugu unlocks the door with a key, pokes a few numbers into the keypad and places his thumb on a fingerprint scanner, all before pushing open the door. He walks through.

"Come on," he says. "The doctor's up here. The door will close by itself."

He heads up the staircase as I pass through the doorway. There's a keypad on the other side as well. I can't get out of here. I can't get past this door. I place the wooden pole in the doorway, blocking the door from closing fully and hurry on my way. I caution a glance behind me to see the door slightly ajar. A thrill shivers up my spine. I did that. I've got this.

To my relief the door at the top of the staircase is not locked with the same care and attention as the bottom one. Gugu opens it simply with the turn of an ornate heavy brass handle. Once you're past certain barriers, I guess all doors open more easily.

In contrast to the door downstairs, this one is a dense oak. Honestly, I have no clue. I don't really know that much about wood, but this seems like expensive oak. It's the kind of wood you'd find in an old rich and suspiciously white country club, filled with gentlemen of leisure exchanging stories of their houses in the colonies. Perhaps they might discuss currency manipulation with one another, gerrymandering, or some light human trafficking. They'd laugh as they tap their cigars into ashtrays.

Behind this door is an office of the same old wealth. It doesn't scream money: screaming would be far too undignified. It softly purrs wealth and power. It's slight, but unmistakable. It's a simple leather couch that costs a family of four's annual grocery budget. It's the frames on the paintings. It's the casual trinkets, each solid and precious metal. It's the stories behind it all: old, money. How did this all get here? And why?

Sitting behind the desk is a tall, white European man with the air of intellectuality and the niceties of a gentleman. He rises to meet me, a courtesy he would never neglect.

"It is good to see you again, Gabi," the doctor says, walking around his desk to greet me. "I am glad you're safe."

He smiles at me. I still don't understand where I stand with this man. I'm not sure if he's my protector, friend, teacher, a suitor or wants to have me killed. Perhaps he's all these things.

This must be what life is like in the top inner circles of the world. Perhaps powerful friends are not only friends, but potential enemies and betrayers. Perhaps this ambiguity is just the nature of the world I have entered. Or perhaps it's all in my head.

"Good afternoon doctor," I reply. "I'm glad I made it here safely as well. I would be lying if I didn't think for a moment that your friend Gugu here would push me off the roof."

"Gugu would never do that," the doctor replies with a smile. "That would be far more spectacular than necessary."

"So he said," I reply.

"Drink?" the doctor asks, readying a bottle of whisky. Lagavulin.

"Like we used to?" I say, as I walk over to the window.

"Just like we used to," he says.

The view is intoxicating. Even the other skyscrapers barely manage to tickle the horizon. Boats dot the water like pond skimmers, their wakes dragging behind them. The people below mill around like ants. Each has such a specific purpose. Each has their own history dragging behind them like their own wake. Each tiny little person has their own life, their own dreams. This is just the place they all intersect. That intersection gives rise to a city, an entity of its own. I wonder if the city itself dreams.

Lady Liberty looks conspicuously small, perched on her island surrounded by water.

"Here you go," the doctor says. He holds out the glass of whisky.

"Thanks," I say, turning around. "You always go for a place with a view, I've noticed."

He holds up his whisky glass to toast me. "I find that looking down from a great height gives me a different perspective of the world," he says.

I look at Gugu. "Don't you want one?"

Gugu takes a sip of water, standing by the bar. "I don't drink," he says.

The doctor casts a glance his way. "Gugu is far more disciplined than either of us. I fear that I am nowhere near as good at foregoing my vices as he."

"Everyone has their own vices," Gugu replies without expression. "Alcohol just happens not to be mine."

While they talk, I stare at the glass. Should I be drinking this? Maybe I should just hold it and not drink it.

"Gabi," says Gugu. "You said that you needed to see the doctor... why?"

The doctor turns back to me.

"What is it?" he says.

I look at Gugu and back at the doctor. Can I trust them? I guess I have no choice at this point. I take a sip of whisky and lean back into the leather chair facing his desk.

"I need your help," I ask.

"Oh?" says the doctor, putting down his drink and looking at me earnestly. He's been so earnest and yet so dishonest.

"The Knife," I say. "It's attacking Karin. It's destroying her."

"The Knife..." says the doctor.

"It's been visiting her dreams every night. Attacking her. Torturing her. Tormenting her."

The doctor looks at me with a concerned expression on his face. I continue.

"I think he's doing it to get to me," I say quietly. "After I saved her from him in the dreamworld, when you came, I think he realized that he could use her. I don't know why, though. I don't know why he wants me."

"Neither do I," says the doctor, leaning back into his chair and sighing. "But he does. He seems to want you in particular."

"What is he? Or it?" I ask. "I've heard him referred to as a Mara. What is a Mara?"

The doctor laughs. "Who told you that?"

I frown at him.

"Oh yes, Busi. I guess that is not exactly wrong. Mara is the old English word for a demon, an incubus, that causes bad dreams. That is where the word nightmare comes from, after all. There were many Germanic legends about evil creatures that would sleep on one's chest at night, causing nightmares."

"But is it actually a demon?" I ask. Normally I would scoff at such a thought, but... "Do demons exist?"

"I do not think the Knife is actually a demon in the sense that you are thinking," the doctor continues. "Although I guess that depends on your definition of a demon. I do not know what it is. It could be a dreamer. It could be a manifestation of fear or pain or something that's taken some sort of form in the dreamworld. It seems to wander amongst dreams inflicting as much pain as possible. That certainly sounds like a demon to me. As I said," the doctor shrugs. "You are not exactly wrong. What are demons if not the manifestation of our deepest fears?"

"So, what can we do about it?" I ask. "I mean, so you're part of this grand, world-controlling secret society, surely you can kill this thing? Demon or not."

I turn my head to Gugu, who shakes his head. "I deal with humans exclusively. I ain't fucking with no demons."

"Doctor?" I ask.

"Busi is one of the few who scare it," he replies. "And you've been hiding yourself, most of the time, so it hasn't been able to find you. Karin must seem like the weak point in your armor. I didn't know it was so... calculating."

"So maybe we can hide Karin too," I say. "We can teach her to hide herself, like I did."

"She's not a lucid dreamer, though," the doctor says.

"We can teach her to be lucid," I say, emphatically. "We can tell her about the dreamworld. Then she can learn to defend herself. In the meantime, she'll be safe because we'll be with her in her dreams. It's perfect."

My idea leaves the room in silence: A pained silence.

"Right?" I ask. "I mean, she's intelligent and strong-willed. If anyone can become lucid, she can."

As I look at them, I can already feel that the answer won't be yes.

"Oh, what the fuck?" I stand up. "Really? Is this because of the whole: You don't talk about Dream Club thing?"

Gugu automatically rears up from where he's leaning against the wall.

"It's not that simple, Gabi," says the doctor, in his placating tone.

I stare at the doctor, leaning onto his desk. "Isn't it? Is it ever? So, tell me. I've got time. Why can't we help Karin?"

"We can help her," he says. "And we will. Now sit down and stop acting like a petulant child."

"What?" I gasp.

"Sit down, and listen to what I have to say. We... I have treated you respectfully and attempted to help you every step of the way and you have offered me frequent contempt in return," he says, his voice level, but his tone sharp. "We can help you with this, but why should we?"

"What do you mean, why should we?" I ask.

"Why should we?" he replies simply. "If we are truly what you think, a malignant and manipulative shadow government, then what makes you think we would go out of our way to help your friend? Especially when you have made it abundantly clear that not only will you not help us, but rather you oppose our aims directly. Surely your new friends would have warned you not to come here. Warned you not to meet us? Why did you come to us? Why do you think we will help you?"

I open my mouth to respond, but instead I hesitate.

"Gugu," says the doctor, turning to his partner. "Would you do me a favor and give us the room?"

Gugu looks at the doctor, the doctor looks back. Neither of them change their expressions, and yet somehow, I can feel something communicate between them. I am between them, after all. Whatever it is, maybe it went straight through me.

Gugu pulls himself off the wall and puts his water down. His eyes meet mine, narrow.

"Don't sit too long on a fence, Gabrielle Rivers," he says, "You might fall."

He pushes the wall and disappears quickly through a hidden door. Of course, this room has a hidden door. How could it not?

This leaves the doctor and me alone in an office that ironically feels more threatening without the assassin in it.

"Are you going to help me or not?" I ask. "Because if not, I'm leaving. If not, I'm going to leave and tell Karin and the rest of the world about this ivory fucking tower of yours. So, either help me or kill me."

"Kill you?" the doctor says. "Is that what you think we're going to do? No, no Gabi. We will help you. On the condition that you do not tell anyone anything."

"Anything?"

"About lucid dreaming, about the dreamworld, about us... about me," he says.

"And if I refuse?"

"Then you will find out what will happen if you refuse," he says. "And The Knife will continue to haunt both you and Karin."

"So, it's true," I reply. "They were right about you. You're evil."

"Why? Because we will not let you blackmail us?" he replies. "Because we will not let someone who has been dreaming for a few short months decide the future of the dreamworld, fueled by some sense of misplaced rebellion. For that reason, we are evil?"

"What?" I reply. "You think that's why I don't want to join you? You think that's why I don't know if I want to be a part of your secret society? Because I'm a rebellious teenager? It's not because you've manipulated elections, assassinated people or instigated revolutions for your own aims?"

"Where are you getting your information from?" the doctor asks. "What exactly is it that you think we have done? Kevin Young is not the most reliable of sources. He's a dangerous man, and misinformed. That's why we tried to protect you from him."

"Just because I don't trust you, doesn't mean I'm on his side," I say.

"Then whose side are you on?" says a third voice.

It comes from behind me. The doctor's gaze darts over my shoulder and I spin around. Kevin Young is standing in the doorway. A gun. His gun pointed directly at my head.

CHEKOV'S GUN

"Answer the question." Kevin says, his voice shaking with anger.

"I mean, I know what side he's on." He points the gun towards the doctor, sniffs. "He thinks the world is better off being ruled, so long as he's the one ruling it."

"Kevin," the doctor says sternly. "You continue to..."

"Shut up," Kevin says, barely containing himself. "You talk and talk. You say all this shit. We're making the world a better place. We're the only ones who can do it. Do you really think I'm going to buy that shit? I'm not an idiot."

He signals for us both to stand, waving the gun in our direction recklessly. He shepherds us to stand next to one another by the window, while he moves to the desk.

"Hands on your fucking head," he says. His face is covered in sweat, hair sticking to his forehead. How did he get up here?

"Kevin..." I start to say.

"Did I say you could fucking talk? You fucking bitch. You pretended like you were on my side. You lied to me. You drugged me."

"What!?!" I say. "You kidnapped me."

"You know. I guess I should have known. You know. Fuck!" Kevin shouts the end of his sentence. "I know what I sound like now. I sound like I'm the crazy one, don't I? But I'm really not. I feel like I'm the only sane person left. We can't just stand by and let them do this, Gabrielle. How can you just let them do this? That's not something a sane person would do. Is it because of the doctor? Are you fucking him?"

He points his gun back at the doctor. "Are you fucking her?"

"Jesus, Kevin," I say. "What the fuck are you talking about?"

"We can't let them do it, Gabrielle," he says again. "We can't."

"You're right," I say, dropping my hands slightly so they're in front of me. "You're right, we can't."

"Don't pretend like you're on my side," he spits. "You just admitted you weren't. I heard you. You'd rather become a part of Le Réveil than fight it. I understand. They can give you everything you've always wanted."

"I'm not on anyone's side," I say. "I'm just trying to help my friend, that's all."

"Karin? You know that they set the Knife on Karin, don't you?" he says. "That's their game. They set the Knife on Karin just like they set the Knife on you. They use him as their fucking attack dog. What better way to ensure that they have leverage over you?"

"What?" I say.

"They set the Knife on her so that they could draw you out. Easiest thing in the world. Draw you out and get leverage. I never said they weren't smart," Kevin rambles on.

I turn to the doctor, who has a pained look on his face.

"Do you still want to sit here and talk to him?" Kevin says. "This fucking scumbag."

"It's not true," says the doctor, meeting my eyes intentionally. "I promise that I didn't."

"Really?" Kevin replies. "Have you noticed how everything seems to just happen in a way that suits them?"

"Don't listen to him, Gabi," the doctor replies. "He has no clue what he's talking about."

"What about Feda?" Kevin asks. "He mysteriously died when he threatened to expose your secrets. Convenient, huh?"

"Feda?" snaps the doctor. "What do you mean?"

Kevin continues, "You might not have killed him yourself, but you know. You know things you cannot pretend not to know, right?"

The doctor's face betrays only complete surprise and confusion.

"Doctor," I say. "Did you know Feda?"

The doctor sighs.

"Okay. Okay. Yes," the doctor says, turning to me and looking very uncomfortable. "I'm sorry I did not tell you the truth. I met Feda before you, in a manner of speaking. He is the reason I sought you out in the first place. But I did not murder him, I mean, how could I murder him. That does not make sense. Nor have I used the Knife as a weapon. I would not and quite frankly, could not, do that."

"Perhaps you couldn't, but the Frenchman could," Kevin says.

"The Frenchman?" the doctor replies.

"Don't pretend like you don't know who I'm talking about," Kevin spits. "I know he exists. I know he is behind everything you do."

"Who told you that?" the doctor replies.

Kevin smiles. "Who else, but Feda."

"That's impossible," the doctor says, furiously searching his mind. "How could you have met Feda?"

"It seems you aren't quite as all-knowing as you pretend," Kevin laughs. "That's why I want to speak with your boss after all. The one who pulls the strings. I want to meet the Frenchman."

"Meet the Frenchman?" I say. "That wasn't your plan."

"Feda's plan was shit," he shouts. "And without you, it's pointless. Now I've got a new plan."

"Feda's plan?" asks the doctor.

Kevin shouts. "God, you're so far behind. Forget about that. I'm here for one reason. I'm here to see the Frenchman. I want you to take me to him."

"You want me to take you to the Frenchman?" the doctor replies as if it's a question.

"Yes. That is exactly what I said," Kevin says sarcastically. "Now's the part where you explain to me that it's not possible."

"It is not possible," the doctor says. "And I guess you know why."

"Entertain me."

"I do not know where the Frenchman is. There is no reason I would. I do not know who the Frenchman is. If I did know, I certainly would not tell a gun-wielding madman who obviously intends to kill him. So, in summation, I cannot, and I will not, tell you."

"I'm going to make a guess that threatening your life won't change that."

"Well, it could not change the former and would not change the latter, so yes, you are correct," says the doctor. He somehow sounds more formal when he's angry.

"And what if I kill her?" he says, directing the gun at me. "Your surrogate daughter. Or is she your surrogate wife? Which one died, both? Which one is she replacing?"

"That would not change anything," the doctor says. "I still could not help you. I still would not help you. If you want to meet the Frenchman, you know how to. Just call him in the dreamworld. He may come to you."

Kevin laughs. "How stupid do you think I am?"

As cool as he is trying to play it, the gun is shaking in Kevin's hand. I can tell because I'm staring directly at it. How peculiar a thought, to know that all that stands between you and death is a quick squeeze of a trigger. The slightest of movements. A simple gesture. The will behind it must be so much more, but the physical action? That's nothing. As easy as a swipe of a pen, crossing out a name.

"Well, I guess if you won't take me to him, all I can do is get as much information out of you as possible."

"Have you ever killed anyone before?" I ask. I don't quite know where it came from. It just erupted out of my throat. "Or would I be your first?"

His eyes shift to mine, but they have a difficult time holding them.

"I regret that you've been pulled into the middle of this," he says. "But I've given you the opportunity to do the right thing. You have chosen to be complicit."

"You've never shot anyone before, have you?" I say, more bravely than I understand. "You're not going to shoot me, Kevin."

"Gabi..." warns the doctor.

"I will," Kevin says. "Unlike you, I actually have the strength to take a stand. To do something. The right thing."

As I open my mouth to respond, the entire room stops. At that very moment, we all hear the sound of the secret door opening. Gugu enters the room.

It seems to happen in slow motion, though not slow enough for me to react in any way. Instead of reacting, I watch. I watch stupidly while standing perfectly still. Kevin spins instinctively towards Gugu, bringing the gun up. Gugu reacts in turn, instantly ducking and rushing forwards.

BAM!

It's so fucking loud. Even louder than I thought. Louder than it was in my dream. The door behind Gugu erupts as a bullet tears through it.

BAM!

Another shot. Gugu reaches Kevin, grabbing the gun. Wrestling. It's going quickly. But slowly.

BAM!

I must have bumped the table. Kevin goes down, Gugu holding him somehow. I can't hear, but there's shouting. It sounds far away. I've never heard a gunshot without ear protection before. It was so loud. I hope my ears are okay. I try to say something, I'm not even sure what. I can barely hear my own voice. God, I hope I'm not deaf.

On the ground Gugu manages to wrestle the gun out of Kevin's hand and proceeds to batter his face with it. Blood spurts and Kevin gurgles words of protest. God, he's going to kill him. Don't kill him. I need answers.

I step forward.

I feel funny. Something doesn't feel right.

The doctor rushes over to me.

"Gabi!"

Oh god. I sink to the ground. What's happening? I feel down to my stomach. Wetness. I think I might have been shot. I can't have been shot. Kevin wouldn't shoot me. I can't get shot. I can't get shot. Right?

Is this it? I've been shot. I can't get shot. Is this it? Am I going to die? I'm not really going to die. Am I going to die? I can't die.

The doctor is holding me. I ask him. He's a doctor. Am I going to die? I don't want to die.

"Hold on, Gabi," he says.

There's blood. There's a lot of blood. It's pouring out of my stomach. No, not pouring. It's spurting. Like ketchup out of a squeezy bottle. Every squeeze causes another spurt out. That must be my heartbeat. Interesting. Interesting how it spurts out like that.

Am I going to die? I don't want to die. I'm not done yet. This can't be real. Is this it? I need to wake up. I must be dreaming.

I don't know if I'm talking or thinking.

I'm tired. Am I going to die? I guess that's okay. I don't want to die, but I guess that's okay. Everyone dies. Everyone dies in the end. I knew I was going to die up here. I guess that's okay. I'm tired. I just want to sleep. Maybe I'll dream. Maybe this was a dream.

"Is this it?"

A DREAM OF HELL

The Bamiyan valley stretches out before me, green and lush and flanked by beige walls. Did those walls protect it from the world at large? That large, self-perpetuating and all-consuming world that swallows and absorbs peoples, cultures and innocence? How long could those walls possibly have stood against that tide? That unstoppable tide. Feda had no chance in this little valley. Before the soldiers and planes came, the world leaked in ever more indirectly.

My feet feel the grass. It tickles my toes. It tells me something of beauty, but I don't listen. I am distracted by the ripping apart of flesh, families and histories. Women dragged out. Sons kidnapped. Homes put to the torch, all to consolidate power. A violence that was so close to home.

"It wasn't always like this," Feda says. "Even then."

He's standing by me in the way he always does, hands behind his back like he's holding something secret there.

"There was life here still," he continues. "Under it all. Under Enduring Freedom. Under the Taliban. Under the Mujahadeen. Under the Soviets. We all still lived."

"How could you live like this?" I ask. "In this world."

"Don't ask me," he laughs. "I died."

We stood silent as countless others in front of us did the same. They died. They were killed. They killed one another.

"Who killed you, Feda?" I ask.

He shrugged. "I don't really know. I was too busy dying."

Fire and blood erupt from homes as they explode. The blasts deafen me. I clutch my ears as the earth shakes around me. Missiles dart in from just above the beige caverns, ending in these plumes of fiery smoke and death. I cannot even see the helicopters in the distance. They must be there, though. I fall to the ground. Feda sits next to me.

Dying. That seems so familiar.

The explosions grow closer. The men and women who were previously fighting each other are now fleeing from the valley. Bullets rip up the ground at their feet. Most fall and shudder as they are torn into shreds.

"Is everything okay, Gabi?" Feda asks. "You seem different? What happened with Kevin?"

Kevin. Dying.

"Kevin shot me," I say. "I don't think he meant to, but he shot me."

"He shot you?" Feda's eyes widen. "Gabi, did he kill you?"

"I don't know."

I run my hand over my stomach. It's wet. Red. Blood. There's screaming and shouting.

"Did you die, Gabi?" Feda asks. "Try to remember."

My mouth feels so dry. And there's a dull pain.

"You're going to be okay. You're going to be okay," says someone's voice, chorused by a siren. "Just breathe. Can you hear me, Gabi?"

I recognize that voice. There are others I don't.

Feda looks around in a panic. "We need to leave now. We must not die here."

The explosions light up all around Gabi. She can barely keep track of them. Feda takes her hand and leads her up into the sky, away from the eruptions of earth below them. Fire traces over their position. Feda weaves between streaming orange missiles.

Feda is holding her hand. So is the doctor. There's a tube going into her arm and the world is throwing her around. She can see other people around her. She doesn't know what's going on, but she's not confused. She's just floating.

"Stay with me!" shout two people from two different worlds: Feda and someone else. They are both shouting at her. Why?

Feda calls to someone else as he drags her through the sky. Busi, he says. She feels like a ragdoll, trailing behind a boy in a park. She feels just as lifeless, without her own volition or will. Just a doll along for the ride. Floating idly in the tide.

Floating idly in the tide.

Floating idly in the tide.

"Gabi!" he shouts. "I need you here. I need you to focus. I need you to stay with me. Concentrate."

"Feda," she says. "Feda. Feda."

She repeats herself. I don't know why. She seems a little odd. This all seems a little odd, a little off. It doesn't feel right.

Feda drops Gabi onto sand. Sand again. The beach. He crouches over her, talking to her.

"Just hang on, Gabi," he says. "Just hang on until she gets here."

"Feda," Gabi says. "He's coming. He's coming for me. For the last time."

"Who's coming?"

Gabi moans in pain. It's the only sound in the silence. Not a breath of wind. No roar from the ocean. Instead, the ocean retreats, creeping down the beach away from the two of them. Every wave laps lower. It reveals the hidden shells and dips where once water washed. Soon the water is barely visible in the distance. Steam seems to rise from the remaining pools of water. The sun dips far in the horizon, hiding from what is still to come. To arrive.

"Fuck," says Feda, looking out where once was the seaside. He screams for Busi.

"Shhhh," says Gabi. She puts her hand up to his face. "It's okay."

Blood is pouring out of her stomach. It runs down the beach towards the ocean. A red carpet. A red carpet for death. Upon it, the silhouette of death walks towards them. Slowly, he steps atop the blood in unstained black boots. Feda stands up and faces him. He blocks the path towards Gabi. Arms outstretched.

"Leave her," he shouts. "She is on the verge of death. If you hurt her, you will kill her. Then you will lose her."

The Knife stops. Is it considering what Feda said? Can it consider things? It's impossible to tell, it's as featureless as night. There are only vague hints at what it might contain. After only a moment, the Knife continues. Feda stands his ground.

"Stop," Feda shouts. "Someone, help! Please! Busi!"

The Knife swipes at him. A chain springs from the sand beneath Feda, but he's already gone. Feda darts across the sand in a wide arc, ending up behind the Knife. The chain that emerged from the sand looks like it belongs to a shipwreck, rusted old iron. It hovers where Feda stood only seconds before, one end still trailing into the sand.

The Knife doesn't move to follow Feda at all. He simply continues lumbering forwards towards Gabi's body.

"Get away from her!" Feda screams, as if my life was his. He flies at the Knife. He spins his body around as the Knife's chain pierces the empty space where he was a heartbeat ago. Feda's kick connects with the Knife as it would with a rock. The silhouette is completely unfazed.

Feda springs back and lands in the sand. "Gabi, I need your help," he says. "Please."

Who is he talking to?

The Knife kneels down next to Gabi's body. He holds his hand in front of him, coal embers burning hot. The air around it shimmers in heat; smoke rises from it. He thrusts it down onto her stomach, holding it against her wound. It burns. It burns. My skin bubbles and pops. My wound fuses together.

Oh my fucking god, it hurts. I scream. The pain is impossible to ignore. It's all-consuming. I look around in a panic. There are people around me. People in blue masks. Just eyes staring. Doctors. The doctor! Pain. Fuck. I see the doctor.

"Help me," I mumble. "The knife. Hurts. Me."

I flail around, but the Knife holds me down. Finally, and in an instant, he is swept away. I hear him falling into the sand nearby. Feda stands over me.

"Are you okay?" he says.

"Feda?" I ask. "I'm alive. I'm still alive. I'm not dead, not yet."

"Good," he smiles. "Unfortunately, I am dead, Gabi. I have no power here. My will cannot overpower others, not without you." He turns away to face the Knife. "I cannot fight him off without you."

The Knife is back on his feet, for the moment only watching us.

"Get up, Gabi," Feda says. "You need to fight him."

"I cannot fight him," I say. "I cannot fight him."

"You have to," Feda says. "You can."

"How?" I ask. "I don't even know what he is."

"I will help you," he says. "Just get up."

I struggle to my feet. Still feeling the ache in my side. "I'm injured," I say.

"You're dreaming," Feda shouts. "You're fine. Don't think you are, know you are."

I laugh and cough. "Still acting like you're Morpheus, hey?"

"Morpheus..." Feda says, his eyes lighting up. "Morpheus will help us. You must tell the doctor."

"Morpheus?" I ask. "What?"

We are both interrupted by the sound of a deep foghorn emanating from the Knife. The force of the blast blows sand in our eyes. The Knife rockets from his spot towards me.

"Fuck!" I shout, dodging to the side. I'm not quite quick enough. As he slides past me, one of his chains wraps around my foot. I feel my momentum shift as it slams me into the sand. I can feel my skin burning where it touches me.

For a second, I can see a different world. The doctor and other faces hover all around me. Poking and prodding.

"Gabi!?" he says. "Are you okay?"

"I need Morph.."

The world disappears and I'm back on the sand. I try to grab hold of the ground to crawl away, but the chains pull me into the air. Handfuls of sand spill out between my fingers as I cling to the earth. The Knife holds me there for a moment, just looking at me as I dangle upside down.

Feda darts forwards between us, flashing a sword through the chain. It slices through, causing me to collapse face-first into the sand.

"Get up!" Feda shouts, as he attacks the Knife with his sword.

I push myself onto my feet, wavering a bit. I turn quickly enough to see Feda's sword strike. The Knife raises his arm and blocks it with ease. He grabs Feda by the throat and holds him in the air. He disarms Feda of his sword.

"Feda!" I run forward. He raises the sword. He's going to kill Feda.

"Don't!" shouts Feda, barely.

It's too late. A large spike attached to one of the Knife's chains emerges from the sand in front of me. I can't stop in time. I'm dulled. I'm so slow. I run into it. It impales me through my stomach. I stop in my tracks, skewered like a kebab. Like a kebab, I giggle a bit at the thought.

I feel the blood rush out of my mouth. Feda reaches out his hand to me.

"Gabi!" he shouts.

I reach down in front of me, grabbing the chain that has pierced its way through me. The strange thing is... it doesn't hurt as much as I thought it would. Is that because I'm dying?

Feda drops to the ground as the Knife walks towards me, still holding Feda's sword. I have a chance to look at him properly. It's almost as if he doesn't exist: A vacuous space where there would otherwise be matter or light. He's literally nothing.

I laugh, blood dribbling down my lips. He stops.

"You're nothing besides pain," I say, still laughing. "I get it now. All you are is pain."

I grab the chain and rip it apart with my hands. Instead of dropping to the ground, I remain floating in the air where he previously held me. I feel no heat from him now, though he is so close.

I kick, but he ducks down in time to avoid it. He dodges below it. If he dodges that means I can hurt him. I drop to the ground in front of him, launching a flurried attack. He retreats backwards, replaced by his barbed chains emerging from the sand below. They crisscross between us, blocking the way. I spin through them, and they take their toll. They rip open my skin as I pass by them, but I don't care. I press forward. Reaching through the chains, I nearly touch the darkness that is the Knife.

But the chains enclose around me, like a snug and spiky blanket. It's cozy. I'll keep it. I charge forwards again, this time slamming into the black figure that once held me paralyzed. It makes no utterance as I hit him, merely rolling off the blow. I shatter the chains around me, letting the rubble fall to the sand. What is going on? How can I do this?

"Morpheus," says Feda, now sitting on the sand, watching. "The god of dreams."

What does he mean? Is the Knife the god of dreams? Morpheus? Oh... I realize. I am Morpheus. I am the god of dreams.

I reach down to my leg. Holstered along my ankle is a gun. I pull it up and aim directly at the Knife.

I fire once, twice, three times. The gunshots are loud, but it doesn't bother me this time. Unfortunately, the bullets don't seem to do anything to this crazy black void of a man.

"What are you? I ask, dropping the gun idly into the sand.

He raises his arms and the sand flares up from the beach, a wall of sand, blinding me. Fuck off! I shield my mouth, take a deep breath in, and blow. The sand scatters.

He is gone.

I spin around, searching for him. When I find him again, he's standing right behind Feda, who looks up at me.

"Behind you!" I scream.

Feda's eyes meet mine. I can see the moment that the realization hits him. There's a moment when he understands exactly what has just happened, and what's about to. He doesn't seem afraid. He opens his mouth to say something, to utter his last words.

The Knife brings down the sword, slicing down Feda's neck, through half his torso. Instead of blood, smoke escapes from his body. He slumps down, and his body dissolves like dry ice across the sand. He simply lies on the ground, fizzling. Within five seconds he is gone, like he never existed in the first place.

As he disappears, I understand. I understand exactly what he was, and what I am.

The Knife just stands there. He is motionless over where once was my friend. There's no expression. There's no humanity. There is no reason. There is only pain.

Despite myself, I feel the weight of it. More than the blood spilling out of my stomach, more than my skin ripped off in patches, this truly hurts. I still feel this pain.

This is what he feels. He is sharing it with the world.

MARA, THE KNIFE

I have no choice. Well, I guess I do. We always have a choice. To do, or not to. Perhaps we don't. Perhaps it isn't really a choice. Perhaps it's just an illusion of a choice. Perhaps we just act. Perhaps the distinction between unconscious and conscious is superficial. Perhaps at the end of the day, all we do is what our neurons are trained to do. Perhaps all we are is a predictable pattern of stimulus and response. Define: algorithm.

Maybe that's why I'm going to do what I'm going to do. Maybe this is the way that the story ends. My will has nothing to do with it. I am unfamiliar with this sort of certainty. I've seen it in others: a terrifying sight. It's not confidence. Confidence means understanding your own abilities. This is about knowing what's going to happen. There is only one possible future from this moment.

I know that's why he did it. He killed Feda so that I would try to kill him. He wants me to try. He wants me to try so that he can inflict as much pain on me as he can. He knows that I won't stop until he's dead or destroyed or whatever is relevant to whatever he is. He wants me to try so that he can defeat me. Utterly defeat me. Crush me. I assume it's less fun to hurt someone who's given up. He wants to make me give up. He knows he can beat me. I know he won't.

He's going to regret giving me this opportunity.

We pace around each other like lions. We aren't sizing each other up. We've already decided we're going to fight to the death. No, we're stalling and probing one another.

I rush forward, headlong into him. His chain pierces my upper thigh. Another rips open my arm. I continue, unfazed, towards him. He steps back as I reach him, raising his hands to meet mine. I throw my body against him, knocking him backwards onto the sand. His chains rear up behind me, piercing into my back as if it would stop me.

Sitting on top of him, I punch his face. It's like hitting a wall. I guess so, at least. I've never punched anything in real life before, least of all a wall. I punch again. And again. I punch him repeatedly as hard as I can. His chains pierce through my chest, hooking around me and flinging me off. I feel chunks of my flesh land with me, as I jump to my feet. The Knife stumbles to his, a distinct crack running down the front of his obsidian exoskeleton.

He can be beaten. There's something underneath that darkness. It's a shell.

He's not nothing, after all. There's something there. Something to kill.

"What are you?" I ask. "Are you human?"

He doesn't make a sound.

I charge forward again. Almost instantly, my feet dig deep into the sand, up to my ankles. It stops me in my tracks. I try to rip my legs out, but I start sinking deeper into the quicksand. The Knife clicks his finger and creates a spark in his hand. It ignites a flame that runs down his body, hits the sand and trails towards me. It engulfs the area in fire. Burning hot flames cover me, though I cannot feel the heat. I can smell my hair and clothes burning.

Water! I call a storm to save me. I ask it to happen, and it does. It starts with the gentle pitter-patter of drizzle, steadily growing stronger and louder. The fire flickers in the rain. In a flash of lightning, I see the dark silhouette approaching me, followed by the crack of thunder. I start scrambling up out of the waterlogged sand that's forming around me. The Knife is almost on me. I call on the storm to help me, and once again she does. The next lightning strike hits the Knife. He flies into the darkness on the crest of an explosion. I manage to rip myself out of the ground, out of the waterlogged quicksand that was sucking me down. The Knife is getting back to his feet, smoke rising from him. More lightning hits the sand around us, more cracks of deafening thunder, more rain falls from the sky.

"Are you going to leave me alone now?" I call out to the creature. "Are you going to leave Karin alone?" I don't expect anything from him, this being of pain.

He reaches his hands in the air, as if calling to the heavens. He wants to steal my storm.

I rush forward again and feel the effects of his call. The rain sizzles on my skin as I run through it. I can smell my flesh burning, though I can't feel a thing. He's turned the rain against me, against both of us. The same thing is happening to him. His black shell shimmers as the acid rain burns through the outer layer. It's weakening him.

There is something in the sand between him and I, buried there. It's a gift for me. I know it is. I reach down and grab it as I run towards him. I already know what it is. I've seen these before. A fulgurite: Hard, but brittle remnants of where lightning kissed sand. This one is ensiform and about four and a half feet in length. It spikes irregularly at the bottom, like some demented glass trident. This was a gift to me from the storm. From Zeus to Morpheus.

I continue towards the Knife, scrambling through burning sand, doused in acid and dragging this new weapon behind me as if I am Zeus' vengeance incarnate. I see the Knife step back, unsure of what to do. This is it, my opening. His uncertainty, the first I have seen, is weakness. His chains flail at me and tear at my skin. It doesn't stop me.

I pull my fulgurite sword in front of me and spear it into the Knife's chest. It instantly splinters and shatters in places. Barbs of razor-sharp glass scatter. But it rips through his darkness, his outer darkness at least. He collapses onto his back, and I twist my sword. His obsidian armor falls apart around him. The shrill sound of metal scraping erupting from him. Screams layered upon screams layered upon screams. Beeps and crying. All sorts of sounds mingled together like the accumulated noise of an entire life escaping at once.

As his darkness collapses, it reveals a small man inside: A man still. A shriveled naked man. A still Japanese man where once there was a demon. His eyes are unfixed, staring into nothingness.

He does not stir. He lies in the black wreckage of his body without the slightest hint of movement. His limbs look incapable of movement, atrophied and withered. But he's breathing. Shattered fulgurite litters his body and surrounds. He hasn't moved in years.

"You're a human?" I ask and kneel down next to him, this pathetic sack of flesh on the ground. "Is this your sarcophagus?"

The acid rain has cleared without me noticing, leaving only the two of us. The fire has died, although the battlefield around us remains. I reach down and put my hand behind his head and raise it. It offers no resistance, again when I let it go. It flops down lifelessly, although still noticeably alive.

It's peculiarly lonely without him, even though he was trying to kill me. Like the relief when the last guest leaves your party, only equaled by the pervasive hole they leave behind. The light shines in through a hole in the clouds, onto the hole of a person lying before me. He lights up like I'm playing a game of Operation!

Beep.

I pull up the blue gown over his body and tuck it around his neck, a hospital gown. I understand now.

Beep.

I lean against his bed, a hospital bed. I can smell it. Hospital smell. I can hear it, feel it. Hospital sounds echoing down the bare and sterile walls. It's distinct. There's nothing like it.

Beep.

He's tucked in, but there are no flowers on his bedside. It's just a cold hospital room, him and machines and not much else. Save me.

Beep.

He lies motionless in his bed, barely an inch of movement. His lip curls ever so slightly, occasionally. How is this the monster that has haunted my dreams? This sack of meat can't piss for itself. How is this a demon of pain?

Beep.

I watch his lip curl again. Pain. Pain! He's in pain. Oh my god! He is in constant agony, unable to end it, unable to communicate with the outside world.

Beep.

I can feel it in him. That's all there's left inside him. The pain has blocked every other part of him. There's no love, no fear, no understanding or thoughts. He cannot even escape it in his dreams, so all he does is share it.

Beep.

My hatred for this creature does not disappear, but sympathy creeps in alongside it. How does one survive knowing nothing but pain? What if there was no relief? Not even a break in the torture so that you can understand what is happening? Just relentless suffering.

Beep.

How long has he been like this? He should not be alive. No one should be alive through this. I look around the hospital room. It's just us, alone.

Beep.

I reach up to his face and place my hand on it. He doesn't flinch. I cover his mouth and hold his nose with my other hand.

Beep.

His eyes remain closed. His body remains still.

Beep

I clamp tightly. No air.

Beep.

I watch the heart monitor.

Beep.

Beep.

It increases in frequency. I can feel the heartbeat in his chest pounding.

Beep.

He doesn't struggle, except his heart.

The door swings open, revealing a white coat, a doctor.

He shouts at me in Japanese, rushing forwards to stop me.

Beep. Beep. Beep.

He's followed by more, more coats, reaching at me to stop.

His breaths are shallow and panicked. His heart is racing, but I am growing tired. And I feel the aches of a thousand wounds in the distance. I desperately hold onto his mouth as the doctors try to pry my hands off him. The whole room lurches. I hear my flesh being sliced by scalpels, little knives stabbing and cutting, but I hold on still. My vision is starting to blur. I can feel something.

Beeeeeeep. A long continuous tone. Then silence.

He lets go. I let go. His body remains on the hospital bed.

I feel the doctors fade away and I collapse against the wall and slide down onto the floor and the room is spinning like I'm drunk. There is still only silence.

I did it. He is dead. So why am I?

I nearly forgot. The colors spill into one another, the walls are no longer perpendicular to one another. I'm losing it. Am I waking up?

No, I'm not waking up. Quite the opposite. I'm dying. I was so distracted by the fight that I forgot. I'm dying, just like Feda.

"Voulez vous vivre?" It's the only sound in the silence. It's a voice. "Do you want to live?"

He speaks French, but I understand him.

"Am I dying?" I reply, but the words sound odd. I am also speaking French. It flows out effortlessly.

"Yes," the voice continues. "But I can change that if you like."

"Who are you?" I ask, trying to keep a grip of my senses. I feel like I'm falling asleep. How can that be? I can't fall asleep. I am asleep, how can I fall asleep?

"I'm sure you can guess who I am," the voice replies, with an air of humor.

Ahead of me, as much as I can perceive a direction in the swirling kaleidoscope of colors and form, a white light, a ring, a white ring, it grows, it grows. The light.

"Are you God?" I ask, the light at the end of the tunnel growing brighter and closer.

Laughter echoes around me. God is amused.

THE FRENCHMAN

"That isn't the first time I've been asked," he says.

The white light explodes into color. What color! Like nothing I've ever seen before; new colors. These are not even ones I could have imagined. They are not mixed from the primary ones either. They are entirely different. Are they ultraviolet? Are they infrared? Are they something else? It's miraculous. Despite my ache, despite my confusion, I can't help but smile at the beauty. It's intoxicating. This myriad of colors, all new and breathtaking. Awe inspiring. Mind blowing. How could this not be heaven? What else could it be?

Only one person could do this.

"You're the Frenchman, aren't you?" I ask, the name sounding odd on my lips.

"That is one of my names, yes," he says. "And you are Gabrielle. Gabrielle Rivers. The scribe of Feda Ahmed. Disciple of the good Doctor Sivers. Slayer of the Knife. Mouthpiece to the world. The Angel Gabrielle."

He walks out of the light, in sharp relief against the colors swarming around him. Just for a moment, he is a silhouette, but the light fades and leaves only a man behind. He looks distinctly normal, human in comparison to his entrance. He is flanked by daylight and sky. It lends warmth to his face, his hair is thick and messy, brown and gray, and covers his head and chin. He looks almost biblical, as if Moses just appeared at the top of the mountain, or God to Moses. I feel myself barely clinging to my mind, to my awareness.

"What happened?" I ask. "I was fighting... He killed Feda. I killed... Is, is he dead? Am I dead?"

"He is dead," The Frenchman replies. "Don't worry. You killed him. Nagato. That was his name. He's been waiting for someone to kill him for years. To end his pain. I'm sure he appreciated it. One of your finest moments, I might add."

Nagato, his name was Nagato. Who was he?

"Congratulations. Killing him was not an easy feat," the Frenchman says. "But you did the world, and him, a favor. Suffocating a man whose life was nothing but agony, whether it was his or others. You saw the opportunity to make the world a better place and took it. Good on you. That's what I hoped you would do."

"You were watching me?" I ask. "Why? Why didn't you help me?"

"Who said I didn't help you, young one? Anyway, you were lucky enough to have a unique advantage," he says, shrugging. "Thank the doctor who sent you the help of Morpheus. The god of dreams, so they say."

"Morpheus?" I ask. "He sent me Morpheus?"

He stops for a moment, as if it should be obvious.

"Morphine, my dear, morphine. How else do you think you managed to beat Nagato?" he laughs. "The doctor loaded you up with morphine. Not being able to feel pain is useful when fighting someone whose signature weapon is pain. He must have been so envious of you: being unable to hurt. Talk about rubbing it in his face. You're still on morphine now, as a matter of fact."

"Morpheus..." I mumble.

"Who would have thought that dying would be the key to defeating Nagato," he says. "And saving Karin."

"Dying," I sigh. "So, I am dead."

"Not dead, dying. It's a small, but crucial line," the Frenchman corrects. "I can stop you from crossing it, however, if you would like?"

"Um, yes," I reply, confused. "Of course, I want to live."

"Of course?" he says. "Not all people want to live. I believe you just saw how much some can crave death. You should know better than most. Are you sure you want to live?"

"Yes," I say. "Yes. Yes, I want to live, but I mean, what's the catch? Why save me?"

The Frenchman crouches down next to me and sits cross-legged on the rocky ground.

"I need you to understand a few things, Gabrielle," he says, quietly and firmly. "First and most importantly: This is probably the only time you ever get to speak to me. Choose your questions carefully, because you won't be able to ask all of them. Lie down."

"What?" I reply.

He stops and looks at me sternly. "That was a very ill-considered question, but I'll let it slide. Lie down, so I can save your life."

I slide off the rock that has replaced the wall behind me. I slip to the ground. I'm not in pain, but it is uncomfortable. I feel kinda floaty. Almost like I'm a little drunk, but far too self-aware for that. The Frenchman holds his hands over me. My whole body feels weird and tingly; my skin feels like it's crawling all over my flesh, like there are insects on me.

"I am going to save your life," he says. "I will do this for you without condition, but afterwards you will face a choice. It's a simple choice, really."

I strain my eyes at the sun to try to look at his face.

"You can join Le Réveil," he says. "You can help me. We can work together to make the world better, to guide humanity to a future where we survive and, hopefully, even thrive. By joining me, you will help guide what this future looks like."

"This will not be achieved through confrontation. It will not be taken by direct force. We will not be evil. We will use whatever power we have at our disposal to influence world events, leaders and, perhaps most importantly, the population towards their own benefit."

With that last sentence, his eyes meet mine. It sends a jolt through my body.

"We will captain the ship so that it does not hit the reef," he continues. "For without that, humanity is doomed. Cursed to die alone on a rock we've destroyed. If you join us, we will do whatever we can, whatever it takes, to stop that from happening."

He smiles like a father finishing a story.

"However, you do have another choice," he says, more sternly than before. "You can have no role in Le Réveil. If you don't want to be a part of our goal, our future, for whatever reason, you are free to walk away."

I raise my eyebrow.

"You will be left alone. You can carry on with your life, both in the dreamworld and the physical world. You will never need to give me, or any of us, a second thought. You can live happily ever after, trusting that humanity will find its way on its own somehow. Or perhaps you feel that it should not. Your life, your thoughts and beliefs, will be yours to do with what you will."

He lowers his voice.

"The only condition of this... is that you never tell a soul. You do not say, or write, a word about me, about Le Réveil or about the dreamworld to anyone. No one. Not Karin. Not your family. Not the public."

He looks away to the sky and pulls his hands away from me.

"How do you feel?"

I don't know. "Um... I feel conflicted, I mean..."

"I was talking about your wounds," he says, chuckling a bit through his smile. "Do you feel better?"

"Oh," I say, feeling around my body. "I actually do."

"Good!" He claps his hands together. "You can stand up then."

He holds a white shawl for me as I stand up, and he looks away from me. Looking down, my body is whole and clean. Where once I was leaking blood and flesh, there is now just torn clothing. The extent of the tearing reveals just how badly injured I was. I'm half-naked now.

"Thank you," I say, pulling the shawl around myself. It does help me feel more secure, but it also reminds me of victims in cop dramas. The woman is being comforted while sitting at the back of an ambulance. She has a cup of coffee in her hand. She has just killed the bad guy.

"It's my pleasure," he says. He holds out his arm for me to take and sweeps over the landscape with his other.

"Should we take a walk?" he asks, like it is another time, like we are about to walk the grounds of the estate and discuss to whom I will be married. "Will you indulge an old man with your company?"

I reach my arm through his. "Sure," I reply. "I guess it's the least I can do after, you know, I mean, after you saved my life."

"Think nothing of it," he says, leading me down the mountain.

The landscape shifts as we start to walk.

"No doubt you have questions for me," he says. "You have this walk to ask them."

"Oh..." I rack my brain to try and distill my thoughts into a well-crafted question.

"I guess, the first one is: Why should I trust you over any other would-be dictator? Even if your aims are as noble as you claim, which itself is a wholly different question, why would I support the most abhorrently undemocratic rule imaginable: a secret and all-powerful dictatorship."

He smiles as we take a few steps.

"That's a good question," he says.

It is a good question, isn't it?

"Le Réveil is not a dictatorship as the world has seen before, nor should I ever hope for us to rule the world as such. Although not beholden to the will of voting, as those who are democratically elected, dictators are beholden to the positions and structures that keep them in place. Dictators have no choice but to consolidate power. Unless their power is absolute, which is never the case, dictators must use most of their power to keep themselves where they are. They are as much a part of a system as democratically elected leaders."

"No, we are nothing like a dictatorial government. We do not rule. We do not govern. We influence. We guide. Yes, we even manipulate. But we do so indirectly and unchallenged. Because of this, we are so much more powerful than those who govern. We can actually effect change. We can sway votes at any level. We can sway individuals. We can sway the entire public. And we don't have to consider parties working directly against us. This power and security make us untouchable, immune to corruption, bureaucracy and brutality. We are not limited to one country or seat of power. We have practically limitless resources. We are uncompromised. We are powerful enough to be noble. We can enjoy the luxury of being moral, because we are unthreatened."

He smiles proudly.

"It sounds counter-intuitive, but it's only by rising above politics and popularity that anyone can have the freedom to help humanity."

"Absolute power corrupts absolutely..."

He sighs.

"These guarantees humanity puts in place, these checks and balances put on governance, inherently prohibit change. What is valued above all else at the end of the day is the maintenance of the status-quo. Although this benefits those with a stake in the system, it does not benefit the society as a whole. More importantly, it serves to protect society against sweeping changes, even when sweeping changes are necessary. Conversely, when the system breaks, it breaks hard. Revolution and war can bring sweeping changes, but at the expense of lives and infrastructure. With modern weapons, it can even be at the expense of the planet or the human race. The only way to move the world forward within such structures is through secret and powerful influence."

He continues.

"At the end of the day, this is all academic. You asked what makes us better than every other dictator. The truth is: It is us. We are better. You must believe in us. You must have confidence, not faith, that having someone in control is better than having no one, even if that someone is imperfect. Then you need to accept that we are the only ones who can fulfill that function."

"That's not particularly reassuring."

"The only way you can truly reassure yourself that we tack the correct course is to join us," he continues. "That way you yourself can ensure that we are not corrupt."

"Assuming I can trust myself."

"If you can't trust yourself in power, let alone anyone else, then how can you ever expect anything to change?"

Arm-in-arm, we continue our stroll. Throughout our conversation, the Frenchman casually, and without visible effort, illustrates our conversation. Sand builds cities and governments, leaders and masses of people. Trees sprout and landscapes change. The world bends to his will around him, all save me. I remain an actor in a world now beyond my control. I can sense it enough to not even bother trying. Even my own agency... it's only mine at his discretion. If it even is? Would I know? He's trying to convince me, but I think he could literally change my mind if he so wanted. Forcibly change it.

"Did you kill Feda?" I ask, as if to prove my own agency to myself.

He stays quiet for a moment. The sand before us shows a familiar valley: The Bamiyan valley. Plumes of sand erupt from the ground. The question doesn't surprise him. In fact, I'm not entirely sure whether the Bamiyan valley started building around us before I even asked the question. This unnerves me.

"No, I did not," he says. "But I know who did."

"The doctor?"

"Oh no," he continues. "The doctor would not do that, no. You killed Feda."

"What?" I ask. "What do you mean?"

"Don't feel too bad, Gabi," he says. "You created him in the first place."

"I created him?" I ask.

"Feda is what the world thinks he is, what you thought he was," the Frenchman explains. "He's simply a character you created. But he's a character that took on a life of his own, part of your life, in fact."

"But..." I stammer, letting go of his arm and stepping backward. "No. No, that can't be. He taught me. He... he planned all this. He talked to other people."

"He did, indeed. All of these things," the Frenchman says. "I don't think any of them noticed, just like you. It was really quite interesting to watch. When you were attacked by the Knife, all those years ago, you used Feda to protect yourself. You split him off from yourself and let him take the pain. Because you were writing him into existence, you unintentionally reified him. He was so much more concrete than most dream characters, and now imbued with your own will. That's what helped you write such a good book. That and the fact that you're also a fantastic writer, even if you doubt it. You really should stop giving yourself such a hard time about that."

It was me after all. I was the ghostwriter

"The dream character of Feda started developing on his own, he interacted with other dreamers as himself. He was so concrete, in fact, that even the doctor was initially fooled. He tried to recruit him."

The Frenchman laughs heartily, as one would at a friend doing something silly. I shake my head. No. This doesn't make sense.

"Feda himself didn't know, but I suspect you could feel the emptiness inside you," the Frenchman continues. "All this might have ended when you killed him, but instead you made him famous! You put him in the minds of millions of people, millions of people imagined him as you described him."

Feda appears in front of us, home in the Bamiyan valley.

"In the collective minds of the dreamworld, he was reborn. They say that you die twice. Once when your body dies, and again when your name is spoken for the last time. You made him immortal."

"A collective hallucination??" I reply.

"Something like that," the Frenchman continues. "A character in the collective unconsciousness."

"And he fought against you?" I ask.

"Yes. He carried that rebellious spirit that was once yours, that you cherished. He embodied it," the Frenchman says. "Almost by instinct, he sides with the weak, the underdog, the resistance, the rebellion... You wrote him that way. You wrote him to be what you never managed to be."

I look down at the ground.

"Don't be offended," he says. "That was not an insult. Those who have the power to act, inevitably act incorrectly at times. That does not mean they are evil. The weak are not necessarily in the right, and the strong are not always in the wrong."

"Maybe the weak need champions because they cannot fight for themselves."

"That's exactly how Le Réveil came to be. We started as a resistance, as the weak rising up to fight for themselves," he says. "We have succeeded. The underdog inevitably becomes the top dog, if successful."

"Then what do you need me for?" I ask.

We come across the shoreline along our stroll. The beach stretches from horizon to horizon.

"You have a knack for communication, for art," he says. "We want you to help us communicate with the world, to convince them to take action on what is the most pressing matter of our age. As I'm sure you're aware, we're destroying this planet. Unless we take some drastic steps, global ecological damage is going to play havoc with the world. The peace that we have fought so hard to achieve will be weakened."

"You want me to fight against climate change?" I ask, a bit confused. "You want me to write a book about climate change? But, that's what I wanted to do anyway."

"Exactly," he says. "So not much to ask, then"

"Why me?" I ask. "I'm not a scientist, and there are thousands of books about this. What would you want me to write it?"

"You misunderstand. We want you to write a story that will inspire the world to care about the planet. To inspire people to care about environmental issues when they vote, whether with their wallet or ballot," he says. "The same way *Enduring Freedom* helped inspire the world to care about the USA's militant foreign policy. If you could create someone like Feda, but for that purpose, the world would be a better place. Rest assured, your contribution will be part of a greater strategy, the details of which I won't share at this point. Its success does not rely on you, but you would be a valuable asset."

We stop walking and stand on the wet sand. The water is slowly rising up our feet and ankles.

"Is that not something you'd like to do?" he asks, letting go of my arm and turning to face me. "Is that not something you think is important?"

"It is..." I say. "But... is that all I need to do?"

"We will never make you do something you aren't willing to do," he says, smiling warmly.

The water creeps over my ankles and up my shins.

"You don't need to choose now," the Frenchman says. "You have plenty of time to think about it. Consider that my gift to you: Time."

He continues.

"I, however, am out of time."

He holds his hand out for me to shake.

"I have a lot more questions," I say, taking his hand hesitantly. "Is Feda gone now? Did he become a part of me again when he died? Why did Nagato target me? Who are you? Why are we speaking French?"

He laughs at the last one.

"There will always be more questions," he says. "I'll answer just one now."

"I like French," he says, turning his back and walking away. "I guess if I'm going to choose any modern language to speak these days, it might as well be French."

Modern language? How old is he?

"How old are you?" I ask.

"Very old," he says. "We are very old."

What does that mean? A thousand follow up questions run through my mind. What are you? Why are you doing this? Only one slips out.

"Did you trick Nongqawuse?" I ask. "Did you trick her to betray her people?"

He stops. For a moment, he doesn't react. For the first and only time, I think I asked a question he didn't expect. He turns around. He doesn't say a thing. He opens his mouth, pauses, and says...

"Even we have made mistakes. More than a few of them. We are different now."

He turns back and continues away. As he does, his body blows apart into sand, like a statue over time. He scatters in an instant and leaves me alone. Only the wind remains to keep me company, and a voice that it carries.

"Gabi, it's time to wake up."

THE CHOICE OF ENDING

"I brought your laptop," my dad says, handing me my case as if I'm going to use it right now. "I wasn't sure exactly what cables you need so I just shoved them all in."

"Thanks dad," I say, putting it on my lap. I guess that's where it belongs.

"How are you feeling?" my mom asks. "Are the nurses treating you well? What are they feeding you?"

"They're feeding me food," I say, rolling my eyes. "I'm fine mom, if my belly can survive a bullet, I'm sure it can survive hospital food."

"We can bring you something nice if you like," she says. "Your dad made some smoked beef brisket the other night..."

"I'm okay," I laugh. "As delicious as that sounds, dad."

I look at him with a wink. He shrugs.

"We'll make something special for you when you come home," he says. "Whatever you feel like."

"I think I'm still going to be here for a while," I reply. "Hence the laptop."

I pat the laptop case to emphasize my point.

A familiar face pops around the curtain separating me from the other patients.

"Gabi!" Karin calls, her smile beaming warmth onto me.

"Karin!" She quasi-jogs across to the side of my hospital bed and reaches over to gingerly hug me. I wince through it, with no regrets.

"You look so much better than the last time I saw you," she says. "I mean, you're conscious for a start, and your blood is flowing through your face."

"Oh, you're making me blush," I reply weakly.

A few small tears emerge for a brief moment under her eyes. She wipes them away.

"I'm so glad you're okay," she says. "I'm so sorry, Gabi. I'm so sorry I didn't act earlier. You warned me about him! And why didn't you tell me about this when you came to my apartment!"

"It's okay, Karin," I reply. I put my hand up to stop her. "It's not your fault, and I'm fine. How were we supposed to know he was so dangerous?"

"Any progress on finding him?" my mom asks Karin.

Karin shakes her head, a few more tears leaking out. "No, they're still looking for him. They've assured me that you're safe, though. They have men in place to protect you, in case he comes back. They found his car near my apartment, which is..." She shivers.

"Do they know his real name?" my dad asks. "Surely with a face and a name they can find him."

"They just don't know yet," Karin replies. "Or they're not telling me if they do."

"Why wouldn't they tell you?" asks my mom, visibly affronted.

"It's a police investigation mom," I reply. "They could have their reasons."

"Well, I think we have the right to know everything they do," she huffs. "I mean, I feel like you have the right to know who this crazy stalker is, so you can protect yourself. If he's an obsessed fan, then surely he'll come after you again. I mean, it's irresponsible of them not to give you that information."

"We don't even know that they know who it is! Aaaah..." I wince again as I raise my voice at my mother. Only she could rile me up enough to hurt myself.

"Are you okay?" my mom blurts out. All three of them rush to my side.

"I'm fine, I'm fine," I repeat. They back off a bit.

"Listen, mom and dad, do you mind giving Karin and me a chance to talk alone?" I ask. "I just need to talk about some work stuff."

"Work stuff?" my dad says, taken aback. "Do you really need to worry about that now?"

"Please dad," I ask.

My mom takes his arm to lead him out. "Come on. We'll be downstairs. Just give us a call if you need anything."

They disappear behind the curtain and out of the room.

"Gabi, I'm so sorry about not doing something about this man," she says. "I should have been more careful."

"Seriously, don't worry about it," I say, brushing her apologies aside. "Are you okay? Last time I saw you... you..."

"Me?!?" she says, laughing. "You're worried about me. You're the one that was shot and you're worried because I had a few bad dreams. I'm fine. I just had a rough patch."

"Really?" I ask.

"Yeah," she says. "To be honest, as soon as I heard about you getting shot, I focused on that. I forgot all about those dreams. I have been able to sleep again. I guess there's nothing like real problems to help you get over imagined ones. I guess it was all just in my head."

"That doesn't mean it wasn't real," I reply. "In fact, all you truly know is real is what happens in your own head."

Karin blinks at me. "You're right Gabi," she smiles. "And... well... you're right."

I smile back.

"You seem different," she says, through her grin.

I motion down at my body and hospital gown, obviously.

"It's been an interesting few months," I laugh. "But I've got good news."

"Yeah?" she asks.

"You're not going to need to organize a ghostwriter. I know the novel I want to write, and I think that I'm the only one who can write it."

Her smile breaks broadly. "Really?" she gasps. "If I knew all it would take is shooting you in the stomach, I could have done that years ago."

We laugh together. It hurts, but I don't really mind.

"That's great, Gabi," she says. "But you really don't have to worry about it right now. Just focus on getting better. The board will understand delays in the case of being shot by a crazed fan. Also, and I hate to say it, but you're all over the news again. This shooting has generated a lot more publicity and... well, created a certain mystique about your upcoming book."

"The Salman Rushdie effect?" I chuckle.

"Exactly," she replies.

I look right to the awe-inspiring collection of flowers, get-well cards and gifts. Karin notices me looking at them.

"They're not all from fans," she says.

"Don't tell me I'm getting hate mail after getting shot?" I ask

"Oh no, not that," she laughs. "No, there are some from friends. And one from the happily engaged couple."

I can see it. It towers over the others with the compensation of the Burj

Khalifa. I can't help but laugh at the absurdity of it, and how absurd it was to bother me so much.

"Of course," I smile weakly.

Karin doesn't say anything for a moment, but just looks at me endearingly.

"So, what are you writing? What's the new book about?"

"Knock knock."

Karin and I turn towards the end of the curtain. The doctor's face peers around. Not a doctor, the doctor. Doctor Sivers.

"Sorry to disturb you. I can come back later," he says.

Karin looks to me for my reaction. Should she get rid of him, or do I want to see him?

"It's fine, doctor," I say. "I seem to be very popular again these days. Come in."

He emerges from behind the curtain, carrying a bouquet of flowers. He and Karin shake hands and she takes the flowers to put in the vase next to my bed.

"You should not call me 'doctor' in here," he says. "People might get me confused."

"Fine, but calling you Jakob feels weird," I reply.

"How are you feeling?" he asks.

"Pretty good, considering," I reply. "I've been having some weird dreams, but I'm okay now."

"That's normal, though," Karin says, before realizing she was right next to an actual expert on the topic. She turns to him. "Isn't it?"

Jakob eyes me. "It is not unexpected. But we can talk about them if you like."

"Oh no," I reply. "It's fine. In fact, I think they've inspired me. That's where I got the inspiration for my new novel."

"Oh really!" exclaims Karin, clapping her hands together. "You were inspired by your dreams? That's incredible. Isn't that something like how you wrote *Enduring Freedom*? It's amazing what our unconscious minds can come up with, don't you think, doctor?"

Jakob continues to eye me coolly. "It certainly is. What's it about, Gabi?"

I smile. "You'll have to wait to find out," I say. "But I'm pretty confident that it's going to change the world. I mean, it's a message that everyone really needs to hear."

"Are you really going to keep us in suspense like that?" says Karin.

"I would prefer you to read it fresh," I reply. "I think that makes for better criticism and editing. Don't worry, doctor, I'll send you a copy too when it's finished. Our sessions together have really helped inspire me. I'm sure you'll be dying to read it."

The doctor chuckles to himself. "I already am, but I'm confident that you will write the book we know that you can. I am sure you will not disappoint us."

"I wouldn't dream of it," I reply.

Karin looks between the two of us, as if noticing that there's something underneath our words, but not knowing what it is. No one says a word for a moment. As if summoned by the silence, the nurse takes the opportunity to enter.

"Okay okay, I need to do some tests," she says, shooing my visitors away. "And there are too many of you here anyway."

"I'll come around to see you tomorrow, Gabi," Karin calls, picking up her things as she leaves.

"Yeah," I say. "Okay, see you then."

The doctor lingers at the curtain. He opens his mouth to say something to me, but resists.

"I'm sure I'll see you soon too, Jakob," I say.

He nods his head to me and walks out, leaving me with an inexplicably stern nurse. After confirming my painkiller dosage, a few checks and minutes, I'm left alone in my bed.

There's nothing else to do but do it. After all, no one else should write my story, but me. No ghostwriter. Not Feda. No, everything he was, has become a part of me once again.

My only co-writer is my laptop. Just a blank white Word document and me, my hands and a keyboard. A white canvas of untold potential, of absolute pure perfection. Let's see how I can ruin it.

THE END

Special Thanks

To my wife and cheerleader Kristen
You saw me through oodles of edits, temper tantrums and doubts.
Thank you for your patience and love, while I gnashed
my teeth at myself and anything nearby.
I could have never finished this without you.

To Sage and Doug
Thank you for being my beta readers.
I appreciate the delicacy of the job, and you both handled
it with grace and empathy.
Your criticism and love were heard and felt, respectively.

ABOUT THE AUTHOR

M J Stone

MJ Stone is a South African novelist, currently based in Brooklyn, NY

His first novel, The Ghostwriter, represents the culmination of ideas formed at the University of Cape Town, where he studied English Literature and Psychology, with a focus on dreaming. It developed over the subsequent years, following him from his hometown to a new life in Moscow, where he would meet his American-born wife. It shadowed him home, to Barbados and finally to New York, where he would eventually finish and prepare it for release, more than a decade after starting it.

MJ Stone currently resides in Williamsburg, Brooklyn, with his wife and day job. He continues to write. His second novel, a modern love story told through the lens of a sci-fi thriller, is presently titled Ark.

Made in the USA
Coppell, TX
30 April 2022

77237567R00184